WAR STORIES

WAR STORIES

Edited by
Hayden McAllister

Illustrations by

Malcolm Barter

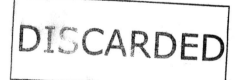

octopus

Contents

First published 1979 by
Octopus Books Limited
59 Grosvenor Street
London W1

This collection © 1979

ISBN 0 7064 0998 1

Printed in Czechoslovakia

Designed by Brian Austin Associates

The March on Aqaba

Alistair MacLean

The Arabs had been terrorized by their Turkish overlords too long. By 1917 they were ripe for revolt – and involved in this uprising was a hitherto little known Englishman; T. E. Lawrence – later to become world famous as Lawrence of Arabia.

This passage by Alistair Maclean describes one successful stage of the Arab revolt, and in it Lawrence is aided by the great desert fighter Sheik Auda abu Tayi in his attempt to March on Aqaba . . .

At first their route lay through a burning desert of pure white sand. The reflection of the sun on the gleaming sand hurt their eyes as cruelly as the dazzle from frozen snow. Water there was none; they had to carry their own. But the toughened Bedouin could go for an entire day without water and get by with only a pint on the second. Lawrence, dressed as always like an Arab in his hooded, flowing white robes, rode uncomplainingly on camel-back with the best of the Bedouins. (Only those who have tried it can appreciate how horribly uncomfortable camel riding can be.) He sought no favours for himself in the way of food and water. The toughening of his early youth, when he had trained himself in stoical endurance and the ability to go without food and drink, was paying off indeed.

Then they entered a region of red sandstone, furnace-hot in the pitiless white glare of the sun. It was so hot that several camels eventually weakened and died and had to be cut up for meat. This sandstone was followed by long, indescribably bleak and barren stretches of lava,

7

where both men and animals suffered tortures of heat and thirst. Finally they came to an oasis, with water and shade, but even here their troubles were not over. As happened so often to Lawrence in Arabia, they were attacked by hostile tribesmen. These hostile Bedouins had, of course, no means of knowing that the very men they were attacking were those who would at last bring freedom to their land.

The long, bitter, exhausting ride went on. They came to the Hejaz railway, where they blew up sections of the line and destroyed the telephone wires. Lawrence tells us how on this occasion the tireless and indestructible Auda composed a long poem in praise of the dynamite that had wrought such damage to the railway!

Then on again they went into the depths of the desert, a desert that was at times of hardened shining mud that hurt their eyes even more cruelly than the reflected light from white sand. Sometimes vast stretches of sand itself were whipped up by the burning wind into a driving, scorching, stinging wall of a million flying needles. It blinded men and camels alike and brought visibility down to only a few feet. But those men were Bedouin, men who could survive in incredibly cruel, desperate conditions that would have killed almost any European – all but Lawrence. He was as enduring, as immune to pain and thirst and exhaustion as the iron men who travelled by his side. They rode steadily on.

After two weeks of this brutally inhuman riding, Lawrence had an opportunity to prove to the Bedouins that he was as tough and tireless as any Arab alive. They were trudging along through the sand – they had dismounted to save the strength of their exhausted camels – blinded by the driving sand and weak from heat and lack of water. Sometime during the day Lawrence saw that one of the party was missing. To turn back, weak and worn out as he now was, into that sand-swept unmarked wilderness, could have been just another way of committing suicide. But Lawrence turned back to look for the missing man. And he turned back alone.

By one chance in a thousand Lawrence found the man, exhausted, blinded and half dead from thirst, took him in charge and turned back again to rejoin the party. Even then Lawrence might have been lost, might have failed to find his friends in that blind and featureless wilderness of flying sand. The saga of Lawrence of Arabia would then have ended before it had properly begun. But Auda, who had noticed Lawrence's absence, turned back and found him. After this, Lawrence's prestige among the Bedouins was secure for all time.

A few days later – eighteen days after the beginning of this journey – they reached the Howietat area where Auda's tribesmen lived. Even in those last few days they had run into constant trouble, losing men from sniper's bullets and snake bites. The Howietat area was alive with poisonous snakes and the local cure for such a bite was to cover the wound with snakeskin and read chapters of the Koran over the invalid. After a few hours of this, the unfortunate sufferer almost invariably died.

Sheik Auda now went ahead to rouse his tribesmen and get the permission of the Emir of Ruwalla to use the Wadi Sirhan as a base. He took along with him £6,000 in gold to help the Emir to make up his mind.

While Auda was doing this, Lawrence undertook a strange long ride to the north, far beyond Damascus. He rode alone.

Lawrence's solitary excursion into the heart of Turkish-occupied territory remains a mystery. If any man knows or ever has known the reason for this journey, or the details of it, he has kept silent. So did Lawrence. In his famous book of the Arabian war, *Seven Pillars of Wisdom*, there is no mention whatsoever made of it.

The only certain fact that seems to be known is that he blew up a bridge at Baalbek, on the Damascus–Aleppo railway – the northern continuation of the Hejaz railway. Beyond that fact, all is guesswork. It is said that he conferred with revolutionary-minded leaders in Syria to see how ready they were to join the Arab cause. And it is said that he dropped many hints, without being too careful about his choice of confidants, that the Arabs would be operating up north in the Damascus direction before very long.

It is highly probable that Lawrence was seeking to give the impression – to which the blowing up of the bridge added – that the next thrust of the Arabs would be towards Damascus, the heart of Turkish Arabia. This impression would effectively prevent the Turks from even beginning to have any suspicions about a forthcoming attack on Aqaba.

This guess is confirmed by what happened on his return when he was met by the Emir of Ruwalla. In spite – or perhaps because – of the £6,000 he had received from Auda, the Emir was still very nervous. He feared what might happen to him if the Turks found out that Arabian tribes were mustering in his Wadi Sirhan. Lawrence told him that he was to worry about it no longer. On the contrary, he should at once inform the Turks of the presence of the gathering Arab forces!

The Emir's astonishment can be imagined; but Lawrence's point is easily seen. The northern part of the Sirhan is as near to Damascus as it is to Aqaba. The known presence of Arab forces there would almost certainly be thought by the Turks to herald an attack on Damascus. Their first reaction to the news would be to prepare to intercept the Arabs on their supposed northward march from the Sirhan. And by sending troops to block this non-existent attack, the Turks would leave the way wide open to the southwest for the attack on Aqaba.

There was no question about it: Lawrence was a master of intrigue and deception.

To increase the deception still further, Lawrence and a picked band of men set out from the Wadi Sirhan and reached the railway line in the vicinity of Deraa, half way between the Sirhan and Damascus. They blew up the track there, derailed a train and captured a Turkish-manned station. There could be no doubt now in the minds of the enemy that the Bedouins were heading for Damascus.

But quickly the Arabs wheeled and thrust south for their original target – Aqaba. On the way there they heard that a squadron of 400 Turkish cavalry was hunting for them. The news didn't worry Lawrence overmuch, for the same messenger told them that a local sheik had thoughtfully provided the Turks with a guide who was leading them in a completely wrong direction.

Then came a serious hold-up in their plans. They learned that they were not going to be able to thrust straight on to Aqaba. The block-house at Abu el Lissal, which lay on a direct line between Maan and Aqaba, was in the hands of the enemy.

As planned beforehand, this enemy blockhouse had been taken by another detachment of Arabs. But by sheer bad luck an entire battalion of Turkish troops happened to be within a few miles at the time. They heard of the capture of the blockhouse, advanced on it, retook it in a massed attack and drove off the occupying Arab tribesmen. Then, by

They blew up the track and derailed the train.

way of revenge, they went out to a little, unsuspecting Arab encampment in the neighbourhood and killed everyone there, women and children included.

Such was the situation that Lawrence, Auda and Sherif Nasir found on their arrival. Their feelings at discovering the massacre can be imagined. They immediately besieged the blockhouse, pouring in a heavy fire on the defenders. But so well placed were the Turks, so determinedly did they fight back that it seemed impossible they could ever be dislodged. But dislodged they were, and by so small a thing as an insult offered Auda by Lawrence.

In the middle of the day, when it was so intolerably hot that most of the Arabs could fire only very occasionally, Auda came to Lawrence. He pointed to his own still rapidly firing clansmen and asked proudly: 'What think ye of the Howietat now?'

'Indeed,' Lawrence replied, 'they shoot a lot and hit a little.'

Auda stared at him, then ripped off his headcloth in berserk rage and dashed it to the ground. Shouting at Lawrence, 'Get your camel if you want to see the old man's work,' he rushed away shouting hoarsely for his tribesmen to follow him. Before Lawrence could stop him Auda was leading fifty horsemen in a breakneck suicidal downhill charge against the enemy.

There was nothing for the horrified Lawrence and Nasir to do but mount their camels, gather 400 tribesmen and charge after him. Lawrence, on a famous racing camel, soon outdistanced the rest. He was rapidly overtaking Auda and his men, who had already smashed headlong into the Turkish positions, when his camel was shot through the head. Lawrence was pitched a great distance forward over the dying animal's head, to crash unconscious to the ground. He should at least have broken some limbs or ribs – if not his neck – but Lawrence, as the Arabs were beginning to discover, was very tough indeed.

When he recovered consciousness, the battle was over. The Arabs, mad for revenge, had killed 300 Turks and taken 150 more as prisoners – in return for the loss of exactly two of their own men. It was incredible.

The spectacle of the triumphant Sheik Auda, when he came to ask Lawrence what he thought of his Howietat tribesmen now, was even more incredible. One bullet had smashed his treasured field glasses, another had pierced his pistol holster, others had reduced his sword scabbard to mangled strips of leather. Six more had passed through his clothing, and his horse had been shot dead under him. But Auda himself was completely unharmed. Even for a man supposed to bear the charmed life Auda did, it was indeed a miracle. Auda himself gave the entire credit for his survival to a copy of the Koran which he always carried with him.

It is an interesting sidelight on the basic simplicity of this amazing man that his Koran was a cheap reproduction made in Glasgow and sold for exactly eighteen-pence. Many years previously some unscrupulous salesman had talked Auda into paying £120 for it.

From Abu el Lissal the Arab forces pressed on to Aqaba. And the capture of Aqaba, after the fight at the blockhouse, turned out to be a complete anticlimax. Many more tribesmen, swayed by this latest Arab victory, had flocked to join Lawrence's banner on the last stages of the march. The Turkish garrison at Aqaba, who were already being bombarded from the sea, had heard of the fate of their comrades at Abu el Lissal. So when they saw the hordes of Arabs advancing upon them, they surrendered without even the semblance of a fight.

Aqaba was now in the hands of the Arabs. The Army of Revolt had secured a base and the way was open for a thrust into the heart of the enemy's land.

Against the King

Howard Jones

This morning I rode out to the moor with Elizabeth and found my father's grave beyond the great ditch that was our undoing.

In this high springtime the kingcups make a golden tapestry from end to end of the shallow mound. I fashioned a cross from reeds and placed it there; and sat and wept, namby that I am, as I recalled the terror of a summer's night five long years ago.

6 July 1685. Somewhere in memory I am flying through darkness, my heart hammering as if it must explode within my breast. I stumble and fall flat on my belly, and I think how sweet to lie here, to let the sedges and the reeds lap me; or to sink a yard into the earth, and there find eternal rest. But the militiamen are all about me, shouting, shooting. They are near, nearer than before. I rise and run like a madman through the night.

So now consider me in this flood-tide of my misfortunes. My name is David Harry Linton; my age, eighteen years and three months. My face, not handsome in the best of times, is now daubed devilish ugly by the mud of Sedgemoor and the bleeding of a scalp wound. My hair is cropped close, and dark – almost black. My eyes are my mother's eyes, a steely grey.

My mother died when I was born. My father, my good, gentle

father whose death weighs so heavily on me now, wanted nothing more than to farm our fields at Middlezoy in peace. But he surrendered to my arguments in the name of liberty, and so enlisted with me in the rebel Monmouth's army, he at once a captain, I a soldier of the line.

We numbered a bare six thousand, a raggle-taggle of tinkers, tailors, oafs and labourers, with a sprinkling of gentry to give us a show of respectability and discipline. But oh, how we roared and ranted up and down the highways, how we scorned and threatened the King, that unspeakable James Stuart who would turn us all into shameful Papists and bind us slaves to France! How we cheered our handsome leader when he proclaimed himself true Protestant and King! How we marched for him – on Bristol, Bath and Bridgwater – singing our lusty songs for Liberty and England!

And then, Sedgemoor.

We thought to surprise the King's army snugly encamped there; and we attacked by night under a waxing moon. As we stood, peering, probing, arguing amongst ourselves, a volley of fire raked us. I saw my father topple head first into the ditch. I think he must have died in the instant. Then I heard the thunder of cavalry, I saw the black belly of a horse above me. My sergeant fell down on me with a scream, his left arm hacked off at the elbow.

Terror seized us all. We turned and ran, a screaming hopeless rabble now. We ran we knew not whither. At last I floundered into the marsh. I fell, I picked myself up. I prayed for easy death. But still I ran.

Presently a cottage loomed up through the night. I stumbled into the porch and pummelled at the door. None answered me. So, in a moment, I took up a stone, crashed it through a window, and scrambled in.

As I lay sprawling on the floor, an old woman called shrilly from the darkness: 'Who is it? Who's there?'

I recognized the voice of Widow Green.

'It's David Linton,' I whispered. 'For God's sake hide me!'

I heard her scuffling bare-footed in the room. She lit a candle and stared at me with watery eyes, like a grey wraith in her long night-shift. She did not speak, but went to a cupboard, took out a bottle of some amber wine and passed it to me.

I drank. Then said she: 'There's blood on tha face, Davey. Dear Lord, the Devil's abroad this night!'

'A thousand devils,' said I. 'On foot, on horse. You must hide me, Widow!'

'Where? Where in these two rooms? Th'art for Monmouth, Davey?'

'I and my father, both.'

'Tha feyther? Where's he?'

'In Sedgemoor ditch. A bullet in his heart.'

She looked around her helplessly. A tear jerked on her cheek. Suddenly I heard the scrape of a boot in the porch outside. The door shook and a man's voice shouted:

'Open, Mrs Green! Open in the King's name!'

I seized a hatchet from a basket of logs by the hearth and backed against the wall. The man lifted a boot several times against the door. 'I hears ye in thar, Mrs Green! Open or ye'll suffer!' The widow glanced at the bolt shivering in its hasp, then swung towards me, her face softened with pity. She took the hatchet from me, flung it down, clasped my wrist, and whispered:

'The back way, Davey – hasten, hasten!'

So she led me, as if I were a child, to the back door. In those few precious seconds which for me were the difference between life and death, I seemed no longer conscious of myself, no longer aware of my fears and pains. The old woman's bobbing white shoulders, the slither of her naked feet, the man at the front shouting and pummelling: these were like incidents in another man's dream.

Then the back door stood open.

She whispered: 'The river's yonder – swim if tha've strength. They'll not seek ye over the river.'

I ran. And the river embraced me, swift, and cold as charity, cold as the King of England's heart.

★   ★   ★   ★

In this way, then, I became an outlaw. My misdeeds were known; my name had been proscribed and a warrant issued against me. My father's house, his fields, and every beast that grazed in them, had been claimed in the King's name.

To be caught was to be summarily tried and hung. So I became a creature of the night, venturing out from the woods at dusk to plunder the larder of some nearby farmhouse or cottage. My only comforts at this time were a dagger and a brace of pistols which I filched from a gentleman's house at Staple Fitzpaine.

Sometimes the way of burglary was made easy for me; a door would be left unbarred or a window open. But none would shelter me, and few, except solitary woodsmen, would so much as acknowledge my existence. Can you blame them? Can you blame them with the King's men combing all the countryside between Exeter and Winchester? With the unspeakable Lord Chief Justice Jeffreys hanging Monmouth rebels by the hundred, and whipping wives and mothers, sweethearts and sisters, for harbouring us poor devils?

Such was the terror which followed upon Sedgemoor.

You may well ask why I did not escape from the West, as did some, for the safety of other parts. Well, for one thing, escape was not easy. Informers abounded; the hills were well watched, and the bridle paths, and the rivers. Militiamen guarded every bridge and turnpike.

But more than this, the fate of Widow Green lay heavy on my conscience. For I had learned from a soft-headed boy whom I met in the woods of Clavelshay, how Mrs Green had been arrested and taken to Taunton Gaol to await her trial.

And so, on a fine August morning I mingled with the crowds outside the Castle Hall in Taunton, where the Lord Chief Justice had opened the Assize. I wore no disguise (indeed, I had none to wear), but my weeks in the fields and woods had given me a long growth of curling hair and a wiry black beard. For an hour or more I lounged against a sunny wall, watching the prisoners come and go. I watched and I listened, speaking seldom in case someone might recognize my voice.

Presently, I became aware of a fellow watching me from the tail of his eye. He was a tall, red-headed man in his forties, respectably dressed in a suit of blue broadcloth. I looked at him, and he quickly looked away, scratching at his chin. I did not care at all for this furtive inspection, and I sidled up to him with my hands thrust into the waist of my breeches.

'Have you been inside, master?'

'I have that,' says he.

'Has Mrs Green been called?'

'Aye.'

'And what's her punishment?'

'She's to be whipped,' says he, with a sort of satisfaction.

'That's murder,' says I. 'A whipping will kill her, certain sure. When will the whipping be?'

He swung his eyes lazily from my tattered shoes to my face. He smiled. Then he answered deliberately:

'I dunnaw, Davey Linton.'

It was as if he had touched my heart and stopped its beating. For a second I was terribly afraid. But my miserable existence had induced in me a sort of savage despair. I pulled my dagger from its sheath and pressed it to his midriff. He gasped as the point prickled his flesh. He did not move, but stared at me with his ugly mouth agape, so that I could see his tongue folded tight against his teeth.

'What's your name?' I whispered.

'Coke, Coke . . . Ben Coke.'

'Where from?'

'Why, Blagdon. Atop Blagdon Hill.'

So this fellow had seen me in other days at Blagdon. Now I could place him.

He had a tidy farm on Blagdon Hill: a farmhouse, barn, sheep, a dozen head of cattle. And I had heard from a woodsman how Ben Coke had betrayed one Billy Haynes, a Monmouth rebel who used to labour for him; so that Billy was hanged in Bridgwater with a dozen more; and Ben received a guinea for his service to the King.

I remembered this tale; and, looking into his heavy-lidded eyes, I believed it to be true. I gave a twist to the dagger, and he caught up his breath sharply, and his tongue drooled over his lower lip.

'That's for Billy Haynes,' I said. 'Now listen carefully what you are going to do.'

I told him then that he must go back into the courtroom, and there inquire, in his own artful way, when and where the sentence on Mrs Green would be carried out. In an hour he must return to the spot on which we stood and tell me everything he had learned.

'And mark this,' I concluded. 'If you send the militia in your stead, they'll not find me here. If you fail to return, and to speak God's truth,

I'll find opportunity to slit your gizzard, as you deserve on Billy's account. That's my solemn oath. What do you say, Ben Coke?'

'Aye. Aye, I'll do so.'

'Swear it.'

'Honest to God, I'll do as ye say.'

He straightened, turned quickly from me, and lumbered away. Once he had vanished through the Castle gates I did not linger, but walked at a smart pace through the little alleys of the town, keeping a wary eye behind me in case he had set the militia at my heels.

However, when I returned to the Castle after an hour, he was standing alone by the wall, his hands deep in his coat pockets.

I went up to him.

'Tomorrow, Davey,' he muttered. 'She'll be whipped from Taunton to Bridgwater.'

'What time?'

'Eight of the forenoon. From Corn Market.'

I put my lips to his ear, and said softly: 'If this is false, you're a dead man, Ben Coke.'

' 'Tis all God's truth,' he answered simply.

I left him there, leaning on the wall, whilst expressions of fear, relief and guilt passed swiftly across his big brown face.

* * * *

From Taunton to Bridgwater is a long eleven miles. I felt certain that Mrs Green would not survive a quarter of the distance: and that therefore, if I was to rescue her, I must make my attempt within a mile or two of Taunton.

I knew the road well. I knew that shortly after leaving Taunton it bends sharply leftwards and runs straight through the straggling length of Yeoman Spinney towards Thurloxton. I walked immediately to the spinney, counting six hundred paces to the bole of an ancient beech tree. I sat there, cradled in the tormented roots, and as I watched the sunbeams flickering and dancing through the branches, there came to me, for the first time in many weeks, a sense of ease, almost of contentment.

It was as if God's hand had led me there. This is the place, I thought;

19

this is where I shall save Mrs Green, where I shall crown my hatred of a wicked king and a merciless judge. This is where I shall become a man again!

At dusk I went out from the spinney and retrieved my pistols from a barn at Staplegrove where I had hidden them. It was after midnight when I returned. I crept again into the bole of my beech tree and slept a dreamless sleep until the dawn.

I primed my pistols, and waited. It was terrifying, that long wait. Because when you wait, you think; and when you think, the hobgoblins of prudence, fear and remorse can so easily torment you.

From afar off I heard the clock of St Mary Magdalene chiming the hours. Five. Six. Seven. A quarter to eight. She's at the Cornmarket now, I thought. She's having her wrists tied to the wagon tail, the driver's climbing to his seat, there's a gaunt brute fingering the whip.

Suddenly I heard a horse galloping through the spinney. I seized my pistols and leapt up, wondering who this solitary horseman might be and what his business was at such an hour. Then, peering round the broad trunk of the tree, I saw that it was not a he but a she.

A young woman, so far as I could judge. Her cloak billowed in a grey canopy above the lifting haunches of her horse. I scarcely glimpsed her face shrouded in the hood. She passed me, the horse cantered away and away. All was silence. My hands were shaking as if I had been stricken with a palsy.

I heard the chime of eight o'clock. I waited, gripping my pistols so fiercely that I could feel the pulse throbbing in my palms. And at last, I heard the rumble of the wagon, the slow, steady rhythm of the wagon horse. Then a scream and the thwack, thwack of a lash, sounds that sent fire flashing through my blood.

Not yet, I thought.

Wait, wait, I thought.

But I could wait no longer. I stepped into the road, calling, 'Halt! Halt!'

Such a sweat of excitement possessed me that I scarcely realized what I was doing. The driver eyed me in astonishment. I can recall only his startled eyes and that his shirt sleeves were rolled back. Whether he was young or old, fair or dark, I cannot say. A shaft of sunlight lit up the whipman gazing round the tail of the wagon: a black-bearded,

I stepped into the road and cried 'Halt'.

thick-shouldered lout, with a head of downy baldness. Behind him, a long way behind, a handful of spectators was spread across the road.

But, above all, it was the silence, the stillness, which impressed me. For a few seconds that seemed eternity, we were all turned to stone. Then the driver called on me to give way in the King's name.

I put a bullet over his head. He tumbled to the ground so swiftly that I thought I must have killed him. But he was up at once and scampering away beyond the wagon, screaming, 'Treason!' Then everyone was running and yelling. I let fly with my second pistol, God knows why, and I saw the ball kick up a feather of dust on the crown of the road.

In a moment all had vanished. And again, the silence.

I ran to the tail of the wagon. Mrs Green stood motionless, looking at me through her tears. I slashed through the cord on her wrists, picked her up bodily, and thrust her on to the plank which served as a driving seat. Then I climbed up beside her, grabbed the reins and whipped up the startled horse.

For a long time neither of us spoke.

My concern was to reach some place where we could lie in hiding. The hills to the west, with their thick overspread of forest and scattered farmsteads, offered the best possibilities, and I soon turned from the road into a lane which in a couple of miles brought us into Deadman Wood. The flanks of the horse were dark with sweat, and as soon as we reached the cover of the trees, I slowed it to a walk.

'Oh, Davey, what madness is in tha?' piped Mrs Green suddenly.

'A madness that saved your skin, old lady,' I answered tartly. 'The whipping would have killed you.'

The Beginning of the End

Anthony Buckly

I was falling gently into the heartland of the German enemy. As the Mosquito droned away into the moonless winter night, I guided my parachute towards the pinpoint of light which flickered in the fields below.

It was 1942. Hitler's forces were terrorizing the Northern world and Japan had erupted to draw the entire globe towards death and destruction. It seemed that only a miracle could halt these juggernauts of war.

A garbled message had reached British Intelligence from Germany. It seemed that someone was claiming that he could provide a solution to end the war and my superiors were ready to clutch at any straw at that time.

It was my job to drag him from under the noses of German Security and bring him back to London . . .

I hit the turf, rolled over and hauled on the parachute lines. The Resistance man who had been signalling was nowhere to be seen. Peering into the darkness, I rose to my feet. Then my eyes picked out the shaded lights of a vehicle which stood a few hundred yards away. Suddenly a searchlight stabbed the night. A second later I was caught in its blinding glare. A voice shouted; 'Halt! or we shall open fire!'

The whole thing had been a trap to capture a British agent! Or so it seemed for a moment. But the next instant a voice from the trees behind rasped: 'Release your parachute and run!'

I obeyed without thinking. As I raced for the forest a machine gun chattered and bullets smacked the earth round my feet. I stumbled and went headlong in the grass. I knew that if I rose I would be a dead man.

Then, directly ahead, a figure darted from the trees, exposing himself to the full blaze of the searchlight. It swept after him as he sprinted away to my left drawing the Spandau's fire away from me. For a few vital seconds, I was no longer the target and I crashed into the foliage.

I crouched, panting, in the almost total darkness. The firing had stopped and all I could hear were the cries of the German soldiers as they began to close in. Then a hand gripped my elbow. 'Follow!' said a voice. We zig-zagged between the firs. Branches lashed at my face. My rescuer halted abruptly. We stood beside a black car, its bodywork gleaming dully in the faint light. A little beyond, the trees ended.

'Jump in,' he hissed, 'they're not far behind!'

The next moment we were bumping across an open field, then out onto a deserted road where the ancient Mercedes raced along at top speed. I struggled out of my flying suit to reveal the inconspicuous jacket and trousers which was my disguise whilst in Germany.

We were safe for the time being.

I turned to the driver. With surprise, I saw that he was no more than seventeen years old. There was an alertness about him, however, which belied his youth.

'Sorry about the unwelcoming reception,' he said. 'They must have spotted your plane.' He thrust a flask at me. 'Have some brandy.'

He introduced himself as Franz and revealed that it was his grandfather whom I was to bring out of Germany. His grandfather was a famous professor and a brilliant scientist. However, since he had once expressed his hostility to the German Reich, he was confined within the research station where he worked. As he was never allowed out, it was my job to go in and get him.

Franz said I should stay with him and his sister until I made the rescue. He then inquired how I intended to get his grandfather out of Germany.

I described how, if the rescue was successful, I was to signal to a captured Heinkel which would pass over the desolate Kleinhartz moor on the next three nights. We hoped that this German aeroplane, stripped of its armament and modified for long-range transport, would fool the enemy anti-aircraft batteries. Once across the English Channel, a pre-arranged signal from our pilot would get us through the British defences.

The countryside dropped away. We sped past a few blacked out houses and entered an unlit town. A few minutes later Franz pulled into the driveway of a large old house.

The front door was opened by a pretty young woman. Her name was Anna and I judged she was a couple of years older than her brother Franz. We ate breakfast as the early morning sun began to slant through the window shutters. I heard how, when their parents had died in the Berlin air raids of 1940, Franz and Anna had come to live at their grandfather's house. We talked about the professor and finally, Anna handed me a photograph of an old, white haired man. He looked completely harmless.

She confirmed that he was a total prisoner in the research station and added that two armed guards were always present when she visited him.

Then Franz and I spent six hours making up for lost sleep.

On awakening, I decided that I must reconnoitre the research establishment before I could plan a rescue. Since the place was twelve miles away, Franz offered to drive me there but I thought that the big Mercedes would be too conspicuous.

'There is a motorbike in the garage,' said Franz. That was ideal. Franz gave me directions and soon I was thundering through the streets on the magnificent BMW motorcycle. This fine piece of machinery could prove a powerful ally; it was fast and would out-distance most pursuers in time of trouble.

$$\star \qquad \star \qquad \star \qquad \star$$

Twenty minutes later I was on a straight length of road in open countryside. A quarter of a mile ahead I could see the research station. Slowly, I drove closer and saw that it was ringed by a double width of high wire fencing. Prowling guard dogs and a dozen sentry towers added the final touch of impregnability.

My heart dropped at the sight; there could be no question of the

blackened face and wire cutters approach which my Commando training had at first suggested.

As I racked my brains for a solution, a covered truck hooted at me
to pull over to the right. As it passed I translated the German Gothic
lettering; 'DANGEROUS CHEMICALS' printed on the tailboard.
A minute later it entered the main gate of the research station and
disappeared inside.

The germ of an idea formed in my head. I made a U turn and rode
back the way I had come until I reached a crossroads. There I propped
up the motorcycle and made a pretence of tinkering with the engine
for the benefit of any passers-by.

Twenty minutes later the empty chemical lorry rattled past. I gave
it a thirty second lead then followed. It turned off onto the main
Bremen autobahn and a few minutes later, pulled into a roadside café.

I parked and followed the massive driver into the murky interior.
He was a plain, open sort of fellow and I found it easy to get into
conversation over our beer and sausages.

We talked about this and that then he mentioned that he did the same
journey to the research station every day, always arriving at two o'clock
in the afternoon. This was the information I needed. We chatted for a
minute more then I said goodbye. His 'Aufwiedersehen' was truer than
he knew for I hoped to meet him again under much less friendly
circumstances.

*　　　*　　　*　　　*

Over an early supper with Franz and Anna I outlined my plan:

The next day, Franz would drive his sister to the research station.
Anna would ask to visit the professor and, if she could do it unseen,
slip him a note. This would tell him to meet the chemical truck in the
unloading bay at two o'clock. I intended to be aboard the truck, using
the driver as cover to get myself past the guards on the gate. During
unloading, I hoped to sneak the professor into the back of the lorry.
Once safely out of the research establishment it would simply be a
matter of driving to our rendezvous with the aeroplane.

Eagerly, Franz asked how I planned to ambush the lorry. He had
somehow acquired a sub machine-gun and ached to use it against the

Nazi tyrants. I pointed out that a bullet-riddled truck would be of little use and, grudgingly, he agreed to my scheme: I was to stage an accident at the crossroads near the research station; motorcycle on its side and me lying in the road feigning unconsciousness.

The lorry driver should stop and, with the help of my Luger, I would persuade him to take me to the professor.

Despite Franz's protestations, I insisted that they should go into hiding immediately after Anna had delivered the message.

The following afternoon I sat alone in the house, smoking heavily.

It was one thirty. The telephone bell rang. Anna's tense voice came over the wires:

'Grandfather has your message.'

'See you when the War's over!' I replied.

They had done their part. Now it was my turn.

★   ★   ★   ★

I kicked the motorcycle into life and its throaty roar pounded back at me from the buildings as I raced to keep my assignment with the unsuspecting truck driver.

After only two miles, I skidded to a halt at a level crossing. A policeman barred my path. Behind him a convoy of grey tanks bearing the cross of the German army rumbled slowly past on the back of a train. The procession seemed endless. I glanced at my watch. The delay could ruin my timing.

At last the tail end of the train had gone. I waited impatiently for the half-barriers to lift. Nothing happened. The policeman still stood there. He noticed my agitation.

'There's another right behind,' he shouted. 'You may as well switch off your engine and save fuel!'

I could see the next train coming but I had only fifteen minutes in which to cover ten miles. That decided me. I kicked into first gear, opened the throttle and jinxed round the nearest barrier. The train was almost on me. The open-mouthed face of its driver remains like a snapshot in my mind. My back wheel skidded on the smooth rails for an instant, then gripped. I flew across the front of the engine with just inches to spare and narrowly skirted the far barrier.

His words froze on his lips when he saw the Luger.

The road ahead was fairly straight for about three miles. I urged every gear to its utmost limit until the needle flickered at 140 kilometres an hour. The rest of the road was all twists and turns demanding constant braking and leaning followed by the thumping roar as I accelerated out of the bends.

Then the crossroads was in sight at last. But the following moment I saw that my carefully laid plan was in ruins; I was too late – the chemical truck had just swung out ahead of me onto the road to the research station.

In the next few seconds I wondered madly how I might retrieve the situation. There was only one possible decision: I had to stage the accident for real!

Head down, I raced past the lorry. There was just one corner between here and the research station and it was right ahead. As I leaned into the bend I released the throttle and let the machine slew away across the road. Simultaneously, I pulled up my legs and rolled.

My parachute training saved me from a bad injury but my right knee was bloodied and my head spun madly. I lay directly in the truck's path and prayed it could stop in time.

With a shudder it screeched to a halt within a few feet of me. The next moment I was heaved to a sitting position. The driver's concerned eyes recognized me immediately from the day before. Then the solicitous words froze on his lips as he saw the Luger.

I rose shakily to my feet and made for the passenger door of the truck. It was open. 'Get this thing moving!' I snarled.

He obeyed, white-faced.

As we approached the main gate I slid from my seat and crouched in the floor well. As long as my door was not opened, I could not be seen from outside.

We stopped and I heard the gateman's voice; 'A bit late today aren't you Karl!' I prodded the driver's leg with my gun.

'Ja . . . Delay the other end,' he replied hoarsely. We drove on and cautiously I returned to my seat. I was gambling that anyone who now saw me within the complex would assume that the guard on the gate had already cleared me for entry.

The lorry threaded its way between large industrial buildings from which came the heavy rumbling of machinery at work. Then we turned into a goods yard.

Instantly I recognized the professor standing a few yards ahead of us. Things looked bad; he was surrounded by several other men.

'Stop the truck, leave the engine running and get out!' I snapped at the driver. I followed suit.

The indignant voice of a helmeted soldier came from the group.

'You have no right to be here, Herr professor. It is strictly forbidden. Please return to your section immediately!'

I elbowed my way towards the old man and spoke with all the authority I could muster; 'The professor is here to discuss a complaint about our last delivery of chemicals.'

It was a flimsy trick but sufficient to momentarily confuse the others. For a few vital moments it had them wondering if the professor did indeed have a right to be in this part of the research station. We pushed past them and walked quickly to the lorry. The soldier took only a moment to recover his composure. Unslinging his rifle, he sauntered towards us. In a voice which dared us to disobey he said heavily:

'I have not been informed of an instruction which countermands the order that research staff are not allowed in this sector. You will please accompany me to the Commandant's office to obtain verification at once.'

This one knew his stuff and we had no time to argue. I pulled out the Luger and shot him in the leg. He spun round and crashed to the ground, screaming loudly.

I glanced round, looking for the truck driver. He had slipped out of sight during the commotion. I cursed. He was our passport through the gate and, having shot the guard, we could not afford the time to look for him. The place could fill with more soldiers at any moment.

'Get in!' I yelled to the professor and simultaneously flung myself up into the driver's seat.

I crunched the gearstick into second and, heaving on the heavy wheel, swung the truck in a wide arc. With tyres squealing, I followed the circuitous route back to the main gate. In minutes we were within two hundred yards of the exit. I had been praying that we could ram our way through the gate but it was a massive iron construction and now I doubted that this was possible. I stamped on the brakes, looking desperately to right and left for an alternative escape route.

The next moment the professor shouted; 'Go on. Go on!' I looked where he was pointing and to my astonishment saw a uniformed figure pulling back the enormous gate and beckoning to us. At this distance the gateman could not see who was in the cab. He had simply recognized the truck which came in and out every day and opened up as usual!

Hardly daring to hope we could fool him long enough to get out, I said, 'Duck down in case he spots you, professor.' With that, I put my foot down and the diesel engine gathered speed. As we lumbered forward, I waved a hand in front of my face in an effort to hide it. At the last moment the guard realized his mistake. He was too late. We were out!

We had a bit of a lead and escape now depended on the Nazi's being slow to respond. I pushed the truck as hard as it would go. It was like urging an ambling elephant to break into a gallop after the sprightly pace of the motorbike.

We had made a couple of miles when I glanced in the rear view mirror; five black specks were on the road. The enemy had not lost a second in getting their pursuit under way. With despair, I calculated that it could only be a matter of minutes before we were captured.

'Our only chance is to take to the fields,' I shouted to the old man. We were nearly at the crossroads and, braking viciously, I hauled rapidly on the steering wheel. The truck went into a wheeling skid which ended with it spanning the road, effectively blocking the route to the following soldiers.

'Get out!' I yelled and, scrambling across the seats, followed the professor through his door. As we ran up the road, I desperately scanned the horizon ahead for some trees, a wood perhaps, where we might throw our pursuers off the scent.

The old man could not move fast and I gave little chance for our survival. We had covered only a few hundred yards when the crackle of machine-guns told me that we were finished. Bullets flew off the road. I turned to see that several soldiers stood between us and the truck. They could hardly miss! I flung myself at the professor and we both fell to the ground. Shots whipped over our heads.

I was dimly aware of the squeal of tyres and machine-gun fire close by. Then a terrific explosion and a rush of searing heat engulfed me.

Slowly, stupefied, I began to move. With amazement I realized that I was being helped to my feet by Anna. Then, further up the road I recognized Franz's Mercedes.

I turned round. Flames licked into the sky from the shattered remains of the truck. The vehicle must have been loaded with TNT because it had detonated like a massive bomb. There was not a Nazi in sight – they had been literally blown to bits.

'That should hold 'em up!' came the satisfied voice of Franz. He dropped the sub machine-gun which had caused the explosion and half carried the shaking professor to the car.

As we raced towards the Kleinhartz moor, a glance at my watch told me that we should reach it in time to signal the Heinkel. I laughed as Franz explained how he and Anna had decided to delay their own escape to 'keep an eye on me' as he put it.

Three hours later, as we winged over Surrey, Franz turned to the professor. 'Now that you're in safe hands grandfather, can you tell us something about this miracle discovery of yours?'

The old man hesitated, peering at us in silence for a full minute. Then a look came into his eyes which frightened me more than all the forces which were then terrorizing the world.

As we heard his words for the first time, I know we all thought that we were listening to a madman's horrific fantasy. His voice rang out like that of a biblical prophet of doom:

'Mankind will never again dare to make war for I can build a machine to unleash the strongest forces of the Universe . . . If used for evil, it will turn the globe to ashes, every spart of life shall be wiped from the face of the Earth!

'This mighty power is held within the smallest particle . . . The Atom . . .'

The trouble with Camels

V. M. Yeates

In the First World War, the Camel aircraft was a scourge to the enemy. Unfortunately it was also a terror to trainee allied pilots, for in practice, this strange and unpredictable aircraft had a 30 percent casualty rate . . .

Flying Camels was not everyone's work. They were by far the most difficult of service machines to handle. Many pilots killed themselves by crashing in a right-hand spin when they were learning to fly them. A Camel hated an inexperienced hand, and flopped into a frantic spin at the least opportunity. They were unlike ordinary aeroplanes, being quite unstable, immoderately tail-heavy, so light on the controls that the slightest jerk or inaccuracy would hurl them all over the sky, difficult to land, deadly to crash: a list of vices to test the stoutest courage, and the first flight on a Camel was always a terrible ordeal. They were bringing out a two-seater training Camel for dual work, in the hope of reducing that thirty per cent of crashes on the first solo flights.

Tom Cundall very well remembered his own first effort. Baker, his instructor, had given him a preliminary lecture.

'I suppose you haven't run a Clerget engine before.' (It was a Clerget Camel.) 'You'll find it just like a Le Rhone; you've taken up the Le Rhone Pup, haven't you? You'll find it a bit fierce to start with: you've got another forty horse-power and plenty more revs. You'll soon get to like that. Be careful with your fine adjustment, they're a bit tricky on that. Ease it back as much as you can as soon as you're off the ground, and the higher you get the less juice you'll find she wants. I expect you've heard all about flying them. Be careful of your rudder. You may find it a bit difficult to keep straight at first. Keep just a shade of left rudder on to counteract the twist to the right; when you're on anything like full throttle you can feel the engine pulling to the right all the time. Remember to use the rudder as little as possible, you hardly want any when you turn. But don't be afraid of putting on plenty of bank. A Camel's an aeroplane, not a house with wings, and you can put 'em over vertical and back again quicker than you can say it. I expect you'll find three-quarter throttle or so best for getting used to it. Keep her between eighty and ninety at first. Don't get wind up, and you'll be quite happy. Now this is what I want you to do. Take your time in running the engine on the ground, so as to get used to it, then go straight up to five thousand all out. You'll be up there in no time. You're not to turn or do anything except ease the fine adjustment back below five thousand. Climb at eighty-five. Then you can try turning to the left, all out or throttled down, just as you like. Don't be afraid of spinning. If you do spin, you know how to get out: pull off the petrol and give her plenty of opposite rudder and stick. Have the stick well forward, but don't keep it too far forward when she's coming out, or you'll dive like hell and lose a lot of height and jerk yourself about and lord knows what.'

Tom had got in and run the engine. There wasn't any difficulty about that. He taxied out and turned round. The wind being easterly he had to take off over the hangars. He opened the throttle and the engine roared. Then it spluttered. Hell! He caught a glimpse of people jumping about with excitement. Too much petrol, his hand went to the fine adjustment. By the time he had got the engine running properly he was almost into a hangar with his tail hardly off the ground. He pulled the stick back and staggered into the air just clearing the roof: if the engine gave one more splutter he would stall and crash. But the engine continued to roar uniformly. His heart, having missed several beats, thumped away to make up for them, and he felt emulsified; but he was flying.

The engine was pulling like a chained typhoon. He seemed to be going straight up. Two thousand feet, and he had only just staggered above the hangars! It was difficult to hold the thing down at all; the

34

His heart missed several beats, but he was flying.

slightest relaxation of forward pressure on the stick would point it at the very zenith. The day was excellent for flying, there being no wind or bumps. A grey mist was still weakly investing the world, limiting the field of vision, wrapping the horizon in obscurity. At his back the south-westerly sun was touching the greyness and changing it into a haze of golden light, blinding to peer into; in front the mist hung like a solid wall, ending abruptly in a straight line at some three or four thousand feet, and on it stood the base of the pale grey-blue vault of the sky, seeming only a degree less solid.

He soon became aware that he was not flying straight. At first the sensation peculiar to side-slipping had been lost in the major sensation of flying a strange machine, but when his senses were less bewildered by the strangeness of it he became aware of a side-wind, of a secondary vibration within the normal vibration of the engine, of the particular feeling of wrongness that is associated with side-slipping. He had seen beginners doing this sort of thing. A few days previously someone had taken off in a Camel and gone across the aerodrome almost like a flying crab, while everyone held their breath and waited for the side-slip to become a spin and the pilot a corpse; but he had got away with it. Tom had been scornful at the time, but here he was doing much the same sort of thing; he had no idea why. He could fly any ordinary aeroplane straight enough. He experimented with the rudder, but soon came to the conclusion that side-slipping was a vice of Camels; at any rate of this one. It would not fly straight for more than a second at a time.

At five thousand feet he put the machine on a level keel in order to try to turn, but flying level brought such an increase of speed and fierceness that he was forced to throttle down the engine considerably before he could bring himself to put on bank. Then, very carefully, he pressed the stick towards the left and the rudder gently the same way. What happened was that all tension went out of the controls, there was an instant of steep side-slip, and the earth whizzed round in front of him. A spin! At once his hand went to the fine adjustment to shut off the petrol. Full forward opposite stick and rudder stopped the spinning, but he found himself diving vertically and side-slipping badly at the same time. He had fallen from the seat and was hanging in the belt. He pulled himself back into the seat by means of the joystick and set about getting out of the dive. Gradually he brought the nose up to the horizon, or to where it was hidden in the mist, and restarted the engine which roared away furiously.

Looking at the pitot he found the speed was a hundred and twenty, so he eased the stick back and climbed. For some minutes he didn't care to do anything but fly as straight as he could, and it cost him an effort of will to decide to try again to turn. This time he was ready for a spin, and as soon as he felt the controls going soft he came out of the turn. By this means he succeeded in turning through a few degrees without actually spinning, and after a few more such turns he let his strong desire to get back to earth have its way. He made out that he was some way east of Croydon, and it was necessary to turn west. To do this he shut off the engine and brought the machine round in a long sweeping glide. The thing would turn on the glide without spinning, anyhow: that was something. He flew towards the sun until he judged the aerodrome must be close ahead, though it was invisible in the golden haze, and stopped the engine again and soon found himself gliding over the aerodrome at a thousand feet. He started the engine, throttled right down, and buzzed the engine on the thumb switch. To get into the aerodrome he had to perform another complete half-turn, which he did on the glide, not without some qualms about the nearness of the ground. He wouldn't have stopped up any longer for the wealth of all Jewry. He would never make a Camel pilot. He would give up flying and go back to the PBI.[1] He drifted on downwards to land, approaching the aerodrome correctly from leeward, but rather fast, being afraid of stalling and spinning into the ground. He floated across the aerodrome. He suddenly realized he would never get in. His wheels touched the ground and he bounced like a kangaroo. Desperately he opened the throttle. The engine spluttered. He was heading for that same hangar again. He would hit it this time. He moved the fine adjustment and the engine roared. He pulled up and once more staggered over the roof, having caught a glimpse of Baker shaking a fist at him. He held on his way shakily up to three thousand feet, and then shut off the engine and glided back.

This time he hardly reached the aerodrome at all, and opened the throttle, but the engine wouldn't pick up. He just floated over the

[1] PBI, Poor Bloody Infantry (Oxford Dictionary).

boundary hedge and pancaked on to the rough ground at the edge of the aerodrome. Luckily the undercarriage stood it. His prop stopped, and he sat there waiting for mechanics to come and swing it: safe, profoundly glad to be back on earth, but feeling a perfect fool.

It took the mechanics a long time to reach him, and that gave Baker time to cool down. All he said was, 'Well, how d'you like it?'

'Oh, not too bad,' Tom lied. 'I spun turning.'

'You'll soon get over that, but for the love of heaven don't do that comic take-off act of yours any more, or you'll smash the only Camel I've got left, and we shall have to scrape you off with a knife.'

But that was long ago: four months in fact. Or was it four years? Camels were wonderful fliers when you had got used to them, which took about three months of hard flying. At the end of that time you were either dead, a nervous wreck, or the hell of a pilot and a terror to Huns . . . All you had to do when caught miles from home by dozens of Huns was to go into a vertical bank and keep on turning to the right until the Huns got hungry and went down to their black bread and sauerkraut, or it got dark: the difficulty was that you might run out of petrol and have to shoot them all down on the reserve tank, so that it might be as well to shoot them all down at once, as recommended in patriotic circles! . . .

Escape or Die

Charles McCormac

1942. Seventeen escape from a Japanese prisoner of war camp on Singapore Island. They hope to reach Australia –

Two fall immediately to Japanese tommy-guns. Seven more are killed by a Japanese beach patrol. Eight reach the open water in a boat. But the waters are shark infested and the skies are suddenly filled with Zero fighter planes coming in for the kill, machine-guns blazing. This attack leaves four out of the original seventeen, and they've barely covered twenty of the two thousand miles to Australia.

Through enemy patrolled jungle and crocodile patrolled swampland the four survivors continue their struggle. After a seemingly endless terror-filled journey they come to a native village in Sumatra. Here the fourth member of their party dies of exhaustion, and still they are miles from their goal.

McCormac and Skinner, two Britishers; along with Donaldson the Australian are the three survivors. Skinner has met a native girl . . .

McCormac and Donaldson want to reach Java. McCormac approaches the head man of the village . . .

We waited anxiously for nearly an hour, then back came the headman with his friend, a powerful, thick-set fisherman.

'Tuan, this is the man who will take you and your friend to the island. His brother has a pukpuk boat which will pick you up from there and carry you to Java; it is too far for him to go himself.'

There was no alternative but to accept his offer. At least we should be a step further on our journey, a step, albeit a small one, closer to

39

Australia. Even if the worst happened and we were left stranded on the island, we could probably think up some way of getting ourselves off it. We had, after all, escaped from far worse situations.

'Thank you,' I said to the headman. 'We will go with your friend; but I have no more money to reward you with; I can only give you a letter, which you must hide until the Japanese are driven out; then you must show it to an English tuan who will give you money.'

I turned to Don.

'Got anything I can write on?'

'Only a scrap of chocolate carton.' Out of the tattered pocket of his shirt he produced a yellow, sweat-stained piece of cardboard and a stub of blue pencil.

On the back of the cardboard I wrote:

'The village has today (I don't know the date) helped R. G. Donaldson (Australia), C. E. McCormac (Great Britain) and Chris. Skinner (Great Britain) to leave Sumatra and further their escape from the Japanese. Please pay them a reward.'

Don and I signed it, but Skinny held back.

'I don't think I ought to,' he said.

'Why on earth not?'

He muttered something unintelligible and turned restlessly away.

'Come on, man. What's the matter with you?'

'Well, it's like this chaps. Reckon I'll stay behind.'

'I knew it!' Don smacked a fist into his palm. 'You poor, silly fool.'

Skinny looked uncomfortable and shifted from one foot to the other.

'Well, this is how it is,' he mumbled. 'See, I've been doing a sort of line with Li-Tong and I reckoned I'd ask her to marry me.'

'Well, for God's sake!' shouted Don. 'You must be mad.'

'Well, what's wrong with that?' Skinny muttered defiantly. 'She's pretty and she's nice. You two can get along without me.'

'But think of it, man,' I pleaded. 'You've always been grousing about living in the jungle; do you want to spend the rest of your life squatting under a lot of palm trees!'

Skinny began to look sulky.

'Well, I've made up my mind, and that's that.'

'What about your folks?'

'That's my affair.'

'Suppose the Japs catch you?'

'Don't worry. They won't.'

It was fantastic. Far into the night we argued and argued, until at last the old man and the fisherman returned. They said they were ready.

Don and I each stuck a parang into our rough rope belts and followed them out of the hut and down to the water's edge. It was raining steadily, with pale moonlight filtering through a layer of thin, diaphanous cloud. Drawn up on to the shelving beach was a sturdy ten-foot launch, with mast, sail and a small diesel engine. Skinny, with Li-Tong clutching nervously at his arm, followed us down to the water's edge. No one spoke, but as Don and I climbed over the gunwale, Skinny seemed suddenly to change his mind.

'Hold it! Hold it!' he shouted. 'I'm coming too.'

He started gesticulating to Li-Tong, lisping at her incoherently in broken Malay. She cottoned on pretty quickly, and at once started up a high-pitched wailing, clinging to his waist like a limpet. For several minutes there was pandemonium, with Li-Tong working up to a fine soprano shriek and Skinny jabbering away in a combination of broken Malay and choicest Anglo-Saxon. It was the old man who finally settled the argument. In one of the rare seconds of silence his thin voice quavered along the shore.

'If the Skinner tuan does not stay, the fisherman will not take the other tuans across the water.'

Hurriedly I pushed off. 'Looks like you've had it,' I said.

I thought he would start another tirade, but Li-Tong nestled up to him and he seemed to recognize the inevitable. 'OK then, reckon I'll have to stay.'

'Suppose we get through,' I asked him. 'Whom shall I notify?'

'No one.'

'What regiment were you in?'

He smiled artfully. 'Signals.'

The engine fired; in a gentle arc the launch drew away from Sumatra; the three of us waved until the coast-line faded and the last we saw of Skinny was a tiny, rain-blurred figure, arms outstretched, stumbling into the little waves that lapped with heartless regularity onto the palm-fringed shore. Never have I been quite certain that our escape was not bought at the price of his captivity. What, I have often wondered, were his thoughts as the launch's outline faded into nothingness and he was left alone?

But though of course we never saw Skinner again we did hear of him, and his story has a heartening postscript.

Towards the end of the Far Eastern war I found myself serving with SEAC Intelligence. Part of my duties was to interrogate personnel who had escaped through Japanese-occupied territory, and one day six Fleet Air Arm officers were brought to me for routine questioning. Theirs was a strange story. They had, it seemed, been taking part in a carrier-borne shipping strike against Jap merchantmen off Telok Betong. Opposition had been unexpectedly fierce and four Fireflies, badly damaged, had crash-landed in the jungle. One was never found, but the other three had managed to touch down in clearings and their crews had escaped serious injury. In each case the pilot and observer had hidden in the jungle for only a short time before they were contacted by natives, who had led them to a bearded white man. This white man, the officers said, was living like a king in a little fishing village on the south-east Sumatran coast. He had cared for them, entertaining them, and finally arranged for their safe transportation, via the 'underground', back to Australia. Each of them could describe the white man and his wife in some detail. Obviously it was Skinny and Li-Tong. They were, I gathered, idyllically happy, with two children, an imposing bamboo atap hut and a small fishing vessel. The man had scorned the idea of returning to civilization, he was far too happy, he had said, where he was. So perhaps my qualms about our having left 'the Skinner tuan' are without foundation.

We headed out to sea, and in soft, persistent rain the launch chugged southward into a dying ground-swell. Gradually the huddled figures on the Sumatran shore lost definition and merged into the darkness. Don and I sheltered from the rain under a layer of ragged coconut matting.

'Seventeen little nigger boys,' I said. 'Then there were two.'

'There'd still be three,' grunted Don, 'if Skinny had a grain of sense.'

We lay in the bottom of the boat listening to the slap of waves and the steady patter of rain. After about an hour the dark mass of an island took shape on our starboard bow; then dead ahead I made out the outline of another smaller island and soon our keel grated harshly onto a gravel beach.

'Where's this?' I asked the fisherman.

He only grunted and waved his hand towards the sombre rocky beach. 'Wait here,' he said.

'For how long?'

'Tonight.'

We clambered out, our clothes sticking damply to our bodies, and as we made our way across the mud and stones of the beach to a protecting outcrop of rock, the taciturn native pushed off and, without another word, set course for Sumatra. We spent the night dozing fitfully in the shelter of the rocks, which offered some degree of protection against the driving rain. When we woke there was no sun and the sky was pewter-coloured and overcast. It was unpleasantly sticky and hot.

'We'd better not move,' I said. 'Cheerful Charlie's brother will expect to pick us up here.'

'If he ever comes,' grunted Don.

We stayed by the beach for several hours but finally decided to explore the island, keeping the beach in sight. Climbing some twenty or thirty feet up the boulders, we looked down through a thin veil of mist on to a volcanic island two or three miles long. Over the water to the southward we were just able to discover the hazy outline of another stretch of land.

On the eastern shore of our island were several fishing huts raised on stilts at the water's edge, but there was no sign of human life, which was hardly surprising as the vegetation was restricted to a handful of stunted shrubs which struggled with difficulty out of the barren rock. We searched for food, but after an hour or so our sum total was only twelve berries, which tasted bitter and were therefore suspect, and a handful of anaemic-looking roots. But in a natural hollow between the rocks we found a pool of water which did not taste over-salty.

About noon the mist cleared rapidly and we saw in the brilliant sunlight, only about a mile offshore, seven or eight Japanese flying-boats, which seemed to be practising take-offs and landings. Early in

A few minutes later the boat nosed ashore.

the afternoon a small naval vessel steamed past two or three hundred yards offshore and we could see the Japanese flag fluttering in the slow tropic wind. Hour followed hour. At first I thought we might have been marooned but Don argued that with signs of Jap activity only a few hundred yards offshore our friends would not risk picking us up by day, but would wait for the coming of darkness.

He was right. About two hours after sunset, we heard the chug-chug of an approaching launch; a few minutes later the boat nosed ashore, and we recognized our fisherman, and with him a younger man whom we took to be his brother. We waded out and climbed aboard.

'Boy, are we glad to see you!' grinned Don.

The younger native gave a non-committal grunt and started tinkering with the engine. After a few moments it speeded up and we again headed out to sea. After a long silence I tried to open the conversation.

'How do you manage to own a motor-boat?'

'It belongs to the Japanese.'

'How come you have it then?'

'I work for them. I look after the flying-boat anchors.' Obviously he meant buoys. I had a sudden idea.

'Are there many flying-boats?'

'Twelve or fifteen, perhaps.'

'Are you taking us near them?'

Don realized what I had in mind. 'Now don't start getting any damn silly ideas,' he grunted.

'OK, cobber. But just think of the fun we'd have pulling the stoppers out of their hulls.'

The elder fisherman motioned us to be silent. He leant over the port gunwale, listening. The distant purr of a motor-launch came whispering over the water. We were pushed into the bottom of the boat, covered with matting and told to keep silent – not that we needed any telling. After a few minutes the launch slowed down almost to a stop. We heard the muttering of voices, perhaps from a waterborne patrol; then we were again under way. Neither of the fishermen would tell us exactly what had happened, but we assumed we had met a Japanese patrol and the brothers had somehow convinced them of the harmless nature of our voyage. Shortly afterwards the engine was throttled back once more and in the gloom we could pick out the soft, waving branches of trees and palms. The launch nosed gently onto the sand.

'Java,' said Cheerful Charlie.

He whispered a few words to his brother. 'Wait,' he said, and they vanished into the darkness.

'Not exactly a talkative couple, are they?' Don grunted as together we squatted on the shingle, some fifty yards from the launch.

'Why should they be? It's usually the people who've talked the least who've helped us the most.'

'I can't make out why they help us at all,' muttered Don. 'Much easier for 'em to stick a knife in our backs and claim the Jap reward.'

'I know they're scared of the Japs; but maybe they're more scared of something else?'

'Such as?'

'This Army of Independence, perhaps.'

After about an hour our two fishermen returned; with them was a Javanese, a surly, taciturn man. He seemed annoyed – not unreasonably I thought – at being dragged out of his bed.

'He will look after you now,' said the elder brother. 'We must go.'

We shook hands with the fishermen, who were obviously anxious to be on their way, and watched their launch disappear into the darkness of Sunda Strait. Then we followed the Javanese. He led us through a tangled mass of mangroves into a belt of thick undergrowth which in turn gave way to an endless, swampy scrub. How he knew where he was going we were quite unable to fathom, for there seemed to be no defined track or path. On and on we went, until at last dawn broke in a flood of pale golden sunlight which shimmered in the countless pools and sparkled brightly on the dew-wet foliage. In the daylight we increased our pace through thickening vegetation. Our guide began to show signs of nervousness. We made good time for about three miles through scrubby secondary jungle; then quite suddenly came to a belt of dark, primeval forest. For about three hundred yards we followed a well-defined track. Then the Javanese stopped.

'Friends here,' he said.

I looked around at the dank, impenetrable jungle.

'Where?'

He shrugged his shoulders and pointed down the track.

'What's the name of this place?'

'Merak.'

He was a man of few words. He again pointed down the dark, hemmed-in trail. 'Friends there. You walk.' And he turned on his heel and strode rapidly away. Don and I looked at each other. Then we burst out laughing. Obviously we had no alternative but to follow his advice. We walked for about another mile, then found some fruit and, tired out, lay down to rest.

But we were stupid. We stretched out only a few yards from a gradual curve in the trail. We could not have chosen a less suitable spot. After our long run of luck we had perhaps become careless and less cautious. We had a good rest and were on the point of moving off again, when less than thirty yards away a man swung into view, walking rapidly towards us. Idiots that we were, we had loitered on a blind corner; he was almost bound to see us, and he carried a revolver.

Don dived into the undergrowth on the opposite side of the track. I froze motionless on the spot where we had been lying.

The man stopped; he took a few paces towards Don; I saw his finger curled over the trigger. He was a youngish man, black-haired and barefooted. His skin was burned brown from the sun, but it was not the brown of an Indonesian. He wore grey slacks and a whitish shirt. Obviously, I thought, a European. I watched uncertainly from my inadequate hideout.

'What are you two fairies doing here?' The voice had a rich, Australian twang. Its owner was entirely self-possessed. He waved his gun towards me.

'Out you come.'

And out I came.

'You next.' The gun circled round to Donaldson who scrambled ignominiously from underneath a thorn bush.

'Who the hell are you?' he muttered sheepishly.

'Who the hell are *you*?' The stranger had an air of definite authority. 'If you want any help, maybe I can do something for you. I heard you were around. Where are you from?'

'Singapore,' I said.

'I heard there was a big break there. Were you in it?'

'Yes,' said Don. 'Unless there was another.'

'No, there was only one.'

'You seem to know a lot.' Don eyed him speculatively. But the stranger let the remark pass.

'Where are the rest of you?' he asked curtly.

'Dead,' answered Don. 'All except one, and his fate was worse than death.'

'Torture?'

'No. He got married.'

The stranger grinned. 'Jesus,' he drawled. 'This is a terrible war.'

'How did you know we were here?' I asked.

'We don't answer questions around here,' he said. 'We only ask them.' He led us down the track. 'Come on, we can talk while we're walking. I'm taking you to a chap who runs a guerrilla band.' . . .

The Scarlet Pimpernel

Baroness Orczy

Paris:
September 1792

A surging, seething, murmuring crowd, of beings that are human only in name, for to the eye and ear they seem naught but savage creatures, animated by vile passions and by the lust of vengeance and of hate. The hour, some little time before sunset, and the place, the West Barricade, at the very spot where, a decade later, a proud tyrant raised an undying monument to the nation's glory and his own vanity.

During the greater part of the day the guillotine had been kept busy at its ghastly work: all that France had boasted of in the past centuries, of ancient names, and blue blood, had paid toll to her desire for liberty and for fraternity. The carnage had only ceased at this late hour of the day because there were other more interesting sights for the people to witness, a little while before the final closing of the barricades for the night.

And so the crowd rushed away from the Place de la Grève and made for the various barricades in order to watch this interesting and amusing sight.

It was to be seen every day, for those aristos were such fools! They were traitors to the people, of course, all of them, men, women and children who happened to be descendants of the great men who since the Crusades had made the glory of France: her old *noblesse*. Their ancestors had oppressed the people, had crushed them under the scarlet heels of their dainty buckled shoes, and now the people had become the rulers of France and crushed their former masters – not beneath their heel, for they went shoeless mostly in these days – but beneath a more effectual weight, the knife of the guillotine.

And daily, hourly, the hideous instrument of torture claimed its many victims – old men, young women, tiny children, even until the day when it would finally demand the head of a King and of a beautiful young Queen.

But this was as it should be: were not the people now the rulers of France? Every aristocrat was a traitor, as his ancestors had been before him: for two hundred years now the people had sweated, and toiled and starved, to keep a lustful court in lavish extravagance; now the descendants of those who had helped to make those courts brilliant had to hide for their lives – to fly, if they wished to avoid the tardy vengeance of the people.

And they did try to hide, and tried to fly: that was just the fun of the whole thing. Every afternoon before the gates closed and the market carts went out in procession by the various barricades, some fool of an aristo endeavoured to evade the clutches of the Committee of Public Safety. In various disguises, under various pretexts, they tried to slip through the barriers which were so well guarded by citizen soldiers of the Republic. Men in women's clothes, women in male attire, children disguised in beggar's rags: there were some of all sorts: *ci-devant* counts, marquises, even dukes, who wanted to fly from France, reach England, or some other equally accursed country, and there try to rouse foreign feeling against the glorious Revolution, or to raise an army in order to liberate the wretched prisoners in the Temple, who had once called themselves sovereigns of France.

But they were nearly always caught at the barricades. Sergeant Bibot especially at the West Gate had a wonderful nose for scenting an aristo in the most perfect disguise. Then, of course, the fun began. Bibot would look at his prey as a cat looks upon the mouse, play with him, sometimes for quite a quarter of an hour, pretend to be hoodwinked by the disguise, by the wigs and other bits of theatrical make-up which hid the identity of a *ci-devant* noble marquise or count.

Oh! Bibot had a keen sense of humour, and it was well worth hanging round that West Barricade, in order to see him catch an aristo in the very act of trying to flee from the vengeance of the people.

Sometimes Bibot would let his prey actually out by the gates, allowing him to think for the space of two minutes at least that he really had escaped out of Paris, and might even manage to reach the coast of England in safety: but Bibot would let the unfortunate wretch walk about ten metres towards the open country, then he would send two men after him and bring him back stripped of his disguise.

Oh! that was extremely funny, for as often as not the fugitive would prove to be a woman, some proud marchioness, who looked terribly comical when she found herself in Bibot's clutches after all, and knew that a summary trial would await her the next day, and after that the fond embrace of Madame la Guillotine.

No wonder that on this fine afternoon in September the crowd round Bibot's gate was eager and excited. The lust of blood grows with its satisfaction, there is no satiety: the crowd had seen a hundred noble heads fall beneath the guillotine today, it wanted to make sure that it would see another hundred fall on the morrow.

Bibot was sitting on an overturned and empty cask close by the gate of the barricade; a small detachment of citoyen soldiers were under his command. The work had been very hot lately. Those cursed aristos were becoming terrified and tried their hardest to slip out of Paris: men, women and children, whose ancestors, even in remote ages, had served those traitorous Bourbons, were all traitors themselves and right food for the guillotine. Every day Bibot had had the satisfaction of unmasking some fugitive royalists and sending them back to be tried by the Committee of Public Safety, presided over by that good patriot, Citoyen Foucquier Tinville.

Robespierre and Danton both had commended Bibot for his zeal, and Bibot was proud of the fact that he on his own initiative had sent at least fifty aristos to the guillotine.

But today all the sergeants in command at the various barricades had had special orders. Recently a very great number of aristos had succeeded in escaping out of France and in reaching England safely.

There were curious rumours about these escapes; they had become very frequent and singularly daring; the people's minds were coming strangely excited about it all. Sergeant Grospierre had been sent to the guillotine for allowing a whole family of aristos to slip out of the North Gate under his very nose.

It was asserted that these escapes were organized by a band of Englishmen, whose daring seemed to be unparalleled and who, from sheer desire to meddle in what did not concern them, spent their spare time in snatching away lawful victims destined for Madame la Guillotine. These rumours soon grew in extravagance; there was no doubt that this band of meddlesome Englishmen did exist; moreover, they seemed to be under the leadership of a man whose pluck and audacity were almost fabulous. Strange stories were afloat of how he and those aristos whom he rescued became suddenly invisible as they reached the barricades, and escaped out of the gates by sheer supernatural agency.

No one had seen these mysterious Englishmen; as for their leader, he was never spoken of, save with a superstitious shudder. Citoyen Foucquier Tinville would in the course of the day receive a scrap of paper from some mysterious source; sometimes he would find it in the pocket of his coat, at others it would be handed to him by someone in the crowd, whilst he was on his way to the sitting of the Committee of Public Safety. The paper always contained a brief notice that the band of meddlesome Englishmen were at work, and it was always signed with a device drawn in red – a little star-shaped flower, which we in England call the Scarlet Pimpernel. Within a few hours of the receipt of this impudent notice, the citoyens of the Committee of Public Safety would hear that so many royalists and aristocrats had succeeded in reaching the coast, and were on their way to England and safety.

The guards at the gates had been doubled, the sergeants in command had been threatened with death, whilst liberal rewards were offered for the capture of these daring and impudent Englishmen. There was a sum of five thousand francs promised to the man who laid hands on the mysterious and elusive Scarlet Pimpernel.

Everyone felt that Bibot would be that man, and Bibot allowed that belief to take firm root in everybody's mind; and so, day after day, people came to watch him at the West Gate, so as to be present when he laid hands on any fugitive aristo who perhaps might be accompanied by that mysterious Englishman.

'Bah!' he said to his trusted corporal, 'Citoyen Grospierre was a fool! Had it been me now, at that North Gate last week . . .'

Citoyen Bibot spat on the ground to express his contempt for his comrade's stupidity.

'How did it happen, citoyen?' asked the corporal.

'Grospierre was at the gate, keeping good watch,' began Bibot, pompously, as the crowd closed in round him, listening eagerly to his narrative. 'We've all heard of this meddlesome Englishman, this accursed Scarlet Pimpernel. He won't get through *my gate*, morbleu! unless he be the devil himself. But Grospierre was a fool. The market carts were going through the gates; there was one laden with casks, and driven by an old man, with a boy beside him. Grospierre was a bit drunk, but he thought himself very clever; he looked into the casks – most of them, at least – and saw they were empty, and let the cart go through.'

A murmur of wrath and contempt went round the group of ill-clad wretches who crowded round Citoyen Bibot.

'Half an hour later,' continued the sergeant, 'up comes a captain of the guard with a squad of some dozen soldiers with him. "Has a cart gone through?" he asks of Grospierre, breathlessly. "Yes," said Grospierre, "not half an hour ago." "And you have let them escape," shouts the captain furiously. "You'll go to the guillotine for this, citoyen sergeant! that cart held concealed the ci-devant Duc de Chalis and all his family!" "What!" thunders Grospierre, aghast. "Aye! and the driver was none other than that cursed Englishman, the Scarlet Pimpernel." '

A howl of execration greeted this tale. Citoyen Grospierre had paid for his blunder on the guillotine, but what a fool! Oh what a fool!

Bibot was laughing so much at his own tale that it was some time before he could continue.

' "After them, my men," shouts the captain,' he said, after a while, ' "remember the reward; after them, they cannot have gone far!" And with that he rushes through the gate, followed by his dozen soldiers.'

'But it was too late!' shouted the crowd, excitedly.

'They never got them!'

'Curse that Grospierre for his folly.'

'He deserved his fate!'

'Fancy not examining those casks properly!'

But these sallies seemed to amuse Citoyen Bibot exceedingly; he laughed until his sides ached, and the tears streamed down his cheeks.

'Nay, nay!' he said at last, 'those aristos weren't in the cart; the driver was not the Scarlet Pimpernel!'

'What?'

'No! The captain of the guard was that damned Englishman in disguise, and every one of his soldiers aristos!'

The crowd this time said nothing: the story certainly savoured of the supernatural, and though the Republic had abolished God, it had not quite succeeded in killing the fear of the supernatural in the hearts of the people. Truly that Englishman must be the devil himself.

The sun was sinking low down in the west. Bibot prepared himself to close the gates.

'En avant the carts,' he said.

Some dozen covered carts were drawn up in a row, ready to leave town, in order to fetch the produce from the country close by, for market the next morning. They were mostly well known to Bibot, as they went through his gate twice every day on their way to and from the town. He spoke to one or two of their drivers – mostly women – and was at great pains to examine the inside of the carts.

'You never know,' he would say, 'and I'm not going to be caught like that fool Grospierre.'

The women who drove the carts usually spent their day on the Place de la Grève, beneath the platform of the guillotine, knitting and gossiping, whilst they watched the rows of tumbrils arriving with the victims the Reign of Terror claimed every day. It was great fun to see the aristos arriving for the reception of Madame la Guillotine, and the places close by the platform were very much sought after. Bibot, during the day, had been on duty on the Place. He recognized most of the old hags, 'tricotteuses', as they were called, who sat there and knitted whilst head after head fell beneath the knife, and they themselves got quite bespattered with the blood of those cursed aristos.

'Hé; la mère!' said Bibot to one of these horrible hags; 'what have you got there?'

At the first mention of smallpox Bilbot stepped back.

He had seen her earlier in the day, with her knitting and the whip of her cart close beside her. Now she had fastened a row of curly locks to the whip handle, all colours, from gold to silver, fair to dark, and she stroked them with her huge, bony fingers as she laughed at Bibot.

'I made friends with Madame Guillotine's lover,' she said with a coarse laugh, 'he cut these off for me from the heads as they rolled down. He has promised me some more tomorrow, but I don't know if I shall be at my usual place.'

'Ah! how is that, la mère?' asked Bibot, who, hardened soldier though he was, could not help shuddering at the awful loathsomeness of this semblance of a woman, with her ghastly trophy on the handle of her whip.

'My grandson has got the smallpox,' she said with a jerk of her thumb towards the inside of her cart, 'some say it's the plague! If it is, I shan't be allowed to come into Paris tomorrow.'

At the first mention of the word smallpox, Bibot had stepped hastily backwards, and when the old hag spoke of the plague, he retreated from her as fast as he could.

'Curse you!' he muttered, whilst the whole crowd hastily avoided the cart, leaving it standing all alone in the midst of the place.

The old hag laughed.

'Curse you, citoyen, for being a coward,' she said. 'Bah! what a man to be afraid of sickness.'

'Morbleu! the plague!'

Everyone was awe-struck and silent, filled with horror for the loathsome malady, the one thing which still had the power to arouse terror and disgust in these savage, brutalized creatures.

'Get out with you and with your plague-stricken brood!' shouted Bibot, hoarsely.

And with another rough laugh and coarse jest the old hag whipped up her lean nag and drove her cart out of the gate.

This incident had spoilt the afternoon. The people were terrified of these two horrible curses, the two maladies which nothing could cure, and which were the precursors of an awful and lonely death. They hung about the barricades, silent and sullen for a while, eyeing one another suspiciously, avoiding each other as if by instinct, lest the plague lurked already in their midst. Presently, as in the case of Grospierre, a captain of the guard appeared suddenly. But he was known to Bibot, and there was no fear of his turning out to be a sly Englishman in disguise.

'A cart . . .' he shouted breathlessly, even before he had reached the gates.

'What cart?' asked Bibot, roughly.

'Driven by an old hag . . . A covered cart . . .'

'There were a dozen . . .'

'An old hag who said her son had the plague?'

'Yes . . .'

'You have not let them go?'

'Morbleu!' said Bibot, whose purple cheeks had suddenly become white with fear.

'The cart contained the ci-devant Comtesse de Tournay and her two children, all of them traitors and condemned to death.'

'And the driver?' muttered Bibot, as a superstitious shudder ran down his spine.

'Sacrê tonnerre,' said the captain, 'but it is feared that it was that accursed Englishman himself – the Scarlet Pimpernel.'

Blazing Cockpit

Richard Hillary

3 September dawned dark and overcast, with a slight breeze ruffling the waters of the Estuary. Hornchurch aerodrome, twelve miles east of London, wore its usual morning pallor of yellow fog, lending an added air of grimness to the dimly silhouetted Spitfires around the boundary. From time to time a balloon would poke its head grotesquely through the mist as though looking for possible victims before falling back like some tired monster.

We came out on to the tarmac at about eight o'clock. During the night our machines had been moved from the Dispersal Point over to the hangars. All the machine tools, oil and general equipment had been left on the far side of the aerodrome. I was worried. We had been bombed a short time before, and my plane had been fitted out with a new cockpit hood. This hood unfortunately would not slide open along its groove; and with a depleted ground staff and no tools, I began to fear it never would. Unless it did open, I shouldn't be able to bale out in a hurry if I had to. Miraculously, 'Uncle George' Denholm, our Squadron Leader, produced three men with a heavy file and lubricating oil, and the corporal fitter and I set upon the hood in a fury of haste. We took it turn by turn, filing and oiling, oiling and filing, until at last the hood began to move. But agonizingly slowly: by ten o'clock, when the mist had cleared and the sun was blazing out of a clear sky, the hood was still sticking firmly half-way along the groove; at ten-fifteen, what I had feared for the last hour happened. Down the loud-speaker came the emotionless voice of the controller: '603 Squadron take off and patrol base; you will receive further orders in the air: 603 Squadron take off as quickly as you can, please.' As I pressed the starter and the engine roared into life, the corporal stepped back and crossed his fingers significantly. I felt the usual sick feeling in the pit of the stomach, as though I were about to row a race, and then I was too busy getting into position to feel anything.

Uncle George and the leading section took off in a cloud of dust; Brian Carbury looked across and put up his thumbs. I nodded and opened up, to take off for the last time from Hornchurch. I was flying No. 3 in Brian's section, with Stapme Stapleton on the right: the third section consisted of only two machines, so that our Squadron strength was eight. We headed south-east, climbing all out on a steady course. At about 12,000 feet we came up through the clouds: I looked down and saw them spread out below me like layers of whipped cream. The sun was brilliant and made it difficult to see even the next plane when turning. I was peering anxiously ahead, for the controller had given us warning of at least fifty enemy fighters approaching very high. When we did first sight them, nobody shouted, as I think we all saw them at the same moment. They must have been 500 to 1,000 feet above us and coming straight on like a swarm of locusts. I remember cursing and going automatically into line astern: the next moment we were in among them and it was each man for himself. As soon as they saw us they spread out and dived, and the next ten minutes was a blur of twisting machines and tracer bullets. One Messerschmitt went down in a sheet of flame on my right, and a Spitfire hurtled past in a half-roll; I was weaving and turning in a desperate attempt to gain height, with the machine practically hanging on the airscrew. Then, just below me and to my left, I saw what I had been praying for – a Messerschmitt climbing and away from the sun. I closed in to 200 yards, and from slightly to one side gave him a two-second burst: fabric ripped off the wing and black smoke poured from the engine, but he did not go down. Like a fool, I did not break away, but put in another three-second burst. Red flames shot upwards and he spiralled out of sight.

At that moment, I felt a terrific explosion which knocked the control stick from my hand, and the whole machine quivered like a stricken animal. In a second, the cockpit was a mass of flames: instinctively, I reached up to open the hood. It would not move. I tore off my straps and managed to force it back; but this took time, and when I dropped back into the seat and reached for the stick in an effort to turn the plane on its back, the heat was so intense that I could feel myself going. I remember a second of sharp agony, remember thinking 'So this is it!' and putting both hands to my eyes. Then I passed out.

When I regained consciousness I was free of the machine and falling rapidly. I pulled the rip-cord of my parachute and checked my descent with a jerk. Looking down, I saw that my left trouser leg was burnt off, that I was going to fall into the sea, and that the English coast was deplorably far away. About twenty feet above the water, I attempted to undo my parachute, failed, and flopped into the sea with it billowing round me. I was told later that the machine went into a spin at about 25,000 feet and that at 10,000 feet I fell out – unconscious. This may well have been so, for I discovered later a large cut on the top of my head, presumably collected while bumping round inside.

The water was not unwarm and I was pleasantly surprised to find that my life-jacket kept me afloat. I looked at my watch: it was not there. Then, for the first time, I noticed how burnt my hands were: down to the wrists, the skin was dead white and hung in shreds: I felt faintly sick from the smell of burnt flesh. By closing one eye I could see my lips, jutting out like motor tyres. The side of my parachute harness was cutting into me particularly painfully, so that I guessed my right hip was burnt. I made a further attempt to undo the harness, but owing to the pain of my hands, soon desisted. Instead, I lay back and reviewed the position: I was a long way from land; my hands were burnt, and so, judging from the pain of the sun, was my face; it was unlikely that anyone on shore had seen me come down and even more unlikely that a ship would come by; I could float for possibly four hours in my Mae West. I began to feel that I had perhaps been premature in considering myself lucky to have escaped from the machine. After about half an hour my teeth started chattering, and to quiet them I kept up a regular tuneless chant, varying it from time to time with calls for help. There can be few more futile pastimes than yelling for

I saw that I was going to fall into the sea.

help alone in the North Sea, with a solitary seagull for company, yet it gave me a certain melancholy satisfaction, for I had once written a short story in which the hero (falling from a liner) had done just this. It was rejected.

The water now seemed much colder and I noticed with surprise that the sun had gone in though my face was still burning. I looked down at my hands, and not seeing them, realized that I had gone blind. So I was going to die. It came to me like that – I was going to die, and I was not afraid. This realization came as a surprise. The manner of my approaching death appalled and horrified me, but the actual vision of death left me unafraid: I felt only a profound curiosity and a sense of satisfaction that within a few minutes or a few hours I was to learn the great answer. I decided that it should be in a few minutes. I had no qualms about hastening my end and, reaching up, I managed to unscrew the valve of my Mae West. The air escaped in a rush and my head went under water. It is said by people who have all but died in the sea that drowning is a pleasant death. I did not find it so. I swallowed a large quantity of water before my head came up again, but derived little satisfaction from it. I tried again, to find that I could not get my face under. I was so enmeshed in my parachute that I could not move. For the next ten minutes, I tore my hands to ribbons on the spring-release catch. It was stuck fast. I lay back exhausted, and then I started to laugh. By this time I was probably not entirely normal and I doubt if my laughter was wholly sane, but there was something irresistibly comical in my grand gesture of suicide being so simply thwarted.

Goethe once wrote that no one, unless he had led the full life and realized himself completely, had the right to take his own life. Providence seemed determined that I should not incur the great man's displeasure.

It is often said that a dying man re-lives his whole life in one rapid kaleidoscope. I merely thought gloomily of the Squadron returning, of my mother at home, and of the few people who would miss me. Outside my family, I could count them on the fingers of one hand. What did gratify me enormously was to find that I indulged in no frantic abasements of prayers to the Almighty. It is an old jibe of God-fearing people that the irreligious always change their tune when about to die: I was pleased to think that I was proving them wrong.

Because I seemed to be in for an indeterminate period of waiting, I began to feel a terrible loneliness and sought for some means to take my mind off my plight. I took it for granted that I must soon become delirious, and I attempted to hasten the process: I encouraged my mind to wander vaguely and aimlessly, with the result that I did experience a certain peace. But when I forced myself to think of something concrete, I found that I was still only too lucid. I went on shuttling between the two with varying success until I was picked up. I remember as in a dream hearing somebody shout: it seemed so far away and quite unconnected with me . . .

Then willing arms were dragging me over the side; my parachute was taken off (and with such ease!); a brandy flask was pushed between my swollen lips; a voice said, 'OK, Joe, it's one of ours and still kicking'; and I was safe. I was neither relieved nor angry: I was past caring.

It was to the Margate lifeboat that I owed my rescue. Watchers on the coast had seen me come down, and for three hours they had been searching for me. Owing to wrong directions, they were just giving up and turning back for land when ironically enough one of them saw my parachute. They were then fifteen miles east of Margate.

While in the water I had been numb and had felt little pain. Now that I began to thaw out, the agony was such that I could have cried out. The good fellows made me as comfortable as possible, put up some sort of awning to keep the sun from my face, and phoned through for a doctor. It seemed to me to take an eternity to reach shore. I was put into an ambulance and driven rapidly to hospital. Through all this I was quite conscious, though unable to see. At the hospital they cut off my uniform, I gave the requisite information to a nurse about my next of kin, and then, to my infinite relief, felt a hypodermic syringe pushed into my arm . . .

The Man with the Donkey

Sir Irving Benson

As a boy, John Simpson Kirkpatrick used to lead donkeys along the sands at South Shields, Co. Durham. When he was eighteen, he left home for Australia to seek his fortune. After a variety of jobs he enlisted in 1914 in Perth. The war took him to Egypt, Lemnos, and finally to Gallipoli.

It was Gallipoli where plain private John Simpson, stretcher-bearer, became a hero.

On the day of landing he found a donkey, and used it to carry wounded men from the top of Shrapnel Gully, down to the ambulance station on the beach.

Day after day, and many a night, without stint, Simpson brought hundreds of injured men through death valley on his donkey.

It was as if his whole life had been a training for this last unforgettable dream . . .

Simpson became the glowing symbol of the courage and service of the stretcher-bearers. On the day of the Landing he carried with the other bearers, but was reported missing from his unit on the second day. Having carried two heavy men in succession down the awful slopes of Shrapnel Gully and through the Valley of Death he annexed a donkey that he found nibbling in one of the gullies. It responded to the sure touch of the friendly man with the experience he had gained as a boy in far-away summer holidays on the South Shields sands and probably welcomed his company after the terrors of the Landing and the pandemonium that followed. They were a quaint pair and from that day they were inseparable.

So he began to work as a lone unit and his Colonel, recognizing the value of his service, allowed him to continue and required him to report only once a day at the Field Ambulance.

His daily trail was up Shrapnel Gully and into Monash Gully and the deadly zone around Quinn's Post. He brought out the men to where he had left his donkey under cover and took them to the dressing-station on the Beach. Fearless for himself, he was always considerate for his donkey. On the return journeys he carried water for the wounded.

He called the donkey by a variety of names according to his mood. Sometimes it was 'Abdul', mostly 'Duffy', occasionally 'Murphy' – reminiscent of Murphy's Circus at South Shields. Brigadier-General C. H. Jess remembered one night when he heard a quick patter of feet outside his dugout and the cheerful voice of Simpson calling, 'Come on, Queen Elizabeth' – calling his donkey after the great battleship.

He himself was variously called Scotty, Murphy, Simmie and generally 'The Man With The Donk'.

General C. H. Brand described Simpson with his donkey as he often saw him wending his way to the Beach.

Almost every digger knew about him. The question was often asked: 'Has the bloke with the donk stopped one yet?' It seemed incredible that anyone could make that trip up and down Monash Valley without being hit. Simpson escaped death so many times that he was completely fatalistic. He seemed to have a charmed life.

Simpson was frequently warned of the peril he ran, for he never hesitated or stopped in the most furious shrapnel fire. His invariable comment as he went on his way was 'My troubles.'

E. C. Buley tells how:

When the enfilading fire down the valley was at its worst and orders were posted that the ambulance men must not go out, the Man and the Donkey continued placidly at their work. At times they held trenches of hundreds of men spell-bound, just to see them at their work. Their quarry lay motionless in an open patch, in easy range of a dozen Turkish rifles. Patiently the little donkey waited under cover, while the man crawled through the thick scrub until he got within striking distance. Then a lightning dash, and he had

65

Even when the firing was at its worst they continued their work.

the wounded man on his back and was making for cover again. In those fierce seconds he always seemed to bear a charmed life.

Once in cover he tended his charge with quick, skilful movements. 'He had hands like a woman's,' said one who thinks he owes his life to the man and the donkey. Then the limp form was balanced across the back of the patient animal, and, with a slap on its back and the Arab donkey-boy's cry for 'Gee', the man started off for the beach, the donkey trotting unruffled by his side.[1]

Most of his casualties were wounded in the legs and so could not walk to the clearing-station. Sometimes he was seen holding an unconscious man with one arm and guiding the donkey with the other, and having handed him over to the Medical staff he returned for more.

I have talked with several men who rode on the donkey. One of them is P. G. Menhennett who told me how:

On the evening before our first attack on Quinn's Post (2 May) we came down from Pope's Hill, which our Battalion – the 16th – had occupied since the Landing to prepare for the dawn attack. It was fierce and many of us were soon out of action and placed out of the line of fire for evacuation when possible. After a terrible night daylight eventually arrived and soon after came Simpson. Some of our cases were pitiful, but this cheerful digger[2] had a word and a smile for all. He came to me and asked me what was wrong and when I told him I'd been shot through the right leg just above the knee, he asked me could I walk. I told him I might have been able to a few hours before had I known the way down, but now it had got cold and stiff I doubted my ability to do so. He re-bandaged my leg and helped me to his famous donkey. Two or three times on the way down he grinned at me and said, 'That was a very nasty spot we have just passed. Jacko's snipers are wonderful shots. It doesn't do to loiter in such spots.' When you realize that he knew the extreme dangers to which he so constantly exposed himself in his self-imposed errands of mercy you can only marvel at the cheerful way in which he carried out his duties. He brought me safely to the

---

[1] *Glorious Deeds of Australia in the Great War*, by E. C. Buley.

[2] Australian soldier.

Beach clearing station and when I thanked him he smiled and said 'Glad to help you.'

An officer he brought down to the Beach fumbled in his pocket and produced a gold sovereign which he held out to him. 'Keep your blinking quid. I'm not doing this for money,' said Simpson.

Time after time he climbed the gully. Day after day and into the night he smiled and carried on. He was always cheerful and never tired.

In the official record there is this entry:

1 May: No. 202 Pte Simpson has shown initiative in using a donkey from the 26th to carry slightly wounded cases and has kept up his work from early morning till night every day since.

There is some evidence that in his eagerness to help he sometimes used a second donkey.

It is quite clear that Simpson made a profound impression on those who saw him at work. Reinforcements soon heard of him when they landed.

Padre George Green said: 'If ever a man deserved a Victoria Cross it was Simpson. I often remember now the scene I saw frequently in Shrapnel Gully of that cheerful soul calmly walking down the gully with a Red Cross armlet tied round the donkey's head. That gully was under direct fire from the enemy almost all the time.'

Durham men can be dour but no portrait of Jack would be true to life without a sense of his ready wit, gaiety of heart and infectious cheerfulness. Mixed with his strong, vibrant manliness and hard-headedness was a tincture of the mother he adored and in whose heart was a vast, catholic compassion. The words of cheer and comfort which he gave to the succession of men who rode on his donkey were not the least quality of his calm, compassionate service to the wounded.

When he spoke in his cheering, comforting way as he bent over a wounded soldier, his voice sounded like a voice from Heaven.

F. W. Dyke, one of the Gallipoli originals, told me of a rare occasion when his donkey was proving obstinate. A Padre was standing by waiting to accompany Simpson, but with all his coaxing the donkey wouldn't move. At last Simpson turned to the Padre and said, 'Padre, this old donkey has been tied up with some mules and has acquired some of their mulish habits. Would you move along the beach a little way, as I'll have to speak to him in Hindustani, and, Padre, I wouldn't like you to think I was swearing at him.'

He camped with his donkey at the Indian Mountain Battery Mule Camp and seemed very much at home with them. But he slept little and begrudged time to eat. The Indians had their own name for him – 'Bahadur' which, being interpreted, means 'the bravest of the brave.'

Not all the men he took down to the Beach were wounded. One day he saw a figure moving in the bush and shouted: 'Halt! there, who are ye?'

'I'm a warrant officer of the 3rd Field Engineers.'

'Come out, then, and let's have a look at ye,' replied Murphy. He examined the suspect and bluntly said, 'I don't like the looks of ye.'

The warrant officer stared and said: 'Don't be foolish. I'll report you. I'm making levels for the excavations for a new road here.'

'Maybe, maybe, but ye'll come down to the station with me all the same.' Arrived there, the warrant officer was, of course, identified.

'Oh, well,' said Simpson, flicking the donkey as he spoke, 'he's dirty enough to be a Turk even if he ain't one, isn't he, Duffy?'[1]

Apparently Jack wrote no letters from Gallipoli. But, on 9 May, he sent off a printed Field Postcard to his mother in South Shields. He crossed out with indelible pencil the irrelevant words leaving the lines: 'I am quite well. I have received your letter dated March. Letter follows at first opportunity. Signed Jack Simpson, 3rd Field Ambulance.'

On Saturday, 15 May, General Bridges set out at 9 a.m. on his daily excursion to see his men, accompanied by Colonel C. B. B. White and Lieutenant R. G. Casey. They took their way into Shrapnel Gully and on through Monash Valley. Bridges stopped to talk to the medical officer at his aid post. When they moved on he was hit.

Lord Casey (then Lieutenant R. G. Casey), who saw Simpson a number of times, tells me that Simpson came up to the dressing-station with his donkey soon after General Bridges was mortally wounded. Simpson made a friendly remark to the General as he lay on the ground with a medical officer trying to stop the dreadful bleeding from the wound in his groin: 'You'll be all right, Dig. I wish they'd let me take you down to the Beach on my donkey.'

---

[1] I owe this incident to Ernest Bailey, Chief Librarian of South Shields.

Bridges had said to Captain Clive Thompson: 'Don't have me carried down. I don't want to endanger any of your stretcher-bearers.' But Thompson said: 'Nonsense, sir, of course you've got to be carried down.'

In the middle of May, the Turks made their most violent attempt to drive the Anzacs[1] from the cliffs and throw them into the sea. They had greatly increased their guns, all well posted and concealed. The German General, Liman von Sanders, had brought up reinforcements amounting to 30,000 and he personally took command. When the moon set on the night of the 18th–19th a tremendous fire of guns and rifles burst from the Turkish lines. Then at 3.30 a.m. a mass of silent figures were detected in the darkness creeping towards the Australian trenches.

Directly the sentries fired, masses of the enemy came rushing forward, yelling their battle cry of 'Allah!' The assault, though most intense at Quinn's and Courtenay's Posts, extended along the whole front. The Turks came across the narrow strip in such masses – in places only a few yards between the confronting trenches – that the Anzacs firing point-blank into the darkness could not miss the enemy.

Morning came, the sun rose behind the teeming hosts, machine-guns and rifles mowed them down in rows and piled them into barriers. Still they came on, rushing wildly at the sandbag lines, scrambling over them, only to die at the ends of rifles which scorched their skins.

The conflict raged on until nearly eleven o'clock in the morning. The great assault had finished and failed. No trench was taken.

It was on the final fling of the attack on the morning of the 19th that Simpson made his last journey with his donkey up the Gully.

That morning Simpson went up the valley to the water-guard where he usually had breakfast, but it was not ready so he went on his way. 'Never mind,' he called cheerily to the cook, 'get me a good dinner when I come back.'

On the way down he was shot through the heart by a machine-gun bullet at the very spot where General Bridges was killed on the 15th. Andy Davidson and others who were carrying from the top of the Gully had just spoken to him as they were going up. When Simpson fell beside the donkey, Davidson says: 'We went back and covered his

[1] *ANZACS:* the code name derived from the initial letters of Australian & New Zealand Army Corps.

body and put it in a dugout by the side of the track and carried on with our job. We went back for him about 6.30 p.m. and he was buried at Hell Spit on the same evening.' They made a simple wooden cross and set it on his grave with the name 'John Simpson' – nothing else.

One of the First Battalion missed him from the Gully that day and asked 'Where's Murphy?'

'Murphy's at Heaven's gate,' answered the Sergeant, 'helping the soldiers through.'

There was a hush through the trenches that night when the news was given that the man with the donkey had 'stopped one' at last. He had been so much a part of Peninsula life that it was hard to realize that he had gone.

Colonel (later General Sir John) Monash wrote to Headquarters, New Zealand and Australian Division:

I desire to bring under special notice, for favour of transmission to the proper authority, the case of Private Simpson, stated to belong to C Section of the 3rd Field Ambulance. This man has been working in this valley since 26 April, in collecting wounded, and carrying them to the dressing stations. He had a small donkey which he used, to carry all cases unable to walk.

Private Simpson and his little beast earned the admiration of everyone at the upper end of the valley. They worked all day and night throughout the whole period since the landing, and the help rendered to the wounded was invaluable. Simpson knew no fear and moved unconcernedly amid shrapnel and rifle fire, steadily carrying out his self-imposed task day by day, and he frequently earned the applause of the personnel for his many fearless rescues of wounded men from areas subject to rifle and shrapnel fire.

Simpson and his donkey[1] were yesterday killed by a shrapnel shell, and inquiry then elicited that he belonged to none of the Army Medical Corps units with this brigade, but had become separated from his own unit, and had carried on his perilous work on his own initiative.

Dr C. E. W. Bean noted in his diary a remark of Monash that Simpson was worth a hundred men to him.

[1] This was a mistaken report. The donkey was not killed . . . The donkey became the pet of the 6th Mountain Battery Indians who took him with them at the evacuation.

Entries in the Diary of Lieutenant-Colonel Alfred Sutton;[1] Commanding Officer of the 3rd Field Ambulance, reveal that he endeavoured to secure recognition of his heroic services:

19 May: Attended funeral of poor Simpson.

24 May: I sent in a report about No. 202 Pte. Simpson J., of C Section, shot on duty 19 May 1915. He was a splendid fellow and went up the gullies day and night bringing down the wounded on donkeys. I hope he will be awarded the DCM.

1 June: I think we'll get a VC for poor Simpson.

4 June: I have been writing up poor Simpson's case with a view to getting some honour for him. It is difficult to get evidence of any one act to justify the VC the fact is he did so many.

How many lives he saved only the angels know – some say scores, some hundreds.

No posthumous decoration was awarded.

There were frequently wild flowers on his grave – the tributes of the men who admired and even reverenced his spirit. The Indians brought their wreaths and solemnly laid them in honour of his heroic spirit.

Pilgrims to Gallipoli invariably seek the grave of this most symbolic figure of the campaign. In after years a commemoration stone replaced the simple cross set up by his mates on that May night long ago. The inscription reads:

John Simpson Kirkpatrick served as 202 Private J. Simpson, Aust. Army Medical Corps. 19 May 1915. Age 22. He gave his life that others may live.

---

[1] Deposited in the Australian War Memorial Library.

Fight in the Fog

Pierre Closterman

29 June 1944

It was pouring with rain and on the rounded perspex of my cockpit flowed a thousand rivulets that seemed to appear from nowhere. Under the pressure of the air the water infiltrated through the cracks and collected in small streams which ran on either side of the sight and landed on my knees. A damp patch gradually spread on each of my trouser legs.

I came down lower still among the trees, which in the murk I could sense rather than see. Scraps of cloud hung on the hilltops. Half unconsciously I kept on repeating to myself: I am going to hit a high-tension cable . . . I am going to hit a high-tension cable . . .

Suddenly the fog receded and emerging from the rain-cloud I found myself in a gloomy cavern with greenish reflections like an aquarium, bounded by pillars of rain. A funereal light succeeded in penetrating through chinks in the clouds, producing tiers of rainbows hanging from the lowering cloud ceiling like spider's webs.

Then once again I plunged into a thick vapour which blurred the landscape and hid its dangers. Rivulets once again began to course over my cockpit. Each time I turned to avoid a shower I got more lost. My compass, shaken up by my violent manoeuvres, turned slowly and erratically like a diseased top, stopped for a second, then almost regretfully started off the other way. I no longer had the foggiest idea where the north was. My restricted horizon merely showed a row of unknown hills bathed in twilight; anonymous roads and cross-roads succeeded one another, villages drowned in the mist all looked the same. Through an open door I caught a momentary glimpse of warm firelight.

Impossible to get my bearings. I daren't ask for a course by radio. I expected to emerge into a flak zone at any moment or over an airfield or a strongly defended marshalling yard. I began to feel the terror of being alone in a hostile world. I began to expect a deadly stream of tracer bullets from every hedge, every cross-road, every wood.

Lost . . . lost . . . lost.

Oh well, to hell with it. I began to climb through the treacle. My artificial horizon was still all of a dither but I had to risk climbing.

The cockpit was now quite steamed over. I climbed straight up, my eyes on my instruments. My aircraft was swallowed up. I couldn't even see my wing-tips, though I could feel them shaken by invisible eddies of warm air. I came out at 10,000 feet into a maze of clouds. Enormous towering cumuli rose up in the blue sky to vertiginous heights, forming canyons, gigantic corridors walled in dazzling white. The shadow of my Spitfire, projected by the sun, looked like some frolicsome porpoise. It jumped from cloud to cloud, hugging the contours, came near, receded, disappeared in the crevasses, scaled the white ramparts.

Setting course on north and out of range of the flak I made for the coast, where it would be easier for me to pinpoint my position. All the same I felt very alone, and the feeling of independence which you get when operating on your own gave way to a vague feeling of anxiety. The Huns had reacted strongly recently in this neighbourhood and, for once, I would have been glad of company.

I began to keep a close watch on the sun and the blue of the sky. To anyone above me my Spitfire must be visible miles off against this cloud background. A glance at the petrol – still about fifty gallons.

The minutes ticked by. I must now be fairly close to the coast, and on the whole I would rather come out under the clouds over France than risk coming out in the middle of the Channel above some trigger-happy naval convoy. I hadn't fired one shell yet and I might perhaps keep my hand in on a German lorry.

As I turned round a cloud I suddenly discovered a dozen black spots coming towards me at full speed – at such speed that they were on top of me before I could make the slightest move. They passed on my right. Jesus! Focke-Wulfs!

They had spotted me too, and broke up in perfect formation, two by two, to cut off my retreat. I was just cruising along, they were doing about 350 mph – no hope of getting away by climbing; in any case two of them were already immediately above me, waggling their wings. My only hope was to reach the clouds and throw them off by IF. For one fraction of a second I found myself spiralling down with one pair of Focke-Wulfs above, another turning into me from in front, another one below me and a last one preparing to cut off my retreat. The bomb-rack hanging between my two radiators was an unnecessary drag and reduced my speed. I must get rid of it. I pulled desperately on the emergency handle but it wouldn't shift – probably iced up. Sweating, I braced myself and tugged desperately – the handle came away in my hand with part of the cable. I avoided a lateral attack by a quick skid and before another section had time to attack, putting my whole weight on the stick I reversed my turn. Damn! My safety-catch was still on, so although I instinctively pressed the button the Focke-Wulf in my sights slipped by 10 yards away. Christ! What about all those other Huns? I couldn't see more than four. Indistinctly I remembered the vital rule. Look out for the Hun you don't see; that's the one that will shoot you down!

I pulled so hard on the stick that I partially blacked out. I couldn't even turn my head, but I felt that those who had disappeared were up there, just waiting for the moment to pounce.

I just avoided a stream of tracer by breaking sharply upwards – unfortunately this manoeuvre put me back just as far from my cloud as I had been at the start. I was in a lather. A nervous tremor in my left leg made it useless. I crouched down in my cockpit with my elbows into my side and keeping my head down so as to be better protected by my back plate. My oxygen mask, pulled down by the g, had slipped over my nose, and I couldn't get it up again, as I had both hands on the controls. I tried breathing through my mouth and felt a trickle of saliva running down my chin into my scarf.

It was now only a question of time. They had me taped; their attacks, perfectly co-ordinated – one from the right followed by one from the left – were going to catch me flat-footed at any moment. My limbs stiffened, the muscles in my neck contracted, I felt the arteries thumping in my temples, in my wrists, under my knees . . .

The dust, the earth accumulated under my seat, loosened by the violence of my manoeuvres, flew about in the cockpit. A drop of dirty oil went slap into my eye.

Suddenly a stream of tracer shot past, pretty close. I looked at the rear mirror and nearly passed out; a Focke-Wulf 190 followed by three others was less than fifty yards behind me, its wings lit up by the fire of its four cannon. I vaguely remember being paralysed for a second, frozen to the marrow of my bones and then suddenly feeling a hot flush. The instinct of self-preservation had returned in a flash; a big kick on the rudder bar, stick right back, then sideways, in one continuous movement. The violence of the manoeuvre took me by surprise too. A black veil passed in front of my eyes. I felt something tearing into the fuselage and then an explosion. Luckily my back plate stopped the fragments.

I found myself on my back and saw my four assailants, surprised at my unexpected movement, pass by beneath me. Now or never. I pulled the stick and straightening out on the ailerons hurled myself vertically towards the clouds.

Saved! I stabilized my plane as best I could – none too easy: my instruments were completely haywire. I heaved a sigh of relief. I tried the controls. Everything seemed to answer. Normal engine temperature – nothing vital seemed to have been hit, at least not seriously.

I flew around for three or four minutes, changing course every thirty seconds. They must have been thrown off the scent by now; however, better come out under the clouds than above, where they must be waiting for me.

I was now rather worse lost than before and I only had thirty gallons of juice left. No possibility of pin-pointing my position as my map didn't cover the area I was over. I set course north-east, thinking I had drifted westwards during the fight. I crossed a broad river which could only be the Seine; but that didn't help much. The Seine meanders and the visibility was practically nil. I daren't risk following it down to Le Havre as the Germans had put up strong flak all along its banks, to protect the bridges against the constant attacks from Thunderbolts and Typhoons.

I had to make up my mind: the petrol was getting low. I reduced boost to the minimum and set my propeller to coarse. I had a vague idea I was about thirty miles south-east of Rouen. I flew just below the clouds so that I could nip back into them if any flak started firing at me, and followed a railway line which ought to get me to Rouen without too much trouble. I might even, if a suitable opportunity arose, take a pot-shot at a locomotive.

★ ★ ★ ★

I was mulling over this prospect when 1,000 yards ahead, an aircraft hove into sight, also following the railway line. I waggled my wings to have a better look at my find. It was a German plane, a Focke-Wulf 190.

I was sure he hadn't seen me. It was certainly one of the bastards who had put me through the hoop – he must have lost contact with the others in the fog.

A discreet glance round me to make sure I was alone. Cautiously, 'on tip-toe', I prepared to take my revenge. I daren't open up too much to catch him up, as I was short of juice. But I could turn my 1,300-feet altitude into speed by going into a shallow dive.

I got right behind him, 300 yards away, in the blind area behind his tailplane. The pilot, unaware of what was going on, was having a fine time, jumping over telegraph poles and hedges along the track and jinking to right and left, incidentally presenting me with a difficult target.

I pulled the stick slightly to get out of his slipstream and got him plumb in the middle of my sight. I really felt like a murderer when I pressed the button. The first burst – the only one – was a bull and the Focke-Wulf disappeared in a cloud of fragments. When the smoke cleared, I saw him go into a left-handed turn, one leg half down, engine blazing. He mowed down a row of trees along a road by a level-crossing and crashed into the next field, where he exploded.

When the smoke cleared I saw her, engines blazing.

A couple of runs over the burning remains to photograph them – for confirmation – and then I made for home.

★   ★   ★   ★

The return flight was a nightmare, as I only had just enough juice. Wing Commander Yule encouraged me over the radio and gave me a direct course, adding that, if I'd rather, he could direct me towards a convoy where I could bale out.

I decided I preferred trying to get back. On the way I recognized the viaduct at Merville, which we had dive-bombed a few weeks before. The Germans had begun to repair the two arches we had destroyed. As I passed I let fly at the scaffolding with a few shells.

I landed at B11 with just under a gallon of juice in my tanks and had a large strip torn off me for wandering off so far by myself without letting anybody know.

A Three Day's Chase

Captain Basil Hall

On 8 November 1810, when we were lying in that splendid harbour the Cove of Cork, an order came for us to proceed to sea instantly, on a week's cruise off Cape Clear, in quest of an enemy vessel reported to have been seen on the west coast. Off we went, but it was not till the 11th that we reached our appointed station. Towards evening it fell dead calm, at which time there were two strange sails in sight – one of them a ship which we supposed to be an American, from the whiteness of her sails; the other a very suspicious, roguish-looking brig.

As the night fell a light breeze sprang up, and we made all sail in the direction of the brig, though she was no longer visible. In the course of the middle watch we fortunately got sight of her with our night-glasses, and by two in the morning we were near enough to give her a shot. The next instant her booms were rigged out and her studding-sails set. The most crack ship in His Majesty's service could hardly have made sail more smartly. For our part, we could set nothing more, having already spread every stitch of canvas.

The two forecastle guns – long nine-pounders – were now brought to bear on the brig; and orders were given to fire at the sails, which, expanded as they now were before us, offered a mark that could not well be missed. Nevertheless, the little fellow would not heave to for all we could do with our forecastle guns. How it happened that none of her yards or masts were brought down by our fire was quite inexplicable.

About half-past four the breeze began gradually to die away, after which the chase rather gained than lost distance. By five o'clock it was almost entirely calm, and the chase thrust out his sweeps, as they are called – huge oars requiring five or six men to each. These give a small light vessel an advantage over a large ship when there is little wind. In less than an hour he was out of shot. As soon as he had rowed himself from under the relentless fire of our guns, he was busily employed in bending a new suit of sails and repairing his damaged spars. By noon next day he was at least ten miles ahead of us, and at two o'clock we could just see his upper sails above the horizon.

In the course of the afternoon we perceived from the mast-head, far astern, a dark line along the horizon – the first trace of a breeze coming up. Soon the sails were filled, and as we raced along we had the malicious satisfaction of observing that the poor little privateer had not yet got a mouthful of the charming wind which was setting us all a-skipping about the decks. In the spot where the brig lay there was a belt of clear white light, within which the calm still lingered, with the privateer sparkling in its centre. Just as the sun went down, however, this spot was likewise ruffled by the wind, and the brig, like a hunted hare roused, sprang off again.

It was not till about two o'clock in the morning that we once more came within good shot of the brig. She appeared, however, to possess the same invulnerability as before; for we could neither strike her hull, so as to force her to surrender, nor bring down a yard, nor lop off a mast or a boom. It was really a curious spectacle to see a little bit of a thing skimming away before the wind, with such a huge monster as the *Endymion* tearing and plunging after her, like a voracious dolphin in pursuit of a flying-fish.

At last our captain became impatient: he gave orders for the whole starboard broadside to be got ready; and then, giving the ship a yaw, poured the whole discharge, as he thought, right into his wretched victim.

Not a man on board the frigate expected ever to look on the poor brig again. What, then, was our surprise, when the smoke blew swiftly past, to see the intrepid little fellow gliding away more merrily than before! There was a general murmur of applause at the Frenchman's gallantry. Next instant, however, this sound was converted into hearty laughter, when, in answer to our thundering broadside, a single small gun, a six-pounder, was fired from the brig's stern.

Instead of gaining by our manoeuvre, we had allowed the privateer to gain several hundred yards upon us; and his funny little shot, which had excited so much mirth, passed through the lee foretop-sail yard-arm. Had it struck on the windward side, where the yard was cracking and straining at a most furious rate, the greater part of the sails on the foremast might have come down quicker than we could have wished, for we were now going at a great rate, with the wind on the quarter.

Soon another shot cut through the weather maintop-gallant sheet; and so he went on, firing away briskly, till most of our lofty sails were fluttering with the holes made in them. His own sails, I need scarcely add, were by this time so completely torn up by our shot that we could see the sky through them all; but still he refused to heave to, and by constantly firing his single stern-chaser, he showed that he meant to lose no possible chance of escape. Had one or two of his shot struck either of our topmasts, I really believe he might have got off.

The breeze had now freshened nearly to a gale, and the distance between us and the brig was rapidly decreasing, for most of his sails were in shreds. The guns were reloaded, and orders given to depress them as much as possible – that is, to point their muzzles downwards – but that not a shot was to be fired till the frigate came actually alongside of the chase. We were resolved to make him surrender, or to run him down; such was our duty, and that the Frenchman knew right well. He waited, however, until our jib-boom was almost over his taffrail, and not till then, when he must have seen into our ports and along the decks, which were lighted up fore and aft, did he give the signal of surrender.

It may be supposed that the chase was now completely over, and that we had nothing further to do than to take possession of our prize. Not at all! It was found impossible to board the brig, or at least it seemed so dangerous that our captain was unwilling to hazard a boat and crew till daylight came. The gale increased before morning to such a pitch that there was a doubt if any boat could live, and the intention

At last the captain gave orders for the starboard broadside to be made ready.

of boarding our prize was of course further delayed. But we took care to keep close to him, a little to windward, in order to watch his proceedings as narrowly as possible. It did not escape our notice in the meantime that our friend went on quietly, even in the height of the gale, shifting his wounded yards, reeving new ropes and bending fresh sails.

About three o'clock in the afternoon a furious squall of wind and rain came on, and the brig suddenly bore up and set off once more right before the wind. At the height of the squall we totally lost sight of our prize; and such a hubbub I hardly recollect to have heard in my life before.

'Where is she? Who was looking out? Where did you see her last?' and a hundred similar questions were poured out in abundance. Sail was made at once, and off we dashed into the thick of the squall in search of our lost treasure.

For about a quarter of an hour a dead silence reigned over the whole ship, and every eye was strained to the utmost, for no one knew exactly where to look. There was, indeed, no certainty of our not actually running past the privateer, and it would not have surprised us much when the squall cleared up had we seen him a mile or two to windward, far beyond our reach. These fears were put an end to by the sharp-eyed captain of the foretop, who had perched himself on the jib-boom end, calling out with a voice of the greatest glee –

'There he goes! there he goes! right ahead! under his topsails and foresail!'

Sure enough there we saw him, springing along from wave to wave, his masts bending like reeds under the pressure of the sails. In a very few minutes we were again alongside of him. Nothing daunted, however, by the style in which we bore down upon him, the gallant commander of this pretty little egg-shell of a vessel placed himself on the weather-quarter, and with a speaking-trumpet in his hand, indicated a wish to be heard.

'I have been compelled to bear up,' he called out in French; 'otherwise the brig must have gone to the bottom. The sea broke over us in such a way that I have been obliged, as you may perceive, to throw all my guns, boats and spars overboard. We have now several feet of water in the hold in consequence of your shot. If, therefore, you oblige me to heave to, I cannot keep the vessel afloat one hour in such weather.'

'Will you make no further attempt to escape?' asked the captain of the *Endymion*.

'As yet I have made none,' he replied firmly. 'I am your prize; and, as a man of honour, I do not consider myself at liberty to escape even if I had the power. I bore up when the squall came on, as a matter of necessity. If you will allow me to run before the wind along with you till the weather moderates, you may take possession of the brig when you please; if not, I must go to the bottom.'

At eight o'clock in the evening it began to moderate, and by midnight we succeeded in getting a boat on board of the prize, after a run of between three and four hundred miles. Such is the scale of nautical sport! The brig proved to be the *Milan* privateer from St Malo, of fourteen guns and eighty men, many of whom were unfortunately wounded and several killed by our shot. In the morning we stopped the leaks, exchanged the prisoners for a prize crew, and put our heads towards the Cove of Cork again, and we returned right merrily to tell our long story of the three days' chase. The captain's name was M Pierre Lepelletier of St Malo; and wherever he goes, I will venture to say he can meet no braver or more resolute man than himself.

The Expert comes Tomorrow

George Martelli

Michel Hollard was such a courageous and resourceful allied agent during the Second World War, that almost single-handed he helped save London from large-scale flying-bomb attacks.

This particular story from George Martelli's book relates an episode involving Michel and another agent called Bart . . .

In the summer of 1943 Michel was requested by his British contact to investigate the aerodrome at Cormeilles-en-Vexin. This was a very large airfield not far from Paris used by the *Luftwaffe*. It had twenty miles of runway and was believed to be divided into three sections. One of them, skilfully camouflaged, was used for operations; a second appeared to be out of service; while a third, surrounded by fencing, was equipped with searchlights and AA. The directive given to Michel was to plot the limits of the three sectors, and to discover the exact function of each.

He decided to entrust the job to Bart. The latter had distinguished himself by his work, particularly on the Channel coast, and was now based on Paris and available to be sent on special missions.

Although partly enclosed, the aerodrome was too vast to guard, and Bart had no difficulty in approaching its perimeter. Carrying a large-scale map in one hand and a pair of field glasses in the other, he proceeded methodically, noting the various features.

After fixing the boundaries of the neutral sector and shading it in on his map, he reached a part of the ground where there were some curious buildings. Nobody being in sight he decided to explore it. The results were interesting. For example, a church steeple made of wood surmounted a large storage tank, while what looked like a row of cottages were in reality repair shops.

A little farther on two haystacks next aroused Bart's curiosity. Scraping away the soil he discovered at first a layer of concrete and then a padlocked manhole. He guessed these were ammunition lockers and was just proceeding to mark the position on his map, when suddenly a German soldier concealed in a silo landed on the ground and covered him with his rifle.

There was no question of flight. The German was only a few yards away and must have been watching him for some time. With his hands above his head he was marched off to the guardroom; and from there taken before an officer wearing air force uniform.

Bart had already prepared his story. He was cycling past the airfield when he noticed a church and some cottages that had not been there when he was last in the neighbourhood. Obeying a natural curiosity he had stopped to investigate.

What about the map – and the glasses?

Well, the glasses had been given him by a friend in the neighbourhood whom he was visiting (this was true, he had borrowed them for the occasion from the curé of the next village), and he was taking them back to Paris.

As for the map, why, he had picked it up off a bench on arriving at the station. It was already marked – in fact it was that which had aroused his curiosity in the first place.

During an hour's interrogation, accompanied by some knocking about, Bart stuck to this story. Finally he was informed that the explanation was not accepted and that he was to be sent to Maisons-Laffitte for questioning by the Sicherheits-Dienst.[1]

That night he spent in a police post at Pontoise. Towards dawn, seeing that his escort were asleep, he rose and crept towards the door. He had stepped across two of the men without disturbing them when the third sat up. All he could do then was to request to be taken to the lavatory.

[1] Security Police to be distinguished from the Gestapo (*Geheimnis Staats Polizei*) or Secret State Police. The latter however worked with the Security Police and were always called in for cases of espionage or subversive action.

At Maisons-Laffitte he was mercilessly 'grilled' all day. Different interrogating officers succeeded one another with progressive brutality: at first face slapping and blows of the fist, then beating with various implements. With desperate courage, Bart stuck to his story. He had found the map at the station; the writing on it was not his.

Paper and pencil were put before him and he was ordered to write down some sentences which his interrogator dictated. Guessing the purpose of this he wrote in a faked hand, but weak as he was with pain and exhaustion the effort was not very successful.

'Right,' said the German. 'Now we'll send for the hand-writing expert. He'll soon tell us if you're speaking the truth.'

As it happened the expert could not be found. He would not be available, apparently, until the next day; but if the writing on the map was identified as his, Bart was informed, he would be shot immediately as a spy. He was then conducted to Houilles, a small town just outside Paris, and locked up for the night.

His cell was on the third floor of the building, about fifty feet above ground. High up in the wall there was a small rectangular window protected by a network of wire. The wire was stretched taut across a wooden frame which was secured by wire lashings to bolts in the wall. In the door was the usual spy-hole enabling the guard to look in.

All thought of escape seemed hopeless. And yet one phrase spoken by his interrogator kept recurring in his head: 'The expert comes tomorrow.' He was convinced his faked hand-writing would not delude the expert. Unless he got away, there could be only one end to it.

He looked at the window again. It appeared inaccessible – and yet perhaps not quite. The guard had just looked through the Judas, and Bart had heard his retreating footsteps. Presumably he would hear them coming back. He had the impression that he was the only prisoner on that floor, so visits to it might not be very frequent.

Placing the truckle bed on its side, he stood on it and just managed to reach the window. He started to unravel, strand by strand, the wire lashings which attached the frame to the opening. With only his hands to help him it was a slow and painful business and soon his nails were ripped and his fingertips bleeding. But he worked on steadily, only pausing to listen for footsteps outside. Once the guard returned and he just had time to drop on the bed and feign sleep before the judas was opened. By midnight he had the frame dismounted.

The opening measured about sixteen inches by twenty inches – large enough for the slight form of Bart to pass through. But what then? A drop of fifty feet – in the dark – on to what – not to mention the noise of the fall?

At that moment the sound of a train could be heard in the distance. This gave Bart an idea. He had already heard several pass quite close, making the night hideous with their clatter. If he could time his leap to freedom when this one approached, the noise of it would deaded that of his fall.

It might be suicide, but the alternative was to face the expert – and it was not as though the Germans would shoot him at once, either. Convinced of his guilt they would want some more out of him, and by now he knew enough of their methods to feel that death was preferable to another 'grilling'.

Anyhow, there was no time to calculate the risk. The noise of the train was growing louder every moment. In a few seconds it would have passed. Without a clear idea of what he meant to do with it, Bart seized his blanket and pulled himself up to the window. He squeezed through the opening feet first until he was sitting on the ledge outside. Then he spread the blanket above his head to act as a parachute, kicked with his heels to take him clear of any obstructions . . . and jumped.

By a miracle he was not killed – nor even knocked unconscious. He had fallen into a garden on to soft ground. As he lay on his back in an agony of pain, groaning audibly, he heard the train go by in a shattering inferno of sound.

Soon after he heard footsteps approaching. Pushing inside his mouth a corner of the blanket which he was still holding, Bart succeeded in rolling to a hedge. The sentry, as he guessed it must be, was patrolling on the other side.

By a supreme effort Bart managed to get on all fours, and, sometimes crawling and sometimes dragging himself on his stomach, reached the end of the hedge, where there was an opening. This led to another garden at the end of which was a small house.

How he got there Bart never knew, but he eventually arrived at a door, under which he could see light. He had just sufficient strength to knock feebly before collapsing; and as the door opened his unconscious form fell across the threshold.

When he came to he was lying on a couch in a sitting-room. Two elderly people, a man and a woman, were standing over him. The woman had a cup of coffee ready and raised his head to help him drink. His back hurt atrociously – although he did not know it yet, he had broken his spine in three places – but it got some support from the rough bandages made of sheets with which the occupants of the house had bound up his torso.

Bart's first question was to ask the time.

His hosts tried to calm him. There was nothing to worry about. They would look after him, and he must just lie still until they could send for an ambulance.

'Impossible,' said Bart, 'I've just escaped from the *boches*. They will be looking for me now. Unless I can get to the station I shall be caught and shot.'

'But you can't move,' the man objected. 'We think your back is broken.'

'Yes I can if you'll support me. I feel stronger now. Anyhow, it's my only chance.'

After some more argument it was agreed to try. It was about 5.30 a.m. and there was a workers' train from Houilles at 6.45.

With one arm round the neck of his Good Samaritan, and the other leaning on a stick, Bart set off for the station. To avoid passing in front of his recent prison it was necessary to make a wide detour; and although the station was only a short distance away it took them nearly an hour to reach it.

But they caught the train – Bart's companion buying the tickets – arrived in Paris, took the *métro* to the Gare de Lyons, and eventually reached a small hotel near the terminus where Michel had a room permanently reserved.

He used it occasionally to sleep in, and also to keep the reports brought to Paris by his agents in northern and eastern France. These were hidden on top of the wardrobe and he only collected them just before leaving for Switzerland.

It was here that he found Bart later in the day, stretched on the bed and exhausted with pain.

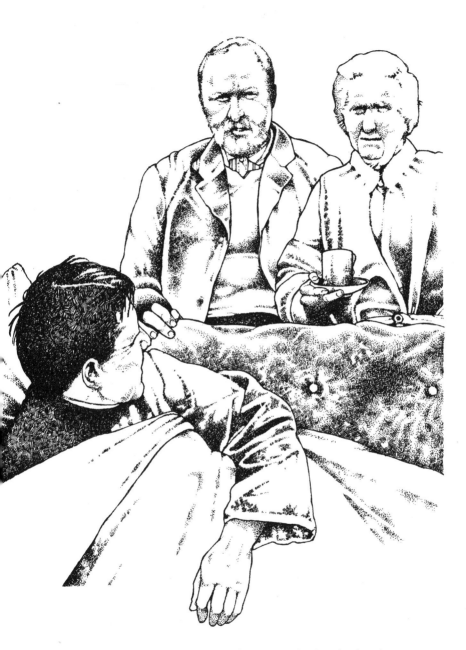

'But you can't move. We think your back is broken.'

By this time the injured man was not making much sense, but his speech was sufficiently coherent to convey roughly to Michel what had happened to him. When he had finished his story Michel looked at him sternly and said: 'Did you tell them anything?'

'Of course not.'

'Are you quite sure?'

'Nothing. I swear.'

'Good,' said Michel. 'In that case we'll attend to your affair.'

Fortunately he knew of a nursing home whose surgeon, Raoul Monod, was a cousin and friend of his. It was run by the Protestant *Association Diaconnesses*, and was not far away, at 18 Rue du Sergent Bauchat.

There Bart was taken the same evening and operated on immediately.

An X-ray revealed three broken vertebrae. These were set by the surgeon and the injured man encased in plaster.

By what seemed not one miracle, but a succession of miracles – the second being the failure of the Germans to discover his escape, and the third his getting to Paris with no spinal column – Bart had so far survived.

But his escape was not yet assured, and every day he lay in the nursing home the risk of discovery increased. The problem was first to find a safe place for him, and then to move him to it.

One of the difficulties was that he would take months to recover and meanwhile would need to be nursed. For this reason he could not be sent to the 'parking place', where there were no facilities for the injured. On the other hand, an invalid always attracted attention and this made Michel's friends reluctant to harbour him. To complicate matters further, Bart was liable for conscription in the labour force.

After considering various alternatives – including a hiding-place in the country – Michel decided that the only solution was to remove Bart to Switzerland, and proceeded to make his plans accordingly. Fortunately it was summer, so he could use the original route across the frontier, where there was no barbed wire to negotiate.

After a week in bed the patient was considered well enough to be moved. It was arranged that his mother should collect him at the clinic and conduct him to the Gare de Lyon where Michel was to meet them. All went well until they were passing the barrier, when the ticket inspector demanded their *fiches d'admission*. These were special passes with which passengers had to provide themselves to gain admission to a particular train. Michel had not had time to obtain them.

'This young man is seriously injured,' he explained. 'He has to leave Paris for urgent treatment.'

'Then you should have brought a medical certificate,' the inspector replied.

At this Bart, who had overheard, pulled up his shirt and displayed his plaster cast. The effect was sensational. Drawn on the white surface with a violet pencil and covering it from neck to waist line was a large Cross of Lorraine – the emblem of the Free French. Below was printed a title: 1ST REGIMENT OF PARACHUTISTS.

The drawing was the work of Bart's neighbour at the clinic, who had waggishly added the title as a tribute to his original method of descent from a third storey window. Michel, who had not seen this artistic effort before, was horrified; but the inspector took one glance, discreetly looked away, and motioned the three to pass through.

Thanks to a friendly guard a corner seat was secured for Bart and he passed a reasonably comfortable night in the train. There was no longer any control at the line of demarcation and the journey passed off without incident.

At Besançon, where they arrived early the next morning, Bart's mother said goodbye to him. He and Michel then continued on the single line railway which runs between Besançon and Morteau.

At La Grande Combe, five miles from the terminus, they left the train to continue the journey on foot. Bart could walk, but only slowly, and the plaster cast weighed painfully on his hip-bones. Michel usually travelled by paths and across country, but this was too difficult for Bart, so they had to keep to the road where the risk increased of meeting a German patrol.

After walking for two hours they arrived at Derrière-le-Mont. Cuenot had been warned and his wife was waiting for them with a meal. Bart had so far stood the journey well, and after the meal and a short rest he was ready to go on.

Now began the real test. The mountain path, which Michel had travelled so often, became progressively steeper and narrower. After a time there was no room for two people and Michel, who had been helping his companion, had to abandon him to his own devices.

The pain caused by the plaster pressing on Bart's hips soon became unbearable. To ease it he took the weight with his hands. This meant abandoning his stick and he had difficulty in keeping his balance. Step by step, sometimes inch by inch, Bart struggled forward, while Michel looked on helpless in an agony of doubt whether his plucky comrade would ever make it.

At last the climb eased as they reached the plateau and hit the track which led to Cuenot's farm. The carter had gone ahead to reconnoitre and Michel saw with dismay that the door and window were closed. This meant that it was not safe to cross the valley.

He looked at his watch. There were five minutes still to go till the agreed time. He watched the farm anxiously, while Bart lay on the ground desperately trying to recuperate his forces.

At last the door opened. Inside he could see Cuenot looking out. It was the 'all clear' sign.

Revived by the news, Bart struggled to his feet and with Michel again supporting him they resumed the march.

From the edge of the forest there was an easy descent of about a hundred yards to the stream at the bottom of the valley, and this was accomplished without too much difficulty. But when they started to climb the farther slope Bart soon began to show signs of distress. For a little way he struggled on and succeeded in reaching the shelter of the trees. Then he stopped. For the time being his strength was finished.

The worst was still ahead – a quarter of a mile at least of stiff climbing through scrub and rock. Dropping on his knees Michel took his companion on his back; then advancing on all fours, a foot at a time, half carried, half dragged him the rest of the way. By the time they reached the wall which marked the frontier, he had just enough strength to lift Bart over and pull him under cover of some trees before he himself sank down completely exhausted.

There they lay together, without an ounce of strength left but savouring the sweet taste of another victory, gained by sheer 'guts' over an all-powerful enemy.

When they had recovered their strength sufficiently, they resumed their walk and eventually arrived at La Brevine. From there Michel telephoned one of his friends in the Swiss Army, who immediately left by car to meet him. A few hours later he and Bart were both installed comfortably at a hotel in Neûchatel.

The next day Bart was admitted to hospital, while Michel returned to Paris. He had made many secret and dangerous journeys to Switzerland, but none had taken more out of him than this, nor afforded him so deep a satisfaction.

Nelson's Last Day

John Simpson

The cold rain came in such heavy squalls that not a solitary star showed above the restless sea. One moment the wind howled like a tormented hound; the next it died to a sigh in the night.

Nineteen miles off Cape Trafalgar, in the thin grey light that comes before dawn, silhouettes of twenty-six British men-of-war could be seen. They were all that stood between the hidden enemy fleet and a possible invasion of England. But where *was* the unseen Armada?

In such an atmosphere of nail-biting tension, none of the British sailors on board dared wager what the morrow would bring. Yet Vice-Admiral Nelson's sixth sense told him it would produce . . . a battle royal! Four times during the past week he'd predicted to Captain Hardy; 'The 21st will be our day!'

As dawn broke on that twenty-first day of October 1805, the rain suddenly stopped, the sky cleared, and the rising sun carved a pathway of burnished gold across the ocean. Only a heavy swell coming in from the vast Atlantic caused the three-masted men-of-war to roll slightly. Soon the white cliffs of Trafalgar would be seen on the eastern horizon, and already various look-outs were at their stations, eyes straining for a sight of land or enemy sail.

When Nelson left his sleeping quarters on his flagship HMS *Victory* that morning, he was dressed as usual in his admirals coat, but for some reason he did not wear his sword. That still lay on his cabin table below deck. It was to be the one time he fought in a battle without his sword. As he joined Captain Hardy on the poop he was in excellent spirits, and ready to face whatever adventure lay before him. Such was his mood that he declared to Hardy; 'Today, I'll not rest content unless we capture twenty enemy sail-of-the-line!'

Perhaps he was tempting providence, for within ten minutes of those words being spoken, a look-out on morning-watch, perched in the masthead of the HMS *Revenge* spotted a single sail on the eastern horizon. 'Enemy sail on the starboard bow!' he cried. Three minutes later the same sailor called again. This time in alarm. 'There's more than one of 'em! There's about forty of the devils!'

In fact there were thirty-three enemy ships in all; eighteen French and fifteen Spanish, under Admiral Pierre de Villeneuve, who commanded this huge squadron from his flagship *Bucentaure*. Soon, the eastern seascape was crowded with a legion of enemy masts bearing the colourful but ominous French and Spanish ensigns. It was the moment Nelson and the British crew had been waiting for, and hundreds of sleepy-eyed seamen scrambled up the hatchways to catch a glimpse of the hostile fleet.

Admiral Villeneuve had received orders to leave Cadiz Bay and land troops at Naples to strengthen Napoleon's waning military campaign in Southern Italy, but for some time he had hesitated before attempting to pierce the blockade of British ships. His orders were *not to go in search* of the enemy. But if his fleet should meet the British warships – then he was to fight to the death. Already the great Napoleon Boneparte had insulted him, calling him a coward. Well, he would show his Emperor; and what better way to do that than with a decisive victory over the British squadron?

So far there had been many encounters between his own ships and those of Lord Nelson, and each time because of successive setbacks, Napoleons plans to invade England had to be delayed. But now, if Villeneuve could crush the British war-dogs once and for all, then surely a victory would open wide the floodgates for a full-scale invasion of England.

The French Admiral looked through narrowed eyes at the distant

British fleet showing indistinct in the morning light. He estimated in his own mind that with the gentle northwest wind continuing to blow against his own ships it would take five hours before the rival squadrons would be close enough to engage in battle. Plenty of time to prepare. Time to call his captains together and remind everyone of them of their duty; especially the Spaniards! *'Vive le Empereur!'*

Six miles across the waves, on board HMS *Victory*, Lord Nelson's order was to hoist the signal, 'The British fleet are to sail in two columns.' Owing to the squalls of wind overnight, many ships had lost way. Now they began to close up and form two columns as part of Nelson's pre-arranged battle-plan.

Although the confrontation was still hours away, the gun crews began checking canons and bringing ammunition up from the magazines. Marines were cleaning their muskets; some of the men thinking what would be their last thoughts of their wives, children and sweethearts. Then they waited; tense and apprehensive as time ticked relentlessly away. One captain turned to his first lieutenant and calmly advised; 'You'd better wear silk stockings like me, for if you get shot in the leg it will be so much more manageable for the surgeon.'

At 9.30 a.m., the enemies were five miles apart, each ship showing full sail. British officers met over breakfast, but few could eat. There was a nervous expectancy in the air. Final plans were laid, for better or for worse. Then came the sound of the drum, beckoning the men to their posts, a little light headed after their pot of beer.

The ships of the combined fleets of Spain and France could be seen clearly now. Some flying the *tricolor*, others the red and yellow ensigns of Spain. At about eleven o'clock, the black snouts of the enemy guns slipped into view. Some of the Frenchmen were three-deckers, showing a terrifying one hundred and twelve guns. Young British hearts quailed at the sight. But the more experienced 'salts' merely grinned. They'd seen it all before. Someone called for a shanty to be sung and the sound of salt water ballads floated over the rippling water. Soon it would be the hissing noise of canonballs whipping through smoke filled air, the heaviest of which could smash right through three feet of solid timber, or leave a hole the size of a small football where a man stomach had been. Then there was chain shot, two half canonballs, to be fired at the rigging; or the raking grape-shot which could maim a dozen crew members in one firing. One hour more and all kinds of devilish destruction would be let loose.

Lord Nelson knew full well the fervid heat of battle. At Cape St Vincent he had directed his ship into action, alone and unsupported, and single-handed held two Spanish squadrons apart. At one time he was fighting seven enemy ships. Not content with such heroics, he managed to board and capture one enemy brig, and then from her deck board and take yet another!

The Battle of Cape St Vincent had earned Nelson a Knighthood – but all was not plain sailing in his naval career, for in his very next action, whilst engaged in an assault on Tenerife, a grapeshot smashed through his right elbow. Below the decks of his flag-ship in stifling heat, the arm was amputated. Nevertheless, further successful campaigns followed his recovery, and even before the approaching Battle of Trafalgar, Lord Nelson was England's most lauded hero.

Such a man as Nelson had destiny on his side. He commanded respect from officers and men alike. Every decision he made had to be carefully weighed, for its effect would be far reaching. Naturally he made mistakes, but these errors were by far eclipsed by his triumphs. However, his next decision on that sunlit morning off Cape Trafalgar was to prove most fateful. He decided that his own flagship HMS *Victory* would be *first* to break the enemy line.

Captain Hardy was appalled! He pointed out that Nelson, as the fleets commander-in-chief would be exposed to every possible danger. Not only canon and grape-shot, but musket fire too! But Nelson was absolutely convinced that only while he was *at the head* of an attack, could he exercise full control over the British squadron. He was adamant, and Hardy soon realized that further argument was useless. However, the Captain did point out that his commander made an excellent target for snipers, and he indicated the bright stars upon Nelsons splendid uniform, suggesting that perhaps His Lordship might change his coat? 'I agree Hardy,' returned Nelson, as he gazed upon the converging enemy. 'But it's too late now to be shifting a coat.' Then he turned calmly to his signals officer and ordered a communication to be sent to the whole fleet. It was the immortal message; 'England expects that every man will do his duty.' The very next order was; 'Prepare to engage the enemy in close action!'

By now the French and Spanish ships were 600 yards away and advancing menacingly in the battle formation of a crescent – as if to swallow up the British fleet in a crushing pincer movement.

Their broadsides turned to reveal rows of deadly iron barrels, ready at a given signal to discharge tons of venomous shot. Painted all colours, some ships had yellow sides, others blood red. A few were funereal black. Many sported decorative ribbons between their coloured decks. Some had carved figures on their prows. All looked proud, graceful and deadly, like cobras of the sea.

At twelve noon the first broadside was discharged.

Abruptly one French ship, the *Santa Ana* was towering over the British *Royal Sovereign* like a sword of Damocles. Yet miraculously, within a few minutes, the British guns had brought the *Santa Ana*'s masts crashing down.

Across the two fleets it was the same grisly tale of destruction. On almost every deck: Fire! Death! Headless bodies. A living nightmare. Flying splinters and grape shot. The stink of burnt flesh. The shrieking agony of wounded men. Disfigured corpses scattered everywhere, and the soft moans of the dying. This was the hideous outcome of war, and soon the salt waters were streaming with the blood of three nations.

At one broadside a hundred men would be shredded into mincemeat, with ropes and tackle lying in a twisted mess across the decks. The once varnished sides of the men o' war were now puckered with shot; the wounded piled high – and already there were as many dead as would sink three barges. The surgeon was the busiest man on board ship and if he died – then God help the wounded! In one private confrontation HMS *Revenge* had been rammed by a Spanish three-decker. The Spaniards bowsprit hung over the *Revenge*'s poop, with a whole party of men in her fore-rigging ready to board. Only the British marines with their rifles and carronades saved the day. But at that instant, with one minor battle won, a two-decked French ship appeared on the *Revenge*'s starboard side – while on the larboard bow yet another. Yet luck was still with the British ship for many of the French gunners shots struck their own ships, killing and wounding their compatriots.

Meanwhile, on board HMS *Victory*, death was already waiting in the wings for the gallant Nelson. He had but two hours to live. As his flagship attacked the enemy formation, the French and Spanish guns began an incessant raking fire. A shot struck the quarterdeck and passed between Lord Nelson and Captain Hardy. A splinter bruised the Captain's foot and tore the buckle from his shoe. Realizing that Hardy was not badly injured Nelson observed: 'This is much too frantic to last for long.'

The *Victory's* mizzen mast was now gone. All her studding sails shot clean away. Thirty lay dead amidst the flying shot and thick acrid smoke. Nevertheless, *Victory* steered resolutely for a small gap in the enemy line. Passing directly between Admiral de Villeneuve's *Bucentaure*, and the Frenchman *Redoubtable*, HMS *Victory* was at the mercy of both her protagonists' guns. But with a defiant gesture, *Victory* fired double and treble shot into Villeneuve's great cabin windows, passing so close to the *Bucentaure* that her main yard-arm caught in the French leader's rigging. All her guns blazing, *Victory* pulverized the French commanders ship, putting at least thirty of her guns out of action. On the Frenchmans decks the dead were thrown back in heaps, with fresh shot further mangling the already mutilated bodies.

With *Bucentaure* behind her, the *Victory* moved into line with *Redoubtable*, and smashed the enemys masts to smithereens with devastating starboard broadsides. Now the English *Temeraire* joined the fray. Following the *Victory*, she was soon stationed on the opposite side of the *Redoubtable*, with the French *Fougueux* on her starboard bow. Four men o' war, two from each side were locked together in murderous combat.

Muskets spat from the mast-tops of the *Redoubtable*, decimating the *Victory's* crew. Scarcely a sailor on the *Victory's* foredeck escaped injury as Tyrolean snipers cooly picked off man after man. So close were the ships that there was the awesome prospect of the *Redoubtable* catching fire from the *Victory's* blazing guns – and the possibility of the flames consuming both *Victory* and *Temeraire*.

With scenes of carnage on all sides, and the *Victory* filled with so many holes that she looked like a floating colander; Nelson ordered his marines to open fire on the snipers. The canons joined in this barbarous return of fire.

Suddenly *Redoubtable's* main-mast swayed, seemed to falter, then came thundering down to smash across her decks. Only seconds afterwards her stern was stoved in. The rudder was fractured beyond repair. All the guns were broken or dismounted. Both sides of the ship were shattered. Most of the pumps were useless and the ladders which connected the decks were in ruins. Those same decks were littered with the victims of war. Yet still the survivors stubbornly cried; 'Vive le Empereur! Vive le Empereur!'

At 2 p.m. the French ship was so badly holed that she was in danger of sinking. At last her captain decided to surrender, ordering the colours to be hauled down. But even before this could be done with dignity, the main mast had crashed to the ground. Nearly 500 of *Redoubtable*'s crew were killed or wounded already and she was to have the worst casualty list in the battle.

Now, all over the frenzied waters, French and Spanish captains began striking their colours. Once *Victory* had broken the enemy line, it signalled the beginning of the end of the enemy.

Through blankets of thick smoke, fire balls descended. Men fought blindly on, others looked to survival. Nelson walked the *Victory*'s quarterdeck in the midst of that raging holocaust alongside Captain Hardy. He was in the act of turning. His eyes were directed towards the stern of the ship. Then the fatal musket ball was fired from the enemys mizzen top.

The ball struck the badge on his left shoulder and bit deep into his chest. He fell face down upon the deck. As Hardy approached, Nelson cried, 'They have done for me Hardy. My backbone is shot through!'

Captain Hardy immediately ordered two seamen to carry the Vice Admiral below. But before he left the deck Nelson still had the presence of mind to give an order regarding tiller ropes. He then covered his face with his handkerchief in the hope that his crew would remain ignorant of his injury. But within a minute, the news was all over the ship. Lord Nelson had been hit. In spite of this disaster, the great man had done enough . . . The tide of battle had turned.

★   ★   ★   ★

In a dim illumination cast by lantern candles, Nelson passed his last minutes. The Surgeon, Mr Beatty approached him and removed the handkerchief. Nelson looked up and muttered. 'Mr Beatty. You can do nothing for me. Attend to the others.' Beatty replied: 'I hope the

'They have done for me,' cried Nelson. 'My backbone is shot through.'

wound is not as bad as Your Lordship imagines.' Nelson answered feverishly. 'Doctor, I told you – I am gone.'

Beatty probed at the wound in the half light. But when he discovered no injury to the skin of the Admiral's back, he realized that the musket ball must have lodged in the spine. He then inquired how His Lordship was feeling. 'I experience a gush of blood every minute within my breast.' said Nelson. 'I cannot feel the lower part of my body. I can hardly breathe. I believe my back is broken.'

These symptoms told Beatty that the wound was fatal. Although he tried to cheer his Admiral with hope, Nelson was not to be fooled. He sensed life ebbing from his body. But there were still questions to be answered! He had to hold on long enough to find out. He must speak with Captain Hardy. 'Will no-one bring Hardy to me?' he moaned. 'He must be killed? Surely Hardy is dead?'

But Captain Hardy was not only captaining the *Victory*, but also conducting the battle on behalf of Nelson. He would, he said, come below as soon as his duties allowed.

An hour gone and Hardy was at last bent over the broken body of Nelson. 'Well Hardy. How goes the battle?' 'Very well my Lord,' answered Hardy. 'We have fourteen of the enemys ships in our possession.' 'I trust none of our ships have lowered their colours?!' cried Nelson. 'None my Lord. Not one.' replied Hardy.

Twenty minutes after Captain Hardy had visited his wounded Admiral for a second time, Nelson's hands had grown quite cold. Soon, his heroic heart beat no more.

★　　　★　　　★　　　★

The dismasted HMS *Victory* was now anchored. The sun was lowering in the western sky. All over the seascape, the ruins of once magnificent sailing vessels strove to stay afloat. Captains counted their dead. Crew members cleared up the wreckage and tended the wounded.

In the eerie quiet following the clamour of battle, the young midshipman of the watch on board HMS *Victory* pencilled in the log. 'Partial firing continued until 4.30, when a victory was reported to the Right Honourable Lord Nelson. He then died of his wound.'

So Nelson had been right. The 21st had been the day – a day of victory that became immortal.

A Bicycle Ride

Henry Williamson

This story is taken from Henry Williamson's novel, 'A Fox Under my Cloak' . . . 1914 . . . The front-line during the First World War was a desolate place. Barbed wire. Devastated areas, pock-marked with shell craters. German troops trying to drive the British troops back, using heavy artillery, rifles and even hand to hand combat. The British, like-wise, pushing forward, trying to capture enemy outposts.

Christmas is approaching. The German soldiers each receive a meerschaum pipe as a gift from Crown Prince Wilhelm. The British troops all receive a gift-package from Princess Mary – a brass box containing a packet of cigarettes, another of tobacco and a small Christmas card.

On Christmas eve, the firing stops. There is a truce. Suddenly German and British soldiers are mingling with one another, smiling and laughing in No Mans Land. Someone suggests a football match should be played between the opposing armies. The idea is welcomed, and the match takes place behind the German lines. The 'war' becomes so unreal that Philip Maddison of the London Highlanders is left wondering, 'Why are we fighting each other?' It is a sad reflection because already some of his best friends are victims of the war.

In this strange atmosphere he borrows a bicycle and goes for a ride behind the German lines. But confused by the bleak landscape he realises he is lost. His heart is in his mouth . . .

When the road forked, or rather the tram lines turned to the left, he found he could not decide which way to go, so he followed the lines. Whatever he did, he must not stop.

The road sloped down; he could free-wheel. Where did it lead? He must think. The sun would be west of south now, as it was about half an hour since he left White Sheet, round about twelve thirty. So it must now be one o'clock. O, what was he trying to think? Start again. If the sun was sou'-sou'-west, and on his back, as it was, then he was heading nor-nor'-east, *which was straight behind the German lines*. Where did the steam-tram go to – Lille?

It was an alarming thought. Then he saw, not very far away and below, the dim suggestion of a fairly big wood. This must be the one south of Wulverghem, where the London Rifles were. Yes, as the road curved, so that the sun was on his right cheek once more, he could see that it led down to level ground extending to the distant wood. There was a little bridge in front, slightly hump-backed; he rattled over it, seeing a narrow stream below.

Phillip's misgivings had made of the ride an ordeal; but the worst was to come. His mouth went dry when he saw in front, where the road went through a small cutting that gave cover from view, some field-grey figures standing; and pedalling nearer, he saw wheels, spade-trails, the barrels of field guns, under wooden shelters roofed with faggots. A German battery!

He was being stared at. They were all smoking new meerschaum pipes. Feeling a little French beard on his chin, he sliced a hand upwards from the elbow, and cried out, in a voice thin and throaty, 'Bon jour, messieurs! Kronprinz prächtiger Kerl! Hoch der Kaiser!' and rode on past one gun, then, another, and another, hoping that, as obviously they didn't know what to make of him, bare-headed in a goat-skin, kilt and khaki puttees, he would be out of their way before anyone of them might think to stop him. To extend the period of their wonder, he curved his arm over his head and scratched exaggeratedly. He could feel their eyes like potential bullets, directed towards his shoulder blades.

There were some ruined cottages in front. The narrow lane was very rough; shell-holes grey with ice. He must be just behind the German support trench. Yes, there before him, a hundred yards away, was a barricade. He had to walk now, his legs were weak, but he managed to wheel the bike forward, trying not to have a strained expression on his face. He was trembling, he looked straight ahead, deliberately avoiding

He sliced a hand upwards and cried out 'Bonjour.'

a glance at the German trench. The grasses on the road looked very fresh and green, the metalling clean, washed by rains, untrodden. Eyes on the road before him, he pushed on towards the last sandbag barricade besides a roadside cottage.

So near and yet so far. Fear rose out of the ground, all about him, as though of the exhalations of the spirits of the hatless British dead lying on the ground.

Perhaps they had been killed in the attack of 19 December, one of many made all along the line in order to hold down the German divisions which otherwise would have been sent to Russia. Living German faces were looking at him, as he could see from the corner of his eye through a thousand dragging threads of fear, his face feeling transparent, his glance upon the ground. Slowly the big barricade of the German front trench became larger in its fixedness across the lane, beside a white *estaminet*[1] stabbed all over with bullet marks in its plaster. A thin ragged hedge, clipped and cut by bullets, stood on the other side of the lane. How could he get past that solid-looking barricade? It was frizzed with coils of wire above and around it. He must leave the bike there, and try and find a gap. Ah, there was a way between the sandbag'd door of the estaminet and the barricade. Now he was walking on an area, unrecognized as a field, torn up by circular shell-holes in places; and fifty yards away stood a group of mixed and mud-stained soldiers in khaki greatcoats, goat-skins, and *feldgrau* jackets. He was safe; he was in No Man's Land.

'Can you tell me the name of this place, please?'

'St Yves. 'Oo are yer?'

'London Highlanders. Who are you?'

'Warwicks.'

'I'm looking for the London Rifles.'

Thumbs jerked – 'Down there.'

Through the fraternizing soldiers, on the frozen level field, he walked towards some cottages seen in the near distance. He asked again.

'East Lancs, mate.'

He went on, past Somersets, and Hampshires. He saw a peasant in the usual black suit being led away to behind the British lines. He had

---

[1] French cottage with bar-room; used as billets in the war.

come up to look at his property – the white estaminet stabbed all over
with bullets.

'I say, can you tell me where the London Rifles – ?'

'We are the London Rifles!'

'Oh, good!'

'I say – who are you?'

'London Highlanders.'

'London Highlanders? Are they here?'

'No, up north – near White Sheet.'

'Have you just come down from there?'

More men of the Rifles were now gathering round him.

'Didn't you come from behind the German lines?'

'Yes. I came along the Messines crest, on a bike.'

'A bike? From behind the German lines?'

'Where did you leave it?'

'Leaning against their barricade over there.'

'Good God!'

'Were you with the London Highlanders at the battle of Messines?'

Questions followed in quick succession. He looked from one face to
another.

'Give him a chance to speak, you fellows,' said someone, who there-
upon in the silence began to ask his own questions. 'You did say you
were with the original battalion at Messines?'

'Yes.'

The questioner looked at him intently. 'Mean to say you've been a
prisoner ever since the bayonet charge?'

'Good lord, no! I wasn't taken prisoner.'

'Then how did you come to be wandering free behind the German
lines?'

'I just went there for a bike ride.'

'What, right behind their lines?'

'Yes. Some of our fellows went behind them to have a football
match, so I thought I'd have a look round. Then I came on here, on the
off-chance of finding one of your chaps, called Willie Maddison. He's
my cousin.'

'Maddison? What company?'

'I don't exactly know.'

'Maddison? Anyone know Maddison? Sure he's with the first battalion, and not with the second at home?' No-one knew Maddison. 'He may be down in front of the convent.'

Phillip was now the centre of about a hundred men, in khaki and grey. One of the Germans listening to him was a tall officer, who looked steadily at him when he had finished speaking. Phillip felt he was thinking about the battery he had passed in the sunken lane; and this feeling was confirmed when the German officer approached him and said in a quiet voice, 'May I have a word with you? Shall we walk this way, and see the prie Dieu at the Cross-Roads – we "huns" have not yet succeeded in shooting it down, you will be able to observe, to the satisfaction of some of your newspapers,' as he indicated the several new crosses of ration-box wood set up over various new graves in No Man's Land that day.

The tall German officer went on, 'May I count on the word of a London Highlander, that you will regard your recent visit behind our lines as, shall we say, never for a moment approximating to that of an agent?'

'An agent, sir?'

'A spy.'

'Oh no, I wasn't for a moment spying, sir.'

Phillip saw that they were closely followed by a German soldier wearing a green shoulder cord. He looked from the officer's orderly to the officer himself, at the big pink face, the expressionless grey eyes, the clean-shaven lips which had hardly moved during the speaking of the words.

'I am glad to hear it,' the voice went on, 'otherwise you would be my prisoner, do you understand? We are still at war.'

'Yes, sir.'

'Then you give me your word?'

'Yes, sir.'

'Good. Now may I ask you some questions of purely personal interest to myself. How did your government manage to supply you with so many Maxim guns at the battle for Ypern, or as you call it – Ypres?'

'Maxim guns? We had none.'

'No Maxim guns? But everywhere our troops met with withering fire, both frontally, and across – no machine-guns?"

'It was the "fifteen rounds rapid" that did it, sir.'

'And your overwhelming reinforcements.'

'But we hadn't any, sir. We had no reserves, other than local. 'Of course,' he added, 'we've got a great many now!'

'I see. Would it amuse you to know that our High Command broke off the battle because your woods were supposedly full of hidden reserves, while we had no more regiments – we were putting in students, with one rifle among three – War is full of surprises.' He paused. 'Well – auf Wiedersehen, my English, or should I say Scottish friend? This war will not last for ever. Perhaps we may meet again when it is over. Until then, goodbye, I am happy to rely on your word.' The German clicked his heels, and bowed.

Phillip came to attention, and bowed. What an extraordinary thing for the Germans at Ypres to be as exhausted as the British had been – and to think that the machine-guns were all on the British side –

Having asked the way to the convent, Phillip walked on. He was approaching a group of cottages about a cross-roads when he came upon a burial party. They had evidently just finished; for as he drew near, a German officer gave a sharp command, at which a German soldier came forward smartly, carrying an armful of ration-box wooden crosses. The officer pointed to one of the new graves. The soldier snatched off his round grey cap, with its red band, and knelt to put one of the crosses upon the loose earth.

Phillip was reading, *Für Vaterland und Freiheit* in purple indelible pencil, when he felt his arm touched.

'Hullo, Phil!'

'Willie!'

They stared at one another delightedly. Phillip felt warmth spreading over his body. They shook hands, while he thought how very young his cousin looked, his brown eyes large and eager like a child's, with his badgeless cap, his greatcoat with the skirt roughly cut off, his face pale and wan. He was only seventeen, too young to have come out. The friend of his boyhood had recently been killed, one of the first casualties in the battalion.

Willie was full of the strangeness of the Christmas Day.

'I've been talking to a Saxon, Phil, all night. We went out to the wire, at the same time. It's most extraordinary, but the Germans think exactly about the war as we do! They can't lose, they say, because God is on their side. And they say they are fighting for civilization, just as we are! Surely, if all the Germans and all the English knew this, at home, then this ghastly war would end. If we started to walk back, and they did, too, it would be over!'

'I wish it were as easy as that, Willie.'

'But it is true, Phillip!'

'It would be a miracle if it could happen.'

'But this is a miracle now, Phil! Look, "For Fatherland and Freedom"! Isn't that just the same as our side's "For God, King, and Country". They *are* the same things! Both sides are fighting with identical ideas to drive them on. Why then, when everyone wants it to stop, should it have to go on? I'll tell you. Because the people at home do not know the whole truth! They think that the whole truth is one-sided, like Uncle Dick, who says, "Look what they've done to Belgium, raping, Uhlans cutting off children's hands, the burning of Louvain – ." Well, they did burn Louvain, I suppose, out of what they call "Frightfulness", to strike terror into the civilian population, like freezing a gum before pulling out a tooth. But, so far as I can make out, most of the newspaper atrocities never really happened.'

'Oh, none of us believe all that stuff in the papers,' said Phillip. 'We know that they shot Belgian franc-tireurs, civvies who killed some of their scouts when they found them camping, or bivouacking. We'd have to do the same if we were in German territory. Everyone knows that.'

'My Saxon friend told me that a lot of bad things were done by the gaol-birds in their ranks, who did rape and murder, but hundreds were court-martialled for it,' said Willie.

'Well, I can vouch for one thing,' said Phillip. 'A German confirmed just now that some of their mass attacks on Ypres were made by students having only one rifle among three of them. That was a rumour at the time, with us. Christ knows we were untrained enough, but some of the Germans were absolute school kids. They even came over singing. The newspapers talk about German efficiency, but I don't believe it, at least, not as regards preparing for this war. Why, I've talked to dozens of regulars who were at Mons on that Sunday! They said some of our fellows were bathing in the canal, when suddenly they saw horsemen on the skyline above them. They turned out to be Uhlans, as surprised as themselves, as they realized when the Uhlans turned round and bunked! Mons was then being made into our advance base; the staff thought the Germans were a hundred miles away! The Germans thought we were still at Boulogne! In fact, one German this morning, up our way, told one of our chaps that their General Staff didn't know that the British Expeditionary Force had landed in France until they read of it ten days afterwards in a Dutch newspaper! Then the Germans thought that we had many more troops at Ypres than they had, and machine-guns, too – so they broke off the attacks, being out-numbered. It was our "fifteen rounds rapid" that seemed to them to be machine-guns! Shows how even the highest authorities can blunder, doesn't it?'

'I think it is all very simple really, Phil. It's like the wind-up, both sides firing away, thinking the other is going to attack. Yet no-one does attack.'

'Not now, perhaps! – but six weeks ago, I can tell you, it was quite a different story! When I look back, I can't think how I lived through it. Most of our chaps copped it, you know.'

'Yes, we read about it, Phil, at Bleak Hill. We went there after you'd left. Is it terrible, being in a bayonet charge?'

'The thought is terrible before, and after, when you think about it. But when it is happening, it all seems to be like in a bad dream, all the movement, I mean. I don't think anyone can feel anything but awfully queer, but some feel less fear than others. Like Peter Wallace – you know, one of the original Bloodhounds. He really was brave. He went to save the MO, who continued to kneel to attend the wounded when the Bavarians broke through at Messines, and lost his glasses, and couldn't see. So he got hold of a German and went for him with his fists, and was bayoneted. His two brothers went to his aid, and were bayoneted too. Peter would have got the VC, if it hadn't been a defeat, our chaps say.'

'Yes, Aunt Hetty told me. I went there for my twenty-four hours' embarkation leave, the day after the news about Messines came. The rumour was that we were going out at once to help you; but we did a fortnight's training, near St Omer, before coming up here.'

'You weren't at an unfinished convent, were you, by any chance?'

'At Wisques, yes! We got there a week after you'd left.'

There was a pause; then Phillip asked how Jack Temperley was killed.

'He fired through a steel loop-hole, without putting his rifle through the hole, but standing back in the trench. His bullet hit the plate, and came straight back at him.'

'Yes, I saw a chap get killed like that. Poor old Jack.'

'Aunt Hetty told me about your friend Cranmer, Phil. He is "missing", isn't he? At least it means a chance of being a prisoner.'

'It's unlikely. Both our Guards and the Prussians don't take prisoners if they can help it.'

'The Saxons told us this morning that the Prussians are relieving them next week. "Shoot the lot of them," they said, "and the war will be over." They hate the Prussians. I heard that long before the war.'

'So did I.'

The talk had taken place under the broken crucifix at the cross-roads of Le Gheer, about a hundred yards behind the British front line. They decided to take a look inside one of the cottages of the hamlet. German dead lay in the first cottage, surprised in a counter-attack of the Inniskillings the previous October; one whiff was enough. Outside in the flooded ditch, just under the ice, lay a British soldier, on his back his blue eyes open as though staring at the sky, arms extended, fingers spread. A look of terror was still visible through the ice.

'I wonder what he thought as he was killed, Phil. Perhaps he saw himself going farther and farther away, and then he was looking down at his body, left behind.'

'I don't know, Willie, I think one thing one moment, and another the next. By the way, did you see what looked like a round, glowing light, on a pole, behind the German lines last night, by any chance?'

'Yes, the Morning Star!'

'But doesn't that rise just before the dawn?'

'Not always. Do you know, Phil, I have been wondering if it was the same star that the Wise Men saw in the East, at the birth of Christ.'

The frost was settling again in little crystals upon post and wire, new mound and icy shell-hole. It was time to think of getting back.

Having said goodbye to cousin Willie, Phillip set off at a vigorous pace down the road beside the wood into Ploegsteert, with its broken church, and from there to Romarin, and the road to Neuve Eglise. There he had the luck to find an ASC lorry going to Poperinghe. After some discussion, and five francs changing pockets, the driver agreed to go through Kemmel, instead of his usual way through Dranoutre. From Kemmel it was a couple of miles to Vierstraat, he said, on parting; and thanking him, Phillip jumped down and, walking with a rapid, loping stride, got back to the line of bunkers just after sunset. Fires gleamed through the trees as he approached the reserve line, his boots ringing on the frozen cross-pieces of the corduroy path. No-one had noticed his absence.

He set about collecting wood for the night's fire, in the light of the moon tarnishing the iced shell-holes. Soon smoke was arising, turning the moon's horns brown. There he would return, after the carrying party that evening.

Much work was done during the next two nights, in the pale hard air. British and German working-parties put up wire, repaired parapets, carried up trench boards and other material, talking normally. No shot was fired. Then on New Year's Eve a messenger came over with a note addressed to the Officer-in-Command, saying that a staff-inspection was taking place at midnight along the Corps front; the 'automatic Pistolen' would be fired in accordance with orders; but they would be fired high. And at half past ten o'clock, as Phillip was knocking a staple into a post, he and others with him heard German voices calling out, 'Go back, Tommee! Go back! It is nearly midnight!' At eleven o'clock the machine-guns opened up all along the line. The frost broke, the rains came, the truce ended. No more wavings, like children saying goodbye, no more heads above parapets.

Submarine Triad penetrates Oslo Fjord

Sidney Hart

Patrols came and went for *Triad* with the regularity of a peacetime liner crossing the Atlantic. By now a few submarines, like *Salmon* and *Ursula*, had distinguished themselves by torpedoing German cruisers. Others, not so fortunate, had failed to return from their missions. A small part of the Price of Admiralty. *Triumph* had reported back with sixteen feet of her bows blown away through striking an enemy mine; but the majority, like *Triad*, had had little success. They'd battled through rough seas, they'd spent their days under the ocean, their nights on the surface. The crews' nerves were tensed during every moment of their long, silent patrols, expecting any second, during their surfaced periods, to crash-dive their vessels into the deeps before enemy or their own aircraft could spot them and take decisive action.

Came *Triad*'s seventh patrol. Hitler had struck another vicious blow, and Norway had been invaded. That gave British submarines a free hand to act. The order for which we'd waited for several months came, 'Sink on sight.' From now on all vessels in our area would be fair game. Even the sinking of, say, one supply ship by fifty-four men in a submarine might be the equivalent of a battle on land, one shipload of German tanks sent to the bottom would have taken a lot of destroying on shore.

Some days after the fall of Oslo, *Triad* was at periscope depth a few miles off the entrance to Oslo Fjord, waiting for the fall of night. When darkness drew down we surfaced; an extra good charge was forced into our batteries by our powerful Diesels, and just before dawn we dived. The idea was to penetrate Oslo Fjord in the hope of finding there some good targets lying at anchor, and there was also a far from distant hope that a German cruiser might be there.

Triad nosed a cautious way through the entrance, and commenced her long, hazardous journey under water to the top of the fjord. Inside her steel hull were fifty-three men who would see not a thing of the pending adventure. The fifty-fourth, her Captain – Lieutenant-Commander Oddie had now replaced that sterling Commander, Jonus – would only get an occasional peep through the periscope. On the way down, if there was a way down, he would see nothing. We should in all likelihood be the hunted instead of the hunters.

The tiniest sound, a single scrape on *Triad*'s side, made us apprehensive of the much dreaded nets or the even deadlier mines. *Triad* was drawing closer – ever closer – to her goal. Only the Captain's curt orders and the quiet, steady hum of the propeller shafts broke the brooding silence.

And then . . . she was there: she was at the fjord's top end. It was a near miraculous feat of navigation on the part of her Captain; but, alas! to the disappointment of every soul aboard, after such a daring venture, the fjord was bare of the hoped-for cruiser. However, lying at anchor, waiting to unload, was a fat supply ship loaded until even her decks were crammed with army vehicles and tanks. God willing, and with just a smudge of luck, the German Army would never use them!

Our Captain was intent on carrying out his attack on this promising target.

'Up periscope!' came the snapped command. And then . . .

'Down periscope!' followed almost like a flash. Good enough: the show has started. 'Stand by one and two torpedoes!' Here was the crucial moment, the climax of all training, and preliminary patrols. We were in the process of attacking the enemy, and in one of his newly-acquired bases. Question was: Should we score?

'Up periscope!'

And then again the order: 'Stand by Number One; stand by: Fire!'

There was a queer, unreal pressure of air in the submarine; a little shudder as the torpedo left its tube.

'Stand by Number Two; stand by: Fire!'

There was the air-pressure on our ears again; there was the same sharp shudder as the second torpedo left *Triad*'s tube. Came next:

'Down periscope!'

Talk about minutes that seem like hours! A torpedo heading for its target runs at about 1,000 yards per minute. At a range of, say, 3,000 yards, the waiting period can grow unendurable. I suppose every man aboard was silently counting . . . counting. One minute, two minutes, three minutes. Dead silence! We'd missed. There was a look of intense anguish on every visible face – sheer, mortified pain. And the sudden dull 'brump' wiped it away like writing off a slate.

'Got her!'

Faces lit up as if illuminated by an interior lamp. Voices were heard which for a seemingly endless time had been silent. Followed a crisp reminder from the Captain: 'We haven't won the war yet! Silence!'

The calm nonchalance of our commanding officers was a thing better imagined than described.

'Up periscope!' He glimpsed our target through the submarine's magic 'eye' calmly, very deliberately, and reported for the benefit of all: 'She's sinking, stern first!' Just like that, with a never a ruffle on his superb calm. This was the Navy in action.

'Stand by for depth charges!' was the next instruction.

Down to 60 feet, and behold *Triad* was creeping back the way she'd come, and creeping blind. Came quickly the 'brump' of depth charges, and the 'brump' of bombs: none close enough to create any immediate anxiety. There was just the tingling uncertainly of . . . 'would they get really close?' We'd foxed them. They were taken by surprise, never expecting any submarine to strike so far up an occupied fjord. They had no definite contact. Altogether, at random, 135 charges and bombs were dropped as we made our way down the fjord. So we reached the open sea – mildly triumphant in the inexpressive British way.

Not being in the Captain's confidence to any noticeable extent, it is not possible for me to say what his exact orders were, as a sequel to the Oslo Fjord venture. But our patrol area changed forthwith to the Skaggerak. There were others of our submarines already there,

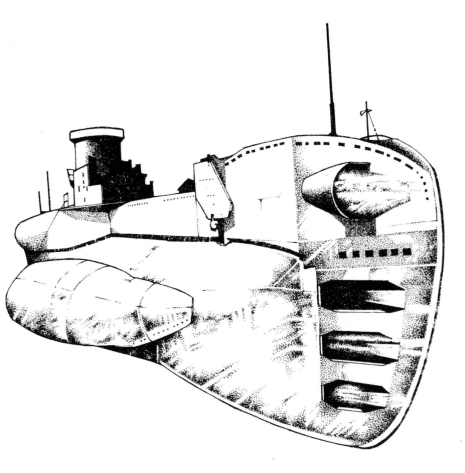

Down to 60 feet and Triad was creeping blind.

where the hunting promised to be good, striking at enemy convoys as they made their harrassed way from Germany to Norway.

Now, mark how Fate administers cruel, tantalizing twists. Our first attack in the Skaggerak was completely ruined by a natural phenomenon that would hardly be credited. Just as our torpedoes were ready to be fired, we ran into a patch of fresh water! *Triad* dipped down to 200 feet depth before she could be checked, owing to the altered buoyancy of the water outside. The attack was utterly ruined. There are no second chances for submarines; we could only hope the 'S' class boat ten miles distant from us would have better luck.

During those tense days the 'brump' of depth charges was continuous. Other submarines were having a bad time in the Skaggerak, but *Triad* had been reasonably lucky until we carried out our third attack of that particular patrol. We closed in towards the convoy at periscope depth. That convoy consisted of two or three supply ships and several motor torpedo-boats – vicious, waspish craft. The order was: 'Diving stations!' Next came: 'Stand by: Five, Six, Seven and Eight!'

There in the engine room we had little or nothing to do beyond sitting and listening, or taking an occasional peep into the control room to note the progress of the attack. I was sitting on the engine room rails when I heard – felt, rather – four quick 'pooshes' of air. Four shudders shook *Triad*; that meant four torpedoes had been fired. A yell from control room followed: 'Shut off shallow water depth gauges!' So we were going deep? That meant the enemy escorts had spotted us. Less than a minute after firing those four torpedoes we were at 150 feet.

It was possible to hear depth charges speeding down through the water towards us, and even before they exploded, easy to realize they were coming annoyingly close. Then, for the fraction of a second, the whole undersea seemed to burst wide open.

The whole of *Triad*'s interior became nothing but a blurred vision, for all the world like a cinema screen when the film being displayed runs off the rails and goes crazy. Paint tore off the bulkheads, lights tinkled down to the deck as if somebody had been using them as targets at an Aunt Sally stall. And before the crashing din of the first attack had died down, a second pattern of depth charges was speeding through the water towards us. All eyes turned up towards the deck-head. Whoomph! Tah-whoomph! Whoomph! There was the same fantastic blur inside our narrow ship; she bucked and plunged as if she were a bronco being spurred to madness. A voice grunted: 'By the b – y hell, those were close!'

I looked first at one, then another of the men in *Triad*'s engine room. There wasn't a sign of fear – stark indifference seemed the characteristic note – and, strangely enough, I wasn't really afraid, although we all knew we'd never get much closer to death without tasting its bitterness. One thing – we'd all go together. That would make it easier; and I felt that *Triad*'s crew would be a pretty good crowd to go anywhere with.

By the engine fuel oil tanks stood Snowy Whitbread – since numbered with the lost – a man on the wrong side of forty, married, with a grown-up daughter; a submarine reservist who after finishing twelve years' service had been called back to the Navy at the outbreak of hostilities. Snowy was the type of man with a rosy complexion who, after weeks at sea, always looked as clean as on the day we sailed. With a brush of his hand over his head his blond hair looked instantly as if it had been combed. On Snowy's lips was the faint suspicion of a smile. Solid as the Rock of Gibraltar, he looked. 'Good old Snowy!' I thought. 'I hope my nerve's as good as yours when I've turned forty!' Whoomph-a-tah! whoomph! The cork chippings came down from the bulkhead, but the dizzy blur that had characterized those first attacks had vanished. We had a fighting chance. Suddenly all depth charging ceased. They'd left us, given up the hunt. Everything was quiet except for the swish of *Triad*'s propellers.

Good news from the Asdic operator gave us the kick of a strong tonic: he had heard two torpedo hits on the convoy through his sound equipment. So our patrol had resulted in one ship definitely sunk, and two probables. Not too bad!

Some few days later *Triad* tied up once again at Rosyth. We had a distance of several hundred yards to walk to *Forth*. And we walked now with an air of confidence, and the feeling of having accomplished a successful patrol. We'd been well and truly depth charged. We had at least one sinking to our credit. What more could heart of man desire?

Alas, aboard *Forth* our success was damped down by the news that our chummy submarine, *Thistle*, had been lost, and *Tarpon*, too, on her very first patrol. Three 'S' class submarines were gone as well, and one of these had been in the next area to ours in the Skaggerak. Five submarines lost! A heavy price to pay for defending Norway; but on the credit side of the account was the fact that British submarines had sunk over a score of enemy ships during those two hectic weeks. Anyway, wars can't be fought in kid gloves.

As a result of our latest patrol, Lieutenant- Commander Oddie was awarded the DSO in recognition of his ship's gallantry in penetrating Oslo Fjord. He well deserved it. The calm efficiency of our submarine commanders can only adequately be realized by those who have served under them – proudly – in action.

A Mile from Freedom

Kendal Burt and James Leasor

Franz von Werra – a German air ace – crash lands in England and is taken prisoner.

After numerous escape attempts he is finally to be transferred to a Prisoner of War camp in Canada; but en-route he escapes by jumping out of a train window during a snow storm.

His plan is to reach the still neutral United States of America.

Surviving more hazards, Von Werra finally reaches a snow covered valley . . .

He walked south and came to what appeared in the gathering dusk to be a wide, flat, snow-covered valley. It was a few seconds before he realized that this was the River St Lawrence. It was frozen over. He was tremendously excited. All he had to do was to wait until it was quite dark and walk across to the United States.

It was far better than a ferry or toll bridge where he would have had to run the gauntlet of customs, passport officials and police of two countries.

But the size of the river was terrifying. How wide was it? Five hundred metres? A thousand? The dusk and the snow made it impossible to judge. But it was a long, long way to the winking lights of the American city on the other side, which he reckoned from his map to be Ogdensburg.

He set out along the bank, wading knee-deep through the snow. He was dead tired and ravenously hungry. He had eaten nothing for nearly twenty-four hours. It had been cold enough all day, but with the approach of night the temperature dropped rapidly. There was a bitter wind at his back. It pierced his clothing like a knife. The cold and fatigue had made him drowsy. He fretted with impatience.

He had travelled so far; now there was only three-quarters of a mile at most between him and final freedom.

He struggled for about two miles along the bank. It was desolate and silent. There was only the hum of the wind round his ears, the occasional flurries of powder blown along the surface of the snow.

He waited until long after dark. A haze of light hung over Ogdensburg. Some distance to the east of it there were three isolated points of light forming a triangle. Perhaps they were street lamps. He made them his objective.

At seven o'clock he left the comparative shelter of the bank and set off across the open ice of the river.

The snow had been blown into deep drifts near the bank. He floundered, fought his way forward foot by foot. Fifty yards out the going became comparatively easy, but the wind swept over the ice straight up the course of the river. It seemed to be laden with splinters of glass. Ice formed on his eye-brows, on the scarf over his head and on the upper part of his coat. Snow from the drifts he had struggled through turned into ice as he walked; the flaps of his coat were like boards.

The glittering stars and the lights of Ogdensburg merged and traced scintillating lines across the snow. The merging of land and sky gave him the illusion that he was about to look over the edge of the world. The illusion vanished as the lights of the city ahead became more distinct.

Now and again he heard the sound of the ice cracking – a sharp snap followed by a rapidly receding rumble. He knew that cracking ice was not dangerous so long as it was freezing. But when he reached what he thought was about half-way, the sounds of cracking became very loud and menacing. Sometimes they were close and he could feel the slight sudden shock wave. An odd sensation.

He tripped over something and went sprawling. The ice was no longer smooth under its thin covering of snow, but jagged and rough as a road surface broken up by a pneumatic drill. He was so numb from cold that it was a minute or so before he felt the full hurt of his tumble.

He was winded and shaken. He lay for a moment, almost overcome by the urge to sleep, his senses pulling one way, his will the other. There came to his mind the memory of a summer evening on a lake near Berlin: green reeds rustling, sun-spangled water, white sails billowing, ripples lapping against glistening, varnished woodwork. Lapping . . . lapping . . .

The wind dropped momentarily and he clearly heard the sound of a car horn. He got up, aching all over, slipping and stumbling on slabs of ice larger than paving stones.

He was only a quarter of a mile from the American shore. Cars rolled along the waterfront, headlights blazing.

He hurried forward eagerly, then paused. Ten, fifteen yards ahead the snow seemed to stop. Beyond was blackness. The shore already? But why was there no snow?

Then he saw the lights reflected on the blackness: water! He could not grasp it. How could there be water when the whole river was frozen over? He frantically hacked with the heel of his boot at a slab of ice. A corner broke off and he tossed it forward into the blackness. It fell with a hollow splash, like a pebble into a well.

There was an ice-free channel between him and the American shore To swim in that temperature meant certain death. He had to go back.

Von Werra returned to the Canadian bank and walked along it towards Prescott. He came to a collection of chalets – a deserted summer holiday camp. He floundered about in the deep snow on the foreshore and eventually found what he was looking for – a long, cigar-shaped mound of snow. He scraped away the side with his boot and came upon something hard. It was an upturned rowing boat.

He went back to the chalets and found a wooden fence. After much kicking and wrenching he managed to free two pailings. They were too wide and too thick and ice made them heavier still, but they would have to do. He used one of them as a shovel to dig away the snow from the boat.

It was a large, cumbersome affair, and was frozen to the ground. He had to lever it free, a little at a time, with one board, using the other as a wedge. When he had freed it he still had to turn it the right way up.

It took all his strength and the aid of the two boards but finally he righted it.

There were no oars or rowlocks. The boat was a six-seater. However was he going to row it – even assuming he could manage to drag it as far as the water?

He groped around, looking for another boat. He found nothing, so returned to the six-seater.

He had got to do it!

In a sudden, desperate rage, he threw himself at the stern of the boat and pushed wildly. It scarcely moved.

He felt a snowflake on his cheek. He looked up at the sky. The stars were obscured. He looked across the river. The lights of Ogdensburg were barely discernible through a curtain of flurrying snow.

It would be fatal to give way to rage and panic. He must conserve his strength, use his wits to spare his muscles, and make every scrap of effort count.

If he tried to *drag* the boat, he would waste a lot of effort, for he would tend to pull the bow down into the snow. He must *push* it. When he got out beyond the drifts, where the snow was only ankle deep on the ice, he could tie his scarf to the mooring ring in the bow and pull the boat behind him.

He tossed the boards into the boat and began pushing it towards the river. He advanced a foot to eighteen inches at a time. At first he thought he would never reach the river. But gradually he stopped thinking. He became an automaton, oblivious to everything except the rhythm of his movements, the rasping of his breath and the taste of his saliva. Fatigue, hunger, thirst and cold were forgotten.

At last he reached the open ice. He crouched down on the lee of the boat out of the wind and the driving snow, resting. When he got up again and tried to push, the keel was frozen to the ice. He had to wrench with all his might to free it. It was wasted effort – he must not rest any more until he reached the pack-ice.

He tried to tie his scarf to the mooring ring, but his fingers were without feeling and for the life of him he could not tie a knot. He would have to continue pushing.

Half-way across.

Sometimes for minutes at a time the lights of Ogdensburg were

*He tossed the boards into the boat
and began pushing it towards the river.*

completely obscured by snow. Von Werra kept pushing. He dared not stop. Now and again he slipped and fell on to his knees. But he got up and went on.

He was brought to a halt by the pack-ice near the water's edge. How could he get the boat over the ice and into the river?

He pulled the boat back a few feet, then pushed it up on to the pack-ice using the two boards as runners under the keel. Again, using the boards alternatively as runners, he managed to push the boat forward, a length at a time.

At last he reached the open river. He tipped the boat three-parts of the way into the water, jumped in and pushed off against the ice with one of the boards. The whole boat slid into the water, rocked violently and in the struggle to regain his balance the board slipped out of his numbed hand.

He sat down and picked up the remaining board, trying to use it as a paddle. But it was too long, too heavy and too clumsy. He could neither feel it nor grip it. It slid out of his hands into the water.

Rudderless, oarless, the boat floated away into the darkness, rocking and turning lazily round and round in the ten miles an hour current. Now and again small icefloes thudded against the sides.

As escaper must have luck. Farther downstream the ice-free channel followed the contour of a toe of land jutting out in the river. The boat, steadied now and facing upstream, gradually slid across the channel and eventually bumped and scraped along the jagged ice bordering one side of the headland.

Von Werra was no stranger to excitement. But even he found the thrill of that trip on the St Lawrence a little too hectic and sustained. Time seemed to stop. He had the impression that the boat was spinning round and round in the darkness, and hurtling down to the sea.

When it bumped and grated against the margin of ice by the headland, he needed no time to make up his mind. The boat grated: he leapt. He managed to fall on the ice. The boat recoiled, then slowly returned. The last he heard of it, it was bumping and scraping slowly downstream.

He got to his feet, staggered across the ice and scrambled up the bank. He was very anxious. It seemed to him that he had been in the boat for hours, and that he had drifted miles. And he knew from the map that farther downstream the USA border was some way south of the St Lawrence – that *both* banks were in Canada. He saw a huge building some distance away on his left. The windows were ablaze with light. Then he had a shock. He noticed that every window was barred. Had he landed in the grounds of a penitentiary?

He moved away to the right as quickly as he could. He was reassured when he saw a car pass by ahead of him. There must be a road. Then he saw two cars parked farther down on the right. He got on to the road and walked towards them. The leading car was unoccupied. The bonnet of the other was raised and a man was tinkering with the engine. A young lady in a snow-sprinkled fur coat stood by him and there was another girl sitting in the car.

On the licence plate of the rear car were the words: 'New York'. It was the same with the other car.

He dared not believe it. He had seen cars in Canada with New York licence plates.

The man went to the car ahead, presumably to get some tools. He looked hard at von Werra but did not speak.

Von Werra moved across the front of the car. The headlamps shone on his overcoat, which was stiff with ice. His legs cast long shadows on the snow. The woman stared at him and then glanced in the direction of the river from which he had come. She laughed and asked lightly:

'What's the matter with you?'

'Excuse me. Is this America?'

'Are you sick, or something?'

'No, truly. What is that house over there? What place is this?'

The woman was struck by his accent and by the tiredness of his voice. She replied straightforwardly:

'That is New York State Hospital. I am a nurse there. You are in Ogdensburg.'

'*Ogdensburg?* But – ' Von Werra could not believe it.

Instead of having drifted miles downstream, he had travelled barely half a mile.

But what did it matter? He was in America.

He smiled wearily.

'I am an officer of the German Air Force,' he said. 'I escape across the river from Canada. I am' – he corrected himself, 'I *was* a prisoner-of-war.'

Duel in the Sun

Alexander Dumas

France in the early part of the 17th Century:
There were nobles, who made war against each other; there was the king,
who made war against the cardinal; there was Spain, which made war against
the king . . .
In these troubled times, D'Artagnan, a young Gascon, wishes to become a
King's Musketeer under Monsieur de Treville. However, by a combination of
mischances, he somehow manages to offend three of the most famous
musketeers, Athos, Porthos and Aramis in one day, and on the morrow is to
fight a duel with all three in turn!
For their part, the musketeers all suspect D'Artagnan of being a spy of the
cardinal.
Athos, already injured in a fight against the cardinals guards the day before,
is the first to duel with D'Artagnan . . .

It was a quarter past midday. The sun was in its zenith, and the spot
chosen for the scene of the duel was exposed to its full ardour.

'It is very hot,' said Athos, drawing his sword in his turn, 'and yet I
cannot take off my doublet; for I just now felt my wound begin to
bleed again, and I should not like to annoy Monsieur with the sight of
blood which he has not drawn from me himself.'

'That is true, Monsieur,' replied D'Artagnan, 'and whether drawn
by myself or another, I assure you I shall always view with regret the
blood of so brave a gentleman. I will therefore fight in my doublet,
like yourself.'

'Come, come, enough of such compliments,' cried Porthos. 'Remember, we are waiting for our turns.'

'Speak for yourself when you are inclined to utter such incongruities,' interrupted Aramis. 'For my part, I think what they say is very well said, and quite worthy of two gentlemen.'

'When you please, Monsieur,' said Athos, putting himself on guard.

'I waited your orders,' said D'Artagnan, crossing swords.

But scarcely had the two rapiers clashed, when a company of the Guards of his Eminence, commanded by M. de Jussac, turned the corner of the convent.

'The cardinal's Guards!' cried Aramis and Porthos at the same time. 'Sheathe your swords, gentlemen, sheathe your swords!'

But it was too late. The two combatants had been seen in a position which left no doubt of their intentions.

'Halloo!' cried Jussac, advancing towards them, and making a sign to his men to do so likewise, 'halloo, musketeers? Fighting here, are you? And the edicts, what is become of them?'

'You are very generous, gentlemen of the Guards,' said Athos, full of rancour, for Jussac was one of the aggressors of the preceding day. 'If we were to see you fighting, I can assure you that we would make no effort to prevent you. Leave us alone, then, and you will enjoy a little amusement without cost to yourselves.'

'Gentlemen,' said Jussac, 'it is with great regret that I pronounce the thing impossible. Duty before everything. Sheathe, then, if you please, and follow us.'

'Monsieur,'' said Aramis, parodying Jussac, 'it would afford us great pleasure to obey your polite invitation if it depended upon ourselves; but unfortunately the thing is impossible, – M de Tréville has forbidden it. Pass on your way, then; it is the best thing to do.'

This raillery exasperated Jussac. 'We will charge upon you, then,' said he, 'if you disobey.'

'There are five of them,' said Athos, half aloud, 'and we are but three; we shall be beaten again, and must die on the spot, for, on my part, I declare I will never again appear before the captain as a conquered man.'

Athos, Porthos, and Aramis instantly drew near one another, while Jussac drew up his soldiers.

This short interval was sufficient to determine D'Artagnan on the part he was to take. It was one of those events which decide the life of a man; it was a choice between the king and the cardinal, – the choice made, it must be persisted in. Too fight, that was to disobey the law, that was to risk his head, that was to make at one blow an enemy of a minister more powerful than the king himself. All this the young man perceived, and yet, to his praise we speak it, he did not hesitate a second. Turning towards Athos and his friends, 'Gentleman,' said he, 'allow me to correct your words, if you please. You said you were but three, but it appears to me we are four.'

'But you are not one of us,' said Porthos.

'That's true,' replied D'Artagnan; 'I have not the uniform, but I have the spirit. My heart is that of a musketeer; I feel it, Monsieur, and that impels me on.'

'Withdraw, young man,' cried Jussac, who doubtless, by his gestures and the expression of his countenance, had guessed D'Artagnan's design. 'You may retire; we consent to that. Save your skin; begone quickly.'

D'Artagnan did not budge.

'Decidedly you are a brave fellow,' said Athos, pressing the young man's hand.

'Come, come, choose your part,' replied Jussac.

'Well,' said Porthos to Aramis, 'we must do something.'

'Monsieur is full of generosity,' said Athos.

But all three reflected upon the youth of D'Artagnan, and dreaded his inexperience.

'We should only be three, one of whom is wounded, with the addition of a boy,' resumed Athos; 'and yet it will not be the less said we were four men.'

'Yes, but to yield!' said Porthos.

'That *is* difficult,' replied Athos.

D'Artagnan comprehended their irresolution.

'Try me, gentlemen,' said he, 'and I swear to you by my honour that I will not go hence if we are conquered.'

'What is your name, my brave fellow?' said Athos.

'D'Artagnan, Monsieur.'

'Well, then, Athos, Porthos, Aramis, and D'Artagnan, forward!' cried Athos.

'Come, gentlemen, have you decided?' cried Jussac for the third time.

D'Artagnan passed his sword through Jussac's body.

'It is done, gentlemen,' said Athos.

'And what is your choice?' asked Jussac.

'We are about to have the honour of charging you,' replied Aramis, lifting his hat with one hand, and drawing his sword with the other.

'Ah! you resist, do you?' cried Jussac.

'S'blood! does that astonish you?'

And the nine combatants rushed upon each other with a fury which however did not exclude a certain degree of method.

Athos fixed upon a certain Cahusac, a favourite of the cardinal's. Porthos had Bicarat, and Aramis found himself opposed to two adversaries. As to D'Artagnan, he found himself assailing Jussac himself.

The heart of the young Gascon beat as if it would burst through his side, – not from fear, God be thanked, he had not the shade of it, but with emulation; he fought like a furious tiger, turning ten times round his adversary, and changing his ground and his guard twenty times. Jussac was, as was then said, a fine blade, and had had much practice; nevertheless, it required all his skill to defend himself against an adversary who, active and energetic, departed every instant from received rules, attacking him on all sides at once, and yet parrying like a man who had the greatest respect for his own epidermis.

This contest at length exhausted Jussac's patience. Furious at being held in check by one whom he had considered a boy, he became warm, and began to make mistakes. D'Artagnan, who though wanting in practice had a sound theory, redoubled his agility. Jussac, anxious to put an end to this, springing forward, aimed a terrible thrust at his adversary, but the latter parried it; and while Jussac was recovering himself, glided like a serpent beneath his blade, and passed his sword through his body. Jussac fell like a dead mass.

D'Artagnan then cast an anxious and rapid glance over the field of battle.

Aramis had killed one of his adversaries, but the other pressed him warmly. Nevertheless, Aramis was in a good situation, and able to defend himself.

Bicarat and Porthos had just made counter-hits. Porthos had received a thrust through his arm, and Bicarat one through his thigh. But neither of these two wounds was serious, and they only fought the more earnestly.

Athos, wounded anew by Cahusac, became evidently paler, but did not give way a foot. He only changed his sword hand, and fought with his left hand.

According to the laws of duelling at that period, D'Artagnan was at liberty to assist whom he pleased. While he was endeavouring to find out which of his companions stood in greatest need, he caught a glance from Athos. This glance was of sublime eloquence. Athos would have died rather than appeal for help; but he could look, and with that look ask assistance. D'Artagnan interpreted it; with a terrible bound he sprang to the side of Cahusac, crying, 'To me, Monsieur Guardsman; I will slay you!'

Cahusac turned. It was time; for Athos, whose great courage alone supported him, sank upon his knee.

'S'blood!' cried he to D'Artagnan, 'do not kill him, young man, I beg of you. I have an old affair to settle with him when I am cured and sound again. Disarm him only, – make sure of his sword. That's it! Very well done!'

This exclamation was drawn from Athos by seeing the sword of Cahusac fly twenty paces from him. D'Artagnan and Cahusac sprang forward at the same instant, the one to recover, the other to obtain, the sword; but D'Artagnan, being the more active, reached it first, and placed his foot upon it.

Cahusac immediately ran to the guardsman whom Aramis had killed, seized his rapier, and returned towards D'Artagnan; but on his way he met Athos, who during this relief which D'Artagnan had procured him had recovered his breath, and who, for fear that D'Artagnan would kill his enemy, wished to resume the fight.

D'Artagnan perceived that it would be disobliging Athos not to leave him alone; and in a few minutes Cahusac fell, with a sword-thrust through his throat.

At the same instant Aramis placed his sword-point on the breast of his fallen enemy, and forced him to ask for mercy.

There only then remained Porthos and Bicarat. Porthos made a thousand flourishes, asking Bicarat what o'clock it could be, and offering him his compliments upon his brother's having just obtained a company in the regiment of Navarre; but, jest as he might, he gained nothing. Bicarat was one of those iron men who never fall dead.

Nevertheless, it was necessary to finish. The watch might come up and take all the combatants, wounded or not, royalists or cardinalists. Athos, Aramis, and D'Artagnan surrounded Bicarat, and required him to surrender. Though alone against all, and with a wound in his thigh, Bicarat wished to hold out; but Jussac, who had risen upon his elbow, cried out to him to yield. Bicarat was a Gascon, as D'Artagnan was; he turned a deaf ear, and contented himself with laughing, and between two parries finding time to point to a spot of earth with his sword. 'Here,' cried he, parodying a verse of the Bible, – 'here will Bicarat die; for I only am left, and they seek my life.'

'But there are four against you; leave off, I command you.'

'Ah, if you command me, that's another thing,' said Bicarat. 'As you are my commander, it is my duty to obey.' And springing backward, he broke his sword across his knee to avoid the necessity of surrendering it, threw the pieces over the convent wall, and crossed his arms, whistling a cardinalist air.

Bravery is always respected, even in an enemy. The musketeers saluted Bicarat with their swords, and returned them to their sheaths. D'Artagnan did the same. Then, assisted by Bicarat, the only one left standing, he bore Jussac, Cahusac, and one of Aramis's adversaries who was only wounded, under the porch of the convent. The fourth, as we have said, was dead. They then rang the bell, and carrying away four swords out of five, they took their road, intoxicated with joy, towards the hôtel of M de Tréville.

They walked arm in arm, occupying the whole width of the street, and taking in every musketeer they met, so that in the end it became a triumphal march. The heart of D'Artagnan swam in delirium; he marched between Athos and Porthos, pressing them tenderly.

'If I am not yet a musketeer,' said he to his new friends, as he passed through the gateway of M de Tréville's hôtel, 'at least I have entered upon my apprenticeship, haven't I?'

The bogus General

Dennis Wheatley

Gregory Sallust is assigned an especially dangerous task by his old friend Sir Pellinore Gwaine-Cust.

Sir Pellinore's plan is for Gregory to enter wartime Germany as a German General in an effort to contact a number of highly placed officials who want a quick end to the war.

So, in a private plane, Gregory is landed in enemy territory – near Cologne. It is dawn. Gregory is now alone. He has no belongings – only his bogus General's uniform, false papers and some money . . .

When he had covered about 400 yards he encountered a fence, on the far side of which he found cultivated land. The crops had been gathered and a rough stubble rustled against his boots as he stroke out across the uneven ground, thanking his stars that the weather had been good during the first week of the war and that the night was fine, for if his boots had been clogged with mud the going would have proved infinitely more tiring and difficult.

After a quarter of a mile the field ended and he struck grass again, but he had to cross several more stubble-fields before he reached a deep ditch and, scrambling across it, found himself on the open road. Turning left, he headed for Cologne.

The country was quite flat and utterly silent. The few houses that he passed showed blank, black windows and their inmates were clearly taking what sleep they could before facing the cheerless prospect of their second war-time Monday morning.

He saw no signs of military activity, but he had not expected to do so as he was nearly forty miles from the Belgian frontier and Germany was still at peace with Belgium. The nearest war zone was far away to the south of Luxemburg, well over a hundred miles distant. The only troops he was likely to encounter in this neighbourhood were anti-aircraft batteries stationed here for the defence of Cologne and the great industrial area further north, where the plants at Düsseldorf, Crefeld and Essen would be turning out munitions day and night. A faint reddening of the sky to northward indicated the innumerable blast-furnaces of Düsseldorf, which could not be entirely screened even in a black-out.

Occasionally a lorry rumbled past or a car with dimmed headlights crawled towards him in the darkness. At one point he encountered a small party of revellers who were singing drunkenly, at another an old woman who was pushing a handcart. But there was little traffic, and each time anything approached he stepped off the road to take cover in the shadows.

The six-mile tramp along the road was a dreary business, but at last the scattered houses merged into disconnected rows and Gregory knew that he was entering the suburbs of Cologne.

Glancing at the luminous dial of his wrist-watch, he saw that it was just on 5.30. This meant that there was nearly another hour to go until sunrise, but the sky was already paling faintly in the east. He had not hurried on his way from the landing-ground because it would have been dangerous for him to be seen, in the conspicuous uniform of a General, drifting aimlessly about the streets of the city before it was astir. Moreover, as an old soldier, Gregory had long since learned to conserve his strength and he never hurried over anything unless he had excellent reasons for doing so.

Where a fence railed off an open field between two blocks of houses he halted and sat down on the stile that gave entrance to it. Plucking a tuft of grass he spent some moments dusting his boots, as he knew that it would be a fatal give-away for a German General to be seen about the streets in boots which were not meticulously clean. Then he took out his case and lit a cigarette.

That was another little slip, he thought, as he drew the fragrant smoke of the Sullivan down into his lungs. Sullivans are not to be obtained in Germany, and if an occasion should arise which necessitated his offering his case this fact might well betray him. He would have to get some of those filthy German ★★★★ as soon as possible.

Fortunately the case was of plain, engine-turned gold without monogram or initials, so he was able to retain it, but with a reluctant sigh he took out the remaining Sullivans and, tearing them into pieces, scattered the tobacco and paper in the long grass behind him.

At a quarter to six a door banged in a nearby house and a shrill voice called out something in German. That brought home to him as nothing had yet done that he really was in Germany. Shortly afterwards a light cart clattered by and Gregory stood up. It would not do for a General to be seen sitting dreaming at the roadside. German Generals were busy, practical people and not given to doing that sort of thing. The uniform would probably have big advantages later, but it had drawbacks as well.

Stubbing out his cigarette he started off again towards the centre of the town and was soon walking on pavement. It was lighter now and there were quite a number of people in the streets. He came to tramlines, and passed a little group of workers waiting at the terminus for a tram to take them into the city. A solitary, grey-clad soldier was among them; steel-helmeted, a gas-mask slung round his shoulders. He drew himself up stiffly and saluted. With a little start Gregory acknowledged the salute and walked on.

The fact that he was wearing a cap instead of a steel helmet did not matter. Actually, it was probably an advantage; for except when actually on parade officers would certainly be permitted such licence behind the war zones, but he ought to have had a gas-mask. Evidently the department which had equipped him had not had one of the latest German pattern, and a British mask would have given him away. He made up his mind to rectify the omission as soon as possible.

The trams were running by now, but he noticed that their clanging, high-pitched bells were silent, doubtless on account of some regulation imposed by the German equivalent of ARP.

He had decided that he would make for the main railway-station, go in by one entrance and come out by another, and then hail a taxi as though he had just arrived by train, in order to reach an hotel where he could breakfast as befitted his rank. But that plan proved quite abortive.

139

The *Hauptbahnhof* yard was full of cars; many were grey ones belonging to Army units and the rest all had some form or other of label pasted on their windscreens, reading 'Supply Service,' 'ARP,' 'Road Control,' 'Police,' and so on. The station buzzed with activity; people, most of whom were in uniform, came and went incessantly, but there was not a single taxi to be seen. Evidently the Germans must have taken them off the streets in order to conserve their petrol supply.

Somewhat cheered by seeing many other officers also walking, Gregory entered the stream of pedestrians moving towards the centre of the town and made his way to the Dom Hotel, which had been used by the British as their Headquarters during their occupation of Cologne twenty years before. A sentry outside it presented arms and Gregory acknowledged the salute, casually now, having become quite used to taking salutes during his walk from the station, but he was informed that the hotel had been taken over by the Administration and was directed to the Excelsior.

On arriving there he went straight through to the gentlemen's cloakroom, picked up the first gas-mask that he saw on a peg and, slinging it round his shoulders, walked out again. Crossing the street, he went round the corner, entered the Edenhof and going into the restaurant proceeded to order breakfast.

If he had had to content himself with the menu which was presented to him he would have fared badly, as rationing was already in force in Germany, but he knew that money would talk there as well as anywhere else in Europe, and in this little matter his rank would protect him from any charge of contravening the laws which some over-zealous witness might bring against him.

Looking the head waiter straight in the eye, he handed him back the menu, which listed only cereals, gave him a two-mark piece and gruffly demanded *Eier mit Schinken*.

'*Jawohl, Herr General*,' replied the waiter swiftly, and turning to one of his minions passed on the order.

While he ate his ham and eggs and drank some passable imitation coffee he considered his next move. If he had entered the country dressed as a private, as Sir Pellinore had suggested, he would have carried a knapsack in which he could have brought a change of linen and other oddments that he might require; but Generals do not carry knapsacks, neither do they carry suitcases, so he had had to content himself with slipping his razor, toothbrush and comb into one of his pockets.

It was clear, however, that he must have luggage if he were to stay in the country for any length of time. He could not just walk into hotels minus even an attaché-case and spend the night without arousing suspicion in the minds of chamber-maids and managers. It had been his intention to take a taxi round the town after he had breakfasted and to purchase his small requirements, but this was now out of the question.

Having paid his bill and had the ration-card with which the department had provided him punched, he went out to the reception-desk and announced to the weedy, C.3-looking clerk who stood behind it: 'I am General von Lettow. My servant did not arrive at the station in Hanover last night in time to meet me with my suitcase, so I had to leave without it. I am now going out to buy a few things and shall have them sent here. See to it that the porter has them all together in his office when I return!'

The little clerk clicked his heels and bowed. 'At your service, Excellency.'

Turning away with a curt nod, Gregory went out to do his shopping. After an hour he had bought at various places a good-sized suitcase, pyjamas, a dressing-gown, two changes of underclothes, bedroom slippers, another pair of boots that fitted him better, and toilet things. He almost gave himself away at the chemist's by inquiring for hair-oil, but remembered just in time that his head was now bald. He tried to get a torch, but without success, as every torch in Cologne had either been commandeered days before for military purposes or snapped up by civilians as part of the ARP outfits.

Having instructed the various shopkeepers that his purchases should be sent at once by hand to the Edenhof, he decided to go and have a drink at the big café on the *Dom Platz* in order to give them reasonable time to make the deliveries, and seated there at a small, marble-topped table with a big mug of the dark *Muniche Löwenbräu* in front of him he studied the surrounding scene with interest.

Workmen, high on a scaffolding, were busily removing the stained glass of the rose-window from the great, twin-towered cathedral opposite, and piles of neatly-stacked sandbags now protected the fine stone carvings on the arches of its doors.

The café was one of those set aside for the use of officers, but a few civilians were sitting about and taking their morning beer. An elderly, grey-bearded man was seated at the next table and Gregory thought that he would try out his German on him, though he had few qualms about it. There are many more dialects and local accents in Germany than there are in England, so that even if his German were not absolutely perfect any peculiarity of inflection would be noticed by his hearer only in the same way that a Londoner might detect a slight touch of the North Country or Cornwall in the speech of an educated Englishman brought up in the provinces.

Having ordered a packet of cigarettes of a popular brand, Gregory leaned across to the bearded man. '*Wüden sie mir Feuer geben bitte?*'

The man quickly fumbled for some matches and Gregory took a light from the sulphurous flame. The thin, loosely-packed cigarette tasted as though it was made of hay, as it probably was, but Gregory knew that he would have to accustom himself to the taste. '*Danke*,' he smiled. 'These are interesting times in which to live, are they not?'

'Yes, indeed, Herr General,' his neighbour replied with nervous haste, and Gregory realized at once that he was too scared to talk to anyone in uniform. Another disadvantage of the kit that he had chosen; but after all, it was not his business to go round seeking the opinions of individual Germans on the war. He must accept Sir Pellinore's statement that a considerable number of Germans were desperately opposed to it and to the Nazi régime, but they would certainly not admit as much to a General, even if there were not dozens of Nazis in brown or black uniforms strutting about within a stone's-throw of the café.

After remarking hurriedly that it was a good thing the weather was keeping so fine for the gallant troops, the elderly man rapidly disposed of his beer, paid his score and departed.

His table was taken shortly afterwards by two younger men, both officers, a Major and a Lieutenant. Having saluted Gregory, and with a formal: 'You permit, Herr General?' they sat down and began to talk together in low voices.

Gregory's hay-filled cigarette had lasted for barely half a dozen puffs, so he took out another and again asked for a light.

The Lieutenant stood up with the rapidity of a Jack-in-the-box, clicked his heels and supplied it. Gregory stood up to take it and, bowing slightly, murmured: 'Von Lettow.' The Lieutenant jerked forward from the waist like an automaton and rapped out: 'Kuhlemann, at your service, Herr General!' The Major sprang to his feet also, and bending abruptly at the waist, snapped: 'Möller!'

Gregory returned their bows and asked if they would join him in a drink. Both accepted, and more beer was brought. Gregory opened the conversation by saying that he had arrived that night from Hanover and was on his way up the Rhine to Coblenz.

'Ha! You are lucky, then, Herr General!' the Lieutenant exclaimed. 'As Coblenz is our base for the Army on the Upper Moselle it does not need much intelligence to guess that to be your destination. You'll see some fighting, whereas we're stuck here in Cologne on garrison duty.'

The Major grunted. 'You'll get all the fighting you want, Kuhlemann, before this war is over. It'll be a long show, just as it was last time. Don't you agree, sir?'

Gregory smiled. 'It is good that young officers should be impatient to serve the Fatherland at the front, but we older soldiers who have seen war may be excused if we are content to wait until we are ordered forward into the battle. The struggle will be a long one, yes; but we shall emerge victorious.'

'*Heil Hitler!*' ejaculated the Lieutenant.

'*Heil Hitler!*' echoed Gregory and Möller promptly, but the latter added thoughtfully: 'It will be hard on the women and children.'

'Yes, it will be hard,' agreed Gregory, 'but they must play their part without flinching.

'The poor devils are having to leave their homes already,' Möller went on. 'Look! There's another batch of them crossing the square.'

Gregory turned in his chair and saw a dejected group of women and children staggering along under the weight of suitcases and bundles. He had seen similar groups in the streets of Cologne earlier that morning, but had been too preoccupied with his own thoughts to wonder about them.

'They're evacuating all the towns in the Saar,' remarked Kuhlemann, 'but the minor discomforts they are asked to face are nothing compared to remaining there to be bombed to pieces by these English swine.'

'They haven't dropped any bombs yet,' replied the Major mildly, 'except on the railway siding at Aachen. They're still busy distributing their leaflets.'

'Have you seen one?' asked Gregory; 'I tried to get a copy in Hanover but people were too frightened of the Gestapo to pass them on to anyone in my position.'

The Major smiled and took out his pocket-book. 'I've got one here, Herr General, if it would interest you to see it. We're supposed to destroy them, of course, but I kept it as an interesting souvenir.'

'*Danke.*' Gregory extended his hand for the slip of paper. 'It is not good that they should be passed freely among the civilian population, but among officers it is another matter. The loyalty of German officers can never be brought into question.'

He read the leaflet through and handed it back. 'What lies these English tell – but between ourselves we must admit that there's just enough truth in it to make it highly dangerous.'

Möller laughed. 'Well, it's not as dangerous as bombs would be, anyway, so we'll hope that they stick to dropping paper.'

Gregory felt that sufficient time had now elapsed for his purchases to have been delivered at the Edenhof so he stood up, the other two following his example. Wishing them good luck, which sentiment they heartily reciprocated, he made his way back to the hotel.

His things had arrived, and he stood by while the porter packed them, in their wrappings, into the suitcase. He then inquired about the sailings of the Rhine steamers and learned to his satisfaction that one was due to leave Bonn for Coblenz at 1.30. The journey could have been made more quickly by rail but Gregory knew that had he actually been a serving officer he would have had a railway pass to his destination. To buy a ticket might create suspicion and to say that he had lost his voucher and ask the RTO to supply him with another would have led to undesirable complications, so he had decided to make the journey by river steamer, on which it was less likely that he would be expected to produce a military chit.

The hall-porter summoned a street porter who took Gregory's bag and preceded him as he walked the comparatively short distance down to the river-side, whence the local electric trains start for Bonn. The line cuts across a bend in the Rhine where the country is flat and uninteresting, so that few people make the river trip from Cologne but

With a big mug of beer in front of him, he surveyed the scene with interest

prefer to board the boat at Bonn, and for a short, local journey of this kind it was quite natural that Gregory should take an ordinary ticket instead of producing a military travelling pass.

The old university town of Bonn was now empty of its students in their gay, many-coloured caps, and in their place were great numbers of refugees, for the colleges were being used to billet the women and children who had been evacuated from the towns immediately behind the Siegfried Line.

With a heavy-footed strut Gregory boarded the big, low-decked steamer and everybody made way for him as he forged ahead to a comfortable seat from which he could enjoy the view as they steamed up the Rhine. He had done the trip on numerous previous occasions, so when they came opposite to the Seven Sisters Mountains on the left bank and the Drakensberg, with its glass-verandahed restaurant situated high above the quiet little town of Königswinter, he went down to lunch.

This consisted of a very small portion of veal, boiled potatoes and carrots, followed by *Apfelkuchen*. There was plenty of bread to go with it, but no butter, cream or cheese. Another square of his forged ration-card was punched, he paid the bill and went on deck again to enjoy a lazy afternoon gazing out across the wide river as bend after bend of it opened out new vistas showing ruined castles perched upon nearly all of the heights that came into view.

At six o'clock they docked at Coblenz, and securing a porter to carry his bag Gregory went straight to the Hotel Bellevue, which stands right on the river-front. He registered at the desk as General von Lettow, and owing to his rank managed to secure a room on the first floor that had just been vacated. Having bought a couple of books from the stall in the hotel lounge he went straight up to his room and unpacked. Then he went out on to the balcony, and as he gazed down upon the scene spread out below memories came floating back to him.

To his left the river divided, and in this direction lay the most beautiful portion of the Rhine, with its famous vineyards of Johannesburg, Marcobrunn, Steinberg, Rudesheim, and the rest. At Coblenz, too, the Rhine was joined by another great river, the Moselle, up which he meant to proceed on the following morning. The Moselle was beautiful also, he recalled, but with a more gentle beauty; passing between less abrupt but more thickly-wooded slopes or lush water-meadows lying level with its banks.

He remembered his first visit to Coblenz, as a boy. It had been over Whitsun in 1913, when his father had taken him with him on a short business trip to Germany. That Whitsun Germany had held her first air pageant, a three-days' rally under the auspices of His Imperial Highness Prince Henry of Prussia, brother of the Kaiser. Over fifty crazy, flimsy planes made of linen and bamboo had gathered from all parts of Germany on the plateau above the town, and seven great Zeppelins had floated like huge, silver cigars above the airfield.

The Hotel Bellevue was then newly built, and had in fact been specially opened in honour of the occasion. Officers of the Kaiser's Army had thronged it, resplendent in their glossy cloaks of grey, green and blue. Their swords and spurs jangling; the gold and silver eagles upon their *Pickelhaubes* glinting in the lights, Death's Head Hussars in fur toques and Jäger in forest green had made the place like a scene from a Viennese musical comedy.

Little Gregory had been thrilled beyond words by the martial splendour of it all, and on the last night he had been allowed to stay up to see the fireworks display at Ehrenbreitstein, the grim old fortress that crowned the hill on the farther side of the Rhine. Twenty-six years had not altered a line of this unforgettable picture save for the addition of hideous steel pylons carrying electric cables.

Yet – so much had happened since. His thoughts drifted to another occasion, a few years after the War, when he had stayed at the same hotel. His companion then had not been his father, but a very lonely lady. What marvellous times they had had together on that stolen holiday in the Rhineland! He wondered what had become of Anita now. She must be getting on, and probably had children. Ah, well! That was the way things went in this world. One could never hold happiness for very long; one had to snatch it whenever it came one's way. With a little sigh he re-entered his room through the long windows and went down to the grill-room of the hotel for a meal.

It was packed with Army officers, but his rank soon secured him a table. As he there sat he sensed the tension about him. Few women were present, and there was no gaiety. The diners talked in low voices and many of them kept one eye on the door, through which an intermittent stream of orderlies hurried, bringing messages or calling officers to the telephone. Coblenz was an important junction and the supply base for the Western Front. And Germany was at war.

As soon as he had finished he went upstairs again and started to undress. It was over twenty-four hours since he had last slept and he was beginning to feel a little tired. He read for a quarter of an hour and then switched off his light.

Things had been easy so far – incredibly easy. He had secured his kit and accomplished over half his journey without the slightest hitch. Protected by his General's uniform, now that he was slipping into the part, he saw no reason why they should not continue so. After all, if one sees an English General in a London hotel or street it does not even occur to one that he might really be a German secret agent.

The red Knight dies

Alexander McKee

The Red Knight, nowadays better known as The Red Baron, was a legend in his own time.

This story by Alexander McKee describes the war situation in 1918. It gives us a glimpse into the lives of famous pilots of the era; shows us how German interrogation methods worked, and ends with Baron von Richthofen's last flight . . .

Russia was out of the war. The Italians had been driven back in rout. The French had been bled white, and their army had mutinied. The U-boat campaign had come close to defeating the British. The American effort was negligible, but would not long remain so. Instead of going sensibly on to the defensive, and forcing some sort of easy peace, the Germans struck the heroic note and decided to risk everything on one final offensive in the west; the last tired blow against another fighter equally weary. There was not much time now before a new, fresh contestant would enter the ring. But four years of fighting had told, and the Allied blockade had had its dire effect; most of the best were dead, the remainder were starving. They gritted their teeth for one more effort, in the spring.

In the early part of 1918, very few of the men who had seen the war in were still at the front; they were either underneath it, or at home. Richthofen was still there, still the greatest name in air fighting; the originator of massed tactics – the *staffeln* stacked in layers, himself at the top, with his No. 2 Wolff, to guard his tail. The method, elaborated and improved, was to be used by the Luftwaffe in 1940, when the RAF had forgotten all about it, and flew Hendon-style. Child critics between the wars were to attack Richthofen for being unsporting; but this was 1918, there was no sport any more.

McCudden was still in action, effortlessly piling up a long score of two-seaters – knocking them down sometimes at the rate of three or four a day. He could get the scouts, too, when he chose; but his 'doctrine', as he called it, was the orthodox military one of inflicting the heaviest casualties with the least risk. On 31 January, with a considerable height advantage, he tackled five scouts single-handed. He knocked out one with his first burst, zoomed into the rest and got another – he had not time to watch the end of their fall, but ground observers confirmed them; he frightened off a third, which went into a spin, and was left with a Pfalz and an Albatros. Then both his guns stopped, the Vickers with a broken belt, the Lewis out of ammunition. 'But I felt awfully brave,' he wrote, 'and as they were very dud, I started chasing them about with no gun, and once very nearly ran into the tail of the Pfalz at whose pilot I could have thrown a bad egg if I could possibly have got one at that moment. I chased these two artists as far as Cambrai . . .' He had come a long way in skill and polish, from the days when he condemned himself for not attacking with sufficient determination.

His respected opponent, 'Green-tail', the leader of a very tough bunch of lads, was still operational; six weeks before, he had killed Maybery, one of 56's flight commanders, who had had a score of twenty. On 18 February, McCudden killed 'Green-tail', but not by way of revenge. He out-manoeuvred an Albatros formation, slipping into the sun above and behind them; as he led the SEs down, he automatically picked the German leader, which at once burst into flames and put one wing straight down, throwing the pilot out – the green tail, the letter K, and the white inverted V on the top wing showed who it was. McCudden shot a second Albatros out of the formation before the Germans even had time to break, and both machines fell together.

In preparation for the March offensive, in which the Germans expected a big haul of captured Allied airmen, they increased the number of intelligence officers available for interrogation duties; one of those chosen was Hans Schröder, who did a short five-day course at Lille under an acknowledged expert, von Karg-Bebenburg. No pressure was used. He decided to use the same methods himself, but to improve on them in one particular – with his flying experience, he could easily pose as the friendly commander of a German squadron. From von Karg-Bebenburg he borrowed the vital tools of the trade – the latest available information on Allied squadrons – and set up his own shop in Douai. It had cells with adjoining listening rooms, and also concealed microphones which were connected up to loudspeakers in the house next door, where the duty interpreter took down all conversations in shorthand.

As the German advance went forward behind the drum-fire of the rolling barrage, and the air forces became fully committed, the customers began to pour in. It was not, of course, the plans of the fortress, which the female spy keeps hidden up her stocking, which Schröder was after; the only information of any real importance in war concerns the enemy's Order of Battle – the number, type, armament and location of his units – and it is necessary always to keep this up to date. If his Order of Battle is known, the enemy's intentions may be deduced from it.

Schröder's first prisoner was a Lieutenant Lomax. A few minutes after he had been shot down, his capture was reported by telephone to Schröder. The machine was a Camel, it had a white triangle painted on the fuselage behind the cockpit. Schröder got out his file on 43 Squadron, RFC, and memorized the contents, which were reasonably full; on average, one officer of this squadron was shot down per week, and each one supplied little items of harmless information. By the time he had closed the file, Schröder probably knew more about that squadron than did Lomax, who had joined it only recently. One thing, however, he did not know – its present location. The British were being pressed back, and information was continually going out-of-date. Well, no doubt Lieutenant Lomax would tell him.

The lieutenant was still being marched to the rear under armed guard when Schröder's car overtook him. Schröder stopped, asked the guard where he was going, then remarked, that as he was going to Douai also, he could give them a left. Casual introduction effected. Then praise for Lomax's gallant attack on the balloon that morning.

The Lieutenant was being marched to the rear when Schröder's car overtook him.

In return, Lomax burst out with a series of questions – could he write home via the Red Cross? – would he be in a camp with other airmen? – and so on. Eventually, they became so friendly that Schröder promised to see if he could pull strings and get Lomax invited round to his place for a few hours before he went off to a proper camp. Lomax was put in solitary confinement in the forward camp at Douai – solitary confinement, because a few days of it encourages the desire to talk, the feeling for companionship of any kind, as every intelligence officer knows.

Then, posing as a squadron commander, Schröder was able temporarily to release Lomax, and take him to visit a local German aerodrome, where everyone had been warned of the imposture, and finally he took the lieutenant back to his own house for tea. In the course of the chat they had, Lomax was astonished about how much Schröder knew of his squadron, the name of its commanding officer, and so on. Then Schröder tried his bluff. He thought that 43 Squadron had probably moved to Avesnes le Compte aerodrome, but he was not sure; he had provided himself with aerial photographs of many British aerodromes; now, he took a chance, and showed Lomax some photos of Avenes le Compte. 'Do you recognize those?'

'But you know all about us!' gasped Lomax in astonishment.

The vital information had been obtained, so Schröder relaxed, asking no questions, just letting Lomax talk. More bits and pieces came out of that, together with an interesting item. The pilots of 43 often went to St Pol, where there was a bar with a very nice girl. 'She's a devil – little Mary,' laughed Lomax. Schröder noted little Mary. She had no military importance, of course, but casually referred to, in conversation with the next British prisoner, she would enable him to pose even more convincingly, as the man who knew so much already, that really there was no need to be too security-minded.

When Lomax left, he was put in a cell with a captured infantry officer, to whom he recounted his version of the interview. He had been warned, he said, that the Germans would try to pump him. 'Well, just let them try it on, they won't get a word out of me.'

A colleague of Schröder's, who operated at Karlsruhe, had a slightly different system, which he maintained was better. He kept a number of informers, unknown to each other, who questioned for him the latest batch of prisoners; a British officer questioned the British, a Frenchman questioned the French; then they came to him with their results. Then, officially, they were put in cells, to explain their absence, but actually they were allowed out into the town, to go to the theatre, and so on. The prize bit of information he had received in this way was advance warning of an air raid on the Ruhr; fighters were grouped to meet it, and the bombers were shot to pieces.

Schröder was under no illusions; if there were British pilots prepared to betray their country, then there must be Germans doing the same thing in British POW camps. Sometimes, Schröder got little enough, except a lecture. Captain Holleran, of 56 Squadron, for instance, gave him a frank account of the difference behind the British and German fronts – the masses of motor transport behind the British lines, the worn-out carts drawn by bony horses, the broken-down lorries, the drawn, starved look of the soldiers, to be seen behind the German lines. 'Germany will certainly lose; must lose,' he said. At first, Schröder found it difficult to believe that Holleran was a pilot, because he had a wooden leg, but he was eventually convinced, when Holleran told him the original article was in Gallipoli, unless a dog had eaten it.

Some of the leading German aces made appointments to meet their opponents at Schröder's house; one of these was Ritter von Schleich, whose base reason was that he coveted the leather coats worn by British airmen and, in spite of his many victories, had never yet managed to lay his hands on one. However, one day in the spring of 1918, he sent down Lieutenant S. B. Reece, who landed more or less intact; von Schleich hurried along to the intelligence officer's house, to meet his opponent and claim his leather jacket. Unfortunately, Reece had been called away unexpectedly from a game of tennis to take part in a patrol. He was still wearing his tennis flannels. Schleich wore terribly, then asked him if he had been playing singles or doubles. When Reece replied that it was a single, Schleich asked the state of the game.

'Three-two for me.'

'Well, if you like, we'll finish it.'

And they did.

On 18 May, a few days before Reece was shot down, Schröder interviewed Lieutenant K. P. Hunt of 65 Squadron. The conversation had only one topic – the death of Richthofen. All the Germans knew, then, was that on 21 April a German balloon observer had made a brief report:

'Red triplane landed on hill near Corbie. Landed all right. Passenger has not left plane.'

Hunt was important, because he had seen the body. Schröder questioned him closely as to what Richthofen was wearing, and Hunt was able to describe the white sweater which Schröder had himself seen when he had given him first aid after he was shot down and wounded the first time. According to Hunt, the Fokker triplane had been hit in the engine, it was not known by whom, and while he was trying to reach his own lines by gliding, Captain Roy Brown, a Canadian of 209 Squadron, had fired at him; he had also been fired on by AA and by Australian machine-guns. Now, they were all claiming to have shot him down, including the crew of an RE8. As in the cases of Immelmann, Ball, and Guynemer – and many others – the death of an ace had ended in a mystery.

In fact, Brown did not claim to have shot down Richthofen. He reported, simply, 'I dived on a pure red triplane which was firing on Lieutenant May. I got a long burst into him and he went down vertically and was observed to crash by Lieutenant May and Lieutenant Mellersh.'

May's own report was equally brief, 'I was attacked by a red triplane which chased me over the lines, low to the ground. While the triplane was on my tail, Captain A. R. Brown attacked and shot it down. I observed it crash into the ground near Vaux-sur-Somme.'

That seemed clear enough. But the fight was witnessed from the ground by many people, none of them appeared to have noticed Brown's Camel, although they all testified to machine-gun fire from the ground. Lieutenant G. M. Travers was in an Australian observation post on top of Corbie Hill. 'They were coming dead to us along the line of the Somme and straight toward Corbie Hill. May was in a bad position, with the red triplane close behind him. They were within a few hundred yeards of us now. Just then, a machine-gun, ahead and below us, fired three or four short bursts, and von Richthofen's plane seemed to turn on its side, right itself again, and then swerve sharply to the right and swoop gradually to the ground, landing about half-a-mile away from us.' Travers was one of the first three to reach the triplane, which was intact; they identified the pilot by an inscription on his watch. Another officer of his unit, Edward Burrow, also went to the machine, and stated 'the bullet which killed him had entered his lower left jaw and had come out behind his left eye.'

D. L. Fraser, intelligence officer of the 11th Australian Infantry Brigade, was also a witness. He saw May with Richthofen behind him, at about 400 feet; he heard a long burst of ground machine-gun fire, and then the triplane flew straight over him, down now to 200 feet. It 'was flying as if not under complete control, being wobbly and irregular in flight. It swerved north, then eastwards, rocking a great deal, and suddenly dived out of sight with the engine running full open.' The triplane came down, said Fraser, about 200 yards away; he ran there, undid the pilot's safety belt, and helped to pull him out. 'He was quite dead and was considerably cut about the face – apparently shot through the chest and body.' On the directions of the divisional commander, Fraser identified the ground-machine-gunner as Sergeant Popkin of the 24th Australian MG Company; but he had also to report that two AA Lewis guns of the 53rd Battery had also fired on Richthofen. Two men from this latter unit, Evans and Bouie, were given the DCM for killing Richthofen. Captain Brown was given a bar to his DFC for doing the same thing. Obviously, they had all fired at him, at one time or another, but only an intensive enquiry on the spot could have come near to settling the matter of whose bullet actually killed Richthofen.

This was attempted. Four medical officers examined the body and decided that Richthofen had been struck by a single bullet, entering his chest on the right, exiting on the left at a slightly higher level; that is, he was shot from the right side by a gun almost on the same level as himself; assuming that the triplane was not stunting, only another aeroplane could have fired the shot. Examination of map positions showed it was unlikely any of the ground gunners concerned could have fired at the triplane from the right. This was the basis of the award to Brown. Statements from other witnesses, that Richthofen had been shot through the head, may have been due to the fact that he had obviously been flung forward when the machine touched down heavily, and had smashed his face against the front of the cockpit. Very possibly, he was already a dying man when the ground witnesses saw him approach in the wake of May's Camel.

Many British squadrons sent representatives to his funeral, carrying wreaths; and photographs of the ceremony were dropped behind the German lines. All his enemies testified to his skill and courage.

The Survivor

Bartimeus

The figures on the bridges of the destroyers wiped the stinging spray from their swollen eyelids and read the message of comfort.

'Return to base. Weather conditions threatening.'

They surveyed their battered bridges and forecastles, their stripped, streaming decks and guns' crews; they thought of hot food, warm bunks, drying clothing, and all the sordid creature comforts for which soul and body yearn so imperiously after three years of North Sea warfare. Their answering pendants fluttered acknowledgment, and they swung round on the path for home, praising Allah who had planted in the brain of the cruiser captain a consideration for the welfare of his destroyer screen.

'If this is what they call "threatening",' observed the senior officer of the two boats, as his command clove shuddering through the jade-green belly of a mountainous sea, flinging the white entrails broadcast, 'if this is merely threatening I reckon it's time someone said, Home, James!'

His first lieutenant said nothing. He had spent three winters in these grey wastes, and he knew the significance of that unearthly clear visibility and the inky clouds banked ahead to the westward. But presently he looked up from the chart and nodded towards the menace in the western sky. 'That's snow,' he said. 'It ought to catch us about the time we shall make Scaw Dhu light.'

'We'll hear the fog buoy all right,' said the captain.

'If the pipes ain't frozen,' was the reply. 'It's perishing cold.' He ran a gauntletted hand along the rail and extended a handful of frozen spray. 'That's salt – *and* frozen . . .'

The snow came as he had predicted, but rather sooner. It started with great whirling flakes like feathers about a gull's nesting-place, a soundless ethereal vanguard of the storm, growing momentarily denser. The wind, from a temporary lull, reawakened with a roar. The air became a vast witch's cauldron of white and brown specks, seething before the vision in a veritable Bacchanal of Atoms. Sight became a lost sense: time, space, and feeling were overwhelmed by that shrieking fury of snow and frozen spray thrashing pitilessly about the homing grey hulls and the bowed heads of the men who clung to the reeling bridges.

The grey, white-crested seas raced hissing alongside and, as the engine-room telegraphs rang again and again for reduced speed, overtook, and passed them. Out of the welter of snow and spray the voices of the leadsmen chanting soundings reached the ears of those inboard as the voice of a doctor reaches a patient in delirium, fruitlessly reassuring . . .

Number Three of the midship gun on board the leading destroyer turned for the comfort of his soul from the contemplation of the pursuing seas to the forebridge, but snow-flakes blotted it from view. Providence, as he was accustomed to visualize it in the guise of a red-cheeked lieutenant-commander, had vanished from his ken. Number Three drew his hands from his pockets, and raising them to his mouth leaned towards the gunlayer. The gunlayer was also staring forward as if his vision had pierced that whirling grey curtain and was contemplating something beyond it, infinitely remote . . . There was a concentrated intensity in his expression not unlike that of a dog when he raises his head from his paws and looks towards a closed door.

' 'Ere,' bawled Number Three, seeking comradeship in an oppressive, indefinable loneliness. ' 'Ow about it – eh? . . .' The wind snatched at the meaningless words and beat them back between his chattering teeth.

The wind backed momentarily, sundering the veil of whirling

obscurity. Through this rent towered a wall of rock, streaked all about with driven snow, at the foot of which breakers beat themselves into a smoking yeast of fury. Gulls were wailing overhead. Beneath their feet the engine room gongs clanged madly.

Then they struck.

The foremost destroyer checked on the shoulder of a great roller as if incredulous: shuddered: struck again and lurched over. A mountainous sea engulfed her stern and broke thundering against the after-funnel. Steam began to pour in dense hissing clouds from the engine-room hatchways and exhausts. Her consort swept past with screeching siren, helpless in the grip of the backwash for all her thrashing propellers that strove to check her headlong way. She too struck and recoiled: sagged in the trough of two stupendous seas, and plunged forward again . . . Number Three, clinging to the greasy beech-block of his gun, clenched his teeth at the sound of that pitiless grinding which seemed as if it would never end . . .

Of the ensuing horror he missed nothing, yet saw it all with a wondering detachment. A wave swpet him off his feet against a funnel stay, and receding, left him clinging to it like a twist of waterlogged straw. Hand over hand he crawled higher, and finally hung dangling six feet above the highest wave, legs and arms round about the wire stay. He saw the forecastle break off like a stick of canteen chocolate and vanish into the smother. The other destroyer had disappeared. Beneath him, waist deep in boiling eddies, he saw men labouring about a raft, and had a vision of their upturned faces as they were swept away The thunder of the surf on the beaches close at hand drowned the few shouts and cries that sounded. The wire from which he dangled jarred and twanged like a banjo-string, as the triumphant seas beat the soul out of the wreck beneath him.

A funnel-stay parted, and amid clouds of smoke and steam the funnel slowly began to list over the side. Number Three of the midship gun clung swaying like a wind-tossed branch above the maelstrom of seething water till a wave drove over the already-unrecognizable hull of the destroyer, leaped hungrily at the dangling human figure and tore him from his hold.

Bitterly cold water and a suffocating darkness engulfed him. Something clawed at his face and fastened on to his shoulder; he wrenched himself free from the nerveless clutch without ruth or understanding; his booted heel struck a yielding object as he struggled surfaceward, kicking wildly like a swimming frog . . . the blackness became streaked with grey light and pinpoints of fire. Number Three had a conviction that unless the next few strokes brought him to the surface it would be too late. Then abruptly the clamour of the wind and sea, and the 'shriek of the circling gulls smote his ears again. He was back on the surface once more, gulping greedy lungfuls of air.

A wave caught him and hurled him forward on its crest, spread-eagled, feebly continuing the motions of a swimmer. It spent itself, and to husband his strength the man turned on his back, moving his head from side to side to take in his surroundings.

He was afloat (he found it surprisingly easy to keep afloat) inside a narrow bay. On both sides the black cliffs rose, all streaked with snow, out of a thunderous welter of foam. The tide sobbed and lamented in the hollows of unseen caverns, or sluiced the length of a ledge to splash in cascades down the face of the cliff.

The snow had abated, and in the gathering dusk the broken water showed ghostly white. To seaward the gale drove the smoking rollers in successive onslaughts against the reef where the battered remains of the two destroyers lay. All about the distorted plating and tangle of twisted stanchions the surf broke as if in a fury of rapine and destruction . . .

Another wave gripped him and rushed him shoreward again. The thunder of the surf redoubled. 'Hi! hi! hi! hi!' screeched the storm-tossed gulls. Number Three of the midship gun abandoned his efforts to swim and covered his face with his soggy sleeve. It was well not to look ahead. The wave seemed to be carrying him towards the cliffs at the speed of an express train. He wondered if the rocks would hurt much, beating out his life . . . He tried desperately to remember a prayer, but all he could recall was a sermon he had once listened to on the quarter-deck, one drowsy summer morning at Malta . . . About coming to Jesus on the face of the waters . . . 'And Jesus said "come." . . .' Fair whizzing along, he was . . .

Again the wave spent itself, and the man was caught in the backwash, drawn under, rolled over and over, spun round and round, gathered up in the watery embrace of another roller and flung up on all fours on a shelving beach. Furiously he clawed at the retreating pebbles, lurched to his feet, staggered forward a couple of paces, and fell on hands and knees on the fringe of a snow-drift. There he lay awhile, panting for breath.

He was conscious of an immense amazement, and, mingled with it, an inexplicable pride. He was still alive! It was an astounding achievement, being the solitary survivor of all those officers and men. But he had always considered himself a bit out of the ordinary . . . Once he had entered for a race at the annual sports at the Naval Barracks, Devonport. He had never run a race before in his life, and he won. It seemed absurdly easy. 'Bang!' went the pistol: off they went, helter-skelter, teeth clenched, fists clenched, hearts pounding, spectators a blur, roaring encouragement . . .

He won, and experienced the identical astonished gratification that he felt now.

'You runs like a adjective 'are, Bill,' his chum had admitted, plying the hero with beer at the little pub halfway up the cobbled hill by the dockyard.

Then he remembered other chums, shipmates, and one in particular called Nobby. He rose into a sitting position, staring seaward. Through the gloom the tumult of the seas, breaking over the reef on which they had foundered, glimmered white. The man rose unsteadily to his feet; he was alone on the beach of a tiny cove with his back to forbidding cliffs. Save where his own footsteps showed black, the snow was unmarked, stretching in an unbroken arc from one side of the cove to the other. The solitary figure limped to the edge of the surf and peered through the stinging scud. Then, raising his hands to his mouth, he called for his lost mate.

'Nobby!' he shouted, and again and again, 'Nobby! Nobby! . . . Nob-bee-e!' . . .

'Nobby,' echoed the cliffs behind, disinterestedly.

'Hi! Hi! Hi!' mocked the gulls.

The survivor waded knee-deep into the froth of an incoming sea.

'Ahoy!' he bawled to the driving snowflakes and spindrift. His voice sounded cracked and feeble. He tried to shout again, but the thunder of the waves beat the sound to nothing.

He retraced his steps and paused to look round at the implacable face of the cliff, at the burden of snow that seemed to overhang the summit, then started again to seaward. A wave broke hissing about his feet: the tide was coming in.

Up to that moment fear had passed him by. He had been in turn bewildered, incredulous, cold, sick, bruised, but sustained throughout by the furious animal energy which the body summons in a fight for life. Now, however, with the realization of his loneliness in the gathering darkness, fear smote him. In fear he was as purely animal as he had been in his moments of blind courage. He turned from the darkling sea that had claimed chum and shipmates, and floundered through the snow-drifts to the base of the cliff. Then, numbed with cold, and well-night spent, he began frantically to scale the shelving surfaces of the rock.

Barnacles tore the flesh from his hands and the nails from his finger-tips as he clawed desperately at the crevices for a hold. Inch by inch, foot by foot he fought his way upwards from the threatening clutch of the hungry tide, leaving a crimson stain at every niche where the snow had gathered. Thrice he slipped and slithered downwards, bruised and torn, to renew his frantic efforts afresh. Finally he reached a broad shelf of rock, halfway up the surface of the cliff, and there rested awhile, whimpering softly to himself at the pain of his flayed hands.

Presently he rose again and continued the dizzy ascent. None but a sailor or an experienced rock-climber would have dreamed of attempting such a feat single-handed, well-nigh in the dark. Even had he reached the top he could not have walked three yards in the dense snow-drifts that had gathered all along the edge of the cliffs. But the climber knew nothing about that; he was in search of *terra firma*, something that was not slippery rock or shifting pebbles, somewhere out of reach of the sea.

He was within six feet of the summit when he lost a foothold, slipped, grabbed at a projecting knob of rock, slipped again, and so slipping and bumping and fighting for every inch, he slid heavily down on to his ledge again.

He lay bruised and breathless where he fell. That tumble came near to finishing matters; it winded him – knocked the fight out of him. But a wave, last and highest of the tide, sluiced over the ledge and immersed his shivering body once more in icy water;

the unreasoning terror of the pursuing tide that had driven him up the face of the cliff whipped him to his feet again.

He backed against the rock, staring out through the driving spindrift into the menace of the darkness. There ought to be another wave any moment: then there would be another: and after that perhaps another. The next one then would get him. He was too weak to climb again . . .

The seconds passed and merged into minutes. The wind came at him out of the darkness like invisible knives thrown to pin him to a wall. The cold numbed his intelligence, numbed even his fear. He heard the waves breaking all about him in a wild pandemonium of sound, but it was a long time before he realized that no more had invaded his ledge, and a couple of hours before it struck him that the tide had turned . . .

Towards midnight he crawled down from his ledge and followed the retreating tide across the slippery shale, pausing every few minutes to listen to the uproar of sea and wind. An illusion of hearing human voices calling out of the gale mocked him with strange persistence. Once or twice he stumbled over a dark mass of weed stranded by the retreating tide, and each time bent down to finger it apprehensively.

Dawn found him back in the shelter of his cleft, scraping limpets from their shells for a breakfast. The day came slowly over a grey sea, streaked and smeared like the face of an old woman after a night of weeping. Of the two destroyers nothing broke the surface. It was nearly high water, and whatever remained of their battered hulls was covered by a tumultuous sea. They were swallowed. The sea had taken them – them and a hundred-odd officers and men, old shipmates, messmates, townies, raggies – just swallowed the lot . . . He still owed last month's mess-bill to the caterer of his mess . . . He put his torn hands before his eyes and strove to shut out the awful grey desolation of that hungry sea.

During the forenoon a flotilla of destroyers passed well out to seaward. They were searching the coast for signs of the wrecks, and the spray blotted them intermittently from sight as they wallowed at slow speed through the grey seas.

The survivor watched them and waved his jumper tied to a piece of drift-wood; but they were too far off to see him against the dark rocks. They passed round a headland, and the wan figure, half frozen and famished, crawled back into his cleft like a stricken animal, dumb with cold and suffering. It was not until the succeeding low water, when the

He clawed desperately at the crevices for a hold.

twisted ironwork was showing black above the broken water on the reef, that another destroyer hove in sight. She too was searching for her lost sisters, and the castaway watched her alter course and nose cautiously towards the cove. Then she stopped and went astern.

The survivor brandished his extemporized signal of distress and emitted a dull croaking sound between his cracked lips. A puff of white steam appeared above the destroyer's bridge, and a second later the reassuring hoot of a siren floated in from the offing. They had seen him.

A sudden reaction seized his faculties. Almost apathetically he watched a sea-boat being lowered, saw it turn and come towards him, rising and falling on the heavy seas, but always coming nearer . . . he didn't care much whether they came or not – he was that cold. The very marrow of his bones seemed to be frozen. They'd have to come and fetch him if they wanted him. He was too cold to move out of his cleft.

The boat was very near. It was a whaler, and the bowman had boated his oar, and was crouching in the bows with a heaving-line round his forearm. The boat was plunging wildly, and spray was flying from under her. The cliffs threw back the orders of the officer at the tiller as he peered ahead from under his tarpaulin sou'wester with anxiety written on every line of his weather-beaten face. He didn't fancy the job, that much was plain; and indeed, small blame to him. It was no light undertaking, nursing a small boat close in to a dead lee shore, with the aftermath of such a gale still running.

They came still closer, and the heaving line hissed through the air to fall at the castaway's feet.

'Tie it round your middle,' shouted the lieutenant. 'You'll have to jump for it – we'll pull you inboard all right.'

The survivor obeyed dully, reeled to the edge of his ledge and slid once more into the bitterly cold water.

Half a dozen hands seemed to grasp him simultaneously, and he was hauled over the gunwale of the boat almost before he realized he had left his ledge. A flask was crammed between his chattering teeth; someone wound fold upon fold of blanket round him.

'Any more of you, mate?' said a voice anxiously; and then, 'Strike me blind if it ain't old Bill!' ·

The survivor opened his eyes and saw the face of the bowman contemplating him above his cork lifebelt. It was a vaguely familiar face. They had been shipmates somewhere once. Barracks, Devonport, p'raps it was. He blinked the tears out of his eyes and coughed as the raw spirit ran down his throat.

'Any more of you, Bill, ole lad?'

The survivor shook his head.

'There's no one,' he said, ' 'cept me. I'm the only one what's lef' outer two ships' companies.' Again the lost feeling of bewildered pride crept back.

'You always was a one, Bill!' said the bowman in the old familiar accent of hero-worship.

The survivor nodded confirmation. 'Not 'arf I ain't,' he said appreciately. 'Sole survivor I am!' And held out his hand again for the flask. 'Christ! look at my 'ands!'

The Battle of Shoreby

Robert Louis Stevenson

Robert Louis Stevenson's book, 'The Black Arrow' follows the fortunes of young Richard Shelton during 'The Battle of the Roses' – (the fighting between the Yorkists under Richard, Duke of Gloucester, and the Lancastrians under Lord Risingham.)

Just prior to this story, Dick Shelton is consulted by the hunchbacked Richard of Gloucester as the Duke draws up his final battle plans for the attack on Shoreby . . .

Richard Duke of Gloucester took his place upon the steps, and despatched messenger after messenger to hasten the concentration of the 700 men that lay hidden in the immediate neighbourhood among the woods; and before a quarter of an hour had passed, all his dispositions being taken, he put himself at their head, and began to move down the hill towards Shoreby.

His plan was simple. He was to seize a quarter of the town of Shoreby lying on the right hand of the high-road, and make his position good there in the narrow lanes until his reinforcements followed.

If Lord Risingham chose to retreat, Richard would follow upon his rear, and take him between two fires; or, if he preferred to hold the town, he would be shut in a trap, there to be gradually overwhelmed by force of numbers.

There was but one danger, but that was imminent and great – Gloucester's 700 might be rolled up and cut to pieces in the first encounter, and, to avoid this, it was needful to make the surprise of their arrival as complete as possible.

The footmen, therefore, were all once more taken up behind the riders, and Dick Shelton had the signal honour meted out to him of mounting behind Gloucester himself. For as far as there was any cover the troops moved slowly, and when they came near the end of the trees that lined the highway, stopped to breathe and reconnoitre.

The sun was now well up, shining with a frosty brightness out of a yellow halo; and right over against the luminary, Shoreby, a field of snowy roofs and ruddy gables, was rolling up its columns of morning smoke.

Gloucester turned round to Dick.

'In that poor place,' he said, 'where people are cooking breakfast, either you shall gain your spurs and I begin a life of mighty honour and glory in the world's eye, or both of us, as I conceive it, shall fall dead and be unheard of. Two Richards are we. Well then, Richard Shelton, they shall be heard about, these two! Their swords shall not ring more loudly on men's helmets than their names shall ring in people's ears.'

Dick was astonished at so great a hunger after fame expressed with so great vehemence of voice and language; and he answered very sensibly and quietly that, for his part, he promised he would do his duty, and doubted not a victory if every one did the like.

By this time the horses were well breathed, and, the leader holding up his sword and giving rein, the whole troop of chargers broke into the gallop and thundered, with their double load of fighting men, down the remainder of the hill and across the snow-covered plain that still divided them from Shoreby.

*   *   *   *

The whole distance to be crossed was not above a quarter of a mile. But they had no sooner debouched beyond the cover of the trees than they were aware of people fleeing and screaming in the snowy meadows upon either hand. Almost at the same moment a great rumour began to arise, and spread and grow continually louder in the town; and they were not yet half-way to the nearest house before the bells began to ring backward from the steeple.

The young duke ground his teeth together. By these so early signals of alarm he feared to find his enemies prepared; and if he failed to gain a footing in the town, he knew that his small party would soon be broken and exterminated in the open.

In the town, however, the Lancastrians were far from being in so good a posture. It was as Dick had said. The night-guard had already doffed their harness; the rest were still hanging – unlatched, unbraced, all unprepared for battle – about their quarters; and in the whole of Shoreby there were not, perhaps, fifty men full armed, or fifty chargers ready to be mounted.

The beating of the bells, the terrifying summons of men who ran about the streets crying and beating upon the doors, aroused in an incredibly short space at least two score out of that half hundred. These got speedily to horse, and, the alarm still flying wild and contrary, galloped in different directions.

Thus it befell that, when Richard of Gloucester reached the first house of Shoreby, he was met in the mouth of the street by a mere handful of lances, whom he swept before his onset as the storm chases the bark.

A hundred paces into the town, Dick Shelton touched the duke's arm; the duke, in answer, gathered his reins, put the shrill trumpet to his mouth, and blowing a concerted point, turned to the right hand out of the direct advance. Swerving like a single rider, his whole command turned after him, and, still at the full gallop of the chargers, swept up the narrow by-street. Only the last score of riders drew rein and faced about in the entrance; the footmen, whom they carried behind them, leapt at the same instant to the earth, and began, some to bend their bows, and others to break into and secure the houses upon either hand.

Surprised at this sudden change of direction, and daunted by the firm front of the rear-guard, the few Lancastrians, after a momentary consultation, turned and rode farther into town to seek for reinforcements.

The quarter of the town upon which, by the advice of Dick, Richard of Gloucester had now seized, consisted of five small streets of poor and ill-inhabited houses, occupying a very gentle eminence, and lying open towards the back.

The five streets being each secured by a good guard, the reserve would thus occupy the centre, out of shot, and yet ready to carry aid wherever it was needed.

Such was the poorness of the neighbourhood that none of the Lancastrian lords, and but few of their retainers, had been lodged therein; and the inhabitants, with one accord, deserted their houses and fled, squalling, along the streets or over garden walls.

In the centre, where the five ways all met, a somewhat ill-favoured alehouse displayed the sign of the Chequers; and here the Duke of Gloucester chose his headquarters for the day.

To Dick he assigned the guard of one of the five streets.

'Go,' he said, 'win your spurs. Win glory for me; one Richard for another. I tell you, if I rise, ye shall rise by the same ladder. Go,' he added, shaking him by the hand.

But, as soon as Dick was gone, he turned to a little shabby archer at his elbow.

'Go, Dutton, and that right speedily,' he added. 'Follow that lad. If ye find him faithful, ye answer for his safety, a head for a head. Woe unto you, if ye return without him! But if he be faithless – or, for one instant, ye misdoubt him – stab him from behind.'

In the meanwhile Dick hastened to secure his post. The street he had to guard was very narrow, and closely lined with houses, which projected and overhung the roadway; but narrow and dark as it was, since it opened upon the market-place of the town, the main issue of the battle would probably fall to be decided on that spot.

The market-place was full of townspeople fleeing in disorder; but there was as yet no sign of any foeman ready to attack, and Dick judged he had some time before him to make ready his defence.

The two houses at the end stood deserted, with open doors, as the inhabitants had left them in their flight, and from these he had the furniture hastily tossed forth and piled into a barrier in the entry of the lane. A hundred men were placed at his disposal, and of these he threw the more part into the houses, where they might lie in shelter and deliver their arrows from the windows. With the rest, under his own immediate eye, he lined the barricade.

Meanwhile the utmost uproar and confusion had continued to prevail throughout the town; and what with the hurried clashing of bells, the sounding of trumpets, the swift movement of bodies of horse, the cries of the commanders, and the shrieks of women, the noise was almost deafening to the ear. Presently, little by little, the tumult began to subside; and soon after, files of men in armour and bodies of archers began to assemble and form in line of battle in the market-place.

A large portion of this body were in murrey and blue, and in the mounted knight who ordered their array Dick recognized Sir Daniel Brackley.

Then there befell a long pause, which was followed by the almost simultaneous sounding of four trumpets from four different quarters of the town. A fifth rang in answer from the market-place, and at the same moment the files began to move, and a shower of arrows rattled about the barricade, and sounded like blows upon the walls of the two flanking houses.

The attack had begun, by a common signal, on all the five issues of the quarter. Gloucester was beleaguered upon every side; and Dick judged, if he would make good his post, he must rely entirely on the 100 men of his command.

Seven volleys of arrows followed one upon the other, and in the very thick of the discharges Dick was touched from behind upon the arm, and found a page holding out to him a leathern jacket, strengthened with bright plates of mail.

'It is from my Lord of Gloucester,' said the page. 'He hath observed, Sir Richard, that ye went unarmed.'

Dick, with a glow at his heart at being so addressed, got to his feet and, with the assistance of the page, donned the defensive coat. Even as he did so, two arrows rattled harmlessly upon the plates, and a third struck down the page, mortally wounded, at his feet.

Meantime the whole body of the enemy had been steadily drawing nearer across the market-place; and by this time were so close at hand that Dick gave the order to return their shot. Immediately, from behind the barrier and from the windows of the houses, a counterblast of arrows sped, carrying death. But the Lancastrians, as if they had but waited for a signal, shouted loudly in answer, and began to close at a run upon the barrier, the horsemen still hanging back, with visors lowered.

Then followed an obstinate and deadly struggle, hand to hand. The assailants, wielding their falchions with one hand, strove with the other to drag down the structure of the barricade. On the other side, the parts were reversed; and the defenders exposed themselves like madmen to protect their rampart. So for some minutes the contest

A third arrow struck the page, mortally wounding him.

raged almost in silence, friend and foe falling one upon another. But it is always the easier to destroy; and when a single note upon the tucket recalled the attacking party from this desperate service, much of the barricade had been removed piecemeal, and the whole fabric had sunk to half its height, and tottered to a general fall.

And now the footmen in the market-place fell back, at a run, on every side. The horsemen, who had been standing in a line two deep, wheeled suddenly, and made their flank into their front; and as swift as a striking adder, the long, steel-clad column was launched upon the ruinous barricade.

Of the first two horsemen, one fell, rider and steed, and was ridden down by his companion. The second leaped clean upon the summit of the rampart, transpiercing an archer with his lance. Almost in the same instant he was dragged from the saddle and his horse despatched.

And then the full weight and impetus of the charge burst upon and scattered the defenders. The men-at-arms, surmounting their fallen comrades, and carried onward by the fury of their onslaught, dashed through Dick's broken line and poured thundering up the lane beyond, as a stream bestrides and pours across a broken dam.

Yet was the fight not over. Still, in the narrow jaws of the entrance, Dick and a few survivors plied their bills like woodmen; and already, across the width of the passage, there had been formed a second, a higher, and a more effectual rampart of fallen men and disembowelled horses, lashing in the agonies of death.

Baffled by this fresh obstacle, the remainder of the cavalry fell back; and as, at the sight of this movement, the flight of arrows redoubled from the casements of the houses, their retreat had, for a moment, almost degenerated into flight.

Almost at the same time, those who had crossed the barricade and charged farther up the street, being met before the door of the 'Chequers' by the formidable hunchback and the whole reserve of the Yorkists, began to come scattering backward, in the excess of disarray and terror.

Dick and his fellows faced about, fresh men poured out of the houses; a cruel blast of arrows met the fugitives full in the face, while Gloucester was already riding down their rear; in the inside of a minute and a half there was no living Lancastrian in the street.

Then, and not till then, did Dick hold up his reeking blade and give the word to cheer.

Meanwhile Gloucester dismounted from his horse and came forward to inspect the post. His face was as pale as linen; but his eyes shone in his head like some strange jewel, and his voice, when he spoke, was hoarse and broken with the exultation of battle and success. He looked at the rampart, which neither friend nor foe could now approach without precaution, so fiercely did the horses struggle in the throes of death, and at the sight of that great carnage he smiled upon one side.

'Despatch these horses,' he said; 'they keep you from your vantage. Richard Shelton,' he added, 'ye have pleased me. Kneel.'

The Lancastrians had already resumed their archery, and the shafts fell thick in the mouth of the street; but the duke, minding them not at all, deliberately drew his sword and dubbed Richard a knight upon the spot.

'And now, Sir Richard,' he continued, 'if that ye see Lord Risingham, send me an express upon the instant. Were it your last man, let me hear of it incontinently. I had rather venture the post than lose my stroke at him. For mark me, all of ye,' he added, raising his voice, 'if Earl Risingham fall by another hand than mine, I shall count this victory a defeat.'

'My lord duke,' said one of his attendants, 'is your grace not weary of exposing his dear life unneedfully? Why tarry we here?'

'Catesby,' returned the duke, 'here is the battle, not elsewhere. The rest are but feigned onslaughts. Here must we vanquish. And for the exposure – if ye were an ugly hunchback, and the children gecked at you upon the street, ye would count your body cheaper, and an hour of glory worth a life. Howbeit, if ye will, let us ride on and visit the other posts. Sir Richard here, my namesake, he shall still hold this entry, where he wadeth to the ankles in hot blood. Him can we trust. But mark it, Sir Richard, ye are not yet done. The worst is yet to ward. Sleep not.'

He came right up to young Shelton, looking him hard in the eyes, and taking his hand in both of his, gave it so extreme a squeeze that the blood had nearly spurted. Dick quailed before his eyes. The insane excitement, the courage, and the cruelty that he read therein, filled him with dismay about the future. This young duke's was indeed a gallant spirit, to ride foremost in the ranks of war; but, after the battle, in the days of peace and in the circle of his trusted friends, that mind, it was to be dreaded, would continue to bring forth the fruits of death.

Dick, once more left to his own counsels, began to look about him. The arrow-shot had somewhat slackened. On all sides the enemy were falling back; and the greater part of the market-place was now left empty, the snow here trampled into orange mud, there splashed with gore, scattered all over with dead men and horses, and bristling thick with feathered arrows.

On his own side the loss had been cruel. The jaws of the little street and the ruins of the barricade were heaped with the dead and dying; and out of the hundred men with whom he had begun the battle, there were not seventy left who could still stand to arms.

At the same time the day was passing. The first reinforcements might be looked for to arrive at any moment; and the Lancastrians, already shaken by the result of their desperate but unsuccessful onslaught, were in an ill-temper to support a fresh invader.

There was a dial in the wall of one of the two flanking houses; and this, in the frosty, winter sunshine, indicated ten of the forenoon.

Dick turned to the man who was at his elbow, a little insignificant archer, binding a cut in his arm.

'It was well fought,' he said, 'and, by my sooth, they will not charge us twice.'

'Sir,' said the little archer, 'ye have fought right well for York, and better for yourself. Never hath man in so brief space prevailed so greatly on the duke's affections. That he should have entrusted such a post to one he knew not is a marvel. But look to your head, Sir Richard! If ye be vanquished – ay, if ye give way one foot's breadth – axe or cord shall punish it; and I am set, if ye do aught doubtful, I will tell you honestly, here to stab you from behind.'

Dick looked at the little man in amaze.

'You!' he cried. 'And from behind!'

'It is right so,' returned the archer; 'and because I like not the affair I tell it you. Ye must make the post good, Sir Richard, at your peril. O, our Crook-back is a bold blade and a good warrior; but whether in cold blood or in hot, he will have all things done exact to his commandment. If any fail or hinder, they shall die the death.'

'Now, by the saints!' cried Richard, 'is this so? And will men follow such a leader?'

'Nay, they follow him gleefully,' replied the other; 'for if he be exact to punish, he is most open-handed to reward. And if he spare not the blood and sweat of others, he is ever liberal of his own, still in the first front of battle, still the last to sleep. He will go far, will Crookback Dick o' Gloucester!'

The young knight, if he had been before brave and vigilant, was now all the more inclined to watchfulness and courage. His sudden favour, he began to perceive, had brought perils in its train. And he turned from the archer, and once more scanned anxiously the market-place. It lay empty as before.

'I like not this quietude,' he said. 'Doubtless they prepare us some surprise.'

And, as if in answer to his remark, the archers began once more to advance against the barricade, and the arrows to fall thick. But there was something hesitating in the attack. They came not on roundly, but seemed rather to await a further signal.

Dick looked uneasily about him, spying for a hidden danger. And sure enough, about half-way up the little street, a door was suddenly opened from within, and the house continued, for some seconds, and both by door and window, to disgorge a torrent of Lancastrian archers. These, as they leaped down, hurriedly stood to their ranks, bent their bows, and proceeded to pour upon Dick's rear a flight of arrows.

At the same time, the assailants in the market-place redoubled their shot, and began to close in stoutly upon the barricade.

Dick called down his whole command out of the houses, and facing them both ways, and encouraging their valour both by word and gesture, returned as best he could the double shower of shafts that fell about his post.

Meanwhile house after house as opened in the street, and the Lancastrians continued to pour out of the doors and leap down from the windows, shouting victory, until the number of enemies upon Dick's rear was almost equal to the number of his face. It was plain that he could hold the post no longer; what was worse, even if he could have held it, it had now become useless; and the whole Yorkist army lay in a posture of helplessness upon the brink of a complete disaster.

The men behind him formed the vital flaw in the general defence; and it was upon these that Dick turned, charging at the head of his men. So vigorous was the attack, that the Lancastrian archers gave ground and staggered, and, at last, breaking their ranks, began to crowd back into the houses from which they had so recently and so vaingloriously sallied.

Meanwhile the men from the market-place had swarmed across the undefended barricade, and fell on hotly upon the other side; and Dick must once again face about, and proceed to drive them back. Once again the spirit of his men prevailed and they cleared the street in triumphant style.

The Man who killed Hitler

Haydon McAllister

'he Boeing B-17 Long-Range Bomber showed no navigation lights
s it passed at altitude over Dymchurch on its secret flight toward the
eartland of Germany.

Sentinels attending the shore batteries along Britain's south coast had
een alerted that a lone aircraft would pass overhead at 23.00 hours on
he 15 August. But the B-17 passed so high above them that only a
oft 'humming', like that made by a honey-bee could be discerned.

Inside the pressurized cabin of the modified high-flying 'plane, Pilot
Metcalfe glanced across at his solitary passenger. It was thirty minutes
o midnight. Switching on the internal intercom he spoke tersely into
he microphone. 'Better turn on your oxygen supply Sergeant Weston.
'ou'll soon be needing it.' Owing to the rarefied upper atmosphere
oth men were experiencing difficulty in breathing.

In his headphones Weston heard the crackle of static as the intercom
vent dead. He did not bother to reply. He felt very cold and his teeth
vere chattering. The B-17 was now flying at 30,000 feet and the
emperature had plunged to *minus* thirty degrees Fahrenheit.

Weston's vision blurred momentarily. Was he on the verge of
lacking out? As he buckled the face mask containing the oxygen inlet
ver his mouth he suddenly remembered that he'd forgotten to kiss

Wendy Turnbull goodbye. Well – that was another good reason fc
returning home safely!

Weston stretched forward to study the control panel. He knew th&
in a short while the pilot would switch on the AN/APQ-9 blocking
transmitter in an attempt to jam the German radar. The bomber drone
on . . . It was ironic to think that the only dangerous object it would b
dropping tonight would be – himself!

His left hand fumbled for the value lever which would release th
flow of oxygen to his air-starved lungs. He only half accomplished th
task and slumped wearily back on his seat. He felt so strange. It was as
he were slipping off the edge of the world.

Anyway, the rest would do him good before they reached th
dropping zone . . .

★   ★   ★   ★

After free-falling nearly a mile, Don Weston pulled the rip-cord of th
parachute. It opened with a bone-jolting crack, and he was left swingin
like a puppet on a string in mid-air . . . then slowly he began to flo&
down towards enemy territory.

In the distance he could see the black bird-like speck of the B-1
fading into the starry August sky above Berchtesgaden – and th&
worried him. It meant that *he* would be visible to anyone watchin
from the ground. His only hope was that here at Untersberg in th
mountainous terrain of Upper Bavaria, there wouldn't be too man
ferret-eyed Nazis prowling around.

He envied the pilot of the plane. In a few hours the lucky devil woul
be back home, snug and warm inside a bunk-bed somewhere in Surre
without a care in the world.

The chill wind whistled derisively in Weston's ears and brought h
thoughts rudely back to the present. He'd taken on something big th
time. The whole might of the Fatherland would soon be set against hir
and he knew that his chances of getting back to England were virtuall
nil. Suddenly Weston was pleased that he hadn't married his regul&
girl Wendy Turnbull. That was one problem out of the way. At lea
he wouldn't be leaving a widow behind – maybe just a broken heart.

As the dark mass of the wooded valley below rose up to meet hir
Weston tensed himself. This was the tricky part. If he got stuck thirt

et up a fir tree like a Christmas fairy, it wouldn't look good in his
emoirs. He tugged on the cords of one side of his parachute and moved
own through the air towards the forest at an angle. The clearing ahead
owed itself in the nick of time and he was able to touch down amidst
hin strip of wild corn and then roll forward to break the full impact
the fall. The black silk of the parachute billowed around him and in
.lf a minute he had freed the harness, crushed the whole contraption
to a ball and stuffed it down a rabbit hole. Then he loosened the straps
taching the pack to his back, stowed it beneath a clump of decaying
acken and crouched in the shadows – listening.
Like a stone Weston remained until his eyes became accustomed to
e post-midnight light, and when at last he'd satisfied himself that his
scent from the skies had raised no alarms, he began to check through
s equipment.
The luger complete with silencer, snug inside his hip pocket. The
rowing knife strapped to his ankle. The dagger at his belt with the
llowed-out handle containing the special fluid.
The strangling wire tucked away in the false heel of the left boot and
e poisonous blow-dart in the right heel.
In his pack was the dismantled long-range 'Specialist' rifle with
escopic lens and spare cartridges wrapped in an oilskin cover. One
ir of clip-on steel-spiked soles. Two handgrenades. Six pounds of
ocessed survival food consisting of crushed chocolate, oatmeal and
sins. A pencil torch – He stopped! Something had moved. He sensed
No! It was nothing but a foraging rabbit . . .
All those hours of training on the Sussex Downs had sharpened
eston's senses to perfection. This was what it had all been in aid of –
give him that one chance in a thousand.
Relaxed once more, Weston went back to itemizing the contents of
pack . . . The pencil torch, map section, hip flask, and the capsule
ntaining the cyanide – in case they caught him.
n a rain-proof packet of the pack was the final item. The signal flare.
he should ever get through, a monoplane flying in from neutral
itzerland would look out for the yellow signal rocket on two
cessive nights. The pick-up point was to be over the frontier in
stria on the shores of a lake six miles outside Saltzburg. If he should
through.

If he could signal 'Mission Accomplished' it would mean so much to Wendy Turnbull.

It would also mean that Adolf Hitler would be dead.

* * * *

During the final briefing at Povey Cross, Commander Burgess had shown Weston six enlarged photographs of the area. One print in particular revealed a chalet nestling like an eagle's eyrie on a mountain slope.

'It's called the Berghof,' he heard the commander say. 'Herr Hitler's mountain retreat at Obersalzburg. From it there's a splendid view over Berchtesgaden. In 1938, Neville Chamberlain was most impressed by the scenery. Apparently he could see the glaciers glinting on the Dachstein mountains.'

Burgess lit a pipe as Weston pointed to a mountain which stood facing the Berghof across a valley.

'Could I use this as a reconnaissance point?' he asked.

'The Kehlstein?' frowned Burgess. 'Doubtful. Height 6,000 feet. It's over three miles from the chalet.'

'Out of range of the high-powered rifle then?'

'Exactly! Unless you happen to catch the Fuhrer out strolling.'

Weston shook his head. 'Too unpredictable. I want to nail the Nazi spider in his web . . .'

'Then you'll need to get within 800 yards to make absolutely sure with the "Specialist" rifle', observed Burgess. 'And that is your main problem Sergeant, for the moment Hitler is hit – or missed! – the whole area will be sealed off, and you'll be trapped like a rat in a trap. SS Guards, police, dogs . . . and a few Gestapo thrown in for good measure.'

'I think I can handle any reception committee,' returned Weston quietly, 'But first I'll need to know more of Hitler's movements in and around the Berghof.'

'Very well,' responded Burgess through a blue wreath of pipe smoke. 'Take a good look at the last photograph will you. It's a close-up of the chalet. It shows a grass covered bunker lined with barbed wire fencing. By the side of this runs an asphalt pathway. Hitler often strolls here. Now directly above the path,' Burgess marked the spot with his finger, 'is the Fuhrer's study. It's on the second floor. Notice the balcony . . .

'Does he use it?'

'Apparently not – but the French windows are large; and occasionally opened – weather permitting. Why not wait until your quarry appears and then – !!' Burgess broke off. He was sweating.

Weston reflected for a time. When he finally spoke his question caught the commander off guard.

'You've met Hitler haven't you?'

Burgess took off his spectacles before replying. He chose his words carefully.

'Yes' I met him briefly at the Nurenburg rally in 1936. Strange character. Can't dress for the life of him. But one glance from those deep blue eyes and you can sense the magnetic power radiating from the man. I'd say – and this is off the record – I'd say he started out with good intentions – then the devil whispered in his ear. He set a snowball of corruption rolling down the mountain. Now it's become a black avalanche – and it could snuff out the light of the world . . .'

'I get the picture,' said Weston.

'Right!' declared Burgess, replacing his spectacles and regaining his composure. 'From now on you're on 24-hour standby.'

★   ★   ★   ★

Moving at speed, yet with all the stealth of a born hunter, Weston reached the woods surrounding Obersalzburg in just over three hours. Once, in the thick bracken he'd almost stumbled on a concealed alarm system. The trip wire had marked the outer perimeter of the security precautions set up to protect the Fuhrer. From that moment on Weston kept his eyes skinned for guard – or guard dogs. He didn't have long to wait.

As he was inching his way forward through the undergrowth he heard the faint sound of snoring. Slowly, raising his head, Weston peered in the general direction of the noise. As yet it was only the vaguest whisper on the wind, but an antelope may well have ignored it. Weston did not.

He moved like the midnight fox. Probing for safe footholds on the pine needle carpet. Gently stepping over stray twigs. Nosing forward toward the source of the sound – all five senses working with the efficiency of radar.

Before he entered the danger zone Weston smeared himself with the scent neutralizing agent contained in the hollow handle of his dagger. As far as a guard dog's sense of smell was concerned – he just didn't exist.

But there was no dog. Instead he saw a uniformed sentry lying, half-propped against the base of a cypress. His greatcoat and a half empty bottle of schnapps at his side. He was as if dead to the world.

Weston crept closer. The only sounds were the steady beat of his own heart rhythm in his ears, the nasal snore of the guard and the thin whine of the breeze in the pine tops.

Weston stole to the far side of the cypress until he became interlocked with the sleeping man's shadow. His fingers slid into the guard's greatcoat pocket. Empty. Weston removed the schnapps and reached down for the coat. The German stirred, scratched at an ear, then continued his contented snoring.

In the other pocket of the greatcoat was a small rectangle of cardboard and printed upon it was a plan of the defence system around the German dictator's den. Weston gazed at it for 20 long seconds, committing every detail to memory. Then he replaced the map, the coat and the schnapps and backed away.

With one rapid check on his compass, the English agent moved to within half a mile of the sleeping Fuhrer.

The German leader was now within rifle range.

*   *   *   *

Fifteen minutes later Weston watched an unsuspecting dog patrol pass within two yards of his temporary hide-out. Then he moved on to select one of the highest evergreens in Obersalzberg.

Unhitching his pack he picked out the steel sole-grips and attached them to his combat boots. After he'd replaced his pack on his shoulders he removed his purpose-built belt from around his waist and once he'd curved it around the base of the tree trunk, he clipped it to his waist and adjusted the tension. Ever so slowly he began to ascend the cleated grey trunk, leaning out at an angle – the steel pitons on his feet biting into the pine wood – the thick leather girdle taking the weight of his body.

The branches were thick and rich with evergreen leaves, but they didn't begin until he'd climbed nearly fifty feet. If a guard or dog should have entered his immediate vicinity, Weston would have had to rely on a whispered prayer.

At last he was able to push aside the thick curtain of pine needles, unfasten the belt and drag himself into the verdant refuge at the top of the tree. As he hauled on the second branch, a wood pigeon's wings exploded in his face as it went careering into space. Weston hung grimly on. A dog barked. Then the night became still once more.

Weston lifted himself into the spread of intertwined branches and a light shower of dead pine needles floated to the floor of the forest eighty feet below. In the vague light he could see something moving beside him. Switching on the pencil torch he saw the young squab of the wood pigeon shifting about in the scattering of twigs the mother bird used as a nest.

Within threequarters of an hour the first glimmer of dawn lit the eastern sky and the sentries could be heard calling out as morning patrols replaced the night watch. At 6.30 a.m. Weston was fastened like a limpet to the pinnacle of the fir tree, and through the detached telescopic sight he observed a house-keeper draw the curtains in the second floor study window of the Berghof. At 7.15 a.m. he saw a half naked Hitler cross to the window in his pyjama trousers. For an instant it looked as if the Fuhrer would step out on the balcony for a breath of fresh air. But a telephone bell jangled, and the German leader was called by his aide to receive a call.

Weston systematically began to assemble the long-range 'Specialist' rifle, while from beneath him came the call of the roosting wood pigeon coo-cooing on the warm breeze.

★   ★   ★   ★

At 10.15 a.m. a German staff car crawled up the thin winding road to the Fuhrer's lair at Obersalzburg. Weston took a sip from his hip flask and idly picked up the telescopic lens. Through it he saw two men climb out of the car and pass through the guard-barrier. The driver remained.

The thick leather girdle took the weight of his body.

Then three men exited from the Berghof. Two of them were generals. They flanked a third man.

All five men exchanged Nazi salutes. Weston grappled with the lens, trying to focus it on the third mans face. Then he saw the clipped moustache and knew it was Adolph Hitler. He wore a brown storm troopers jacket. Black trousers. Jackboots . . .

A sudden wave of inspiration burst upon Weston. Almost feverishly he unhooked the rifle from the shoulder strap, snapping the telescopic sights into place in the same movement.

Already the staff car had begun its slow drive down the narrow precipitous road.

Weston levelled the barrel. The black cross on the optics hovered upon the high ranking officials in the back seat of the Mercedes. Then Weston lowered his aim until the rear wheel entered his circle of vision. The white walled tyre bobbled over a stone. His finger squeezed slowly . . .

There was a dull 'Phut' and a tremendous kick-back against his shoulder. From 500 yards he heard the squealing skidding tyres. There came an eerie silence like when a clock stops ticking in a haunted room.

The staff car nosedived off the precipice, seemed to hang in mid-air and then floundered into the gaping space beyond – the driver still wrestling with the steering wheel.

The sound of splitting branches, buckling metal and an earth shaking 'Keeroomph!' After a count of four the petrol tank exploded like a depth charge.

An alarm bell was ringing from the compound surrounding the Berghof and various running figures converged upon the scene.

Weston unclipped the telescope; unscrewed the still hot barrel from the gun-stock and waited. With luck they would never find the bullet in the burnt-out wreck. He yawned, and decided to stay put till sundown; then sneak over the border into Austria; whence the pick-up point and the yellow signal rocket.

★   ★   ★   ★

By the time the ambulances arrived from Berchtesgaden, guards and officials had formed a tenuous human chain stretching from the roadside down to the deep valley below.

The bodies were brought up one by one. On the first and second stretchers the grey blanket was drawn over the head of the corpses within. Upon the third stretcher Weston could see the unconscious driver.

It seemed like an eternity before the fourth stretcher was borne up the hillside. As it passed by the line of guards Weston could see them doffing their hats and giving the stiff-armed salute. Surely it must mean that Hitler . . . ?

Weston had to be certain. He centred the telescopic lens on the blanket of the stretcher. He seemed to be very near. The bespectacled doctor in the white coat was bending over.

The pine tops swayed in the wind. How his legs ached. He *must* hold his gaze. He *must* make sure.

In his minds-eye the images merged. He became vaguely conscious of a medical blanket around himself also. Suddenly he was very very tired.

★   ★   ★   ★

When Sergeant Don Weston came to in East Grinstead General Hospital, the shadowy figure above his bed told him that he was lucky to be alive . . . Later, Wendy Turnbull sat by his bedside. She looked exactly as he remembered her . . .

Burgess appeared the following afternoon. He explained that the severe lack of oxygen while travelling in the high-flying B-17 may have caused Weston slight brain damage. There would have to be extensive tests. So for six months at least – Adolph Hitler would have to wait.

The Battle of the River Plate

Captain W. E. Johns and R. A. Kelly

'Clear lower deck' had been sounded as usual by the Marine bugler, and we fell in on the quarterdeck facing the ship's officers. Commander Graham waited for the master-at-arms to report, then brought the ship's company to attention and turned smartly on his heel to face the Captain.

'Ship's company correct, sir.'

For a moment after giving his salute of acknowledgment Captain Bell was silent, looking meaningfully along the rows of his assembled crew. 'Hooky' Bell – how appropriate a nickname as he perched there on the grating in front of us with that eagle nose and the penetrating gaze.

'I have received orders that we are to rejoin Commodore Harwood aboard HMS *Ajax* off the mouth of the River Plate, along with the New Zealand cruiser *Achilles.*'

We stood, faces nipped by the cold wind driving from the Antarctic; from bearded three-badgers to smooth-faced sprogs there was the one thought – just what was in store for us? So far our patrols had been fruitless; but this could be our first encounter with the reality of war. It was something for which we were now really prepared. Every morning before dawn the bugler would sound the 'Awake'. Men would roll from their hammocks, groping for cigarettes and matches for a quick 'burn' as they lashed up and stowed their hammocks. Within a few minutes the bugle would sound 'Action stations' – always a slightly unnerving call until we heard the single 'G' note blown at the end to indicate practice only.

Practice or not, we jumped to it with a clattering of iron ladders and a fierce, purposeful scramble to designated stations in the director, on the bridge, in the gun turrets, and deeper in the engine and boiler rooms. Gangways and spaces were cleared to enable fire and repairs parties to move freely.

Twice a day we moved to those action stations. As the ordnance artificer of 'Y' turret I would move to my after gun position and swing automatically into a routine which by this time I could do in my sleep.

Now as we stood on *Exeter*'s upper deck, our hair blown by the wind, some of us thought of 'Monte' – our 'home port' – and wistfully dreamed we were off to the bars and friendly cabarets. But that would not happen either – it would be another of those abortive trips followed by a return to the Falklands with all their bleakness and biting winds.

At 0700 on Tuesday, 12 December, HMS Exeter *joined HMS* Ajax *and* Anchilles *about 250 miles eastward of the River Plate. At noon that day, Commodore Harwood made the following signal:*

'My policy with three cruisers in company versus one pocket battleship. Attack at once by day or night. By day act as two units, 1st Division (*Ajax* and *Achilles*) and *Exeter* diverged to permit flank marking. First Division will concentrate gunfire. By night ships will normally remain in company in open order. Be prepared for the signal ZMM, which is to have the same meaning as MM.[1]

On the Tuesday night we carried out exercises mainly for flank marking – that is, the two divisions attacking from different directions so that each could observe the other's fall of shot. We passed imaginary signals to each other and gained some useful practice on the gunnery fire-control equipment. Then just before 0500 we went to dawn action stations.

It was going to be a beautiful day. The weather had turned warmer as we steamed north, and now the breeze barely ruffled the surface of the sea. As we stood down from our stations I looked ahead at the shapes

[1] MM. Commanders of divisions are to turn their divisions to course . . . starting with the rear division.

of *Ajax* and *Achilles*. We were steaming in line ahead, without the sign of a ship or a wisp of smoke to mar the clean line of the horizon. Then I went below to my mess, to lie down on the lockers – not to sleep, but to think.

At about 0610 a flag signal broke at *Ajax*'s yard, and our chief yeoman, Tom Remmick, dashed to Captain Bell, who was in his sea cabin on the bridge. There was little need to read the signal, as there was now an obvious blob of smoke on the horizon, and soon after *Exeter* broke formation and steamed in the direction of that smoke.

At 1615 the ship making smoke was identified as a pocket battleship, probably Admiral Scheer. *The units divided in accordance with the Commodore's plan,* Exeter *to the NW, the other two cruisers to the NE.*

Suddenly the bugle sounded 'Action stations', and we all listened as usual for the familiar 'G' note, but it did not come. We knew that *Exeter* was going into action for the first time.

There were some who were still sceptical – just another merchant ship; but everyone rushed to action stations collecting gear, opening lockers, donning flash suits. Taut faces revealed the first signs of fear and apprehension. Down below in gangways and spaces the chippies, cooks, and stewards, who formed the fire and repair parties, gripped more tightly than usual their saws, hoses, and axes, and serious-faced they waited.

'A pocket battleship,' said one who always knew what was going on. '*Admiral Scheer*,' said another. In the welter of speculation the beauty of the day was forgotten, and we were all conscious of the increasing throb of the engines as *Exeter* began to pile on the knots. Two minutes later we were in battle.

At 0617 Graf Spee *opened fire on* Exeter *at 20,000 yards with her main armament of eleven-inch guns.*

Even as I ran aft to my turret, my heart pounding, shells were falling into the sea around the ship, and the range was closing rapidly as the two ships sped towards each other. It was a frightening prospect being in the path of 12,000 tons of armour-plated battleship with superior firepower, but it was still odd that she should have chosen to come in and fight when she could have dictated the entire battle at long range.

The gap narrowed. Water and metal sprayed the ship from near misses even before the enemy had come fully over the horizon, and I began to hear the first screams of pain as men were struck down by the hot flying metal. For all of us – teenage sprogs and professional sailors alike – war had become the ghastly reality that it always is.

'Are we in range yet?' Captain Bell repeatedly asked. Then the fire bells rang followed by the single note, and *Exeter* gave a tremendous heave as her two forward eight-inch gun turrets fired their first rounds in anger.

'Ship is now engaging *Scheer*,'[1] said the detached voice over the loudspeakers. Again the shrapnel cascaded onto the exposed and unprotected high-angle gun and torpedo positions. The range had come down quickly, and our three eight-inch turrets were loading and firing with speed and precision – a great tribute to our period of training. The first two salvoes were short, but by the third our eight-inch shells were straddling *Graf Spee*.

My turret came into action just after 0622 – about five minutes after what is now known to be the *Graf Spee* had opened fire on us – just as a shell burst close amidships, on starboard side, killing the torpedo-tube crew on deck. Hot metal sliced through to the Chief Stokers' bathroom, killing members of a decontamination party, while metal peppered the catapult area and cut down my mate 'Bunker' Hill only yards away from the little caboose where he kept his conjuring gear.

Then the forecastle was hit and the paint shop set alight. Smoke obscured the bridge as the fire parties fought the flames abreast of the two forward gun turrets. The reverberation of the gunfire all but burst their eardrums as they clung to their swirling hoses. Through the smoke a man would totter, sway, and fall, then in a moment clear of smoke a figure would rush in and drag the inert body back into the billowing whiteness. Suddenly a blinding flash, a terrible rending sound, and the forecastle lay revealed, a mass of twisted metal and burning timbers. Not a living soul among the debris.

Our first major disaster came with an eleven-inch direct hit on 'B' turret, the one manned by the Royal Marines and the turret which I had left only weeks before. The explosion blasted the two gun barrels apart, where they remained as a 'V' sign of mute defiance. The big, rugger-playing Marines corporal miraculously scrambled clear of the

[1] It was still thought at this stage that the enemy vessel was the *Admiral Scheer*.

They stumbled through the mess deck for the after stern position.

wrecked turret, unaware that another Marine, both legs badly damaged, was clinging around his neck.

'B' turret had been in action for only ten minutes prior to that hit; now, as though to crush the Churchillian gesture, another eleven-inch shell tore through the rear of the turret, spraying the superstructure and the bridge with hot metal, wreaking severe damage on the wheelhouse beneath. Most of the bridge staff were killed, and seven telegraphists in the W/T office were scythed down. What tangled steelwork had remained upright after the first explosion was now flattened, mangled corpses littering the deck of that once immaculate turret. The 'boot-necks' I had worked and joked with had been blasted out of existence.

Deeper down in the ship, in the transmitting station, grim-faced Marines bandsmen anxiously watched the gunnery brain panel. Only four lights winked back at them from the indicator board where normally six lights glowed as guns were brought to the ready. Occasionally the 'Royals' would break into a hoarse cheer as *Exeter* fired another four-gun broadside, rearing up as the shells sped from her barrels.

The ship shuddered as shells tore into the hull, sometimes with such force that they screwed through the thin armour-plating and out of the other side of the ship before bursting.

On the bridge the navigator lay slumped across his compass. The main gyro was out of action and the lower wheelhouse wrecked. Below, Petty Officer Green, the Chief Quartermaster, struggled furiously with the jammed steering-gear. With blood gushing from his leg, he called up to the bridge, 'What the hell's going on up there?'

A frightened voice quavered in reply, 'What shall I do? Everybody is dead up here.'

Answering the order to get below, a young boy seamen fell into the PO's arms, and, helping one another, they somehow got below decks and stumbled through the mess-decks for the after steering position.

They never made it.

Captain Bell, wounded in the head, had moved aft near the emergency steering position, where in that after compartment the Sailmaker and an engine room artificer clung grimly to the huge iron-spoked steering-wheel, turning it now to port now to starboard, but never away from the enemy. Using a boat's compass snatched from a damaged sea-boat, Captain Bell continued to con his ship in action, passing his orders along a chain of seamen, stokers, and Marines to the two men struggling with the great wheel.

Down below, in the gyro-compass room, the young electrical artificer checked his delicate instruments. He felt the ship hit time and time again forward of his compartment, until a terrifying ripping sound ended in an explosion in the compartment above him. His little cubby-hole began to get hot, the air thickened, until he found it increasingly difficult to breathe.

Climbing to the armoured hatch, he sprang the small manhole open and was immediately struck by flames and smoke from above. Quickly he closed the manhole and ran to the phone. He dialled Damage Control HQ, asked for his Chief, and reported, 'There is a fire in the compartment above the gyro-compass room; it is too fierce for me to do anything about it. The compass room is full of smoke, and I am finding it hard to breathe. Can you send a fire party?'

The reply came, 'Wait.'

The young artificer waited, with the fire burning fiercely above, his compartment getting hotter and hotter. For almost an hour he held on, watching the electricity supplies fail and his master gyro compass click erratically to a stop. Then he phoned again to report failure of the gyro compass, but this time the line was dead. In the darkness, scared and alone, with what appeared to be a blazing inferno above him, there was nothing he could do but wait.

In the compartment above, a fire party battled against the flames and eventually brought them under control. When they lifted the hatch the young artificer came out of it like a bat out of hell, continuing at high speed up through the various compartments to the upper deck.

In another part of the ship there was the strange sound of a piano. The padre, George Groves, had stopped to play before he moved on with his bottle of Scotch with a wee drop for all and sundry.[1]

Within the first fifteen minutes *Exeter* had been hit by at least five eleven-inch shells, and her superstructure had been penetrated by thousands of fragments of shrapnel from near misses. At 0632 her starboard torpedoes were fired in local control at *Graf Spee*. Soon afterwards two more eleven-inch shells screamed into her, the first

[1] In peace-time when we did a shoot he always played the piano. He did not like the noise.

putting 'A' turret out of action, the second striking the most decisive blow yet. This second shell penetrated the light plating amidships, cutting through several bulkheads and exploding in the Chief Petty Officers' flat.

At that moment Petty Officer Green, with the young boy seaman, was passing through the flat on his way aft. They and others in the area received the full impact, and virtually everyone was killed or maimed. Terribly burnt, Jimmie Green was to be unconscious for seventeen days, later to be remembered by Captain Bell as the man who 'was burnt the colour of a baked potato but who refused to die'.

The CPO[1] and ERA[2] messes were now a huge, blackened tomb, a space large enough to take at least a dozen London double-decker buses. Wire jumping-ladders now hung where two hours before strong iron gangways had stood. Kit lockers had been rolled by the explosion into battered drums of steel.

All the control positions, whether gunnery or torpedo, forward or aft, port or starboard, had been wiped out. Captain Bell, steel splinters in both eyes, stood soaked in petrol cascading from the punctured petrol tank of the Walrus aircraft above him, by his side Commander Robert Graham, and around him on all sides twisted ironwork and shrapnel-riddled bodies. It is said that at this stage Captain Bell turned to his Commander and said laconically, 'Well, if things get any worse we shall have to ram her.' Two minutes later Commander Graham slumped to the deck with shrapnel in both his legs.

Inside my turret, after firing only two or three rounds, we would find the ship's head slew away, and our target would be lost to us. To regain we would have to swing around on the other beam before we could bear again on the enemy. We did not know at that time that this was because two valiant characters were hanging with great concentration to the massive after wheel in a courageous effort to prevent the ship being hit.

'B' turret had gone early in the action. Now 'A' turret had been hit and its crew scattered in all directions. Exeter's forward guns were silent, and all that was left intact were the engines, racing at almost top speed, and the two guns in my turret.

[1] CPO, Chief Petty Officers.
[2] ERA, Engine Room Artificers.

How ironic that, with all the battering and the slaughter above and below decks, the engines kept running, driving us towards our adversary. My pal Roy Ruse said afterwards, 'To us in the engine room it was just another high-speed run, except for a listing to port or starboard when the ship altered course, a violent shudder when the shells struck home. High speed requires extra vigilance to bearing temperatures and auxiliary engines, so we were kept very busy. Normally we should not have known what was taking place on deck, but Commander (E) Sims took an occasional trip above and came back with a not-so-good report. Then we began to take a list to starboard as the compartments on that side became flooded.'

Aboard *Graf Spee* Commander Rasenack, the gunnery officer, was asking permission from Captain Langsdorff to bring all guns to bear to finish us off. It was as well that we remained in blissful ignorance of this, and also to our advantage that the Captain of *Graf Spee*, badly concussed by gun blast, had apparently not fully recovered from the effects, or sufficiently to be able to give this order.

Now aware of the desperate situation we were in, I wiped the sweat and some of the grime from my face, closed my eyes against the cordite fumes, and muttered, 'My God, these bloody guns have got to keep going now!'

Inside 'Y' turret conditions were getting bad. Both guns were being fired as soon as they were loaded, the confined space beginning to fill with cordite fumes, while the breeches, through lack of cooling water, became fiercely hot.

High up in his gunnery control tower, above the bridge, his eyes red and inflamed from the constant rubbing of the eyepieces of his director sight, Lieutenant-Commander R. B. Jennings surveyed the blackened, silent remains of his two forward gun turrets. Nothing worked in the director; now there were no answering rings as he squeezed the director firing-pistol, and no lights shone back at him from the gun-ready panel. He climbed down from his eyrie and made his way aft to our turret, where he climbed unconcernedly on top of the turret – as we fired another broadside, then focused his binoculars on *Graf Spee*, shouting spotting orders to us through the open centre position. Shrapnel whined about him, burying itself at times in the deck timbers, or, deflected from the metal surfaces, hummed away below decks killing or wounding men in the repair parties.

Shells still whistled through the ship like a red-hot tornado, and in the after medical station, set up in the wardroom, Surgeon Lieutenant Roger Lancashire, RNVR, had a miraculous escape. As he recalls, 'I was sitting on my haunches taking the drugs out of a cupboard when there was a loud crash and a blast of air and I felt something whizz across the top of my cap. I was bowled over backwards. Later in the day I found a part of the fuse cap, which had nearly decapitated me, embedded deeply in the fanlight casing.'

Inside 'Y' turret the water reservoirs for cooling the guns, and the air to clear the fumes, had all but gone. The crew cursed, sweated, and choked as they cried out to me, 'For God's sake, Chief, give us some air and water!'

How could I tell men sweating and toiling under such terrible conditions that the supplies which came from outside the turret had long ago been shot away and there was nothing I could do about it.

From somewhere forward there was the crash and shudder of yet another explosion. The lights in the turret dimmed, went out, and both guns fell mute. The sweat on my body ran cold as I realized that with our last two guns unable to move we were now at the mercy of the enemy.

We waited, helpless in the darkened gunhouse, praying hard that it was not the ship's dynamos which had been damaged. The young midshipman tried to telephone, but the line was dead. Down below the electrical and engine-room staffs shone their torches on the turbine cases, at times lighting up the racing prop shafts, making their way to the dynamo and circuit boards. There they found that the explosion had shaken off the dynamos, and, working feverishly, they had them back on again and the dynamos running. The lights glimmered and came on in our turret, and we were in action again.

Almost at once we found further trouble. The electrical supplies to the gun pointers were now no longer available, and our last link with any other part of the ship had been severed. Quickly, with the help of the local director-layer, we changed over to local control. This meant that we had to obtain for ourselves all the gunnery data we needed – range, deflection, and whether our shells were falling over or short. I had never thought to be in this position, but I knew these guns well and that they, like humans, had their own special weaknesses. How I prayed, as I stood on my tool-bag in that fume-filled centre position, that nothing further would go wrong.

When we opened the centre-position hatch bright sunlight streamed in. I could clearly see *Graf Spee* steaming on a course parallel to ours, flying from her foremast the largest flag I had ever seen, with its great swastika.

Then fate hit out again. The right gun developed trouble after loading, a burr preventing the rammer from returning fully back. I shouted for a handspike and started forcing the rammer-head back, bit by bit. This did clear it and allowed us to fire, but now, every time we rammed, the burr got larger and the rammer more difficult to return.

Then we hit *Graf Spee* – slap in the middle of her huge bridge control. as it erupted in a large reddish-yellow flash the young midshipman controlling the firing cried jubilantly, 'We hit her! We hit her!'

Ajax and *Achilles* closed in as the *Graf Spee* altered course to westward. Just as she had been all set to finish us off the tables had been sensationally turned. But for HMS *Exeter* the blood-bath had ended . . .

. . . Listing heavily to starboard, her forecastle aflame, her bridge a mass of twisted, useless metal, HMS *Exeter* turned towards the Antarctic ice-fields. In a cloud of smoke and flame she dropped over the southern horizon, to be lost completely to the world. As the Battle of the River Plate moved towards its fantastic climax. *Exeter* struggled at eighteen knots on the 1,200-mile journey to the Falklands, a seemingly impossible task for a ship of whom *Ajax*'s officer-observer had said, 'I have never seen such a shambles, anyway in a ship which survived. Her mainmast was moving perceptibly as she rolled.' . . .

Two V.C.s of the air

John Frayn Turner

Rawdon Hume Middleton

Flight Sergeant Rawdon Hume Middleton, No. 149 Squadron. A real New South Wales man, Middleton worked for his father, who was the manager of the Wee Wang sheep station at Brogan Gate, NSW. And the colourful name given to this occupation is Jackaroo. So Rawdon Middleton was a Jackaroo. What stopped him being one we will never know, except that on 14 October 1940, he decided it was time to start to think of the war. He joined up.

This lean, quiet, unassuming chap was also tough. In the RAAF he became an earnest, plodding pupil. All he did was thorough, though unspectacular. He is said to have brooded a lot on the German bombing of unprotected cities, and followed a common trait among out-back Australians in being inclined to bouts of melancholy. But this was actually more apparent than real, as indicated by the entries in his diary.

Middleton's first chance came as a second pilot on the night of 6 April 1942, in No. 149 Squadron. They never reached the target of Essen, and their bombs had to be jettisoned live twenty-five miles north of Aachen. The main cause of this spot of trouble was an attack by a Messerschmitt Me 110, which caused considerable damage to the starboard wing. The bomber, a Halifax, hobbled home from the Dutch coast on three engines, and literally gave up the ghost altogether on landing. According to Middleton's fellow squadron members, this operation seemed to have an astonishing effect on Middleton, shaking him out of his melancholy, and galvanizing him into a mood almost of buoyancy. The probable explanation for that phase is that he, like so many others, got sick of waiting for operations to start. Once they did, there was no time to brood – or certainly far less.

Middleton was in a series of big attacks on Rostock, Lübeck, Duisburg-Hamborn, the Ruhr, and Hamburg, all as second pilot.

On 31 July 1942, he walked into the mess with a broad Australian grin. He had been given the captaincy of a Stirling, and that same night he was airborne on a big one-hour raid on Düsseldorf. He had bad luck, however, because his rear turret went unserviceable, and he had to return early. In his crew were Mackie, Cameron, and Gough, who will also figure in Middleton's last flight.

Then came Osnabrück, Frankfurt, Wilhelmshaven, Munich, Genoa, and Turin, and some steady routine mine-laying-trips around Europe's coast. The previous operation before his final mission also had Turin as its objective; more specifically, the target was the Royal Arsenal there; and the date of this raid: 20 November.

Incidentally, in August Middleton was posted to No. 7 (PFF) Squadron with his crew to become a Pathfinder unit. On his return from a mission to Nuremberg, the CO told Middleton that he could continue as a Pathfinder pilot, but that his navigator was not up to standard, so that navigator and crew would be posted back to No. 149 Squadron. The authorities reckoned without the 'quiet, unassuming man.' Middleton refused to be parted from his crew, and returned to his old squadron with all of them.

His final mission was his twenty-ninth – one short of a complete Operational Tour. Seven aircraft were detailed for this operation on the Fiat Works at Turin, near the Italian Alps. It was just after a week since their previous long-distance onslaught on Turin, on 20 November.

Now the night of 28 November 1942, arrived, and the seven Stirlings set out.

They got airborne from Lakenheath at 1814 hours on that early winter night. Darkness was just falling. The single summer-time kept it light till nearly six o'clock. This was Middleton's crew:

Second Pilot: Flight Sergeant L. A. Hyder, a former Glasgow student.

Nav. B: Pilot Officer G. R. Royde.

Wireless Operator Air Gunner: Pilot Officer N. E. Skinner.

Mid Upper Air Gunner: Flight Sergeant D. Cameron – formerly a gamekeeper.

Front gunner: Sergeant S. J. Mackie.

Rear gunner: Sergeant H. W. Gough – a garage hand in peace-time.

Flight engineer: Sergeant J. E. Jeffery.

Middleton, of course, flew as captain and first pilot. Trouble started before Turin. They experienced great difficulty in climbing to the necessary 12,000 feet to cross the Alps. This led to excessive fuel consumption, which was to make its effect felt later on. Added to this hazard, the night had grown so depthlessly dark that the mountain-peaks around and before them almost faded into invisibility. Only by screwing up their eyes could they distinguish these deadly Alps. It was no night to be trying for Turin. As things turned out, only four of the seven aircraft did get through. At this stage over the Alps Middleton had to decide whether or not to go on, since the drain of fuel through the great climb meant that they would have barely enough for the return. And there were few places to ditch a bomber between Italy and the English Channel.

They sighted flares ahead. These seemed to clinch it for Middleton. He could hardly turn back now, having come so far, and with the flares actually in sight. There would be time to worry about fuel later. Now the raid would take all his mind. He pressed on south, and even dived down to 2,000 feet to identify the target for certain, despite the difficulty of regaining height. Middleton made three flights over the Fiat Works before he was satisfied he had identified in exactly. And more precious petrol burned away in the process.

Now it was 2200 hours and the epic battle began in earnest. All that had gone before became child's play; all that fuss over the Alps in pitch-black. And there was no second from now on in which to think of fuel – or the lack of it.

Light anti-aircraft guns fired at Middleton's Stirling and another one close behind. The first hit came when a large hole appeared in the port main-plane, making it difficult to maintain lateral control, or – more simply – the aircraft would not stay balanced.

A shell struck the cockpit, burst inside it, shattered the windscreen, and wounded both pilots – Middleton and Hyder. Here was war at its worst.

A piece of shell splinter tore into the side of Middleton's face, destroying his right eye totally, and exposing the bone over the eye. He was also wounded in the body and legs.

Hyder got wounds in the head and both his legs, which bled profusely. The wireless operator was also hit in the leg by a splinter. The Stirling started to go down, far from England and Lakenheath. Middleton lost consciousness as the plane dipped down to 800 feet above Italian soil. Hyder snatched the controls just in time and jerked the plane up. They still had the bombs aboard. At 1,500 feet he gave the order, and the welcome phrase came back: 'Bombs gone.'

The flak poured up the short distance from ground to plane. It varied each moment from light to heavy. And the ground gunners could hardly help recording more hits, which they did. The three gunners in the plane fired continuously until the rear turret was put out of action. One more blow, and the four aircraft left the target area with good fires burning in the Fiat Works.

Middleton drifted back to consciousness again. As soon as they were clear of the immediate target zone, he ordered Hyder back to get first aid. Middleton was in obvious agony. Before Hyder had been properly fixed up, he insisted on returning to the cockpit, as he knew that Middleton could only see slightly – and could only barely speak because of the loss of blood and surges of pain.

This magnificent crew set course for base from the other side of Europe. They faced an Alpine crossing, and homeward flight, most of them wounded, and in a badly damaged aircraft without enough fuel to reach the English coast. Here was heroism on the most massive scale imaginable.

They discussed abandoning the plane or landing it in Northern France, but Middleton was adamant.

'I'm going to try to make the English coast,' he insisted, so that the crew could leave by parachute. Mackie sat at Middleton's shoulder all those long, weary, agonizing hours homeward, giving the captain visual assistance. Mackie was on his thirty-third trip – three over the Operational Tour – having volunteered to continue with his captain.

Middleton must have known by now that there could be little chance for him, but he kept going for the sake of the others. The war brought out this close friendship among aircrews. Men who faced death together had the biggest bond between them it was possible to find.

Middleton's wounds worsened, and as those hours circled off his strength ebbed too. Midnight came and went, then 0100, 0200, hours. Even now their ordeal was not yet over. Soon after 0200 hours the Stirling shuddered over the French coast at 6,000 feet. It was asking too much of any man. More anti-aircraft fire attacked them. For eight hours Middleton had kept the plane up. Intense Ack-Ack hit it yet again.

How many more hits could they take? Yet Middleton mustered up enough strength from somewhere – the inner resources beyond the understanding – to take evasive action. The very thought of the crippled bomber being bounced over the sky, out of the way of Ack-Ack, by a mortally wounded pilot seems too wild to be true; yet it happened all right, about 0230 hours on the morning of 29 November.

There was only the Channel now between them and the south coast of England. Could the fuel last out? If not, it would be a wet end to their dreams. As these next twenty minutes ticked off, the fuel gauge read practically zero. 0230, 0240, 0250. Middleton could not last as long as the petrol it seemed – just a matter of chance which drained out first. Somehow, no one will ever know how – not even the crew – Middleton managed to keep the Stirling airborne. Riddled with splinters of shells, it chugged on till the Kent coast loomed dimly into view below them. They gave him an accurate reading of the fuel.

'Five minutes more.'

Summoning up his reserves of strength, Middleton said that he would not take the risk of hitting houses by trying to land the big bomber. So he ordered them all to abandon aircraft while he flew parallel with the coast for a few miles. After that, he said, he was going to head out to sea. Middleton insisted, and this was not the time or place to argue about it. He might still make it, they thought. He had come this far, to the very cliffs of Dover.

Hyder, Royde, Skinner, Cameron, and Gough, all baled out safely and survived.

Mackie and Jeffery stayed to help Middleton till the last minute.

Then they jumped. Their 'chutes opened all right, and they fell into the sea – but they fell too far out. Neither survived the night. The following afternoon, about 1500 hours, a naval launch recovered their bodies with the parachutes open.

At 0255 hours the Stirling ran out of fuel. Middleton might still have been conscious, or he might not. In any case, the Stirling crashed into the sea off Dymchurch.

As the citation ends: 'While all the crew displayed heroism of a high order, the urge to do so came from Flight Sergeant Middleton, whose fortitude and strength of will made possible the completion of the mission. His devotion to duty in the face of overwhelming odds is unsurpassed in the annals of the Royal Air Force.'

All the surviving crew were awarded either the DFC or DFM.

On 15 January 1943, Middleton was awarded the Victoria Cross.

On 1 February 1943, his body was washed up at Shakespeare Cliff, Dover.

★ ★ ★ ★

William Reid

'Oh, hell,' said Acting Flight Lieutenant William Reid, RAFVR, No. 61 Squadron, as he was wounded. Then he set about carrying on to complete his mission.

Reid did not have a long operational career behind him on the night of 3 November 1943. Only six weeks earlier he had been posted on operational duties for the first time.

Now the night of 3 November, with Reid pilot and captain of a Lancaster. Its pilot pressed a stream of fire from the fighter – and Reid's plane took off all right, and reached the flat moonscape of the Dutch coast. Then 'O for Oboe' met trouble. An enemy Messerschmitt Me 110 described an arc in the darkness to come within yards of the Lancaster. Its pilot pressed a stream of fire from the fighter – and Reid's windscreen was shattered in an instant. Because of a failure in the heating circuit, the rear gunner's hands were too cold for him to open fire immediately, or to operate his microphones and so give warning of danger. But after a brief delay he managed to return the Messerschmitt's fire. A hectic few moments followed before the Messerschmitt Me was finally driven off. But by this time the damage was done.

Reid tells exactly what did happen as far as he was concerned behind that shattered screen:

I saw a blinding flash and lost about 2,000 feet before I could pull out again. I felt as if my head had been blown off – just the sort of feeling you get at the time.

Other members of the crew shouted 'Are you all right?' It was no good telling them I felt half dead, and said, 'Yes I feel all right.'

I resumed course again, and managed to get my goggles on. The wind was just lashing through the broken windscreen. Tiny pieces of the 'Perspex' were all over my face and hands. Fortunately, I didn't get any in my eyes, although there was some in my eyelids. I suppose I instinctively ducked.

My shoulder was a bit stiff, and it felt as if some one had hit me with a hammer. Blood was pouring down my face, and I could feel the taste of it in my mouth. It soon froze up because of the intense cold. I didn't turn back because there were lots of other bombers behind us and it might have been dangerous for them.

At this stage it was ascertained that Reid and the aircraft were both hurt more than might be imagined. Reid had wounds in his head, shoulders, and hands. The plane had its elevator trimming tabs damaged by the fighter, and it became very hard to handle. The rear turret too had got badly knocked about, and the communications system and compasses were put out of action. These were all serious setbacks both to the continuation of the operation and the eventual return home.

Reid found out that the crew were so far unscathed, kept completely quiet about his own injuries still, and went on to Düsseldorf.

It was the mid-upper gunner, Flight Lieutenant D. Baldwin, who reported that Reid shouted out 'Oh, hell!' as the fighter's first bursts hit the windscreen and himself.

It was the rear gunner, Flight Sergeant A. F. Emerson, who told how his fingers had been too frozen to reply to the Messerschmitt Me till the German was within 150 yards. Emerson thought he hit him then.

The ordeal of 'O for Oboe' and its faithful crew was still barely beginning on this night over Germany.

Soon after the Messerschmitt was driven off, or shot down, the Lancaster was attacked again, by a Focke-Wulf 190 this time. The enemy's fire raked the bomber from stem to stern. The rear gunner replied with his only serviceable gun, but the chronic condition of his turret made accurate aiming impossible.

Reid takes up the story of this fateful flight again:

My navigator was killed, and the wireless operator fatally injured. The oxygen system was put out of action. I was again wounded. The flight engineer, though hit in the forearm, gave me oxygen from a portable supply.

I looked for the Pole Star and flew on that for a bit. I knew from the flight plan just roughly where we were. Then I could see Cologne on the starboard, and turned for the attack on Düsseldorf.

So Reid refused to be turned from his objective, and he reached the target some fifty minutes later – minutes that must have seemed like days.

After the Focke-Wulf attack Baldwin discovered the wireless operator lying over the already dead navigator.

Meanwhile Reid memorized his course so well that even amid this holocaust the bomb-aimer thought that the plane was proceeding so normally that nothing had happened. He was cut off by the communications failure, and knew neither of the casualties to his comrades or even of the captain's injuries. The bomb-aimer was Flight Sergeant L. G. Rolton, who said that Reid gave him a good bombing run right over the centre of the target. Photographs showed that when the bombs were released the aircraft was exactly in its proper place, so they must have hit their mark precisely. What an achievement, with the navigator dead and the wireless operator dying – and the pilot still nearly fainting from loss of blood!

Steering still by the Pole Star, with the added assistance of the moon, Reid then set course for home. With the windscreen shattered, the cold grew more intense each minute, and he lapsed into semiconsciousness – fatal for the pilot of a plane. Reid continues his own narrative:

After we had bombed I steered a little north to avoid the defences, and headed for England as best I could. I was growing weak from loss of blood, and the emergency oxygen supply had given out.

Because the elevators had been shot away, we had to hold back the stick the whole of the time. That was a tough job. I held both arms round it and clasped my hands, because my shoulder was weak. The

My navigator was killed and the wireless operator fatally injured.

engineer also held on all the time. I did not then know that he had been wounded in the hand.

The bomb-aimer also helped. We went through heavy flak near the Dutch coast and then I saw searchlights over England.

Reid spent that time over the North Sea partly unconscious and then regaining consciousness. Several times when he came round he gave the thumbs-up sign to Rolton, and at one stage the aircraft went round three times in a flat spin until the engineer and Rolton pushed with their knees to control the stick. But at last they were really over England. Reid revived, and took over the controls again. They were losing height all the time now, but he still felt confident that they could make it safely. They spotted an airfield below them, through the silky haze of a ground mist. This mist, however, was helping to hide the runway lights, and added to that, blood from Reid's head wound was running down into his eyes now. Any exertion made it worse, so that as he tried to get the flaps down it gushed out and rushed over his face – a fantastic way in which to try to bring a bomber down, but the only one possible. It was this or not at all.

Reid circled around and flashed a distress signal with the landing-lamp. Then, as the hydraulics had been shot away, they had to use an emergency system to try and get the undercarriage down. Minutes were passing, and the crew still alive thought he was going to faint again at any moment. The bomb-aimer stood behind him, so that he could pull Reid out of the pilot's seat and take over if it became necessary. But Reid kept conscious as the defenceless, damaged Lancaster slowly circled and wheeled in for a landing through the night and the mist – lower, lower. The runway lights leapt and danced about before Reid's blood-blinded eyes, so that the whole scene in the next few seconds seemed like a bad dream – mist, lights, darkness, the Americans' airfield. Could he bring the Lancaster down? It would be a miracle. Slowly the altimeter read less and less, till the fateful moment came.

Touch-down.

And as the Lancaster felt English earth beneath it again – an unlikely possibility a few hours earlier – one leg of the damaged undercarriage collapsed under them as the load came on it. It had been shot through, and could not support anything at all. The plane thumped along on its tummy for about fifty yards, and the grinding, grating noise gradually eased till the Lancaster stopped dead still. Nothing exploded or caught fire. They were down. They clambered out, still somewhat dazed by the ordeal, and the Americans at once attended to their wounds.

As the citation summed it all up:

Wounded in two attacks, without oxygen, suffering severely from cold, his navigator dead, his wireless operator fatally injured, his aircraft crippled and defenceless, Flight Lieutenant Reid showed superb courage and leadership in penetrating a further 200 miles into enemy territory to attack one of the most strongly defended targets in Germany, every additional mile increasing the hazards of the long and perilous journey home. His tenacity and devotion to duty were beyond praise.

And he lived to fight again and survive the war: a tall, fair, smiling man with a moustache, who won the Victoria Cross on one of his first operational flights.

The engineer, Sergeant J. Norris, was awarded the Conspicuous Gallantry Medal. The navigator who was killed was Flight Sergeant J. A. Jeffreys, of Australia.

Welcome to Oflag XXIb

Eric Williams

After bailing out from his crippled bomber over Germany, Peter Howard has many adventures before finally being taken to Dulag-Luft Prisoner of War camp. Here, he becomes friendly with John Clinton, and naturally their conversation turns to the idea of escape.

But no sooner do they draw up plans than they hear that they are going to be transferred. This time to Oflag XXIb in Poland . . .

Every week a list of names of those who were to be 'purged' to a permanent camp was pinned to the notice-board in the dining-room. This week the purge was to *Oflag XXIB* in Poland, and Peter's name was on the list. He was glad to see that John Clinton was going with him. There was something about the young Army officer's quiet self-sufficiency that had captured his respect. He had shaken off the first, almost panic-stricken frenzy to get away and spent most of his time reading. It seemed a complete reversal of his earlier frame of mind, but Peter sensed that he was holding himself firmly in check, realizing that their stay in this transit camp was short, tiding over the time until he could concentrate wholly on the problem of escape.

As soon as Peter knew that at last they were really going, he began to make plans for his own escape. Convinced that he had not made the most of his opportunities, refusing to accept excuses from himself, he vowed that he too would make his getaway.

He sewed special hidden pockets into the lining of his greatcoat, where he concealed the scalpels and the little food he had managed to collect. He spent hours in the library studying an encyclopaedia from which the censor had omitted to remove the maps. He traced some of the maps on to toilet paper and hid them with the other things. But the doctor's[1] death had made him even more pessimistic about jumping trains, and he knew in his heart that this preparation was merely a front to convince himself that he was doing all he could to get away.

At last the purge party was assembled outside the huts, complete with baggage. Peter was amazed at the quantity some of them had managed to collect in so short a time. They were made to march to the station, which was several miles away, and he was glad that he had decided to travel light.

John Clinton carried his luggage in his pockets, including a book that he had taken from the prison library. He marched with an amused expression in his eyes.

'What's so funny?' Peter asked.

'These chaps with their bundles. They look like the lost tribes of Israel.'

'Maybe they've got some sense. You don't know where we might find ourselves.' Peter shifted his small bundle from one shoulder to the other. 'Probably just as well to have something to start life with. It may be a perfectly new camp, with nothing there at all.'

'There's no point in preparing to settle down,' Clinton muttered. 'If you set out with that idea you'll never get away. Look at that chap!' He nodded towards a broad, stocky air-gunner named Saunders, who was staggering along under the burden of an unwieldy bundle wrapped in a blanket. He had a large 'Bomber Command' moustache, and wore a balaclava helmet and flying boots.

'Old Bill looking for a better 'ole,' Peter said. 'I wonder what he's got in the bundle.'

'Doesn't matter what it is. It shows that he's preparing to settle down.'

At the railway station they were lined up by the *Feldwebel* and then addressed by the officer in charge. 'Gentlemen,' he said, 'you will be some days in the train. If you behave reasonably, you will be reasonably treated. If you attempt to escape, you will be shot. This is not an idle threat. The guards have been given instructions to shoot any prisoner

---

[1] The evening before, Peter had heard that a paratroop doctor had been killed while jumping off the train on his way to hospital at Obermassfeld.

who attempts to escape. There is a live round in every barrel. That is all, gentlemen.'

They were herded into carriages which were divided into compartments in the English fashion, but the seats were wooden. Peter found himself squeezed into the corner of a compartment opposite a tall fair flight lieutenant and Saunders, who had arrived triumphant with his bundle, which he put on the floor between their legs. Next to Peter sat Clinton, already reading his book.

'Any more for Margate?' Saunders seemed determined to make it a pleasant journey. He handed cigarettes round, and soon the air was thick and stale with smoke. Four men at the far end of the compartment began a game of cards. Peter wondered which of them had been shot down with a pack of playing cards in his pocket – or had he picked them up at *Dulag-Luft*? Saunders had evidently been laying in a stock of something or other, judging by the size of his bundle. Peter looked at him closely. A red good-humoured face with a mouth that smiled easily under his grotesque moustache, a smile that was half-suppressed like that of a schoolboy. The mass of untidy hair, tow-coloured, and a quick dogmatic way of speaking that was not aggressive. An easy chap to get along with.

The flight lieutenant next to him was of a different breed. Fair and slim, even in his issue uniform he looked immaculate; his moustache was short and carefully tended. His name was Hugo, and he sat now as though the whole trip had been arranged as a sort of pleasure outing in which, although not entirely approving, he felt he ought to play his part.

Two hours later the train was still in the station. They had made several false starts, but had been shunted back to their original position again. At last, as though satisfied with the lesson it had taught them, the engine whistled in derision, and slowly the train pulled out.

Long hours of sitting on a wooden seat . . . nothing to read . . . falling asleep, and waking stiff . . . smoking, yawning, and moving restlessly . . . thinking of home . . . .

Often the train stopped for no apparent reason, miles from any station. Each time it stopped, the German soldiers jumped down on to the track, and stood with tommy-guns at the ready until it started again. Each time it stopped, Peter tensed himself to escape, but each time he saw that it was hopeless. There were raised sentry boxes, fitted with machine-guns, at both ends of every carriage.

John Clinton, when he had finished with his book, which was of no use to the others as it was Latin verse, proved himself a lively and interesting travelling companion. He told them that he had been born in Malaya, that his father owned a rubber plantation where he had lived until he was sent home to school in England. He had just gone up to Oxford when the war started, and he had joined the Army. He kept them amused for hours with stories of his troop of bren-gun carriers. It seemed to Peter that if he needed a partner in his escape he could go a long way and not find a better man than John Clinton.

Saunders, who together with his brother ran a greengrocer's shop in North London, did not appear disturbed at the prospect of several years' captivity. The business would go on and in time he would return to it. He took life as it came, finding it good and full of queer incidents which he invited the others to observe from his own original and slightly derisive viewpoint. Life to him, too, was something to be chuckled at, a chuckle in his case at once suppressed and followed by a quick look over his shoulder. He had started his career with a kerbside barrow off Oxford Street, and still retained that furtive, quick look round for the police.

Hugo on the other hand seemed almost devoid of humour. He was gentle, languid and charmingly self-centred. He made a perfect foil for Saunders. His main concerns at the moment were that there would be no facilities for washing in the camp – as, indeed, there were none on the train – and that he would not be given enough to eat. 'What couldn't I do to a steak,' he sighed. 'With lashings of chip potatoes and red gravy. A T-bone steak.'

'I'd settle for a plate of fish and chips,' Saunders said.

'I'd settle for a tin of spam,' Peter added.

'All you chaps think about is food,' John said. 'When I was in the desert – '

'Look out,' Saunders said. 'There's that sand blowing in again!'

Beyond the steamed-up window miles and miles of pine forest, dark inside but with the tall trunks of the outer trees reddened by the sun; inside the compartment boredom and depression, hunger and thirst, the smell of old socks, the choky heaviness of the smoke-filled atmosphere.

Then the failure of the heating plant, the cold.

The cold.

Icicles, formed by their breath on the window-pane – breaking them off to suck because they had no water.

By the third day they had eaten their rations and Peter had given up all hope of escape from the train. He took the food that he had saved from the hidden pockets in his coat, and shared it round among the men at his end of the compartment. Following his example, John Clinton produced a hidden store of food which he too shared. 'Might as well eat it as let the Germans have it,' he said. They looked at the others expectantly, but apparently any plans they had made to escape did not include a stock of food.

Late in the afternoon of the fourth day the train made one of its customary halts at a small wayside station, but this time it was different. The escort came down the train, shouting ''*Raus, 'raus! Ausgehen, alle ausgehen!*'

Looking out of the open door Peter saw that they had been surrounded by a cordon of soldiers, steel-helmeted and armed with tommy-guns.

'This is it,' Saunders said. 'Full military honours, too.'

It was growing dark as they got down from the train. A fine sleet was falling, powdering their greatcoats and restricting their view. It was colder here than it had been in Frankfurt, and as far as Peter could see there was nothing but a flat unbroken sheet of snow. 'Looks as though we've come to Siberia,' Saunders said.

There were arc lamps hanging by the side of the track and the prisoners were paraded there for roll-call. They were counted three times before the guards could find the correct number and they were able to set out, at a shambling gait, for the camp.

The road led them straight across a plain towards a village whose few pale lights flickered wanly through the falling snow. It was little more than a track, seamed and furrowed by passing carts but improving as it neared the village, until they were marching on cobblestones which rang under the steel of their boots. The guards – there were nearly as many guards as there were prisoners – marched at their side, tommy-guns at the ready, while in front and behind the column were lorries with searchlights and machine-guns.

As they neared the village, some of the men at the head of the column began to sing. Slowly the song crept down the ranks until the whole company was singing. To Peter, it seemed that they were singing to show the villagers that, although captured, they were not defeated; he was thankful that they had chosen, not a patriotic song, but *Bless 'Em All* as their tune.

Leaving the village behind them they climbed a long hill, stumbling and slipping on the icy road. They were tired now, and had stopped singing. Presently they saw the lights of the camp ahead, the great circle of arc lamps, and the searchlights sweeping slowly across the empty compound. As they drew near a searchlight was turned on them, blinding them and throwing long shadows from the unevenness of the snow-packed road. It lit up their pale faces, dark beginnings of beards, the odd shape of scarves tied round their heads and the bundles they carried on their backs.

The gates were thrown open and the long straggling line of prisoners marched into the camp, peering through the darkness for some hint of what they were to expect. They could only see the wire, bright and hard in the light of the arc lamps, and the black and red-striped sentry box. Untidily they closed up on the leading ranks, who had halted. The gates were shut behind them with a creak and clatter of chains.

The prisoners eased the bundles from their shoulders. Some of them lit cigarettes; a *Feldwebel* ran up and down the column telling them not to smoke, but they took no notice. The falling snow settled on their heads and shoulders as they stood waiting in the horizontal beam of the searchlight.

Then they were counted again, several times. Peter heard the Germans arguing about the count, and was filled with a feeling of sick futility. He stood in the cold muddy snow of the compound dumbly waiting for the guards to make a move. All he wanted was to get out of the snow. He thought with nostalgia of the dry room at *Dulag-Luft*. Even the railway carriage would have been better than this.

At last the guards agreed on the count, and the prisoners were marched into a large cement-faced building which stood just beyond the light of the arc lamps.

As he stood in the long queue, Peter wondered why they must be searched again. They had been searched before leaving *Dulag-Luft*;

what would the Germans imagine they would have picked up during the journey? When his turn came, he stood and watched the guard trying to unravel the series of elaborate knots with which he had tied his bundle – the Germans never used knives, too salvage-conscious, he supposed. He wished he had added a few more knots for luck. The things the doctor had given him, together with the small brass compass and the maps he had copied from the encyclopaedia were safe in their hidden pockets, and he managed to get them through undiscovered.

When the last man had been searched the prisoners were taken to a large hall, where they were handed over to the Senior British Officer. There were tables and forms set out in the hall, and the newcomers were given a cup of tea and two slices of black bread thinly spread with jam. When they had eaten they were addressed by the tall lean group captain, whose lined face looked haggard under his battered service cap.

'Gentlemen,' he said, 'before you go to your new quarters I should like to say a few words about the general running of this camp. The organization is simple, and I want to keep it that way. I, as Senior British Officer, am responsible to the German authorities for all that goes on inside the camp; but I'll tell you more about that later.

'The building you are in is known as the White House. It was once a reformatory, but no prisoners sleep here now. It is used for the camp theatre and lecture rooms and for the library. Normally no prisoners are allowed in the building after dark.

'There are ten barrack blocks in the compound. Each barrack block is divided into twelve messes. In each mess there are eight officers. Each barrack block is under the command of a wing commander or a squadron leader. Each mess has a senior officer, who is responsible to the block commander for the conduct of his mess.

'All discipline is self-imposed. You will find, before you have been very long in the camp, that most of our energy is devoted to a ceaseless war against the enemy. To carry on this war, a spirit of loyalty and service is essential. You will find such a spirit in this camp.

'Our foremost activity is – escape. Do not forget that there are men here who have been escaping ever since they were captured. At the moment there is a tunnel half-way towards the wire. No – don't be alarmed. I can speak freely. The guards have gone, and we have stooges posted at every window. I tell you this because I want to warn you against ill-considered attempts at escape. If you rashly take the first chance that offers itself, it is more than likely that you will fail. That is not important; what is important is that, in failing, you may uncover another, long-planned scheme that, but for your interference, might have succeeded.

'There is a special body of officers in this camp known as the Escape Committee. It is their job to co-ordinate and assist all escape attempts. If you have an idea, take it to them. Do not be afraid that by doing so you will lose control of the scheme. It is your scheme, and you will be the first man to leave the camp by means of it, if it succeeds. The Escape Committee will arrange for your forged passports and civilian clothes. We have special departments whose only job is making these things. If you have a scheme of escape, take it to the Committee. They are all experienced men, and they will give you all the help they can.

'The Germans have their own security branch. It is known as the *Abwehr*. They employ specially trained men we call 'ferrets.' You will recognize them in the camp by their blue overalls and the long steel spikes they carry. These men are dangerous. They all speak English and are expert in the discovery of escape activity. You will find them hiding under the floor and in the roof, listening at the keyhole and the windows. Look out for them.

'We have our counter-ferrets. We call them 'stooges.' Every ferret that comes into the camp is shadowed by a stooge. There are stooges standing at every window and door as I am talking. Before I began, they searched every possible hiding-place within hearing distance of this room. You, also, will be asked to volunteer for this duty. It is practically the only duty you will be asked to perform, and I hope you will do it cheerfully.

'If you attempt to escape – and I hope you will – you will find it an ungrateful task. Its greatest function is that it boosts the morale of your fellow prisoners. They feel that while there is an escape attempt in operation we are doing something against the enemy – not just vegetating. As I told you when we first met, there is a wonderful spirit in this camp. I hope that you will foster that spirit.'

When the group captain had gone, the new purge was divided into groups to be distributed among the ten barrack blocks. Peter and John

Clinton made up a party with Saunders, the air-gunner, and Hugo, the tall immaculate flight lieutenant.

As they made their way down the stairs of the White House Peter felt the warmth and integrity of the group captain still with him. Here was a man to follow, a man with something positive to offer. What a difference between this and the weak opportunism of *Dulag-Luft*. He was almost cheerful again, eager to take his part in the war that would continue in this camp.

Outside, it was still snowing. The roofs of the barrack blocks were covered in snow, but the ground inside the compound had been churned into thick black sludge. Duck-board rafts outside the doors of the long low barracks were half under water, and the newcomers cursed as they squelched their way through the darkness.

The door to their barrack block was secured by lock and bar – a modern lock, Peter noticed, and a wooden bar four inches thick, resting in heavy iron brackets. The guard unfastened the door and led them into a small vestibule. The by now familiar stench, which had so astonished them during their first days at *Dulag-Luft*, told them what lay beyond the door which faced them – typical German POW sanitation.

There were two more double doors on their right, and these the guard kicked open without ceremony.

After the freshness of the night, the fug inside was overpowering. The big low room was almost in darkness. Through the gloom of smoke and steam, Peter could see row upon row of two-tier wooden bunks diminishing into hazy perspective. As his eyes grew accustomed to the smoke he noticed that the bunks had been pulled out from the walls to form a series of small rooms. In each room stood a wooden table on which a guttering home-made lamp shed a feeble dull red glow. Smoke from these lamps joined with steam from rows and rows of damp washing which hung on lines almost down to head level, to form clouds which billowed and eddied under the roof. The concrete floor was puddled with the water which dripped incessantly from the rows of washing. There were windows in each of the side walls, but these were covered from the outside by black-out shutters. There seemed to be no ventilation whatever.

Round each small table sat a group of prisoners playing cards or

A figure wearing a worn RAF tunic came towards them.

trying to read by the light of the home-made lamps, which threw weird and distorted shadows on the walls, once white-washed, now grey and smeared by smoke and steam. Most of the men were wearing beards, their hair was long, and they shuffled round in wooden clogs or sat huddled on their bunks, blankets hunched round their shoulders, merging with the shadows that surrounded every feeble light. There was a buzz of conversation which dropped into curious silence as the new arrivals entered.

In one corner of the room a reedy gramophone ground out a dance tune, strident in the sudden hush.

A figure emerged from the shadows, and came towards them. He was wearing a worn RAF tunic on which, below the pilot's wings, was the ribbon of the DFC with bar. On the sleeves, almost worn away, were the three rings of a wing commander. He was dark and bearded, and his feet were thrust into huge wooden clogs which he scraped along the concrete floor as he walked.

'Hallo, chaps – are you the new lot from *Dulag*?'

'Yes, sir.'

'Good show. Sorry about the light – it'll come on again presently, I expect. Goon reprisal. My name's Stewart. Had a rough journey?'

'Pretty grim, sir, yes.'

'Well, we've got some food fixed up for you. And by the way, don't call me "sir" – we dispense with that sort of thing here. You'll want a wash before you eat. Just drop your things and I'll show you round. You've got soap and towels, I expect.'

He took them down the central gangway formed by narrow wooden lockers, which screened off the 'rooms' which lay behind them. 'You'll find us a bit bolshie, I expect, but the morale is pretty good – the Hun can't do a thing with us.'

Peter, glancing in through the narrow doorways between the lockers, which screened off the "rooms" which lay behind them. standing at right angles to the wall. Each mess had a table and two long wooden forms, and seemed isolated, drawn round its own centre of fitful light. The effect of a squalid prolific slum was intensified by the festoons of washing which hung everywhere.

As they entered the washroom at the far end of the block, the electric light came on. There was a round of ironic cheers from the prisoners in the larger room.

'It won't be for long,' Stewart told them. 'The goons do it for fun. You'd better take advantage of it and get washed up while you can.'

Peter looked at the two long cement troughs, above which ran an iron pipe with taps at intervals. There were wooden duck-boards on the floor, which was awash with greasy water. 'The drains have stopped up again,' Stewart explained. 'We complain about it every day, but it doesn't do any good.'

The newcomers set about removing some of the accumulated dirt of the four days' journey. The water was cold. As Peter washed, he thought of the wing commander's description 'bolshie'. What did he mean by bolshie? The place was certainly primitive enough. He looked round him at the flooded floor and dirty walls.

There was a sudden burst of conversation and loud laughter from the large room, as the door opened and a man came out carrying a large tin which he began to fill under one of the taps. He was dressed in a short sleeveless jacket roughly cobbled from blankets. His hair was cropped down to a quarter of an inch in length, and as he waited for the tin to fill he sang softly to himself. Peter watched him furtively; it seemed almost unbelievable that this could be a British officer. He felt as he had felt on his first day at school. When the man had gone, he looked across the trough at John, who was washing his beard. 'What d'you make of this?' he asked.

'Better than the last place,' John said. 'It's got a sort of discipline. You know where you are, in a place like this.'

'Looks pretty grim to me.' Hugo ran a wet comb through his hair, patting the wave into shape with his hand. 'Almost a boy scout atmosphere.'

'It'll be all right.' Saunders was holding his dental plate under the running tap. Without his teeth his face looked old and drawn. 'Better than the flak over Duisburg, any road.'

'I didn't mind the flak.' Hugo was now combing his moustache. 'You can put up with almost anything if you've got civilized living conditions.'

'Listen to him,' Saunders said. 'Civilized living conditions! He doesn't know he's alive.' To Hugo, 'I bet you've never been hungry in your life.'

'Not until I came to Germany.'

'Then you've been lucky,' Saunders told him.

The wing commander called them together. Under the shadow of his beard his face was thin. 'I know you've just had a pi-jaw from the SBO[1], so I'll make mine as short as possible. I'm going to put you chaps in the end mess, but for dinner this evening you will each go to a different mess, partly because we've drawn no rations for you yet and partly' – he grinned – 'so that you can give all the gen about home. You're the first batch from England since we arrived here, so you'll have to answer a lot of questions. Do it as cheerfully as you can – the chaps have been away a long time.

'Flight Lieutenant Tyson is the hut representative on the Escape Committee, and if you want to escape we'll give you all the help we can. Your chances of getting back are practically nil. I'm telling you this because we don't want the game cluttered up with chaps who aren't prepared to put in everything they've got.

'Another thing: Don't be polite to the Hun. Don't let him be polite to you. If we behaved ourselves he could do with a tenth of the number of guards he has to use now. Relax for a moment, say a polite word to him – and you'll find yourself becoming a dead-beat. Don't forget for a single second that these are your enemies. Do everything in your power to make their job as difficult as you can.

'I'm putting you in the end mess. There's a chap there you might find a bit of a strain at first, he's a queer type. But there will only be six of you instead of the usual eight. You should be able to cope. Stick it as long as you can anyway, and if you find it too much let me know.'

'What d'you mean,' Saunders asked, 'a queer type?'

'Oh, he's a bit round the bend, that's all. Strain, y'know. There's a Pole, too; his name's Otto Sechevitsky. He more or less looks after Loveday. If I were you I'd be guided by Otto until you know the ropes. You'll find life a bit strange here at first no doubt, and Otto's got the thing buttoned up as well as anybody. If you follow him you won't go far wrong.'

He took them to a mess at the extreme end of the block, near the entrance and unpleasantly close to the latrine.

Otto and Loveday were playing chess. The wing commander intro-

[1] SBO, Senior British Officer.

duced them. 'I'll leave you now,' he said. 'Otto will look after you.'

As soon as he had gone, Loveday rose to his feet. He was a tall rawboned man and his nose looked as though it had been squashed in below his protuberant forehead. The eyes, deep-set, slanted upwards and outwards, giving the face a cunning look belied by the wide slack mouth which showed red and moist through the tangled beard. He was wearing clogs, a greatcoat and a Balaclava helmet.

He cleared his throat. '*I'll* look after you individuals. You are all suffering from shock. You are all a bit unstrung. But I understand the position.' He spoke slowly, punctuating each word with a stabbing movement of one of his large raw-looking hands. 'I make allowances for newcomers. It's fate that sent you here. And fate that sent me to look after you. Ain't that right, Otter?' He chuckled without mirth and looked at Otto, who smiled in an embarrassed way. 'You may think an individual has free will – but he hasn't. Life's a chess-board and we're all pawns.' He knocked one of the pieces from the board with a sweep of his mittened right hand and looked at Peter. 'Ain't that right?' he said.

Peter hesitated. 'Er – yes,' he said.

Loveday looked at him for a long time, while Peter felt himself coloured with confusion.

'You'll learn,' Loveday said. 'You'll learn soon enough. Won't he, Otter? He'll learn in time.' He looked round at the others. 'You'll all learn.' He looked at the chess-board and chuckled again. 'Little pawns on a big board.' He began to drum his fingers on the table-top.

'All the bunks are free,' Otto said, 'except these two.' He indicated the two-tier wooden bedstead farthest from the doorway. He was a thin brittle-looking man whose grey eyes were calm and patient beneath a mass of straw-coloured hair. He looked oddly military and neat standing there beside Loveday's untidy bulk. 'Just put your things down and I'll make some tea. The other chaps will call for you when they want to take you to dinner.'

Dinner. Peter's stomach contracted and he felt a sudden spasm of nausea. Dinner. He had not eaten a hot meal since leaving *Dulag-Luft*. He hoped that they would not be too long before they called for him.

On each bunk was a sack filled with wood shavings, as a mattress, and a smaller sack, as a pillow. There were thin shoddy blankets, and two sheets and a pillowcase of coarse cotton. He chose the bunk above the one that John had chosen, leaving Hugo to share with Saunders, and began to arrange his few possessions on the rough shelf which the previous owner had fixed above his bunk. All his early enthusiasm had collapsed before the impact of this overcrowded slum. How could one escape, submerged beneath this turmoil? The room was loud with the roar and chatter of a hundred voices, filled with the bustle of a hundred different aims. He worked in silence, conscious of the tall figure of Alan Loveday watching them unpack.

'I've got a book here.' Loveday took down a large book from the shelf above his bunk. 'It tells you how to handle people. An individual has to know how to handle people in a place like this.'

Peter looked down at John and raised his eyebrows.

'What's the book called?' John asked.

'*A Textbook of Psychology*. Psychology is the study of the mind. This is a good place to study psychology, because everybody is suffering from shock. Everybody is a bit abnormal round here.'

'Yes,' John said. 'I suppose you're right.'

'I don't need you to tell me when I'm right,' Loveday shouted. 'I'm telling *you!*' He glared angrily at John. 'Just because you talk with an Oxford accent is no reason for you to tell me when I'm right!'

John was silent.

'This is a different world from the one you've lived in,' Loveday continued. He was standing on one foot, the other resting on a stool at the end of the table. His mittened hands plucked restlessly at his beard. 'This is a world where you have to study other individuals. Things are not the same here. Everybody – '

'Goon in the block!' It was one of the prisoners at the far end of the barrack. Soon the chanted cry was taken up on all sides. 'Goon in the block! Goon in the block!'

'What's that?' Peter asked.

'It's the German guards doing the rounds,' Loveday explained. 'The other chaps always call out when they come in. It's a sort of warning. I always ignore them myself. When an individual . . .'

Peter went to the doorway of the mess, and looked down the central corridor. Followed by the jeers and catcalls of the prisoners, the tall, heavily-built guard walked down the centre of the barrack block, with his dog, a big Alsatian, on a chain.

'Two goons approaching,' someone called, 'one leading the other!'

The guard, ponderous in his heavy jackboots and his long green greatcoat girdled by a thick, unpolished leather belt, walked slowly down the corridor, the dog slavering and straining at the leash.

'What do they do that for?' Peter asked.

Loveday laughed. 'It's psychological. They do it to frighten us. They turn the dogs loose in the compound every night. They're trained to savage everyone except the owner. One man to one dog. No one else can handle them.'

Waterloo

General Cavalie Mercer

Waterloo is a village near Brussels and is famous for the battle which was fought there on 18 June 1815.

Two gigantic forces with about 70,000 soldiers in each army, faced each other across a shallow valley. On one side were Napoleon's French troops, while on the other was the Duke of Wellington's army, composed of various nationalities, (Belgians, British, Brunswickers, Hanoverians, Nassauers), who had never fought together before. Many of the British troops were raw recruits.

Napoleon wanted to defeat the British before the Prussians could arrive in the battle zone. Wellington wanted to hold the French.

Captain (later General) Alexander Mercer was there, and this is how he vividly described some of the battle scenes . . .

We were talking when suddenly a dark mass of cavalry appeared for an instant on the main ridge, and then came sweeping down the slope in swarms, reminding me of an enormous surf bursting over the prostrate hull of a stranded vessel, and then running, hissing and foaming, up the beach. The hollow space became in a twinkling covered with horsemen, apparently without any object. Sometimes they came pretty near us, then would retire a little. There were lancers amongst them, hussars, and dragoons – it was a complete *mêlée*. On the main ridge no squares were to be seen; the only objects were a few guns standing in a confused manner, with muzzles in the air, and not one artillery-man. After caracoling about for a few minutes, the crowd began to separate and draw together in small bodies, which continually increased; and now we really apprehended being overwhelmed, as the first line had apparently been. For a moment an awful silence pervaded that part of the position to which we anxiously turned our eyes. 'I fear all is over,' said Colonel Gould, who still remained by me. The thing seemed but too likely, and this time I could not withhold my assent to his remark, for it did indeed appear so. Meantime the 14th, springing from the earth, had formed their square, whilst we, throwing back the guns of our right and left divisions, stood waiting in momentary expectation of being enveloped and attacked. Still they lingered in the hollow, when suddenly loud and repeated shouts (not English hurrahs) drew our attention to the other side. There we saw two dense columns of infantry pushing forward at a quick pace towards us, crossing the fields, as if they had come from Merke Braine. Every one, both of the 14th and ourselves, pronounced them French, yet still we delayed opening fire on them. Shouting, yelling, and singing, on they came, right for us; and being now not above 800 or 1,000 yards distant, it seemed folly allowing them to come nearer unmolested. The commanding officer of the 14th, to end our doubts, rode forward and endeavoured to ascertain who they were, but soon returned, assuring us they were French. The order was already given to fire, when, luckily, Colonel Gould recognized them as Belgians. Meantime, whilst my attention was occupied by these people, the cavalry had all vanished, nobody could say how or where.

We breathed again. Such was the agitated state in which we were kept in our second position. A third act was about to commence of a much more stirring and active nature.

It might have been, as nearly as I can recollect about 3 p.m., when Sir Augustus Frazer galloped up, crying out, 'Left limber up, and as fast as you can.' The words were scarcely uttered when my gallant troop stood as desired in column of subdivisions, left in front, pointing towards the main ridge. 'At a gallop, march!' and away we flew, as steadily and compactly as if at a review. I rode with Frazer, whose face was as black as a chimney-sweep's from the smoke, and the jacket-sleeve of his right arm torn open by a musket-ball or case-shot, which had merely grazed his flesh. As we went along, he told me that the enemy had assembled an enormous mass of heavy cavalry in front of the point to which he was leading us (about one-third of the distance between Hougoumont and the Charleroi road), and that in all probability we should immediately be charged on gaining our position. 'The Duke's orders, however, are positive,' he added, 'that in the event of their persevering and charging home, you do not expose your men, but retire with them into the adjacent squares of infantry.' As he spoke, we were ascending the reverse slope of the main position. We breathed a new atmosphere – the air was suffocatingly hot, resembling that issuing from an oven. We were enveloped in thick smoke, and, *malgré* the incessant roar of cannon and musketry, could distinctly hear around us a mysterious humming noise, like that which one hears of a summer's evening proceeding from myriads of black beetles; cannon-shot, too, ploughed the ground in all directions, and so thick was the hail of balls and bullets that it seemed dangerous to extend the arm lest it should be torn off. In spite of the serious situation in which we were, I could not help being somewhat amused at the astonishment expressed by our kind-hearted surgeon (Hitchins), who heard for the first time this sort of music. He was close to me as we ascended the slope, and, hearing this infernal *carillon* about his ears, began staring round in the wildest and most comic manner imaginable, twisting himself from side to side, exclaiming, 'My God, Mercer, what *is* that? What *is* all this noise? How curious! – how very curious!' And then when a cannon-shot rushed hissing past, '*There! – there!* What *is* it all?' It was with great difficulty that I persuaded him to retire: for a time he insisted on remaining near me, and it was only by pointing out how important it was to us, in case of being wounded, that he should keep himself safe to be able to assist us, that I prevailed on him to withdraw. Amidst this storm we gained the summit of the ridge, strange to say, without a casualty; and Sir Augustus, pointing out our position between two squares of Brunswick infantry, left us, with injunctions to remember the Duke's order, and to economize our ammunition. The Brunswickers were falling fast – the shot every moment making great gaps in their squares, which the officers and sergeants were actively employed in filling up by pushing their men together, and sometimes thumping them ere they could make them move. These were the very boys whom I had but yesterday seen throwing away their arms, and fleeing, panic-stricken, from the very sound of our horses' feet. Today they fled not bodily, to be sure, but spiritually, for their senses seemed to have left them. There they stood, with recovered arms, like so many logs, or rather like the very wooden figures which I had seen them practising at in their cantonments. Every moment I feared they would again throw down their arms and flee; but their officers and sergeants behaved nobly, not only keeping them together, but managing to keep their squares closed in spite of the carnage made amongst them. To have sought refuge amongst men in such a state were madness – the very moment our men ran from their guns I was convinced, would be the signal for their disbanding. We had better, then, fall at our posts than in such a situation. Our coming up seemed to reanimate them, and all their eyes were directed to us – indeed, it was providential, for, had we not arrived as we did, I scarcely think there is a doubt of what would have been their fate. Our first gun had scarcely gained the interval between their squares, when I saw through the smoke the leading squadrons of the advancing column coming on at a brisk trot, and already not more than one hundred yards distant, if so much, for I don't think we could have seen so far. I immediately ordered the line to be formed for action – *case-shot*! and the leading gun was unlimbered and commenced firing almost as soon as the word was given: for activity and intelligence our men were unrivalled. The very first round, I saw, brought down several men and horses. They continued, however, to advance. I glanced at the Brunswickers, and that glance told me it would not do; they had opened a fire from their front faces, but both squares appeared too unsteady, and I resolved to say nothing about the Duke's order, and take our chance – a resolve that was strengthened by the effect of the remaining guns as they rapidly succeeded in coming to action, making terrible slaughter, and in an instant covering the ground with men and horses. Still they persevered in approaching us (the first round had brought them to a walk), though slowly, and it did seem they would ride over us. We were a little below the level of the ground on which they moved – having in front of us a bank of about a foot and a half or two feet high, along the top of which ran a narrow road – and this gave more effect to out case-shot, all of which almost must have taken effect, for the carnage was frightful. I suppose this state of things occupied but a few seconds, when I observed symptoms of hesitation, and in a twinkling, at the instant I thought it was all over with us, they turned to either flank and filed away rapidly to the rear. Retreat of the mass, however, was not so easy. Many facing about and trying to force their way through the body of the column, that part next to us became a complete mob, into which we kept a steady fire of case-shot from our six pieces. The effect is hardly conceivable, and to paint this scene of slaughter and confusion impossible. Every discharge was followed by the fall of numbers, whilst the survivors struggled with each other, and I actually saw them using the pommels of their swords to fight their way out of the *mêlée*. Some, rendered desperate at finding themselves thus pent up at the muzzles of our guns, as it were, and others carried away by their horses, maddened with wounds, dashed through our intervals – few thinking of using their swords, but pushing furiously onward, intent only on saving themselves. At last the rear of the column, wheeling about, opened a passage, and the whole swept away at a much more rapid pace than they had advanced, nor stopped until the swell of the ground covered them from our fire. We then ceased firing; but as they were still not far off, for we saw the tops of their caps, having reloaded, we stood ready to receive them should they renew the attack.

One of, if not the first man who fell on our side was wounded by his own gun. Gunner Butterworth was one of the greatest pickles in the troop, but, at the same time, a most daring, active soldier; he was No 7 (the man who sponged, etc.) at his gun. He had just finished ramming down the shot, and was stepping back outside the wheel, when his foot stuck in the miry soil, pulling him forward at the moment the gun was fired. As a man naturally does when falling, he threw out both his arms before him, and they were blown off at the elbows. He raised himself a little on his two stumps, and looked up most piteously in my face. To assist him was impossible – the safety of all, everything, depended upon not slackening our fire, and I was obliged to turn from him. The state of anxious activity in which we were kept all day, and the numbers who fell almost immediately afterwards, caused me to lose sight of poor Butterworth; and I afterwards learned that he had succeeded in rising and was gone to the rear; but on inquiring for him next day, some of my people who had been sent to Waterloo told me that they saw his body lying by the roadside near the farm of Mount St Jean – bled to death! The retreat of the cavalry was succeeded by a shower of shot and shells, which must have annihilated us had not the little bank covered

One of the first men who fell on our side was wounded by his own gun.

and threw most of them over us. Still some reached us and knocked down men and horses.

At the first charge, the French column was composed of grenadiers à cheval[1] and cuirassiers, the former in front. I forget whether they had or had not changed this disposition, but think, from the number of cuirasses we afterwards found, that the cuirassiers led the second attack. Be this as it may, their column reassembled. They prepared for a second attempt, sending up a cloud of skirmishers, who galled us terribly by a fire of carbines and pistols at scarcely forty yards from our front. We were obliged to stand with port-fires lighted, so that it was not without a little difficulty that I succeeded in restraining the people from firing, for they grew impatient under such fatal results. Seeing some exertion beyond words necessary for this purpose, I leaped my horse up the little bank, and began a promenade (by no means agreeable) up and down our front, without even drawing my sword, though these fellows were within speaking distance of me. This quieted my men; but the tall blue gentlemen, seeing me thus dare them, immediately made a target of me, and commenced a very deliberate practice, to show us what very bad shots they were and verify the old artillery proverb, 'The nearer the target, the safer you are.' One fellow certainly made me flinch, but it was a miss; so I shook my finger at him, and called him *coquin*, etc. The rogue grinned as he reloaded, and again took aim. I certainly felt rather foolish at that moment, but was ashamed, after such bravado, to let him see it, and therefore continued my promenade. As if to prolong my torment, he was a terrible time about it. To me it seemed an age. Whenever I turned, the muzzle of his infernal carbine still followed me. At length bang it went, and whiz came the ball close to the back of my neck, and at the same instant down dropped the leading driver of one of my guns (Miller), into whose forehead the cursed missile had penetrated.

The column now once more mounted the plateau, and these popping gentry wheeled off right and left to clear the ground for their charge. The spectacle was imposing, and if ever the word sublime was appropriately applied, it might surely be to it. On they came in compact squadrons, one behind the other, so numerous that those of the rear

---

[1] These grenadiers à cheval were very fine troops, clothed in blue uniforms without facings, cuffs, or collars. Broad, very broad buff belts, and huge muff caps, made them appear gigantic fellows.

were still below the brow when the head of the column was but at some sixty or seventy yards from our guns. Their pace was a slow but steady trot. None of your furious galloping charges was this, but a deliberate advance, at a deliberate pace, as of men resolved to carry their point. They moved in profound silence, and the only sound that could be heard from them amidst the incessant roar of battle was the low thunder-like reverberation of the ground beneath the simultaneous tread of so many horses. On our part was equal deliberation. Every man stood steadily at his post, the guns ready, loaded with a round-shot first and a case over it; the tubes were in the vents; the port-fires glared and sputtered behind the wheels; and my word alone was wanting to hurl destruction on that goodly show of gallant men and noble horses. I delayed this, for experience had given me confidence. The Brunswickers partook of this feeling, and with their squares – much reduced in point of size – well closed, stood firmly, with arms at the recover, and eyes fixed on us, ready to commence their fire with our first discharge. It was indeed a grand and imposing spectacle! The column was led on this time by an officer in a rich uniform, his breast covered with decorations, whose earnest gesticulations were strangely contrasted with the solemn demeanour of those to whom they were addressed. I thus allowed them to advance unmolested until the head of the column might have been about fifty or sixty yards from us, and then gave the word, 'Fire!' The effect was terrible. Nearly the whole leading rank fell at once; and the round-shot, penetrating the column carried confusion throughout its extent. The ground, already encumbered with victims of the first struggle, became now almost impassable. Still, however, these devoted warriors struggled on, intent only on reaching us. The thing was impossible. Our guns were served with astonishing activity, whilst the running fire of the two squares was maintained with spirit. Those who pushed forward over the heaps of carcasses of men and horses gained but a few paces in advance, there to fall in their turn and add to the difficulties of those succeeding them. The discharge of every gun was followed by a fall of men and horses like that of grass before the mower's scythe. When the horse alone was killed, we could see the cuirassiers divesting themselves of the encumbrance and making their escape on foot. Still, for a moment, the confused mass (for all order was at an end) stood before us, vainly trying to urge their horses over the obstacles presented by their fallen comrades, in obedience to the now loud and rapid vociferations of him who had led them on and remained unhurt. As before, many cleared everything and rode through us; many came plunging forward only to fall, man and horse, close to the muzzles of our guns; but the majority again turned at the very moment when, from having less ground to go over, it were safer to advance than retire, and sought a passage to the rear. Of course the same confusion, struggle amongst themselves, and slaughter prevailed as before, until gradually they disappeared over the brow of the hill. We ceased firing, glad to take breath. Their retreat exposed us, as before, to a shower of shot and shells: these last, falling amongst us with very long fuses, kept burning and hissing a long time before they burst, and were a considerable annoyance to man and horse. The bank in front, however, again stood our friend, and sent many over us innocuous.

Lieutenant Breton, who had already lost two horses and had mounted a troop-horse, was conversing with me during this our leisure moment. As his horse stood at right angles to mine, the poor jaded animal dozingly rested his muzzle on my thigh; whilst I, the better to hear amidst the infernal din, leant forward, resting my arm between his ears. In this attitude a cannon-shot smashed the horse's head to atoms. The headless trunk sank to the ground – Breton looked pale as death, expecting, as he afterwards told me, that I was cut in two. What was passing to the right and left of us I know no more about than the man in the moon – not even what corps were beyond the Brunswickers. The smoke confined our vision to a very small compass, so that my battle was restricted to the two squares and my own battery; and, as long as we maintained our ground, I thought it a matter of course that others did so too. It was just after this accident that our worthy commanding officer of artillery, Sir George Adam Wood, made his appearance through the smoke a little way from our left flank. As I said, we were doing nothing, for the cavalry were under the brow re-forming for a third attack, and we were being pelted by their artillery. 'D – n it, Mercer,' said the old man, blinking as a man does when facing a gale of wind, 'you have hot work of it here.' 'Yes, sir, pretty hot'; and I was proceeding with an account of the two charges we had already discomfited, and the prospect of a third, when, glancing that way, I perceived their leading squadron already on the plateau. 'There they are again!' I exclaimed; and, darting from Sir George *sans cérémonie*, was just in time to meet them with the same destruction as before. This time, indeed, it was child's play. They could not even approach us in any decent order, and we fired most deliberately; it was folly having attempted the thing. I was sitting on my horse near the right of my battery as they turned and began to retire once more. Intoxicated with success, I was singing out, 'Beautiful! – beautiful!' and my right arm was flourishing about, when some one from behind, seizing it, said quietly, 'Take care, or you'll strike the Duke'; and in effect our noble chief, with a serious air, and apparently much fatigued, passed close by me to the front, without seeming to take the slightest notice of the remnant of the French cavalry still lingering on the ground. This obliged us to cease firing; and at the same moment I, perceiving a line of infantry ascending from the rear, slowly, with ported arms, and uttering a sort of feeble, suppressed hurrah – ankle-deep in a thick tenacious mud, and threading their way amongst or stepping over the numerous corpses covering the ground, out of breath from their exertions, and hardly preserving a line, broken everywhere into large gaps the breadth of several files – could not but meditate on the probable results of the last charge had I, in obedience to the Duke's order, retired my men into the squares and allowed the daring and formidable squadrons a passage to our rear, where they must have gone thundering down on this disjointed line. The summit gained, the line was amended, files closed in, and the whole, including our Brunswickers, advanced down the slope towards the plain.

Although the infantry lost several men as they passed us, yet on the whole the cannonade began to slacken on both sides (why, I know not), and, the smoke clearing away a little, I had now, for the first time, a good view of the field. On the ridge opposite to us dark masses of troops were stationary, or moving down into the intervening plain. Our own advancing infantry were hid from view by the ground. We therefore recommenced firing at the enemies' masses, and the cannonade, spreading, soon became general again along the line. Whilst thus occupied with our front, we suddenly became sensible of a most destructive flanking fire from a battery which had come, the Lord knows how, and established itself on a knoll somewhat higher than the ground we stood on, and only about 400 or 500 yards a little in advance of our left flank. The rapidity and precision of this fire were quite appalling. Every shot almost took effect, and I certainly expected we should all be annihilated. Our horses and limbers, being a little retired down the slope, had hitherto been somewhat under cover from the direct fire in front; but this plunged right amongst them, knocking them down by pairs, and creating horrible confusion. The drivers could hardly extricate themselves from one dead horse ere another fell, or perhaps themselves. The saddle-bags, in many instances, were torn from the horses' backs, and their contents scattered over the field. One shell I saw explode under the two finest wheel-horses in the troop – down they dropped. In some instances the horses of a gun or ammunition waggon remained, and all their drivers were killed. The whole livelong day had cost us nothing like this. Our gunners too – the few left fit for duty of them – were so exhausted that they were unable to run the guns up after firing, consequently at every round they retreated nearer to the limbers; and as we had pointed our two left guns towards the people who were annoying us so terribly, they soon came altogether in a confused heap, the trails crossing each other, and the whole dangerously near the limbers and ammunition waggons, some of which were totally unhorsed, and others in sad confusion from the loss of their drivers and horses, many of them lying dead in their harness attached to their carriages. I sighed for my poor troop – it was already but a wreck.

I had dismounted, and was assisting at one of the guns to encourage my poor exhausted men, when through the smoke a black speck caught my eye, and I instantly knew what it was. The conviction that one never sees a shot coming towards you unless directly in its line flashed across my mind, together with the certainty that my doom was sealed. I had barely time to exclaim 'Here it is then!' – much in that gasping sort of way one does when going into very cold water takes away the breath – 'whush' it went past my face, striking the point of my pellisse collar, which was lying open, and smash into a horse close behind me. I breathed freely again.

Under such a fire, one may be said to have had a thousand narrow escapes; and, in good truth, I frequently experienced that displacement of air against my face caused by the passing of shot close to me; but the two above recorded, and a third which I shall mention, were remarkable ones, and made me feel in full force the goodness of Him who protected me among so many dangers. Whilst in position on the right of the second line, I had reproved some of my men for lying down when shells fell near them until they burst. Now my turn came. A shell, with a long fuse, came slop into the mud at my feet, and there lay fizzing and flaring, to my infinite discomfiture. After what I had said on the subject, I felt that I must act up to my own words, and, accordingly, there I stood, endeavouring to look quite composed until the cursed thing burst – and, strange to say, without injuring me, though so near. The effect on my men was good. We had scarcely fired many rounds at the enfilading battery when a tall man in the black Brunswick uniform came galloping up to me from the rear, exclaiming, 'Ah! mine Gott! – mine Gott! vat is it you doos, sare? Dat is your friends de Proosiens; an you kills dem! Ah, mine Gott! – mine Gott! vill you no stop, sare? – vill you no stop? Ah! mine Gott! – mine Gott! vat for is dis? De Inglish kills dere friends de Proosiens! Vere is de Dook von Vellington? – vere is de Dook von Vellington? Oh, mine Gott! – mine Gott!' etc. etc., and so he went on raving like one demented. I observed that if these were our friends the Prussians they were treating us very uncivilly; and that it was not without sufficient provocation we had turned our guns on them, pointing out to him at the same time the bloody proofs of my assertion. Apparently not noticing what I said, he continued his lamentations, and, 'Vill you no stop, sare, I say?' Wherefore, thinking he might be right, to pacify him I ordered the whole to cease firing, desiring him to remark the consequences. *Psieu, psieu, psieu*, came our *friends'* shot, one after another; and our friend himself had a narrow escape from one of them. 'Now, sir,' I said, 'you will be convinced; and we will continue our firing, whilst you can ride round the way you came, and tell them they kill their friends the English; the moment their fire ceases, so shall mine.' Still he lingered, exclaiming, 'Oh, dis is terreebly to see de Proosien and de Inglish kill vonanoder!' At last darting off I saw no more of him. The fire continued on both sides, mine becoming slacker and slacker, for we were reduced to the last extremity, and must have been annihilated but for the opportune arrival of a battery of Belgic artillery a little on our left, which, taking the others in flank nearly at point blank, soon silenced and drove them off. Our strength was barely sufficient to fire three guns out of our six.

These Belgians were all beastly drunk, and, when they first came up, not at all particular as to which way they fired; and it was only by keeping an eye on them that they were prevented treating us, and even one another. The wretches had probably already done mischief elsewhere – who knows? My recollections of the latter part of this day are rather confused; I was fatigued, and almost deaf. I recollect clearly, however, that we had ceased firing – the plain below being covered with masses of troops, which we could not distinguish from each other. Captain Walcot of the horse-artillery had come to us, and we were all looking out anxiously at the movements below and on the opposite ridge, when he suddenly shouted out, 'Victory! – victory! they fly! – they fly!' and sure enough we saw some of the masses dissolving, as it were, and those composing them streaming away in confused crowds over the field, whilst the already desultory fire of their artillery ceased altogether. I shall never forget this joyful moment! – this moment of exultation! On looking round I found we were left almost alone. Cavalry and infantry had all moved forward, and only a few guns here and there were to be seen on the position. A little to our right were the remains of Major M'Donald's troop under Lieutenant Sandilands, which had suffered much, but nothing like us. We were congratulating ourselves on the happy results of the day, when an aide-de-camp rode up, crying 'Forward, sir! – forward! It is of the utmost importance that this movement should be supported by artillery!' at the same time waving his hat much in the manner of a huntsman laying on his dogs. I smiled at his energy, and, pointing to the remains of my poor troop, quietly asked, 'How, sir?' A glance was sufficient to show him the impossibility, and away he went.

Our situation was indeed terrible: of 200 fine horses with which we had entered the battle, upwards of 140 lay dead, dying, or severely wounded. Of the men, scarcely two-thirds of those necessary for four guns remained, and these so completely exhausted as to be totally incapable of further exertion. Lieutenant Breton had three horses killed under him; Lieutenant Hincks was wounded in the breast by a spent ball; Lieutenant Leathes on the hip by a splinter; and although untouched myself, my horse had no less than eight wounds, one of which – a graze on the fetlock joint – lamed him for ever. Our guns and carriages were, as before mentioned, altogether in a confused heap, intermingled with dead and wounded horses, which it had not been possible to disengage from them. My poor men, such at least as were untouched, fairly worn out, their clothes, faces, etc., blackened by the smoke and spattered over with mud and blood, had seated themselves on the trails of the carriages, or had thrown themselves on the wet and polluted soil, too fatigued to think of anything but gaining a little rest. Such was our situation when called upon to advance! It was impossible, and we remained where we were.

A Day in The Life of 'D' Company

Alex Bowlby

'D' Company had moved to Perugia in Central Italy. Panzer Grenadiers commanded the hills, and they'd already won a victory over the Guards.

This excerpt from a book by Alex Bowlby describes some skirmishes between 'D' Company and the Panzer Grenadiers . . .

A gun fired. Its shell screamed through the trees. The whole orchestra started up – big mortars, small mortars, Spandaus, Brens, rifles, grenades. The tank's 88 fired 'cheesecutters'. Two Spandaus raked the section's position. Our own guns opened up. The whole hill shook with explosions. Then I heard a peculiar 'wurra-wurra!' Small shells smacked into a tree growing out of my trench. I could see the white-hot steel. They were cannon-shells. The tank was using the tree as an aiming post. Hypnotized with fear I watched the tree slowly disintegrate.

'Prepare to withdraw!' shouted Mr Simmonds.

I pulled on my greatcoat over my equipment.

'Withdraw!'

The Platoon fled. Major Henderson was walking the rest of the Company down the hill. He was looking very thoughtful. He halted us in a clearing half-way down the hill.

'They'll probably try a box-barrage,' he said, 'so we'll stop here.'

The Company sat down and waited. Sure enough a murderous barrage came down at the foot of the hill.

'That was a crafty move!' said Baker. 'See that "Tiger"? Big as a house!'

Baker also told me that three out of the four stretcher-bearers had been wounded whilst giving first-aid. No one had been killed outright.

'We ain't done bad,' he added. 'Phillips got three of them with the Bren, and I nabbed a couple. Five Platoon got a stack.'

'All right, "D" Company,' said Major Henderson. 'We'll return to the positions.'

This made me feel cold all over. But Henderson knew his stuff. I climbed the hill wondering if the Germans had occupied our positions. They hadn't. A depleted section – Gibson and Sullivan were helping to carry wounded back to our own lines – dropped into the trenches.

A Bren opened up. The whole show began again. Only this time the noise seemed worse than ever. It hammered my nerves to jelly. I tried to concentrate on the hills rising out of the mist. Noise swept them away. When I heard a rush of feet I lay on my back waiting to be bayoneted. I couldn't even have raised my hands above my head. But the feet passed my trench. Looking out I saw the Platoon running down the hill. Leaping out of my trench I raced after them. I'd gone fifty yards before I realized I had left my rifle behind.

The remnants of the Company were gathered in the clearing. Very conscious of my lack of arms I asked Mr Simmonds if I should go back for my rifle.

'No, I don't think so,' he said. 'I'll ask the Company Commander.'

Major Henderson had a look at me.

'Yes,' he said. 'I think you should get it.'

Back I went, wishing I had kept quiet. I was soon crawling. Every few yards I stopped to listen. Everything was still. The positions were just as we had left them. I could see my rifle lying on the parapet. As I crept towards it someone spoke. I froze. An answering voice came from the same place – higher up the slope. Wriggling over to the trench I grabbed my rifle, jumped to my feet and raced down the slope. I ran so fast I went head-over-heels – and kept going that way, deliberately, for at least thirty yards. I guessed a tumbling target would be difficult to hit.

When I reached the clearing I found it deserted. It was one of the worst moments of the day. I felt horribly lost. Running on down the hill I spotted a rifleman, near the bottom. When I got there I saw seven or eight more running across a field towards a wooded slope a quarter of a mile away. As I ran after them guns opened up. The shell burst amongst us. As if in a dream I saw the others run on unhurt. They kept running. I threw myself flat at every burst. In spite of this I slowly gained on them. Every moment I expected to be blown to bits. How could one survive shells bursting at one's feet? Yet even then part of me was noticing how red the flames were. Nothing could stop me recording. But my bouncing burned me up physically. As I neared the slope my knees stopped working. I fell in a heap. My greatcoat felt like a leaded shroud. With one last effort I got up and staggered to the slope.

Recovering my breath I crawled up the slope in search of the others. They were standing on a path, O'Connor, Mr Simmonds, Swallow and Major Henderson amongst them. Some shells crashed into the undergrowth below us. We moved into a ditch above the path. On my left I had a signaller, on my right Mr Simmonds. Major Henderson was on the extreme left of the group, next to the signaller.

'I think we should clear out now, John, don't you?' he said.

'Wouldn't it be better to wait till it's dark?' suggested Mr Simmonds.

'One up to you,' I thought.

Major Henderson looked at his watch.

'It's only six now,' he said. 'It won't be dark until nine.'

Whilst they continued the discussion I filled my pipe. As I went to strike a match a Spandau opened fire. From twenty yards farther up the slope. The bullets weren't aimed at us. The shock struck almost as hard. I was petrified. Like a Pompeian sentinel. Pipe in mouth, match in hand, I stared at Mr Simmonds. He stared back. Unmoved. A mortar fired. It was in the same place as the Spandau, not more than twenty yards farther up the slope. The bomb sailed off towards our own lines. The Germans began talking. One of them shouted. An answering cry came from the foot of the slope. I counted four voices there, one of them a woman's. Could they be Italians? Mr Simmonds had the same thought. He slowly swivelled round towards the rifleman the other side of him, who spoke fluent German. The rifleman shook his head, and mouthed the word 'German'.

As I glanced at the bushes shielding the ditch, and worked out our chances of leaving it alive, one of the Germans at the top of the slope began singing. It was on the lines of the '*Horst Wessel*', and reeked of victory and '*Deutschland über Alles*'. The singer did it proud. He was a big fellow, by the sound of him. Although very much aware of how easily he could sling us a grenade I couldn't help enjoying the irony. I grinned ruefully at Mr Simmonds. He looked straight through me.

In the middle of the second verse guns opened up from our own lines. The shells landed on the slope. The Germans shouted at one another. The barrage only lasted a few minutes but it was enough to make them dig in. I thanked God for the gunners. Whilst the Germans were digging we could afford to relax a little, to straighten our legs, and move an arm. When they stopped only snatches of conversation broke the silence. Finally everything was quiet. The slightest rustle could give us away. And there were two hours to go.

As I sat in the ditch I was aware of a *creeping* fear. The longer the silence the worse the fear. I longed for noise, any noise, even the noise on the hill. In lieu of it I began praying, a stream of promises of what I would do if God would let me leave the ditch alive.

'And if I do get out,' I thought, 'I'll desert. Anything's better than this.'

Footsteps began crunching down the slope. They were heading straight for the bush in front of me. I released the safety-catch of my rifle. As I pointed it at the bushes Mr Simmonds put a finger to his lips. I wondered whether the German would surrender or if I would have to shoot him.

'One shot and we've all had it,' I thought.

I also decided that a Tommy would have been much more useful than a rifle. I made a mental note to get myself one – if we ever got out of the ditch.

The German halted behind the bush.

Had he twigged?

Then I heard a steel belt-buckle being loosened. Other noises followed;

I grinned at Mr Simmonds. Again he looked straight through me. The German re-buckled himself, and walked back up the slope. The wood began to roar with silence. After more prayers I looked round to see how other people were taking the strain. Mr Simmonds was as poker-faced as ever. The German-speaking rifleman was bowed down by the weight of an enormous wireless. Behind him O'Connor was clutching a spare Bren barrel and looked ready to conk the first German

I wondered if the German would surrender or if I would have to shoot him.

he saw. When I looked at the signaller I had a shock. He was asleep! Major Henderson was looking at his watch. As the light faded he mouthed a message warning us that we were moving out in five minutes; we were to leave the ditch in single file, one at a time.

Deciding that our chance of survival would depend more on speed than guile I began shedding my greatcoat. To do this in silence required time, and I had only just managed it when Major Henderson stood up. As I stood up myself Mr Simmonds dug me in the ribs. I turned round. He pointed at my greatcoat. Cursing him silently I picked it up.

Major Henderson stepped gingerly out of the ditch; the signaller followed. A twig cracked under him. As I moved on to the path I trod on another.

'Halte!'

I swung round instinctively. A figure stood silhouetted against the sky. I ran down the slope. The sentry opened fire. As rifle-bullets whistled past the ground gave way under my feet. My greatcoat flew out of my hand.

'Good riddance!' I thought, and then hit the ground like a bomb.

I jumped up quickly, saw that I'd fallen twenty feet – that part of the slope ended in a cliff – then ran after Major Henderson, who was disappearing round the corner of the slope.

The Germans were shouting their heads off.

'That shook the bastards,' I thought.

As the rest of the party joined us two Spandaus opened fire. The bullets were nowhere near us but O'Connor and another rifleman were to come. I was beginning to get worried when O'Connor ran in.

'Ward went down when the Spandau opened up, sir,' he said. 'He's not hurt, but he wouldn't get up.'

For the first time that day Major Henderson didn't have a ready answer. As he stood there, obviously debating whether we should go back for the rifleman or get clear ourselves, I put my oar in.

'If we don't move out, now, sir, we'll never get out.'

To my surprise Major Henderson nodded, then led us into a cornfield. We were half-way across when a Spandau opened up. Tracer bullets lit up the party – I had a split-second recollection of our removing the Bren tracer – and we ran. The tracer whipped between us as if the Spandau-man had orders to just tickle us up.

'Battle-course gone wrong,' I thought, and then my underpants came down.

I went headlong. Scrambling up I plunged forward in child-like rushes, my pants round my ankles. Again and again I crashed into the corn. Sobbing with rage, my face knocked raw by the stubble, I tried desperately to keep up with the others. As I dropped behind it seemed that the Spandau must get me. He didn't, and I caught the others up behind a hedge. Whilst they rested I pulled up my pants.

The Germans tossed us a couple of mortar-bombs. We moved into the next field. I had no idea where we were but Major Henderson was handling a compass with a professional air. He knew.

On the far side of the field we passed a German lorry. No one challenged. I would have shot them happily if they had.

We kept going until we heard track-vehicles on a road. We headed towards them cautiously. Were they ours?

'Whoa-back!' someone shouted.

I've never heard a sweeter sound.

At the Battle Front

Lt.-Col. R. G. A. Hamilton

GRENAY, 21 SEPTEMBER 1915

Today is the first day of the great bombardment. And what a bombardment it is! There must be hundreds and hundreds of French and English guns all concentrated at this one spot. We have an almost unlimited allowance of ammunition and are letting it off at a tremendous rate. I have spent most of the day in my cellar, with my adjutant, surrounded with maps and telephones. Every few minutes I get an order from Group HQ to say that such-and-such an area is being shelled by German batteries in the direction of Loos or St Pierre. I then look up on my coloured tracings which of my batteries can best deal with the particular area and then phone to them to turn their fire on to the place. Since dawn this morning the noise has been appalling. Field-guns, howitzers, large and small, big naval guns, 'mothers', and even 'grandmothers', are all joining in. The poor Hun must be having a rotten time. By evening his fire had distinctly slackened off. I think we must be fairly drowning him with shells. At last we are beginning to get our own back. So far during this war the German has always had the vast superiority of fire; now, for the first time, he is hopelessly outnumbered in guns and shells. After dark the fire was not so continuous, but it is still being kept up fairly heavily, with bursts of intense gun fire every half-hour or so. The French 75 batteries on our right and left seem to keep at it the whole time.

I have been at the telephone all day except for meals. It is very dull down in my dark wine-cellar, with only one small hole up into the air, whilst all the battery commanders are in their Observing Posts, watching the fun. However, my place is at the end of the telephone and my work is of the greatest importance, as from here I direct and control the fire of all the batteries. By dark this evening the batteries had fired over fifty rounds per gun. Late in the evening I had a message from our Group Commander to say that we were keeping down the hostile fire, and that he was pleased with the work of the brigade.

About 10.30 at night I got a message from Harvey, who is now in command of my battery, to say that the Germans were firing down the Grenay-Loos road with machine-guns. We could hear it quite distinctly back here. I at once turned A and C Batteries on to this road and the market square in the centre of Loos. This stopped the machine-guns at once.

'And so to bed' in my horrid cellar.

GRENAY, 22 SEPTEMBER 1915

I woke early this morning to hear the great bombardment continuing. The volume of fire is simply appalling. The whole earth is trembling, and this house shakes the whole time with the concussion of the guns firing. There are French 75 batteries right and left of us and a six-inch howitzer battery immediately behind our house. As I was writing this, I saw Colonel Pereira, who was my company commander in the Grenadiers, so ran out to speak to him. He is commanding a pioneer battalion along our front.

Our bombardment has continued all day and now, after dark, is still being kept up by intermittent bursts of fire, especially by the French batteries around us.

At 10 p.m. I again heard machine-gun fire in the direction of St Pierre, so I went out myself and arranged for a brigade salvo to be fired on my whistle, to be immediately followed by a round of gun-fire. I had all the guns laid on the square in front of the church in St Pierre. The batteries all fired at exactly the same second, and if the German convoys were passing through the town then, which it is practically certain they would be, the result must have been serious to them. If, as I suspect, the square was packed with men and wagons, with food and ammunition for the trenches, we must have caused horrible slaughter. It is a horrible thing to have to do, but war is a horrid thing and the more we kill the sooner it will be over. After all, they have done this sort of thing to us. What is more, it pleases our own infantry to know that our guns are always ready to help them, night and day.

It is a glorious moonlight night, and I could see the reflection in the sky of the bursting shells.

Our forward observing officers report that the whole of St Pierre and Loos is blotted out in smoke, whilst parts of the towns are in flames. I also hear that our heavy guns have been playing havoc with their infantry trenches.

This afternoon they fired one twelve-inch shell, which fell near here, but so far they have not repeated it.

Perhaps they will try again in the middle of the night. We have been firing a great deal of our new high-explosive shells today.

GRENAY, 23 SEPTEMBER 1915

Our batteries did not open fire very early today, as there was a mist. The Hun, on the other hand, shelled us from eight to nine, with eight-inch shells. He fired about twenty shots, which all fell at exactly the same spot – 100 yards in rear of D Battery and 300 yards from my HQ. We were all shaving at the time, and I expected to cut myself every shot, as the whole house rocked with the concussion. Pieces of shell struck our house, but, fortunately, did not come through the windows. I appealed to Group HQ for help, and they at once turned some of our very heavy howitzers on to them. It stopped the Germans at once, and so far (11 a.m.) we have had no more shells near us. The general bombardment is going on merrily again and, as usual, the place is rocking and shuddering with the noise. Our aeroplanes are going to take photos of the enemy's positions between 12.30 and 1 p.m., so we have to stop firing, or else they would see nothing for smoke.

4 p.m. The roar of the guns has increased greatly, and is now simply appalling. The French batteries never seem to stop. I have been watching one gun and found that it was firing continuously at the rate of one

round every three seconds, or twenty rounds per minute per gun. They seem to keep it up for about a minute at a time, then they all run back to their dug-outs, which are some way from the guns. The extraordinary thing about the French batteries is that they do not dig in the guns at all; in fact, they stand out in the open without any protection at all. We, on the other hand, make small forts over each of our guns that will keep out anything under a six-inch shell. This afternoon I have been plastering St Pierre and Loos with shrapnel, by 'search and sweep', *i.e.* each gun in the batteries fires nine shots and three different ranges and three different angles. I am glad I am not there.

7 *p.m.* Things have quietened down again now.

8 *p.m.* The most extraordinary phenomenon is happening. There is a loud wailing in the air, just like the wind in the trees, only louder. It also somewhat reminds me of jackals in the East, or a dog howling. It has been going on for some time now. It is the wierdest and most mournful thing I ever heard, following on the day's bombardment. If one was superstitious, which I am, one would say it was the spirits of the killed, wailing in the air. The true explanation more probably is that the wind has got up and that it is whistling through our broken roof.

Last thing before going to bed in my cellar, I ordered all batteries to sweep the main streets of Loos and St. Pierre with shrapnel. It is a brutal thing to do, but will certainly cause the Germans considerable losses in their supply columns, and, besides that, the moral effect on their infantry in the trenches should be great, if their food fails to arrive.

GRENAY, 24 SEPTEMBER 1915

A letter from G. and some tobacco: both very welcome.

LE RUTOIRE, 27 SEPTEMBER 1915

Nothing happened in the morning. The batteries continued to improve their gun-pits. At lunch time I was sent for to Group HQ, and told that the Guards were going to assault the Chalk Pit and Hill 70. My batteries were ordered to barrage a road on their left. I personally was to go at once to the HQ of the 1st Guards Brigade, and remain with General Feilding during the attack. I worked out the zones for the various batteries, and gave them their orders to keep up a steady fire from 3 to 5 p.m.

There was a shout and the assault commenced.

I had an awful time trying to get up to where General Feilding was. I had to walk about a mile up our own communicating trench and came to our old fire trenches, the ones we had been in till two days ago. After that it was necessary to get out into the open and pass through our wire into the neutral zone. Crossing the space of some 400 yards before reaching the German trenches was simply Hell incarnate. It was being swept continuously by the German heavy guns and also with shrapnel, to say nothing of rifle-bullets which were coming over the crest. This ground presented a terrible sight, the dead lying about everywhere – principally our own men who had been killed in the assault two days before. Besides these were hundreds of rifles and the kits of the wounded. The latter had already been brought in. Needless to say, I lost no time in getting across, and was much relieved when I dropped safely down into the German front-line trench. With great difficulty, I made my way along this, as it was very narrow, and packed with Coldstream Guards, who were waiting to do the assault. Eventually I found General Feilding with his Staff Captain, Lord Gort, and reported that my batteries were barraging the road on his left.

It was now 3 p.m., and suddenly our shells began to come over my head in a continuous stream from the four batteries. The shooting was distinctly good, the great majority of the shells falling near the road or bursting over it. The assault was timed to take place at 4 p.m., and a few minutes before the hour our people on the left sent up clouds of white smoke – a harmless smoke that gave off dense white clouds. The wind was blowing from us to the Huns, and the smoke made a complete screen between our assault and the people on the left. The result was that the assault was completely hidden from the German sight. The smoke screens are very successful, and the infantry were delighted with them.

Precisely at the hour, the officers leaped up on to the parapet, immediately followed by the men – this was the 2nd Battalion Irish Guards. There was a shout of 'They are off!' and the assault commenced. Almost at once they were lost to sight in the valley in front of us, and, so far as we could see, they had very few casualties to start with. The Germans now began to fire fast, with shrapnel and rifle. Our look-out place in the rear parapet of the German trench became unhealthy, and we were all so excited in watching the assault that we continued looking out. We had a Coldstream machine-gun about ten yards on our right, which was firing over the heads of the assaulting troops. Suddenly a shrapnel burst just on our right, and the machine-gun stopped a few moments later. Someone reported that it had just caught the gun crew, and killed and wounded the lot, except the actual man who was working the gun, who was not touched.

After a time some of our wounded began to crawl and stagger back. They said that they had got through the wood, but had been taken in flank by machine-guns, and the assault had been brought to a stop. This turned out to be true, and the brigade had to be content with entrenching themselves on the road at the foot of the hill they had hoped to take. General Feilding went on to see what was happening, but told me to remain in the German trench by my telephone. Whilst I was waiting for him to come back, I had a look round and was astounded to see what a palatial place it was. I was specially struck by the officers' quarters. One of them must have been quite twenty feet under ground, a long, sloping passage leading down to it. The soil is hard chalk a few feet below the surface. A room had been cut out underground some fifteen feet by twelve feet; the floor was boarded, and so were the walls. There were two iron bedsteads, a large table, chairs, and a large looking-glass. The walls were decorated with pictures, and, in fact, there was every luxury. The place was dry and warm; dozens of empty bottles were lying about; also cigar-boxes – but alas! neither wine nor cigars were left. I got a copy of the *Kolnische Zeitung*, three days old, which afforded much amusement when I got back to my dug-out. Also a roll of maps of the district. These were very rough and disappointing.

The walk back was a nightmare. It was about two miles in the dark, partly in the communicating trench and partly across the open; as it was raining, the clay soil had become exactly like vaseline, and for every step one took forward one slipped back six inches – added to which I kept falling into shell-holes in the dark.

Spent a very uncomfortable night in our dug-out in the trench, near the guns. Soon after daylight they started shelling us from the direction of Hulluch. The shelling was done entirely by a six-inch or eight-inch battery with high explosives. However, no damage was done during the morning, although these big shells were falling all among the guns.

At lunch-time I was told that the Guards were going to attack again, and that I was to support them with two batteries, and keep the other two batteries in hand, ready to turn on to anything required. I detailed A and B to fire. No sooner had we begun our bombardment than the Hun got on to us seriously with eight-inch shells. He started on A battery, which was some fifty yards behind my HQ dug-out, where I was. Edmond, the CO, went on firing steadily all through it, till he was hit by a large piece of a shell in the side, which went right through his lungs. The doctor gave him two hours to live. Immediately after, Calderwell was killed by a shell landing on his dug-out, and at the same time Jennings was wounded in some forty places – I hope, however, not dangerously. No officer was now left in A Battery, and the sergeant-major withdrew the men some 300 yards into a trench. As soon as the shelling stopped they came back to the guns, and I went across to them. They had one man besides the officers killed, and about fifteen wounded.

Meanwhile, B Battery was firing away hard, and as soon as I saw that A was out of action I turned on C to deal with the same target. Almost immediately the Germans switched on to B and C, and shelled them hard, about a shell every ten seconds. They got a direct hit on one of the C guns, smashing it to pieces and killing most of the men round it. Suddenly they stopped sending these huge Jack Johnsons into us, and gave us Woolly Bears instead. These are 4·2 howitzers which burst their shells in the air, just over one's head. They were firing gas-shells, which fill the air with some horrible fumes of ammonia and sulphur. One shakes, cannot speak, and the eyes smart and pour tears. It was impossible to keep the batteries in action, and I reluctantly had to go over to Group HQ and say that the brigade had been silenced for the time. I could hardly speak with shaking.

Things quieted down about 6 p.m., and we were able to take stock of what was left, collect the dead, and see what the damage was. I was greatly relieved to find that there was much less damage than I expected. A Battery had lost all its officers except one, who was with the wagon line, and a good many gunners. As the brigade was already short-handed in officers, owing to the colonel being killed, and Kenny and Potter being sick, I decided to break up A Battery for the present. I am sending two of their guns to C Battery, who have had one gun smashed today, and one gun each to B and D. This gives me three five-gun batteries, which in many ways will be easier to handle.

Late at night we buried the killed in a common grave at the farm, with dozens of men who have died after being brought in wounded. It was a mournful business, in pouring rain and standing in six inches of liquid mud. We put Caldwell alongside his men at one end of the grave. It rained hard all night and the water dripped through the roof of our HQ dug-out, making us all very wet and uncomfortable. I have decided to move to our positions at dawn – half a mile the other side of the farm. I cannot move at night as it is imperative that all the batteries should be ready to help the infantry in case of a counter-attack tonight.

Le Rutoire, 29 September 1915

At dawn I rode off with battery commanders to find a new position. It was impossible to do so in the dark as one could not see the lie of the ground. On the other hand, it is almost suicide to drive guns into the open by daylight, in full view of Fosse 8, where the Huns have an observing post. B Battery moved first, and got their horses away safely before the morning mist had cleared off enough for the Hun to see him. C Battery had to wait at the old position till B were ready to fire from the new one. The result was that just as they were moving off, the Germans opened fire with heavy shell. Fortunately, no one was hit, and they came into action in the new place. Within half an hour the German heavy guns had got the range to a yard, and they dropped sixty huge Black Marias right into the battery in thirty minutes, exactly one every half-minute. I was standing with Cammell, in B Battery, at the time. We were about 300 yards to the right of C. I watched Harvey through my glasses. He was standing in the open, apparently taking no notice of the shells which were falling all round him. At last he called his men away, and they all sauntered over towards us, sitting down and eating when they got a couple of hundred yards from the guns. I was watching the shells bursting, when a large piece of steel hit me on the leg above the knee, and knocked me flying. Fortunately, it had me with the flat side, so that my leg was only bruised and not cut at all. However, I have been very stiff all day on that leg.

I expected to find all the guns had been knocked out, but to my surprise found that only one gun and one limber had been damaged. That now makes two of C Battery's guns out of action, leaving them with one section of their own and one section of A.

About two o'clock I was sent for to go to Le Rutoire. On arrival there, I found the Prince of Wales, who had come to visit the Guards Division, which are here. It was an awful risk, as whilst he was there they were shelling the farm hard, just over our heads, with bricks and mortar falling all round. General Feilding was with him. I warned them that I had just come along the road and that it was being heavily shelled. They waited till the burst was over, and then went on. Within a quarter of an hour of the Prince going, the Germans really started shelling the farm in earnest with eight-inch shells, dropping them in regularly, one after another, into the buildings. They really ought not to have let him come to such a place, but I believe he is always trying to get into the front trenches.

Running the Gauntlet

James Fenimore Cooper

Hawkeye, the woodsman-scout, assisted by the Mohican Indians Chinga-chgook and his son Uncas, attempt to lead Alice and Cora Munro and Major Duncan Heyward through hostile territory back to the besieged Fort William Henry.

The Fort, (situated on Lake George) is commanded by the father of the Munro sisters – Lieutenant-Colonel George Munro, and is ringed by both enemy Indian and French soldiers under General Montcalm.

In the pre-dawn darkness, a patrolling French soldier challenges them, but Heyward replies in French, and unwittingly the sentry lets them pass . . .

They moved deliberately forward, leaving the sentinel pacing the banks of the silent pond, little suspecting an enemy of so much effrontery, and humming to himself some words, which were recalled to his mind by the sight of women, and perhaps by recollections of his own distant and beautiful France.

' 'Tis well you understood the knave!' whispered the scout, when they had gained a little distance from the place, and letting his rifle fall into the hollow of his arm again; 'I soon saw that he was one of them uneasy Frenchers; and well for him it was that his speech was friendly and his wishes kind, or a place might have been found for his bones amongst those of his countrymen.'

He was interrupted by a long and heavy groan which arose from the little basin, as though, in truth, the spirits of the departed lingered about their watery sepulchre.

'Surely it was of flesh!' continued the scout; 'no spirit could handle its arms so steadily!'

'It *was* of flesh; but whether the poor fellow still belongs to this world may well be doubted,' said Heyward, glancing his eyes around him, and missing Chingachgook from their little band. Another groan, more faint than the former, was succeeded by a heavy and sullen plunge into the water, and all was as still again as if the borders of the dreary pool had never been awakened from the silence of creation. While they yet hesitated in uncertainty, the form of the Indian was seen gliding out of the thicket. As the chief rejoined them, with one hand he attached the reeking scalp of the unfortunate young Frenchman to his girdle, and with the other he replaced the knife and tomahawk that had drunk his blood. He then took his wonted station, with the air of a man who believed he had done a deed of merit.

The scout dropped one end of his rifle to the earth, and leaning his hands on the other, he stood musing in profound silence. Then shaking his head in a mournful manner, he muttered, –

' 'Twould have been a cruel and an unhuman act for a white-skin; but 'tis the gift and natur' of an Indian, and I suppose it should not be denied. I could wish, though, it had befallen an accursed Mingo, rather than that gay young boy from the old countries.'

'Enough!' said Heyward, apprehensive the unconscious sisters might comprehend the nature of the detention, and conquering his disgust by a train of reflections very much like that of the hunter; ' 'tis done; and though better it were left undone, cannot be amended. You see we are, too obviously, within the sentinels of the enemy; what course do you propose to follow?'

'Yes,' said Hawkeye, rousing himself again, ' 'tis as you say, too late to harbour further thoughts about it. Aye, the French have gathered around the fort in good earnest, and we have a delicate needle to thread in passing them.'

'And but little time to do it in,' added Heyward, glancing his eyes upwards, towards the bank of vapour that concealed the setting moon.

'And little time to do it in!' repeated the scout. 'The thing may be done in two fashions, by the help of Providence, without which it may not be done at all.'

'Name them quickly, for time presses.'

'One would be to dismount the gentle ones, and let their beasts range the plain; by sending the Mohicans in front, we might then cut a lane through their sentries, and enter the fort over the dead bodies.'

'It will not do – it will not do!' interrupted the generous Heyward; 'a soldier might force his way in this manner, but never with such a convoy.'

' 'Twould be, indeed, a fearful path for such tender feet to wade in,' returned the equally reluctant scout; 'but I thought it befitting my manhood to name it. We must then turn on our trail and get without the line of their look-outs, when we will bend short to the west, and enter the mountains; where I can hide you, so that all the hounds in Montcalm's pay would be thrown off the scent for months to come.'

'Let it be done, and that instantly.'

Further words were unnecessary; for Hawkeye, merely uttering the mandate to 'follow,' moved along the route by which they had just entered their present critical and even dangerous situation. Their progress, like their late dialogue, was guarded, and without noise; for none knew at what moment a passing patrol, or a crouching picket of the enemy, might rise upon their path. As they held their silent way along the margin of the pond, again Heyward and the scout stole furtive glances at its appalling dreariness. They looked in vain for the form they had so recently seen stalking along its silent shores, while a low and regular wash of the little waves, by announcing that the waters were not yet subsided, furnished a frightful memorial of the deed of blood they had just witnessed. Like all that passing and gloomy scene, the low basin, however, quickly melted in the darkness, and became blended with the mass of black objects, in the rear of the travellers.

Hawkeye soon deviated from the line of their retreat, and striking off towards the mountains which form the western boundary of the narrow plain, he led his followers, with swift steps, deep within the shadows that were cast from their high and broken summits. The route was now painful; lying over ground ragged with rocks, and intersected with ravines, and their progress proportionately slow. Bleak and black hills lay on every side of them, compensating in some degree for the additional toil of the march by the sense of security they imparted. At length the party began slowly to rise a steep and rugged ascent, by a path that curiously wound among rocks, and trees, avoiding the one, and supported by the other, in a manner that showed it had been devised by men long practised in the arts of the wilderness. As they gradually rose from the level of the valleys, the thick darkness which usually precedes the approach of day began to disperse, and objects were seen in the plain and palpable colours with which they had been gifted by nature. When they issued from the stunted woods which clung to the barren sides of the mountain, upon a flat and mossy rock that formed its summit, they met the morning, as it came blushing above the green pines of a hill that lay on the opposite side of the valley of the Horican.

The scout now told the sisters to dismount; and taking the bridles from the mouths, and the saddles off the backs of the jaded beasts, he turned them loose, to glean a scanty subsistence among the shrubs and meagre herbage of that elevated region.

'Go,' he said, 'and seek your food where natur' gives it you; and beware that you become not food to ravenous wolves yourselves, among these hills.'

'Have we no further need of them?' demanded Heyward.

'See, and judge with your own eyes,' said the scout, advancing towards the eastern brow of the mountain, whither he beckoned for the whole party to follow; 'if it was as easy to look into the heart of man as it is to spy out the nakedness of Montcalm's camp from this spot, hypocrites would grow scarce, and the cunning of a Mingo might prove a losing game, compared to the honesty of a Delaware.'

When the travellers reached the verge of the precipice, they saw, at a glance, the truth of the scout's declaration, and the admirable foresight with which he had led them to their commanding station.

The mountain on which they stood, elevated, perhaps, a thousand feet in the air, was a high cone that rose a little in advance of that range which stretches for miles along the western shores of the lake, until, meeting its sister piles beyond the water, it ran off towards the Canadas, in confused and broken masses of rock, thinly sprinkled with evergreens. Immediately at the feet of the party, the southern shore of the Horican swept in a broad semicircle, from mountain to mountain, marking a wide strand, that soon rose into an uneven and somewhat elevated plain. To the north stretched the limpid, and, as it appeared from that dizzy height, the narrow sheet of the 'holy lake,' indented with

261

numberless bays, embellished by fantastic headlands, and dotted with countless islands. At the distance of a few leagues, the bed of the waters became lost among mountains, or was wrapped in the masses of vapour that came slowly rolling along their bosom, before a light morning air. But a narrow opening between the crests of the hills pointed out the passage by which they found their way still farther north, to spread their pure and ample sheets again, before pouring out their tribute into the distant Champlain. To the south stretched the defile, or rather broken plain. For several miles in this direction, the mountains appeared reluctant to yield their dominion, but within reach of the eye they diverged, and finally melted into the level and sandy lands, across which we have accompanied our adventurers in their double journey. Along both ranges of hills, which bounded the opposite sides of the lake and valley, clouds of light vapour were rising in spiral wreaths from the uninhibited woods, looking like the smokes of hidden cottages; or rolled lazily down the declivities, to mingle with the fogs of the lower land. A single, solitary, snow-white cloud floated above the valley, and marked the spot beneath which lay the silent pool.

Directly on the shore of the lake, and nearer to its western than to its eastern margin, lay the extensive earthen ramparts and low buildings of William Henry. Two of the sweeping bastions appeared to rest on the water which washed their bases, while a deep ditch and extensive morasses guarded its other sides and angles. The land had been cleared of wood for a reasonable distance around the work, but every other part of the scene lay in the green livery of nature, except where the limpid water mellowed the view, or the bold rocks thrust their black and naked heads about the undulating outline of the mountain ranges. In its front might be seen the scattered sentinels, who held a weary watch against their numerous foes; and within the walls themselves, the travellers looked down on men still drowsy with a night of vigilance. Towards the south-east, but in immediate contact with the fort, was an entrenched camp, posted on a rocky eminence, that would have been far more eligible for the work itself, in which Hawkeye pointed out the presence of those auxiliary regiments that had so recently left the Hudson in their company. From the woods, a little farther to the south, rose numerous dark and lurid smokes, that were easily to be distinguished from the purer exhalations of the springs, and which the scout

*'Yonder comes a fog that will
make an arrow more dangerous than a cannon.'*

also showed to Heyward, as evidences that the enemy lay in force in that direction.

But the spectacle which most concerned the young soldier was on the western bank of the lake, though quite near to its southern termination. On a strip of land, which appeared, from his stand, too narrow to contain such an army, but which, in truth, extended many hundreds of yards from the shores of the Horican to the base of the mountain, were to be seen the white tents and military engines of an encampment of ten thousand men. Batteries were already thrown up in their front, and even while the spectators above them were looking down, with such different emotions, on a scene which lay like a map beneath their feet, the roar of artillery rose from the valley, and passed off in thundering echoes, along the eastern hills.

'Morning is just touching them below,' said the deliberate and musing scout, 'and the watchers have a mind to wake up the sleepers by the sound of cannon. We are a few hours too late! Montcalm has already filled the woods with his accursed Iroquois.'

'The place is, indeed, invested,' returned Duncan, 'but is there no expedient by which we may enter? Capture in the works would be far preferable to falling again into the hands of roving Indians.'

'See!' exclaimed the scout, unconsciously directing the attention of Cora to the quarters of her own father, 'how that shot has made the stones fly from the side of the commandant's house! Aye! these Frenchers will pull it to pieces faster than it was put together, solid and thick though it be.'

'Heyward, I sicken at the sight of danger that I cannot share,' said the undaunted, but anxious daughter. 'Let us go to Montcalm, and demand admission: he dare not deny a child the boon.'

'You would scarce find the tent of the Frenchman with the hair on your head,' said the blunt scout. 'If I had but one of the thousand boats which lie empty along that shore, it might be done. Ha! here will soon be an end of the firing, for yonder comes a fog that will turn day to night, and make an Indian arrow more dangerous than a moulded cannon. Now, if you are equal to the work, and will follow, I will make a push; for I long to get down into that camp, if it be only to scatter some Mingo dogs that I see lurking in the skirts of yonder thicket of birch.'

'We are equal,' said Cora, firmly; 'on such an errand we will follow to any danger.'

The scout turned to her with a smile of honest and cordial approbation, as he answered, –

'I would I had a thousand men, of brawny limbs and quick eyes, that feared death as little as you! I'd send them jabbering Frenchers back into their den again before the week was ended, howling like so many fettered hounds or hungry wolves. But stir!' he added, turning from her to the rest of the party, 'the fog comes rolling down so fast, we shall have but just the time to meet it on the plain, and use it as a cover. Remember, if any accident should befall me, to keep the air blowing on your left cheeks – or rather, follow the Mohicans; they'd scent their way, be it in day or be it at night.'

He then waved his hand for them to follow, and threw himself down the steep declivity, with free, but careful footsteps. Heyward assisted the sisters to descend, and in a few minutes they were all far down a mountain whose sides they had climbed with so much toil and pain.

The direction taken by Hawkeye soon brought the travellers to the level of the plain, nearly opposite to a sally-port in the western curtain of the fort, which lay, itself, at the distance of about half a mile from the point where he halted to allow Duncan to come up with his charge. In their eagerness, and favoured by the nature of the ground, they had anticipated the fog, which was rolling heavily down the lake, and it became necessary to pause, until the mists had wrapped the camp of the enemy in their fleecy mantle. The Mohicans profited by the delay to steal out of the woods, and to make a survey of surrounding objects. They were followed at a little distance by the scout, with a view to profit early by their report, and to obtain some faint knowledge for himself of the more immediate localities.

In a few moments he returned, his face reddened with vexation, while he muttered his disappointment in words of no very gentle import.

'Here has the cunning Frenchman been posting a picket directly in our path,' he said; 'red-skins and whites; and we shall be as likely to fall into their midst as to pass them in the fog!'

'Cannot we make a circuit to avoid the danger,' asked Heyward, 'and come into our path again when it is passed?'

'Who that once bends from the line of his march in a fog can tell when or how to turn to find it again! The mists of Horican are not like the curls from a peace-pipe, or the smoke which settles above a mosquito fire.'

He was yet speaking, when a crashing sound was heard, and a cannon-ball entered the thicket, striking the body of a sapling, and rebounding to the earth, its force being much expended by previous resistance. The Indians followed instantly like busy attendants on the terrible messenger, and Uncas commenced speaking earnestly, and with much action, in the Delaware tongue.

'It may be so, lad,' muttered the scout, when he had ended; 'for desperate fevers are not to be treated like a toothache. Come, then, the fog is shutting in.'

'Stop!' cried Heyward; 'first explain your expectations.'

' 'Tis soon done, and a small hope it is; but it is better than nothing. This shot that you see,' added the scout, kicking the harmless iron with his foot, 'has ploughed the 'arth in its road from the fort and we shall hunt for the furrow it has made, when all other signs may fail. No more words, but follow, or the fog may leave us in the middle of our path, a mark for both armies to shoot at.'

Heyward, perceiving that, in fact, a crisis had arrived when acts were more required than words, placed himself between the sisters, and drew them swiftly forward, keeping the dim figure of their leader in his eye. It was soon apparent that Hawkeye had not magnified the power of the fog, for before they had proceeded twenty yards, it was difficult for the different individuals of the party to distinguish each other in the vapour.

They had made their little circuit to the left, and were already inclining again towards the right, having, as Heyward thought, got over nearly half the distance to the friendly works, when his ears were saluted with the fierce summons, apparently within twenty feet of them, of, –

'Qui va là?'

'Push on!' whispered the scout, once more bending to the left.

'Push on!' repeated Heyward; when the summons was renewed by a dozen voices, each of which seemed charged with menace.

'C'est moi,' cried Duncan, dragging, rather than leading those he supported, swiftly onward.

'Bête! – qui? – moi!'

'Ami de la France.'

'Tu m'as plus l'air d'un *ennemi* de la France; arrête! Non! tirez, mes camarades!'

The order was instantly obeyed, and the fog was stirred by the explosion of fifty muskets. Happily, the aim was bad, and the bullets cut the air in a direction a little different from that taken by the fugitives; though still so nigh them, that to the unpractised ears of the two females, it appeared as if they whistled within a few inches of the organs. The outcry was renewed, and the order, not only to fire again, but to pursue, was too plainly audible. When Heyward briefly explained the meaning of the words they heard, Hawkeye halted, and spoke with quick decision and great firmness.

'Let us deliver our fire,' he said; 'they will believe it a sortie, and give way, or they will wait for reinforcements.'

The scheme was well conceived, but failed in its effect. The instant the French heard the pieces, it seemed as if the plain was alive with men, muskets rattling along its whole extent, from the shores of the lake to the farthest boundary of the woods.

'We shall draw their entire army upon us, and bring on a general assault,' said Duncan: 'lead on, my friend, for your own life, and ours.'

The scout seemed willing to comply; but, in the hurry of the moment, and in the change of position, he had lost the direction. In vain he turned either cheek towards the light air; they felt equally cool. In this dilemma, Uncas lighted on the furrow of the cannonball, where it had cut the ground in three adjacent anthills.

'Give me the range!' said Hawkeye, bending to catch a glimpse of the direction, and then instantly moving onward.

Cries, oaths, voices calling to each other, and the reports of muskets, were now quick and incessant, and, apparently, on every side of them. Suddenly, a strong glare of light flashed across the scene, the fog rolled upwards in thick wreaths, and several cannon belched across the plain, and the roar was thrown heavily back from the bellowing echoes of the mountain.

' 'Tis from the fort!' exclaimed Hawkeye, turning short on his tracks; 'and we, like stricken fools, were rushing to the woods, under the very knives of the Maquas.'

The instant their mistake was rectified, the whole party retraced the error with the utmost diligence. Duncan willingly relinquished the support of Cora to the arm of Uncas, and Cora as readily accepted the welcome assistance. Men, hot and angry in pursuit, were evidently on their footsteps, and each instant threatened their capture, if not their destruction.

'Point de quartier aux coquins!' cried an eager pursuer, who seemed to direct the operations of the enemy.

'Stand firm, and be ready, my gallant 6oths!' suddenly exclaimed a voice above them; 'wait to see the enemy; fire low, and sweep the glacis.'

'Father! Father!' exclaimed a piercing cry from out the mist; 'it is I! Alice! thy own Elsie! Spare, oh! save your daughters!'

'Hold!' shouted the former speaker, in the awful tones of parental agony, the sound reaching even to the woods, and rolling back in solemn echo. ' 'Tis she! God has restored me my children! Throw open the sally-port; to the field, 6oths, to the field; pull not a trigger, lest ye kill my lambs! Drive off these dogs of France with your steel.'

Duncan heard the grating of the rusty hinges, and darting to the spot, directed by the sound, he met a long line of dark-red warriors, passing swiftly towards the glacis. He knew them for his own battalion of the Royal Americans, and flying to their head, soon swept every trace of his pursuers from before the works.

For an instant, Cora and Alice had stood trembling and bewildered by this unexpected desertion; but, before either had leisure for speech, or even thought, an officer of gigantic frame, whose locks were bleached with years and service, but whose air of military grandeur had been rather softened than destroyed by time, rushed out of the body of the mist, and folded them to his bosom, while large, scalding tears rolled down his pale and wrinkled cheeks, and he exclaimed, in the peculiar accent of Scotland, –

'For this I thank Thee, Lord! Let danger come as it will, Thy servant is now prepared!'

Flame Tank Commander

Andrew Wilson

When Wilson had reported to the Adjutant, Barrow told him the truth about the Crocodiles; the flame thrower was terrific, but the tank itself a death trap. There followed a little catechism about British and German tanks.

'What do the Germans have most of?'

'Panthers. The Panther can slice through a Churchill like butter from a mile away.'

'And how does a Churchill get a Panther?'

'It creeps up on it. When it reaches close quarters, the gunner tries to bounce a shot off the underside of the Panther's gun mantlet. If he's lucky, it goes through a piece of thin armour above the driver's head.'

'Has anybody ever done it?'

'Yes. Davis in "C" squadron. He's back with headquarters now, trying to recover his nerve.'

'What's next on the list?'

'Tigers. The Tiger can get you from a mile and a half.'

'And how does a Churchill get a Tiger?'

'It's supposed to get within two hundred yards and put a shot through the periscope.'

'Has anyone ever done it?'
'No.'

★   ★   ★   ★

Wilson watched the three long forms of the other troop's Crocodiles move across his front and tailed in behind them.

As they reached the road, the artillery started firing. The guns were positioned all round. Their flashes lit the darkness and the noise came blasting unnervingly over the hedges. Standing with his head and shoulders above the turret flaps, he felt suddenly grateful for the encircling armour and the warmth which began to seep up from the engine.

The troops moved down the road through the wood. At the end of the wood there was a misty greyness. Infantry stood by the roadside with Bren guns, and rifles and mortar-bomb cases; presently they moved off, and Wilson knew that they had gone across the start line.

From time to time there were long bursts of machine-gun fire. Then there was a new noise – a long, low moaning and a succession of crumps, which he knew were mortars. They began to explode in small angry bursts among the Crocodiles, and he closed the flaps, pleasantly conscious that he was now under fire and that the fire could do him no harm.

They stayed there all morning and most of the afternoon. The sounds of battle came from ahead; but wherever you looked, vision was cut off by trees and hedges. The sun was very warm. Alertness gave way to torpor. It was like a Sandhurst field day, about the time when someone said: 'All right, pack up. You've just got time to get clean for dinner . . .'

Suddenly the hum in the headphones cut out. It was Barber calling them forward. They were going in to flame.

The other troop led. They ran along a path marked by tapes. Beside it was something black, swarming with flies, beneath a German camouflage cape. Further on were the first dead British.

At the start of a rise Barber was waiting with the infantry CO. He made an up and down movement with his clenched fish, which was the sign for opening the nitrogen bottles on the trailers. Wilson jumped down.

'Got where we are?' said Barber, pointing to the place on his map.

His finger moved to an orchard four hundred yards away, stayed there a moment, then moved to a field beyond it.

'There are some Spandaus there. Flame them out. The infantry will follow you. A Sherman troop's waiting to cut off the enemy at the back.'

Wilson wanted to ask: How do you spot Spandaus? But it sounded too silly.

With the other troop leader he ran back to the tanks. The crews were closing the trailer doors.

'Mount!' he shouted.

They climbed in and slammed down the hatches.

'Driver, advance. Gunner, load.'

The troops moved forward in line abreast, Wilson's on the left. As they came through a hedge, mortaring started. Everywhere infantry were crouching in half-dug foxholes, trying to protect their bodies from the bursts of the bombs.

All at once it seemed to him that he'd done this before. Perhaps it was the battle course, or the flame runs at Ashford. They went through a couple of fields. Any moment now they should see the beginning of the orchard. He reached down and put on the switch which let up the fuel to the flame gun.

Suddenly it came into view: a bank of earth, another hedge, and beyond it the orchard.

'There you are. Dead ahead, driver.'

The driver slammed down into second gear. The tank reared up for a moment, so that you couldn't see anything but the sky; then it nosed over the bank, and through the periscope he was looking down a long, empty avenue of trees.

Somewhere in this avenue, perhaps at the end, someone must be waiting to kill him. If only he knew what to look for.

The sergeant and corporal moved their tanks into the avenues on each side of him. The other troop started firing their machine-guns, and Wilson took the cue.

'Co-ax, fire!'

There was no target to indicate, just a patch of open field where the avenue ended a couple of hundred yards away. The gun broke into a roar, filling the turret with bitter fumes which made his eyes smart.

Through the periscope he saw the other troop start to flame, the yellow fire sweeping through the trees.

Better get his own flame going.

'Flame gun, fire!'

There was the well-remembered hiss, the slapping like leather. The fuel shot out, spraying the trees, paving the ground with a burning carpet. The tank ran on through it.

Quickly the details of the field became visible; not so much a field as a wilderness of scrub. A hundred yards to go. The forward edge was in range now.

'Slap it on, flame-gunner, all you've got!'

The flame leapt out with an almost unbroken roar. The driver was slowing up, uncertain where to go.

Suddenly the leader of the other troop called across the wireless:

'Hello, Item Two. Don't go into this lot. Let them have it from where you are!'

Wilson saw nothing but blazing undergrowth. Surely no one would have dared to stay there. But he kept the troop at the edge of the field, pouring in the flame, till the fire rose in one fierce, red wall.

Then the gun gave a splutter like an empty soda-water syphon. He looked round. The other troop had finished. They were already heading back through the smoking orchard.

He turned his own tanks and followed.

Beneath the trees with smouldering leaves, the British infantry were coming in with fixed bayonets.

Outside mortar range the troops stopped and formed up in column. Wilson opened his flaps and took off his headset. The other troop-leader walked over the grass towards him.

'Well,' he said. 'That went all right.'

'Sure,' said Wilson. 'But where were the enemy?'

'Don't worry about the enemy. All you've got to do on these jobs is to get in and flame.'

Wilson did a number of actions on the same sector in the next few days. The pattern was always the same. A call to pressure up; a quick conference with the infantry; a run across some fields to flame an enemy you never saw.

Little by little he gathered opinions about the Unseen Enemy from

'*Where the devil did you come from?*'

men in the troop. Some said that as soon as the Germans saw the Crocodile trailers, they pulled out; others that they lay low, hoping that the flames would go over them. But none of them had ever seen the results of a flaming. As soon as the Crocodiles re-fuelled after action, they would be sent somewhere else.

For two days there were no casualties in the tanks.

Then, on the third day, a Sherman in a field ahead was hit by an eighty-eight. Wilson heard the slam of the shot and the rip of a Spandau. From messages on the air, he knew the enemy was shooting up the crew as they tried to bale out. A moment later a great column of black smoke billowed up, and death, which had so far been remote, seemed suddenly to take a step towards him.

The last day the troop spent on that sector, they'd just finished flaming and were coming back to re-fuel, when Wilson's tank gave a sudden lurch sideways and stopped. The final drive had gone. He sent on his other two tanks and wirelessed for the squadron ARV[1] – a turretless tank with special towing equipment.

The Crocodile lay with its tail on the edge of an enemy trench that had been overrun earlier in the morning. A little down the trench you could see a pile of bodies and the bent muzzle of a Spandau. It was curious to look at those bodies, the first recognizable enemy that Wilson had seen.

His operator nudged him.

'I'll bet there's a Luger to be got off that lot.'

Lugers were a great prize; every tank man wanted to get one on his belt in place of the cumbersome British ·45 revolver.

When the mortaring stopped, they got out and walked along the trench. It smelled with a sweet and sickly smell, like a woman's cheap powder.

There were three bodies in the first heap. They'd been caught by a twenty-five pounder burst. One was a young NCO, with a hideous stomach wound. He lay half twisted on his side so that the blood had run out and congealed on his hip where he kept his pistol holster.

Wilson saw the holster first. And the operator saw that he had seen it.

'Your find, Sir.'

All at once Wilson wished he hadn't come. He felt the operator

[1] ARV, Armoured Recovery Vehicle.

274

looking at him, waiting to see him dig in his hand and withdraw the pistol from the mass of dark blood. In a moment it had become a matter of honour.

He bent down and pulled the body till it sat against the wall of the trench. Then, as deliberately as possible, he took the Luger from its holster and wiped the but on a tuft of grass.

'Thanks,' he said, looking at the operator. 'Now find yourself one.'

They went further along the trench. The dead lay everywhere. It was odd how alike they looked: all young, all with strong white teeth in mouths where the flies were gathering, all with the same golden suntan, now like a mask on the bloodless faces beneath. Wilson couldn't help comparing them with the usual British infantry platoon, with all its mixtures which were a sergeant-major's nightmare – the tall and short, bandy-legged and lanky, heavy-limbed countrymen and scruffy, swarthy Brummagem boys with eternally undone gaiters. Even in death, he found something frightening about so much fine German manhood.

The mortaring began again. Wilson and the operator turned to go back.

Suddenly there was a shout. The gunner, who'd been left to do wireless watch, was making frantic gestures from the turret. A Spandau started firing.

They ran to the tank.

'What is it?' shouted Wilson.

'They're expecting a counter-attack.'

Just then Wilson saw the front hatches open.

'Where's the driver?'

'Gone to look for loot,' said the gunner, waving his hand in the general direction of the enemy.

Wilson swore.

At that moment there was a sickening moan in the air and a salvo of mortar-bombs exploded on the trench.

The driver came running across the open, and flung himself in through his open hatch.

'What the hell did you think you were doing?'

The man panted into the microphone.

'There's Jerries in the next field,' he said.

Wilson felt a curious pricking at the back of his collar. The tank had its back to the enemy. He told the gunner to traverse the turret and put a new belt in the Besa.

Where had the infantry got to? Why was the recovery tank taking so long?

They waited. A Bren started firing. Spandaus broke in. Wilson picked a gap in a nearby hedge and directed the gun on it. Every second he expected to see coal-scuttle helmets, the flash of a panzerfaust.

Then he glanced back through the rear periscope, and there was the ARV only ten yards away, in a field of exploding mortar bombs. Its cut-throat crew jumped out with the towing bar, and the fitter-sergeant gave Wilson a big wink.

A few minutes later the ARV and the Crocodile passed back through a line of foxholes, where a platoon stood grimly behind their Bren guns. Wilson never knew what happened to them, except that the counter-attack was held. When they reached a quiet place, the fitter-sergeant came and undid the shackles.

'Thanks,' said Wilson.

'All part of the service,' said the sergeant. He was very pleased with himself.

Next day Wilson took over a replacement tank, and the squadron moved back to a place off the Tilly road.

★   ★   ★   ★

For Army and Corps headquarters the fighting in Normandy might have had a pattern, a significant development. But for the Crocodile crews it was an endless repetition of the same limited actions, varied only by the number of casualties. Among the latest was the handsome Scotsman from Eastbourne. He'd been dragged from his tank horribly burned and wasn't expected to live.

For six weeks the battle went on and on. Then all at once there was talk that the enemy was being pushed back on the Americans' front. The Americans had taken St Lô and Avranches, and the arrows on the war maps were thrusting into Brittany.

About this time, Wilson was sent back to the regiment to collect a replacement tank. Everything at headquarters was much the same except that there was no one left in Reserve. In the mess Drysdale told him that Dixie Dean and a young lieutenant called Beechey had been killed in 'B' squadron.

They had gone out after dark to bring back the crew of a knocked-out Sherman, but when they reached the tank, which was still burning, there was only the dead body of an infantryman on the ground. One of them touched the body and there was a violent explosion. The enemy had attached a charge to it.

Both the officers had been friends of Wilson's; for a long time he'd shared a room with one of them. But now he couldn't fix them in his mind any more. There deaths seemed remote, like strangers'.

After lunch he took over the tank and a crew, and a young lieutenant called Macksey who was coming up to replace Argentine. The squadron was moving during the day, and he went over to the Intelligence tent to get its new location. The sergeant picked up a signal which had just come in and decoded the map-reference.

'Would you like to see it on the map, sir?'

'No thanks,' said Wilson. 'I'll work it out on the way. We're a bit late.'

They went out on one of the 'tank tracks' which had been marked out across country. Wide and straight, they cut for miles through open fields and led the tanks swiftly from the beach area to the front.

Wilson fixed the reference on his map. Apparently the squadron had been moved to a place on the far side of Villers Bocage. It didn't surprise him. In the last few days, in an attack in which the Crocodiles took no part, Villers had been taken and the war was beginning to move. All the fields which had been packed with troops and vehicles were empty. The knocked-out Panthers near the Tilly road were relics of something which had finished. It was very quiet. You couldn't even hear gunfire any longer.

The Churchill VII did thirteen miles per hour. It was twilight as they got near Villers, and dark when they entered it. There were no buildings and no streets – just a bull-dozed canyon through a pile of rubble which stretched for half a mile, and over it all the bitter taste of dust and charred wood.

The next place was called Aunay. It was just the same, except that there were some sappers there, working their bulldozer with shaded headlamps. Beyond Aunay the road went up a steep hillside, and at the top there were some infantry with anti-tank guns. Two miles further on Wilson halted the tank at a cross-roads.

'This is it,' he said. But there was no sign of the squadron.

They pulled the tank into the yard of a deserted farm and took it in turns to mount guard.

As soon as it was light, they pushed on cautiously to a little village which the map showed. It was eerily empty. Then a figure in a cassock appeared on the road, walking towards them. Wilson got down and went to meet him, anxious that no one should hear his stumbling French. He wondered: should he say 'Father'? He wasn't a Catholic. It sounded too silly.

'Good morning, sir.'

'Good morning, my son.'

'Have you seen any English tanks?'

'No, my son. But I heard you arrive last night.' He smiled. 'The Germans also. They have just departed.'

Wilson turned the tank·round and they started back towards the British lines. He hoped the gunners' identification charts had been brought up to date. In case they hadn't, he reversed the turret and hung out the red-white-and-blue recognition flag.

After they had gone a mile they met the first infantry advancing in open order astride the road. A bewildered captain held up a hand to stop them.

'Where the devil have you come from?'

Wilson told him.

The captain beckoned to his wireless operator and spoke with his battalion headquarters.

'You're luckier than you think,' he said, when he'd finished. 'You've just missed being at the wrong end of a divisional artillery shoot.'

Next day, still waiting for orders, they were harboured in a field beside the road. The co-driver was cooking the midday meal over the petrol stove.

'What's it today – stew again?' said Wilson.

The co-driver grinned, making a great mystery. 'Wait and see,' he said.

At last the meal was ready. The co-driver wiped out the mess-tin with a swab of cotton-waste from his pocket and filled them with small lumps of meat, swimming in a rich white sauce. Everyone took a spoonful.

'Like it?'

It was delicious. It turned out to be German tinned rabbit.

In the afternoon, the squadron was called to clear out a battalion of paratroopers who were caught in the trap and refused to surrender. Duffy sent Wilson and Grundy ahead in the scout car to meet the infantry. The squadron followed with its curious additions to the transport echelon.

On the way there were many dead cows: the infantry were shooting up the inflated carcasses with Sten-guns, so that they burst and allowed the nauseous gasses to escape. Suddenly Wilson felt sick, but it wasn't an ordinary sickness. He felt a violent twisting in his guts. Presently he stopped the car and vomited.

At the rendezvous an infantry captain was waiting. He was distressingly cheerful. When they went forward and started to discuss the ground, Wilson had to break off and disappear behind a hedge. He came back trembling, with a curious chill all over him.

'Are you all right?' said the captain.

'It's nothing,' said Wilson. But as the captain went on to explain the plan of attack, the pains gripped his stomach more and more fiercely, and to look at the map made him giddy.

'Zero seventeen-hundred hours,' said the captain.

They went back to the road and waited for the squadron. Wilson could hardly stand now. When the squadron arrived, Grundy passed on the plan to Duffy and they mounted their tanks.

'Anything wrong, sir?' said the operator.

Wilson shook his head, but he had to keep pressing his stomach against the edge of the cupola to deaden the pain. The next thing he knew was that the column had stopped and he was being helped down to the ground.

'Good God,' said the co-driver. 'Have I poisoned you, sir?'

'Pick you up on the way back,' said the troop sergeant.

The tanks drove off. He was lying in the middle of a field. The enemy had started to mortar, and he was being sick again. A little way off he could see the spoil where someone had dug a slit trench.

Several times he tried to crawl towards it, but the pains in his stomach held him motionless.

For a long time he lay with his face to the ground, with the fumes from the exploding mortar bombs drifting all around him. Then the squadron was coming back.

'Pick him up,' said someone. It was the troop corporal.

'Where's the sergeant?'

'Went on a mine, sir. The tank brewed up but they all baled out.'

Everything faded. Then he was being taken into an aid post and someone was putting pills into his mouth.

'Dysentery,' said an MO.

Escape from Campo 12

Brigadier James Hargest

New Zealander Brigadier James Hargest was the highest ranking officer to escape during the war.

Captured in Egypt in 1941, he was finally transferred to Campo 12, near Florence, Italy.

After several unsuccessful escape attempts, the Brigadier and five others mined a tunnel at the bottom of a lift shaft . . .

As we intended going out through the tunnel entrance in heavy rain, we could expect copious mud and we all provided ourselves with overdress. I had an out-sized pair of pyjamas to pull over my clothes, including the raincoat, and a large handkerchief to tie over my cap to keep it clean. We had soft outer material to keep our boots clean and to reduce the noise. Some sewed up large felt overshoes; I slipped two felt soles under my boots and held them in place by two pairs of huge socks which protected my trouser-legs as well. We each had sufficient money and a map, and most of us had compasses.

We also had our identity cards. Over these, G-P[1], our official artist and map-maker, rose to superb heights from which the fact clearly emerged that if he had not chosen to be a respectable major-general he might have had a successful career as a forger. Sketching and painting being his hobbies he was allowed a fairly good assortment of brushes, fine pens, paper, inks and colours. After we had obtained possession of a real Italian identity card he did not seem to have much trouble in

[1] Gambier Parry.

matching the paper and copying the crest, stamp-markings, printed lines, and the signature of the issuing official. He spent hours mixing inks to get exact shades, and improvising stamps. Somehow he managed to procure special glasses which made the fine work possible.

We thought photographs would stump him; not a bit of it. For his weekly gramophone recitals it was necessary to buy records, and by a queer chance he discovered that the artists' photographs in the catalogues were the exact size of, and printed on similar paper to, those on identity cards. He sent for further catalogues and set up a small committee to choose likenesses. The results could not have been better – all six of us seemed to have more or less of a counterpart in German or Italian opera. They found me a celebrated German tenor, and G-P gave him my moustache more painlessly than I cultivated his right-hand hair-parting.

I called myself Angelo Pasco, after my old friend the fish-merchant in my native town of Invercargill; there was no chance of my forgetting it, and it was easy to pronounce. I came from Bologna, and you could see that I was a bricklayer if you looked inside my case and saw trowel and plumbline lying on top.

To provide six identity cards was a long and arduous task. Before they were all ready even G-P's happy disposition showed signs of strain; but they were six perfect replicas – it was impossible for the lay eye to tell the counterfeit from the original.

Miles had acquired a useful tool – a pair of pliers. One day he came to me with the news that a workman had left his pliers on the ground a little distance from his job. By that time we were no mean snappers-up of unconsidered trifles. Miles carelessly threw an old gardening sack over them and after the man departed we hurried them into hiding.

The next matter of importance, and it was very important, was the 1.30 a.m. check. Every night the officer on duty accompanied by a sergeant, came round our rooms and saw us all in bed, the servants as well. We could not expect to leave before nine o'clock, which would only give us four and a half hours' start. On the other hand, if we could evade this check we would not be missed until eleven in the morning at the earliest. We decided to use dummies. As a preliminary, Neame protested against the practice of the inspecting officers of coming right into our rooms; he insisted on their staying in the doorway and using their torches from there. After weeks of squabbling we got them used to this. Then as spring approached we applied for protection against the mosquitoes, and nets were put up, great canopies completely covering each bed and reducing the rays of the torches to impotence.

Then we concentrated on our dummies. They were little masterpieces – all of them. Each had to be different and required different materials. Boyd was grey-haired, O'Connor and Combe fair, I dark and Miles and Carton bald. We persevered to such an extent that we produced tolerably good likenesses. I let my hair grow, and when Howes cut it we stuck it on a handkerchief saturated with glue, not overlooking my bare spot on top. We fixed the handkerchief over a stuffed balaclava and sewed on an ear and the job was complete. Sometimes when we made up the bed it was difficult to believe that I was not really in it. Each week we had a small exhibition of dummies in bed, everyone interested being invited to throw in suggestions.

The last piece of rock was removed early in March. We were ready. All that was necessary was the suitable night, and we settled down to a period of waiting.

★   ★   ★   ★

On Sunday, 28 March, it rained hard. As the day advanced we made ready. There was, of course, a certain amount of tension, and when at church service we found that G-P had included the hymn 'Through the night of doubt and sorrow onwards goes the pilgim band,' we were all a little moved. Right up till seven-thirty we thought there were great possibilities; but with night the rain eased and Neame cancelled preparations. Needless to say there were divergent opinions; but we had agreed to abide by his decision, and there was never any question of the wisdom of this.

Monday morning was fine; but as the day advanced clouds came over and by six o'clock it was raining hard, a silent rain, but very close to what we needed. I was on my bed resting about 7.30 p.m. when Neame looked in and said: 'I think you had better dress, Jim; it looks as though tonight will be a good one.'

At once we got to work and in a very few minutes I was ready. Ranfurly had reserved some sandwiches and hard-boiled eggs for each of us, and at the last I opened a bottle of rum which Stirling and I had kept for this occasion for over a year. I filled six two- or three-ounce medicine bottles, one for each man. There was also room for a small bottle of wine in my case.

Then came the hardest moment of the whole adventure: saying goodbye to Howes. For three years we had been together, in England and in the east. We had fought together; on all my leaves, however short, I had taken him. In the Greek and Cretan campaigns he had never left me for one moment, no matter how weary he was, and in our last fight he had shared my slit trench. He was a big, quiet young fellow who inspired confidence; in Vincigliata every officer and man liked and respected him. Of course he wanted to come with me; I would have given much to take him; but the risks were great and the chances of success so small that I did not feel I had a right to endanger him. So we said goodbye. War is hard in its goodbyes.

Dinner was a quarter of an hour earlier that night and we sat down all together for the last time, some of the boys mounting guard to prevent surprise. While we were dining Neame and Ranfurly passed through the hole into the chapel, Neame to see that all was right in the tunnel, Ranfurly to pull down the timbering at the far end and cut away the remaining earth up to the surface. He took the long knife and made a perfect job.

We were all waiting rather tensely, trying to conceal it beneath the veneer of small talk, when the last alarm came through from Vaughan's room: 'Officer coming.' We six escapees took up our cases and fled upstairs through the living-rooms. It was only an NCO making his round of the battlements. We trooped back to the dining-room. Things ran smoothly from then onwards. We said our goodbyes lightheartedly and one by one filed into the lift-landing and slid for the last time through the panel into the chapel porch. I was fourth man and when I got in the first three had disappeared down the shaft. Ranfurly was sitting, naked except for a pair of shorts, at the head of the shaft, and when I went to shake hands he said: 'For heaven's sake don't touch me, I'm just one greasy slimy mess from head to foot.' Taking out those last five inches of mud had been a dirty business.

I found Neame sitting in the by-pass. He reported that all was well. He had a shaded light there, and I could see Boyd's legs disappearing up the ladder. Each of us had a special task once we appeared on the surface. John Combe went first carrying his suitcase, a stout rope and a blanket. The blanket he spread on the ground to act as a carpet to avoid obvious marks a sentry could see when daylight came. The rope was to be hitched round a post on the top of a stone wall just down the hillside from the battlements. It was our last obstacle, five feet high on the uphill side and about ten feet on the downhill or road side. The rope was to steady us; we could hang on to it while descending. A huge iron gate about twelve feet high opened on to the road. As we had never seen it used in all the time we had been there we had no reason to hope that it might not be locked. Once over, John was to help Miles, who was then to be his assistant on the road. Miles, second man up, was to take a measured three-ply board reinforced for strengthening, to be used as a lid for the hole when the last man was out. Boyd was next and had just his kit. He was to get on to the road and act as scout while the rest came over.

I was number four and in addition to my suitcase had the hooked rope we always used for haulage and a sandbag full of pine needles and soil. I pushed the case up ahead of me, and dragged the sandbag up with my free hand – not easy in that confined space with mud oozing out from every side. When I emerged I had a shock. Instead of the darkness we had expected a couple of concealed lamps made it almost as light as day. Had an Italian been on that side he must have seen each of us as we came up. As it happened, the light certainly made our exit easy.

It was a tremendous experience. Not even the need for action could suppress the wave of exaltation that swept over me. Here was the successful achievement of a year of planning and seven months of toil. I remember thinking, with a new kind of awareness, that whatever the immediate future held, at this moment I was alive and free. I have never been able to recapture in retrospect the fullness of that moment.

I put down my case and sandbag and passed the rope back into the shaft, hook downwards. A tug, and I began hauling up. Carton's large pack appeared. I unhooked it and fished again, this time for O'Connor's pack. All this was according to plan and I had hauled in and was waiting for a head and shoulders to appear when a whisper came up: 'The rope.' A bit surprised, I tried again; up came two walking sticks – I hadn't heard about them. De Wiart came surprisingly easily. As he surfaced I placed his pack on the stump of his left arm and off he went. O'Connor, following, disappeared into the darkness. I threw the carpet back down the shaft and clamped the board over the hole. It fitted perfectly and stood my weight as I pressed it down. I emptied my bag of pine needles on it and smoothed the surface. I even found a few stones and some chickweed to give it a natural appearance. The last job was to level off any remaining footmarks. Then, taking up my case, rope and empty sack, I decamped. It was exactly half-past nine.

They were all waiting at the foot of the little wall. We had had unexpected good luck, as the door to the road was not locked, and we passed through. I gave my rope to Miles, who cached it along with the other one in a place already chosen, not too conspicuous, yet not too well hidden. When our flight was discovered we hoped that they would be found and give the impression that we had come over the top. We wanted to keep the secret of the tunnel as long as possible. Once through the door we found sufficient shadows to make the going safer. We began crossing the road. John, finding the door difficult to close, slammed it; the noise seemed to shatter our freedom.

We filed down through the wet woods in complete darkness, then across a fence into an olive grove. Thick brambles made the terraces difficult to negotiate; but we got down somehow without noise. Half-way down to the deep valley we were making for we stopped and hid our overclothes and my sandbag in some bushes. Six hundred yards lower down a roadway ran at right angles to our path. Here we said goodbye to O'Connor and de Wiart, who were using this as a starting-point for their long walk. We shook hands, and the darkness swallowed them up.

The rain had stopped, and we had no trouble in seeing our way downhill to a bridge above a mill, where we came on a tarred road. We threw our overshoes into the swollen stream. I felt terribly dirty, and seemed to be muddy all over, so I soused my suitcase in the running water and cleaned off the worst of it. Then we set off on our six-mile tramp. The road offered no obstacles, we knew it so well from observation, and we tramped along it like a police squad in pairs, our heavy boots making a tremendous noise. It was the first time in many months we had walked on a road unaccompanied by a guard, although I don't think we gave much thought to that at the time.

Once we got on to the lower ground nearer the city we began to meet people carrying torches or on lighted bicycles. We were a little tense at first; but no one took any notice of us and we soon became accustomed to them. We were dressed in very heavy clothes because we felt certain that if we succeeded in reaching the mountains near the frontier we would find snow and might have to sleep out in it. In addition we wore our greatcoats and before long we felt the heat and perspired like oxen. For some reason Miles and Boyd, who were leading, cracked on a very fast pace that seemed unnecessary and even dangerous. I caught them up and suggested slowing down as we had three hours from the start in which to do six miles, and it would be preferable not to arrive too early and too hot. They were afraid that we might miss our route, and wanted some time in hand. As it was, we arrived at 11.35 p.m. After a little careful reconnaissance, we went boldly into the huge hall of the station.

The ticket gate was at the far end, guarded by carabinieri and railway officials. We did not stay together but moved about separately to get the lie of the land. I wanted to see whether I drew any special attention, so took up a position close to some soldiers in the middle of the great hall; but neither they nor anyone else looked at me or my dirty boots, so I gained fresh confidence and ceased to be afraid of being detected through my dress.

We drifted outside and met in the shadow, Boyd going off to buy three third-class return tickets to Milan. In a few moments he returned rather perturbed. In response to his request the ticket clerk had asked a question or told him something, and Boyd had fled. We thought it could be nothing more serious than instructions about changing at Bologna, so Miles went over and bought the tickets without further trouble. Combe who was better dressed travelled second-class and bought his own ticket. The waiting was trying. To relieve the monotony we walked about the streets in pairs, coming back at intervals to see if there was any alarm. At about twelve-thirty we sauntered through the gates. It was quite simple. Adopting the slowish gait of an elderly workman I walked up and, looking each official in the eye as I reached him, passed safely through.

Then began a long wait. The train did not come in until 1.45 a.m. It was to have left at 12.35 a.m. Contrary to report, Fascism could not even run the trains punctually for us. All that time we walked about the

287

No one took any notice of us and we soon became accustomed to them.

cold, wet platform, afraid to sit down in case we sat on something forbidden – there were no regular seats. When the train arrived it was crowded to the doors, and the chances of getting aboard seemed remote. The seething crowd on the platforms surged towards the doors in solid masses, preventing anyone from alighting. I saw a new technique in train-boarding. Men and women ranged themselves along the platform opposite the compartment windows; a man would heave his lady up until she got a hand-hold which enabled her to go through the window. Then she reached down and hauled in the baggage which the man held up to her, afterwards taking his arms and pulling him up and in. We were well separated by this time and I had no one to haul me in. I determined that if anyone was left behind it wasn't going to be me, and tucking my bag safely under my arm I charged in. I don't know how I managed it, but eventually I got one foot on the step and the crowd behind did the rest, depositing me well into the corridor with Boyd not far behind. All this was done to the accompaniment of shouts, curses, and fierce arguments, in none of which I took part; but I was on board. I did not ask for more.

The Italians are wonderful people. At one moment they can hurl piercing diatribes at each other; at the next they are smiling and all politeness. In five minutes they were laughing and teasing and making room for each other like happy children. My only discomfort was due to the fact that the man next to me, not six inches from my face, was the carabiniere in charge of the carriage. After a while he began to talk to me. I ignored him, but he spoke again. I bent over and said in a whisper such as I've often heard deaf people use: 'I'm sorry, but I am very deaf.' This was in Italian and probably very bad Italian, though I had practised hard; but it was effective and he left me alone.

The train was fast and we did the forty-five miles to Bologna in an hour, arriving at 3 a.m. The slow train to Milan was due to leave precisely at that time, but actually it was twenty minutes past five before we got away. Another weary wait on a cold platform without any seats. Our efforts to find a refreshment buffet were fruitless. Once when the others were seeking food and I was watching the luggage, a policeman came up and asked me if all the bags were mine. I said they were and he walked off. Several people asked me about platforms or trains, but my chief anxiety was the delay. It was growing lighter and our features would become easier to distinguish. We had hoped to be in Milan by six o'clock and at Como by eight; we seemed to be stuck here indefinitely.

When the train did come in the scrimmage was fiercer than at Florence. By this time I had learnt from experience and, putting my head down, drove in, using my elbows on all who came alongside. By this method I got on to the step and mounted to the top; but then disaster overtook me. Someone clutched at my poor little suitcase and tore it out of my hand, leaving me only the handle. I had to make a quick decision – to retrieve it or leave it. I decided on the former, and kicking my legs clear I dropped straight down on the crowd struggling to mount the high steps. The cursing reached a high standard; but I found my bag and butting ahead with it climbed up again. This time I was further along the corridor. I could see Miles's tall figure at the other end and Boyd about six feet behind me. We ignored each other.

I repaired the handle of my bag with a boot-lace, and standing with my back to the outside wall held it behind my neck so that it would not be trampled on. My legs straddled a pile of suitcases on the floor. As soon as we started a little elderly man nearby spoke to me and threatened to become chatty. I looked straight at him with what I thought was a little smile, but was probably more like a foolish grin to him, and said nothing. When he persisted I repeated my formula about being deaf.

He turned away to find another audience, whom he amused by making jokes at my expense, all of which, of course, I had to ignore. He was a mean little man and I would have loved to wring his neck. The train stopped at every station and the journey seemed endless. I had memorized all the larger stations so that in the event of a hasty detrainment I would know where we were in relation to other places and to the frontier. I ticked them off as we passed: Modena, Parma, Piacenza, Lodi – they came and went horribly slowly. From the beginning I had prayed that if we had to run for it we would at least be over the river Po; at last we crossed it. The heavy rain beat drearily across the Lombardy plain. Every stream was in spate, in every hollow lakes had formed; the Po itself was wide and muddy.

In the corridor there was an air of jollity and no one seemed to resent the overcrowding; on the contrary, they enjoyed it. Near the door was a ladies' toilet and as we progressed the women in the carriage kept coming down to it, squeezing past everyone with the greatest difficulty. One cheery old fellow installed himself as doorkeeper and as one woman came out he would call: 'One more!' If a lady overstayed a period he thought reasonable he would knock on the door and urge her to hurry. Everyone enjoyed him. As each woman passed me at my corner I had to crouch to make room and this brought my weight down on the cases below me. After a while I saw my troublesome old man look down intently. He struck a match to see better and held it near by feet. I looked down and a dreadful sight met my gaze. My weight had split the two or three cheap cases from top to bottom and out of the cracks appeared ladies' lingerie, gloves, etc.; worst of all, there was a sickly red mess on the floor that was either red wine mixed with mud or strawberry jam – the match went out before I could decide. My position would have been bad if the old man or anyone nearby had been the owner and involved me in an argument of which the results could only have been disastrous. I prayed hard. The old man looked at me and winked. Obviously the bags weren't his. I determined to be well out of the carriage by the time the real owner could get to them. .

At Lodi, the last stop before Milan, a nice-looking young woman and her husband got in – I don't quite know how they did it. Anyway, she was full of personality and in a very few moments she was the centre of much chattering. She seemed to be re-telling some joke the old man was making at the expense of Lodi, and tried to draw me in to the talk. I smiled back weakly, and the old man came to my assistance:

'It's no use talking to him. He's deaf. Anyway, I think he's a German!'

Blindfold to Memmert

Erskine Childers

It is the turn of the century. Davies, a young English yachtsman, and his friend Carruthers are exploring the East German coast, when they become involved in 'The Riddle of the Sands'.

What dark secret lies hidden amidst the treacherous shoals and sandbanks of the Frisian Islands? Is the German Navy preparing for war? Are they in fact planning an invasion of Britain?

One particular night, Davies and Carruthers and their tiny vessel 'Dulcibella' are fogbound just outside Norderney harbour. The blinding sea-mist prevents the Englishmen from sailing, but what is worse; it stops them from spying on their German protagonists who are meeting at Memmert that very evening.

Their situation seems hopeless until Carruthers (the storyteller) jokingly remarks . . .

'*Why not go to Memmert?*'

'To Memmert?' said Davies slowly; 'by Jove, that's an idea!'

'Good heavens, man! I was joking. Why, it's ten mortal miles.'

'More,' said Davies absently. 'It's not so much the distance – what's the time? Ten-fifteen: quarter ebb – What am I talking about? We made our plans last night.'

But seeing him, to my amazement, serious, I was stung by the splendour of the idea I had awakened. Confidence in his skill was second nature to me. I swept straight on to the logic of the thing, the greatness, the completeness of the opportunity, if by a miracle it could

292

be seized and used. Something was going on at Memmert today: our men had gone there; here were we, ten miles away, in a smothering, blinding fog. It was known we were here – Dollman and Grimm knew it; the crew of the *Medusa* knew it; the crew of the *Kormoran* knew it; the man on the pier, whether he cared or not, knew it. But none of them knew Davies as I knew him. Would anyone dream for an instant – ?

'Stop a second,' said Davies, 'give me two minutes.' He whipped out the German chart. 'Where exactly should we go?' ('Exactly!' the word tickled me hugely.)

'To the depot, of course; it's our only chance.'

'Listen then; there are two routes: the outside one, by the open sea, right round Juist, and doubling south – the simplest, but the longest; the depot's at the south point of Memmert, and Memmert's nearly two miles long.'

'How far would that way be?'

'Sixteen miles good. And we should have to row in a breaking swell most of the way, close to land.'

'Out of the question; it's too public too, if it clears. The steamer went that way and will come back that way. We must go inside over the sands. Am I dreaming, though? Can you possibly find the way?'

'I shouldn't wonder. But I don't believe you see the hitch. It's the *time* and the falling tide. High water was about 8.15: it's now 10.15, and all those sands are drying off. We must cross the See-Gat and strike that boomed channel, the Memmert Balje, strike it, freeze on to it – can't cut off an inch – and pass that "watershed" you see there before it's too late. It's an infernally bad one, I can see. Not even a dinghy will cross it for an hour each side of low water.'

'Well, how far is the "watershed"?'

'Good Lord! What are we talking for? Change, man, change! Talk while we're changing.' (He began flinging off his shore-clothes, and I did the same.) 'It's at least five miles to the end of it, six, allowing for bends; hour and a half hard pulling; two allowing for checks. Are you fit? You'll have to pull the most. Then there are six or seven more miles – easier ones. And then – What are we to do when we get there?'

'Leave that to me,' I said. 'You get me there.'

'Supposing it clears?'

'After we get there? Bad; but we must risk that. If it clears on the way there it doesn't matter by this route; we shall be miles from land.'

'What about getting back?'

'We shall have a rising tide, anyway. If the fog lasts – can you manage in fog *and* dark?'

'The dark makes it no more difficult, if we've a light to see the compass and chart by. You trim the binnacle-lamp – no, the riding-light. Now give me the scissors, and don't speak a word for ten minutes. Meanwhile, think it out and load the dinghy – (by Jove! though, don't make a sound) – some grub and whisky, the boat-compass, lead, riding-light, matches, *small* boathook, grapnel and line.'

'Foghorn?'

'Yes, and the whistle too.'

'A gun?'

'What for?'

'We're after ducks.'

'All right. And muffled the rowlocks with cotton-waste.'

I left Davies absorbed in the charts, and softly went about my own functions. In ten minutes he was on the ladder, beckoning.

'I've done,' he whispered. 'Now *shall* we go?'

'I've thought it out. Yes,' I answered.

This was only roughly true, for I could not have stated in words all the pros and cons that I had balanced. It was an impulse that drove me forward; but an impulse founded on reason, with just a tinge, perhaps, of superstition; for the quest had begun in a fog and might fitly end in one.

It was twenty-five minutes to eleven when we noiselessly pushed off. 'Let her drift,' whispered Davies, 'the ebb'll carry her past the pier.'

We slid by the *Dulcibella*, and she disappeared. Then we sat without speech or movement for about five minutes, while the gurgle of tide through piles approached and passed. The dinghy appeared to be motionless, just as a balloon in the clouds may appear to its occupants to be motionless, though urged by a current of air. In reality we were driving out of the Riff-Gat into the See-Gat. The dinghy swayed to a light swell.

'Now pull,' said Davies, under his breath; 'keep it long and steady, above all, steady – both arms with equal force.'

I was on the bow-thwart; he *vis-à-vis* to me on the stern seat, his left hand behind him on the tiller, his right forefinger on a small square of paper which lay on his knees; this was a section cut out from the big German chart, a section of Juist Memmert and Norderney. On the midship-thwart between us lay the compass and a watch. Between these three objects – compass, watch, and chart – his eyes darted constantly, never looking up or out, save occasionally for a sharp glance over the side at the flying bubbles, to see that I was sustaining a regular speed. My duty was to be his automaton, the human equivalent of a marine engine whose revolutions can be counted and used as data by the navigator. My arms must be regular as twin pistons; the energy that drove them as controllable as steam. It was a hard ideal to reach, for the complex mortal tends to rely on all the senses God has given him, so unfitting himself for mechanical exactitude when a sense (eyesight, in my case) fails him. At first it was constantly 'left' or 'right' from Davies, accompanied by a bubbling from the rudder.

'This won't do, too much helm,' said Davies, without looking up. 'Keep your stroke, but listen to me. Can you see the compass card?'

'When I come forward.'

'Take your time, and don't get flurried, but each time you come forward have a good look at it. The course is sou'-west half-west. You take the opposite, north-east half-east, and keep her *stern* on that. It'll be rough, but it'll save some helm, and give me a hand free if I want it.'

I did as he said, not without effort, and our progress gradually became smoother, till he had no need to speak at all. The only sound now was one like the gentle simmer of a saucepan away to port – the lisp of surf I knew it to be – and the muffled grunt of the rowlocks. I broke the silence once to say, 'It's very shallow.' I had touched sand with my right scull.

'Don't talk,' said Davies.

About half an hour passed, and then he added sounding to his other occupations. 'Plump' went the lead at regular intervals, and he steered with his hip while pulling in the line. Very little of it went out at first, then less still. Again I struck bottom, and glancing aside saw weeds. Suddenly he got a deep cast, and the dinghy, freed from the slight drag which shallow water always inflicts on a small boat, leapt buoyantly forward. At the same time, I knew by boils on the smooth surface that we were in a strong tideway.

'The Buse Tief,' muttered Davies. 'Row hard now, and steady as a clock.'

For a hundred yards or more I bent to my sculls and made her fly. Davies was getting six-fathom casts, till, just as suddenly as it had deepened, the water shoaled – ten feet, six, three, one – the dinghy grounded.

'Good!' said Davies. 'Back her off! Pull your right only.' The dinghy spun round with her bow to NNW. 'Both arms together! Don't you worry about the compass now; just pull, and listen for orders. There's a tricky bit coming.'

He put aside the chart, kicked the lead under the seat, and, kneeling on the dripping coils of line, sounded continuously with the butt-end of the boathook, a stumpy little implement, notched at intervals of a foot, and often before used for the same purpose. All at once I was aware that a check had come, for the dinghy swerved and doubled like a hound ranging after scent.

'Stop her,' he said suddenly, 'and throw out the grapnel.'

I obeyed and we brought up, swinging to a slight current, whose direction Davies verified by the compass. Then for half a minute he gave himself up to concentrated thought. What struck me most about him was that he never for a moment strained his eyes through the fog; a useless exercise (for five yards or so was the radius of our vision) which, however, I could not help indulging in, while I rested. He made up his mind, and we were off again, straight and swift as an arrow this time, and in water deeper than the boathook. I could see by his face that he was taking some bold expedient whose issue hung in the balance . . . Again we touched mud, and the artist's joy of achievement shone in his eyes. Backing away, we headed west, and for the first time he began to gaze into the fog.

'There's one!' he snapped at last. 'Easy all!'

A boom, one of the usual upright saplings, glided out of the mist. He caught hold of it and we brought up.

'Rest for three minutes now,' he said. 'We're in fairly good time.'

It was 11.10. I ate some biscuits and took a nip of whisky while Davies prepared for the next stage.

We had reached the eastern outlet of Memmert Balje, the channel which runs east and west behind Juist Island, direct to the south point of Memmert. How we had reached it is hard to explain, but with the aid of the chart we had at the time, and with a certain amount of luck, we made it. I add this brief explanation, that Davies's method had been to cross the channel called the Buse Tief, and strike the other side of it at a point well *south* of the outlet of the Memmert Balje (in view of the northward set of the ebb-tide), and then to drop back north and feel his way to the outlet. The check was caused by a deep indentation in the Itzendorf Flat; a *cul-de-sac*, with a wide mouth, which Davies was very near mistaking for the Balje itself. We had no time to skirt dents so deep as that; hence the dash across its mouth with the chance of missing the upper lip altogether, and of either being carried out to sea or straying fruitlessly along the edge.

The next three miles were the most critical of all. They included the 'watershed', whose length and depth were doubtful; they included, too, the crux of the whole passage, a spot where the channel forks, our own branch continuing west, and another branch diverging from it north-westward. We must row against time, and yet we must negotiate that crux. Add to this that the current was against us till the watershed was crossed; that the tide was just at its most baffling stage, too low to allow us to risk short cuts, and too high to give definition to the banks of the channel; and that the compass was no aid whatever for the minor bends.

'Time's up,' said Davies, and on we went.

I was hugging the comfortable thought that we should now have booms on our starboard for the whole distance; on our starboard, I say, for experience had taught us that all channels running parallel with the coast and islands were uniformly boomed on the northern side. Anyone less confident than Davies would have succumbed to the temptation of slavishly relying on these marks, creeping from one to the other, and wasting precious time. But Davies knew our friend the 'boom' and his eccentricities too well; and preferred to trust to his sense of touch, which no fog in the world could impair. If we happened to sight one, well and good, we should know which side of the channel we were on. But even this advantage he deliberately sacrificed after a short distance, for he crossed over to the *south* or unboomed side and steered and sounded along it, using the Itzendorf Flat as his handrail, so to speak. He was compelled to do this, he told me afterwards, in view of the crux, where the converging lines of booms would have involved us in total confusion. Our branch was the southern one, and it followed that we must use the southern bank, and defer obtaining any help from booms until sure we were past that critical spot.

For an hour we were at the extreme strain, I of physical exertion, he of mental. I could not get into a steady swing, for little checks were constant. My right scull was for ever skidding on mud or weeds, and the backward suck of shoal water clogged our progress. Once we were both of us out in the slime tugging at the dinghy's sides: then in again, blundering on. I found the fog bemusing, lost all idea of time and space, and felt like a senseless marionette kicking and jerking to a mad music without tune or time. The misty form of Davies as he sat with his right arm swinging rhythmically forward and back, was a clockwork figure as mad as myself, but instructive in his madness. Then the boathook he wielded with a circular sweep began to take grotesque shapes in my heated fancy: now it was the antenna of a groping insect, now the crank of a cripple's self-propelled perambulator, now the alpenstock of a lunatic mountaineer, who sits in his chair and climbs and climbs to some phantom 'watershed'. At the back of such mind as was left me lodged two insistent thoughts: 'we must hurry on', 'we are going wrong'. As to the latter, take a link-boy through a London fog and you will experience the same thing: he always goes the way you think is wrong. 'We're rowing *back*!' I remember shouting to Davies once, having become aware that it was now my left scull which splashed against obstructions. 'Rubbish,' said Davies, 'I've crossed over'; and I relapsed.

By degrees I returned to sanity, thanks to improving conditions. It is an ill wind that blows nobody good, and the state of the tide, though it threatened us with total failure, had the compensating advantage that the lower it fell the more constricted and defined became our channel; till the time came when the compass and boathook were alike unnecessary, because our handrail, the muddy brink of the channel, was visible to the eye, close to us; on our right hand always now, for

'Let her drift, the ebb'll carry her past the pier.'

the crux was far behind, and the northern side was now our guide. All that remained was to press on with might and main ere the bed of the creek dried.

What a race it was! Homeric, in effect; a struggle of men with gods, for what were the gods but forces of nature personified? If the God of the Falling Tide did not figure in the Olympian circle he is none the less a mighty divinity. Davies left his post, and rowed stroke. Under our united efforts the dinghy advanced in strenuous leaps, hurling minature rollers on the bank beside us. My palms, seasoned as they were, were smarting with watery blisters. The pace was too hot for my strength and breath.

'I must have a rest,' I gasped.

'Well, I think we're over it,' said Davies.

We stopped the dinghy dead, and he stabbed over side with the boathook. It passed gently astern of us, and even my bewildered brain took in the meaning of that.

'Three feet and the current with us. *Well* over it,' he said. 'I'll paddle on while you rest and feed.'

It was a few minutes past one and we still, as he calculated, had eight miles before us, allowing for bends.

'But it's a mere question of muscle,' he said.

I took his word for it, and munched at tongue and biscuits. As for muscle, we were both in hard condition. He was fresh, and what distress I felt was mainly due to spasmodic exertion culminating in that desperate spurt. As for the fog, it had more than once shown a faint tendency to lift, grown thinner and more luminous, in the manner of fogs, always to settle down again, heavy as a quilt.

Note the spot marked 'second rest' (approximately correct, Davies says) and the course of the channel from that point westward. You will see it broadening and deepening to the dimension of a great river, and finally merging in the estuary of the Ems. Note, too, that its northern boundary, the edge of the now uncovered Nordland Sand, leads, with one interruption (marked A), direct to Memmert, and is boomed throughout. You will then understand why Davies made so light of the rest of his problem. Compared with the feats he had performed, it was child's play, for he always had that visible margin to keep touch with if he chose, or to return to in case of doubt. As a matter of fact – observe our dotted line – he made two daring departures from it, the first purely to save time, the second partly to save time and partly to avoid the very awkward spot marked A, where a creek with booms and a little delta of its own interrupts the even bank. During the first of these departures, the shortest but most brilliant, he let me do the rowing, and devoted himself to the niceties of the course; during the second, and through both the intermediate stages, he rowed himself, with occasional pauses to inspect the chart. We fell into a long, measured stroke, and covered the miles rapidly, scarcely exchanging a single word till, at the end of a long pull through vacancy, Davies said suddenly:

'Now where are we to land?'

A sandbank was looming over us crowned by a lonely boom.

'Where are we?'

'A quarter of a mile from Memmert.'

'What time is it?'

'Nearly three.' . . .

Dawn Patrol

Arthur Gold Lee

'Quarter to four, sir. You're on patrol in half an hour. And it's a fine morning.'

The orderly batman, himself called by the night guard five minutes earlier, shakes me gently, and speaks in a murmur so as not to disturb the other pilots asleep in the hut.

I tumble from my bed and sit on it, yawning, and feeling more than sluggish after a generous intake of alcohol the evening before. The batman treads silently in his rubber-soled shoes to the opposite corner and stirs out Courtneidge, who is also on the dawn patrol. Satisfied that we are both well awake, he then steals out, carefully closing the door behind him, and creeps on to his next port of call. No clumsy footsteps, no early-morning cheerfulness, no whistling, for everyone else is asleep, and he knows they prefer to stay that way.

It is practically dark, and I can scarcely see what I am doing, but don't like to switch on my torch for fear of waking the two lucky types snoring peacefully in their corners. I dress dazedly, fumbling for my clothes, trying to make no noise. Where the hell did I put my second sweater, my long woolly scarf? Damn, I nearly knocked the blasted table over! Who the devil's moved my helmet and gloves? And so on. Whispered curses coming from the dimness of

Courtneidge's corner proclaim that he's having his troubles too. But in three minutes we are dressed. No time for brushing teeth, no time even for washing, except to wipe my face with a damp sponge. Courtneidge comes across, we leave the hut together. I close the door noiselessly behind me – not that I am excessively considerate by nature, but I am well aware that if I don't play fair, the two sleepers, when their turn for the dawn job comes, will make sure that I am wide awake with them.

As we make for the Mess in the near darkness, we are joined by two other muffled figures, Joske and Odell. We grunt our good mornings, but say nothing else. As we move along, I momentarily shiver, for the air is chilly after the rain, but it is sweet and fragrant, and the damp ground smells of the richness of the soil.

In the Mess the orderly cook, also called by the night guard, has prepared a snack breakfast of tea, hard-boiled eggs, bread and margarine. He puts everything before us without a word. We don't speak either – this is no hour for light chat. We gulp the food down not because we're hungry but because we have to have it inside us, for nobody can fly and fight on an empty stomach. When we come down from patrol we shall have our real breakfast at leisure, porridge, maybe coffee, maybe bacon and sausage and marmalade. Something to look forward to.

We light cigarettes, then, with scarcely a word between us, leave the Mess, wrap our scarves round our necks, for it is still sharp and shivery, and clamber into the waiting Crossley, engine quietly running. There is now a faint steely light – we can see the other huts and the farm alongside which our encampment is scattered.

Five minutes later we are by the hangars at the further side of the aerodrome. Here the mechanics, also pulled from their beds by the ubiquitous night guard, have drawn out our respective Pups, started the engines, and run them up for us. We utter our good mornings morosely to the sergeant and the fitters and riggers and armourers, who regard us bleakly as though it is our fault that they are here at this absurd hour.

The air no longer has the scent of rain, but only of burnt castor oil from the Le Rhône rotary engines. In the flight office, our somnolence dispelled, we don our flying gear while Joske, our leader, gives his

303

instructions. We're on a Line Patrol, but we shall go five or ten miles over, he tells us, and for Christ's sake keep a sharp look-out eastwards when the sun comes up. He doesn't need to tell us, we know what can happen if the Hun comes at you out of a dazzling yellow sunrise.

A light mist hovers low over the aerodrome, but it is not sufficiently dense to bother us. The air is completely still and we need a long run to take off. We leave the ground in quick succession, and join up in formation overhead, and although by now daylight is flooding the empty vault of the sky above, lower down it is still dark enough for us to seek guidance from the flames of each other's exhausts.

As we lift over the sleeping countryside, everything seems snug, rural, tranquil, utterly remote from the notion of war. The pale grey mist still lingers over the low-lying ground, but now, as the world begins to waken and show signs of life, it is mingled with splashes of blue smoke rising from camp-fire and cottages. We pass over a village and the smoke from its chimneys clings to the houses, enveloping them in a ghostly blue veil. It seems incredible that on so peaceful a summer's morning we are riding into the skies to kill other flyers also taking wing into the dawn.

Climbing steadily southwards, we quickly meet the light mounting from the east. At first, a pale yellow flush that marks the dark edge of the earth, then, as the minutes pass, that turns to a pinkish gold. The first diffused rays of the sun, which still hides below the horizon, pierce the steely sky and transform it to pale blue. Below lies Hunland, but I can see nothing of it, for the mist is there too, and the ground is blanketed.

We are not the only early birds. Silhouetted blackly against the eastern glow hangs the motionless sausage-shape of an observation balloon, and the line of them stretching north and south is easily picked up. When we pass over them and look back, they shine yellow in the sun's light. Soon, as we turn eastwards we shall see the line of dark silhouetted enemy balloons some five miles beyond the trenches.

At 8,000 feet we are alone except for a couple of BE2e's beneath us, creeping along their artillery spotting beats. Far below them a double line of spasmodic red flashes, the bursting of British and German shells, marks the course of the opposing trench systems. We move eastwards over the hell that lies there, and on into Hunland. As we enter the archie belt, our practised leader begins a series of gentle, erratic changes of course, and just in time, for archie, with no other customers, gives us his full attention, and at once sends up a sighting salvo.

But our zigzagging has deceived him, and the four black woolly balls, each centred with its red flash, though good for height are over a hundred yards to our right. We hear the quick wuff! wuff! wuff! wuff! plainly enough, but they are much too far away to worry us. Archie is angry, and sends up three more salvos in rapid succession, each one nearer to us than the last. But we are moving eastwards at ninety miles an hour, and as we draw out of his effective range, we hear more bursts behind us, and know that he will now give it up, and allow us to enter Hunland without further trouble.

Mounting smoothly into the sky and the light, and being welcomed not over-warmly by archie, I find that yesterday's cobwebs are quickly vanishing. My spirits rise. The smooth roar of my willing engine is the voice of our challenge to the Huns – come up and meet us, it seems to shout, and join us in a friendly morning scrap!

We look eastwards to greet the sun as its golden rim edges above the horizon. We are seeing it long before the earthbound mortals below, but soon, as it rises higher and its flame floods the eastern sky, it becomes our enemy, for in its dazzle the enemy may be hiding. We cannot see into it, nor can we see downwards towards the earth, for the bright light above gives substance to the early haze, and hides everything from us.

But westwards all is clear. In the distance are groups of small woolly clouds, soon turning to gold as the glinting rays touch them. They look quaintly like flocks of sheep suspended in the sky. They are the forerunners of other clouds, larger, big banks of cumulus looming high behind.

Now full daylight is upon us. The void of the heavens is a deeper blue. We are at 12,000 feet, well inside Hunland. Surely by now some enemy formation is up, looking for prey with all the advantages on their side? I put a thumb close to my left eye to mask the sun, and gaze intently into the golden glow around it. No glittering specks there, so far as I can see.

Abruptly, I am alerted by the sound of shots, but it is only Joske firing a dozen rounds to make sure his gun is working. We spread out and follow his example, firing casually into Hunland. Always I wonder what happens to the bullets when they reach the ground – they are just as likely to hit a Frenchman as a German. Then we close in again to formation. Not that we are in really close formation, there is no need for that, but we're close enough for Joske to be able to twist round and gesture to us and give signals.

Watching out for Huns while going eastwards is not a burden, for at least one's potential troubles are ahead, but when at last we swing southwards, we must then be continuously searching to our left to guard the flank. The same again, but on the other side, when we reach the end of our beat and turn round to the north. But all this is of secondary consequence compared with when we turn westwards, and present our tails towards the sun, for then every one of us must strain his neck to look constantly behind – and not just to glance behind, but stare intently, examining every sector in turn, especially above, for nothing can be more unhealthy than to be caught unawares by a Hun formation diving out of the sun. And of the four of us, it is Odell, at the rear position of our diamond formation, who has the worst job, for if we *are* jumped, he will get shot at first. Naturally he knows this and takes even more interest in his tail than the rest of us.

Looking downwards, I see that under the warmth of the swiftly rising sun, the haze and mist are being put to rout. A strong westerly wind had sprung up, shown by long tails of smoke from towns below us, in German hands. Another enemy, this westerly wind, always carrying us deeper into Hunland.

Until now we have had no excitement whatever. The four of us have patrolled our beat, some five to ten miles in Hunland, at half-throttle, and seemingly scarcely moving at all, as there are no nearby clouds to show up our speed. We are now at 15,000, have been up an hour and have seen no aeroplanes other than the BEs at 6,000 feet, so Joske decides to look for trouble further into Hun territory, and we climb eastwards. The sky is clear, and the sun is still low enough to be a menace, but not nearly so much as during that first hour.

As we swing eastwards in a wide sweep, I suddenly see five specks a little below us coming from the north-east. They are not easy to pick out against the distant patchwork earth below, and in case Joske has not seen them, I dive in front of him, rock my wings and point down.

le at once finds them, lifts a gauntleted hand in acknowledgment,
ıd rocks his wings to warn the others. The two formations are
)proaching each other, the space between us is closing rapidly. Joske
still climbing to gain extra height. They are V-strutters – I recognize
ıem as D–IIIs – there is no mistaking their sleek pigeon-breasted curve.
hey see us and surprisingly turn sharply south.

Joske rocks his wings again and drops into a shallow dive with
ıgine full on. We are four, they five, but we have height, and if only
'e get close enough we shall smash them on the dive. I am sweating
·ith excitement, my finger is on the trigger, my Aldis is lined on the
ft winger, green and white, as I watch for Joske's tracer to flash away.

Then suddenly, just as we open fire, the Huns swing sharply to the
·est and come directly under us. Joske steepens our dive, but we can't
ɔt our sights on to them as they race beneath us, a hundred yards
ɔlow. We swirl round madly, and there they are, plunging away to
ıe northwards. We drop into vertical dives after them, engines full on,
ring wildly at 300 yards' range, but it is hopeless, they gradually draw
·vay from us. Not for the first time, we appreciate that the Albatros
·–III is twenty-five miles an hour faster than the Pup.

I can't understand why they have refused combat, for in a dog-fight,
·en at 15,000, five D–IIIs, each with two fast-firing Spandaus com-
ɪred with the Pup's single, slow-firing Vickers, plus their quicker
imb and speed, could have made mincemeat of us. Afterwards, in the
ɪuadron office, we decided that they must have been four new boys
ɔing shown round the Lines by an experienced hand. *He* knew exactly
:hat to do, but in a free-for-all the others would have been easy victims
·r us.

In chasing them we have dived down to 8,000, and Joske levels out
·hile we take up position behind him. And as we do so, there is the
·arp rattle of gun-fire, and tracers flash among us. We whip round and
:urn steeply to the right, the Pup's best trick to avoid giving the Hun a
·rget. I see them swirling above us, still masked by the low eastern sun
ɪt of which they have attacked us. They are D–IIIs. We have been
ught napping! And in a clear sky!

At first I cannot see how many there are and I don't really care, all
n thinking about is avoiding being hit. Tracers whizz past me,
ɔngside, to port, to starboard, above, below. I seem to be enveloped

in them, but miraculously none hits me. I know it can be fatal to swer
to change direction, for if I bank from one turn to the other I offer a
instant's sitting target, so I continue my steep turning to the righ
meanwhile out of the corner of my eye trying to get my bearings an
spot my attacker.

Tracers flash by again, and the crackle of bullets is so close that
cringe into my cockpit. But the D–III can't turn as tightly as I ca
can't get his guns on to me. Another D–III speeds at an angle across n
front, turning away. I glimpse the curving underside, the pale blu
wings, the black cross on the fin. He is about a hundred yards awa
Instinctively I turn after him, still in a steep turn, and at once find his ta
and fin in the ring sight.

I press the trigger, the tracers jump out towards him, enter his fus
lage halfway up, I edge them towards the pilot – then *crack-ak-*
behind me, I jerk the stick back into my belly, the Pup suddenly kic
sharply and dips down – I have flown into the blue Hun's slipstrear
But my attacker is thrown off and I level out, still on a turn. The blu
Hun has gone, but another is firing at me from three-quarters aster
much too accurately, the tracers slip between the wings to port, tw
yards from me. I kick the rudder and skid clear. I think, Christ, I
never get out of this, I've not had time to draw breath yet.

Dazedly I glimpse other machines banking round me, but I dor
have time to count. A mottled Hun come across my front firing at
Pup. I swing after him, give him a deflection shot, twenty rounds, th
tracers seem to go right into the engine, he lifts suddenly and clim
away. I try to follow, the Pup hangs on the prop, but just can't clin
any steeper.

Suddenly the general crackle of guns increases. But the Albatros
are pulling away. I see them now – only four. And I see why they'
bolting. A trio of FE2b's has spotted the fight and come wading i
their gunners hosing the Hun with long streams of tracer. God,
think, what guts these chaps have got, to join in a dog-fight in su
antiquated tubs as those birdcage pushers. But they do the trick, th
D–IIIs vanish to the east.

I take a deep breath and flop back in my seat. I'm feeling somewh
sick. It all started so suddenly, I had no time to think, and never rea
knew what was happening. I'd made certain we were done for. At 8,0

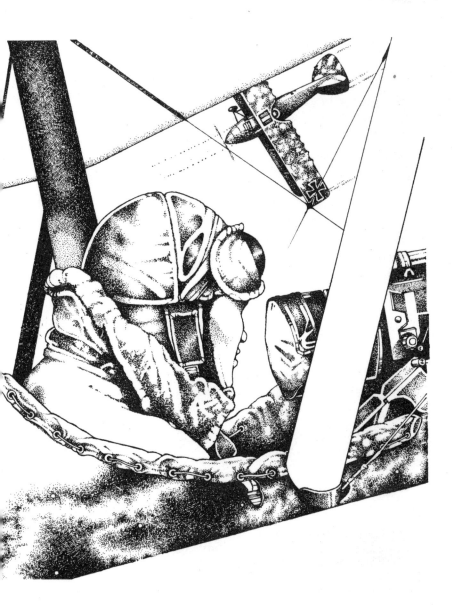

Another D-III speeds at an angle and instinctively I turn after him.

the Pup is completely outclassed by the Albatros. You can't get away
you've got to fight it out – with one gun against two.

We circle close around the FEs and wave our thanks. The pilo
and observers wave back, then join up and pass on westward
Obviously they were on the homeward run from a reconnaissanc
when they saw our scrap. I don't envy them sitting there exposed to th
full blast of air, especially the observer – open cockpit is the word
Far worse than for us. None of the Pups is adrift, and we resum
formation and carry on with the patrol. But we'd been lucky. We ha
allowed ourselves to be taken by surprise, out of the early-morning su
where danger always lies and only the marvellous manoeuvrability of
our faithful Pups, plus the intervention of the FEs, had saved us from
bad mauling.

We still have half an hour's patrol to do, and Joske resumes our be
up and down the Lines. Within two minutes, Odell gives the distre
signal and glides away westwards. His engine has been damaged, as w
learn afterwards. We also learn that we have all taken punishment, b
one has been hit in a vital spot.

By now the sky has changed, for the flocks of sheep have con
swiftly in from the westwards, and have already passed underneat
followed by larger masses of cumulus, whose white billowing to
slide along not far below us. We see no more Huns, and Joske, feeling
a good mood, keeps us skimming close to the solid-looking mountai
of woolly cloud. As we swing round their swelling hills and valleys
realize that not a trace of the dawn hangover remains.

Suddenly I see by the dashboard watch that it is half past six. We'
been up over two hours, and because of the fight and the cloud-hoppin
I've not noticed it. But now that the job is practically finished,
realize that I'm famished, and my thoughts turn to the bacon ar
sausage awaiting me. At this moment, Joske gives the washout sign
and we break up and make our separate ways home. Another dav
patrol is over.

Midshipman Jack Easy and the Fighting Chaplain

Captain Marryat

A sloop of war arrived from the fleet with despatches from the commander-in-chief. Those to Captain Wilson required him to make all possible haste in fitting, and then to proceed and cruise off Corsica, to fall in with a Russian frigate which was on that coast; if not there, to obtain intelligence, and to follow her wherever she might be.

All was now bustle and activity on board of the *Aurora*. Captain Wilson, Jack Easy and Gascoigne, quitted the governor's house and repaired on board, where they remained day and night. On the third day the *Aurora* was complete and ready for sea, and about noon sailed out of Valette Harbour.

In a week the *Aurora* had gained the coast of Corsica, and there was no need of sending look-out men to the mast-head, for one of the officers or midshipmen was there from daylight to dark. She ran up the coast to the northward without seeing the object of her pursuit, or obtaining any intelligence.

Calms and light airs detained them for a few days, when a northerly breeze enabled them to run down the eastern side of the island. It was on the eighteenth day after they had quitted Malta, that a large vessel was seen ahead about eighteen miles off. The men were then at breakfast.

'A frigate, Captain Wilson, I'm sure of it,' said Mr Hawkins, the chaplain, whose anxiety induced him to go to the mast-head.

'How is she steering?'

'The same way as we are.'

The *Aurora* was under all possible sail, and when the hands were piped to dinner, they had neared the chase about two miles.

'This will be a long chase; a stern chase always is,' observed Martin the master's mate.

'Yes, I'm afraid so – but I'm more afraid of her escaping,' said Gascoigne.

'That's not unlikely either,' replied the mate.

'You are one of Job's comforters, Martin,' replied Gascoigne.

'Then I'm not so often disappointed,' replied the mate. 'There are two points to be ascertained; the first is, whether we shall come up with the vessel or lose her – the next is, if we do come up with her, whether she is the vessel we are looking for.'

'You seem very indifferent about it.'

'Indeed I am not: I am the oldest passed midshipman in the ship, and the taking of the frigate will, if I live, give me my promotion, and if I'm killed, I shan't want it. But I've been so often disappointed, that I now make sure of nothing until I have it.'

'Well, for your sake, Martin, I will still hope that the vessel is the one we seek, that we shall not be killed, and that you will gain your promotion.'

'I thank you, Easy – I wish I was one that dared hope as you do.'

Poor Martin! he had long felt how bitter it was to meet disappointment upon disappointment. How true it is, that hope deferred maketh the heart sick! and his anticipations of early days, the buoyant calculations of youth, had been one by one crushed, and now, having served his time nearly three times over, the reaction had become too painful, and, as he truly said, he dared not hope: still his temper was not soured, but chastened.

'She has hauled her wind, sir,' hailed the second lieutenant from the topmast cross-trees.

'What think you of that, Martin?' observed Jack, our hero.

'Either that she is an English frigate, or that she is a vessel commanded by a very brave fellow, and well-manned.'

It was sunset before the *Aurora* had arrived within two miles of the vessel; the private signal had been thrown out, but had not been answered, either because it was too dark to make out the colours of the flags, or that these were unknown to an enemy. The stranger had hoisted the English colours, but that was no satisfactory proof of her being a friend; and just before dark she had put her head towards the *Aurora*, who had now come stem down to her. The ship's company of the *Aurora* were all at their quarters, as a few minutes would now decide whether they had to deal with a friend or foe.

There is no situation perhaps more difficult, and demanding so much caution, as the occasional meeting with a doubtful ship. On the one hand, it being necessary to be fully prepared, and not allow the enemy the advantage which may be derived from your inaction; and on the other, the necessity of prudence, that you may not assault your friends and countrymen. Captain Wilson had hoisted the private night-signal, but here again it was difficult, from his sails intervening, for the other ship to make it out. Before the two frigates were within three cables' length of each other, Captain Wilson, determined that there should be no mistake from any want of precaution on his part, hauled up his courses and brailed up his driver that the night -signal might be clearly seen.

Lights were seen abaft on the quarter-deck of the other vessel, as if they were about to answer, but she continued to keep the *Aurora* to leeward at about half a cable's length, and as the foremost guns of each vessel were abreast of each other, hailed in English –

'Ship ahoy! what ship's that?'

'His Majesty's ship *Aurora*,' replied Captain Wilson, who stood on the hammocks. 'What ship's that?'

By this time the other frigate had passed half her length clear of the beam of the *Aurora*, and at the same time that a pretended reply of 'His Majesty's ship – ' was heard, a broadside from her guns, which had been trained aft on purpose, was poured into the *Aurora*, and at so short a distance, doing considerable execution. The crew of the *Aurora*, hearing the hailing in English, and the vessel passing them apparently without firing, had imagined that she had been one of their own cruisers. The captains of the guns had dropped their lanyards in disappointment, and the silence which had been maintained as the two

Captain Wilson himself pointed each gun after it was loaded.

vessels met was just breaking up in various ways of lamentation at their bad luck, when the broadside was poured in, thundering in their ears, and the ripping and tearing of the beams and planks astonished their senses. Many were carried down below, but it was difficult to say whether indignation at the enemy's ruse, or satisfaction at discovering that they were not called to quarters in vain, most predominated. At all events, it was answered by three voluntary cheers, which drowned the cries of those who were being assisted to the cockpit.

'Man the larboard guns and about ship!' cried Captain Wilson, leaping off the hammocks. 'Look out, my lads, and rake her in stays! We'll pay him off for that foul play before we've done with him. Look out, my lads, and take good aim as she pays round.'

The *Aurora* was put about, and her broadside poured into the stern of the Russian frigate – for such she was. It was almost dark, but the enemy, who appeared as anxious as the *Aurora* to come to action, hauled up her courses to wait her coming up. In five minutes the two vessels were alongside, exchanging murderous broadsides at little more than pistol-shot – running slowly in for the land, then not more than five miles distant. The skin-clad mountaineers of Corsica were aroused by the furious cannonading, watching the incessant flashes of the guns, and listening to their reverberating roar.

After half-an-hour's fierce combat, during which the fire of both vessels was kept up with undiminished vigour, Captain Wilson went down on the main-deck, and himself separately pointed each gun after it was loaded; those amidships being direct for the main-channels of the enemy's ship, while those abaft the beam were gradually trained more and more forward, and those before the beam more and more aft, so as to throw all their shot nearly into one focus, giving directions that they were all to be fired at once, at the word of command. The enemy, not aware of the cause of the delay, imagined that the fire of the *Aurora* had slackened, and loudly cheered. At the word given, the broadside was poured in, and, dark as it was, the effects from it were evident. Two of the midship ports of the antagonist were blown into one, and her mainmast was seen to totter, and then to fall over the side. The *Aurora* then set her courses, which had been hauled up, and shooting ahead, took up a raking position, while the Russian was still hampered with her wreck, and poured in grape and cannister from her upper deck carronades to impede their labours on deck, while she continued her destructive fire upon the hull of the enemy from the main-deck battery.

The moon now burst out from a low bank of clouds, and enabled them to accomplish their work with more precision. In a quarter of an hour the Russian was totally dismasted, and Captain Wilson ordered half of his remaining ship's company to repair the damages, which had been most severe, whilst the larboard men at quarters continued the fire from the main-deck. The enemy continued to return the fire from four guns, two on each of her decks, which she could still make bear upon the *Aurora*; but after some time even these ceased, either from the men having deserted them, or from their being dismounted. Observing that the fire from her antagonist had ceased, the *Aurora* also discontinued, and the jolly-boat astern being still uninjured, the second lieutenant was deputed to pull alongside the frigate to ascertain if she had struck.

The beams of the bright moon silvered the rippling water as the boat shoved off; and Captain Wilson and his officers, who were still unhurt, leant over the shattered sides of the *Aurora*, waiting for a reply: suddenly the silence of the night was broken upon by a loud splash from the bows of the Russian frigate, then about three cables' length distant.

'What could that be?' cried Captain Wilson. 'Her anchor's down. Mr Jones, a lead over the side, and see what water we have.'

Mr Jones had long been carried down below, severed in two with a round shot – but a man leaped into the chains, and lowering down the lead sounded in seven fathoms.

'Then I suspect he will give us more trouble yet,' observed Captain Wilson; and so indeed it proved, for the Russian captain, in reply to the second lieutenant, had told him in English, 'that he would answer that question with his broadside,' and before the boat was dropped astern, he had warped round with the springs on his cable, and had recommenced his fire upon the *Aurora*.

Captain Wilson made sail upon his ship, and sailed round and round the anchored vessel, so as to give her two broadsides to her one, and from the slowness with which she worked at her springs upon her cables, it was evident that she must be now very weak-handed. Still the pertinacity and decided courage of the Russian captain convinced Captain Wilson, that, in all probability, he would sink at his anchor before he would haul down his colours; and not only would he lose more of the *Aurora*'s men, but also the Russian vessel, without he took a more decided step. Captain Wilson, therefore, resolved to try her by the board. Having poured in a raking fire, he stood off for a few moments, during which he called the officers and men on deck, and stated his intention. He then went about, and himself conning the *Aurora*, ran her on board the Russian, pouring in his reserved broadside as the vessels came into collision, and heading his men as they leaped on the enemy's decks.

Although, as Captain Wilson had imagined, the Russian frigate had not many men to oppose to the *Aurora*'s, the deck was obstinately defended, the voice and the arm of the Russian captain were to be heard and seen everywhere, and his men, encouraged by him, were cut down by numbers where they stood.

Our hero, who had the good fortune to be still unhurt, was for a little while close to Captain Wilson when he boarded, and was about to oppose his unequal force against that of the Russian captain, when he was pulled back by the collar by Mr Hawkins, the chaplain, who rushed in advance with a sabre in his hand. The opponents were well matched, and it may be said that, with little interruption, a hand-to-hand conflict ensued, for the moon lighted up the scene of carnage, and they were well able to distinguish each other's faces. At last, the chaplain's sword broke: he rushed in, drove the hilt into his antagonist's face, closed with him, and they both fell down the hatchway together. After this, the deck was gained, or rather cleared, by the crew of the *Aurora*, for few could be said to have resisted, and in a minute or two the frigate was in their possession. The chaplain and the Russian captain were hoisted up, still clinging to each other, both senseless from the fall, but neither of them dead, although bleeding from several wounds.

As soon as the main deck had been cleared, Captain Wilson ordered the hatches to be put on, and left a party on board while he hastened to attend to the condition of his own ship and ship's company.

It was daylight before anything like order had been restored to the decks of the *Aurora*; the water was still smooth, and instead of letting go her own anchor, she had hung on with a hawser to the prize, but her sails had been furled, her decks cleared, guns secured, and the buckets were dashing away the blood from her planks and the carriages of the guns, when the sun rose and shone upon them. The numerous wounded had, by this time, been put into their hammocks, although there were still one or two cases of amputation to be performed.

The carpenter had repaired all shot-holes under or too near to the water-line, and then had proceeded to sound the well of the prize; but although her upper works had been dreadfully shattered, there was no reason to suppose that she had received any serious injury below, and therefore the hatches still remained on, although a few hands were put to the pumps to try if she made any water. It was not until the *Aurora* presented a more cheerful appearance that Captain Wilson went over to the other ship, whose deck, now that the light of heaven enabled them to witness all the horrors even to minuteness, presented a shocking spectacle of blood and carnage. Body after body was thrown over; the wounded were supplied with water and such assistance as could be rendered until the surgeons could attend them; the hatches were then taken off, and the remainder of her crew ordered on deck; about two hundred obeyed the summons, but the lower deck was as crowded with killed and wounded as was the upper. For the present the prisoners were handed over down into the fore-hold of the *Aurora*, which had been prepared for their reception, and the work of separation of the dead from the living then underwent. After this, such repairs as were immediately necessary were made, and a portion of the *Aurora's* crew, under the orders of the second lieutenant, were sent on board to take charge of her. It was not till the evening of the day after this night conflict that the *Aurora* was in a situation to make sail. All hands were then sent on board of the *Trident*, for such was the name of the Russian frigate, to fit her out as soon as possible. Before morning, – for there was no relaxation from their fatigue, nor was there any wish for it, – all was completed, and the two frigates, although in a shattered condition, were prepared to meet any common conflict with the elements. The *Aurora* made sail with the *Trident* in tow; the hammocks were allowed to be taken down, and the watch below permitted to repose.

In this murderous conflict the *Trident* had more than two hundred men killed and wounded. The *Aurora's* loss had not been so great, but still it was severe, having lost sixty-five men and officers. Among the fallen there were Mr Jones, the master, the third lieutenant Mr Arkwright, and two midshipmen killed. Mr Pottyfar, the first lieutenant, severely wounded at the commencement of the action.

Martin the master's mate, and Gascoigne, the first mortally, and the second badly, wounded. Our hero had also received a slight cutlass wound, which obliged him to wear his arm, for a short time, in a sling.

Among the ship's company who were wounded was Mesty; he had been hurt with a splinter before the *Trident* was taken by the board, but had remained on deck, and had followed our hero, watching over him and protecting him as a father. He had done even more, for he had with Jack thrown himself before Captain Wilson, at a time that he had received such a blow with the flat of a sword as to stun him, and bring him down on his knee. And Jack had taken good care that Captain Wilson should not be ignorant, as he really would have been, of this timely service on the part of Mesty, who certainly although with a great deal of '*sang froid*' in his composition when in repose, was a fiend incarnate when his blood was up.

'But you must have been with Mesty,' observed Captain Wilson, 'when he did me the service.'

'I was with him, sir,' replied Jack, with great modesty; 'but was of very little service.'

'How is your friend Gascoigne this evening?'

'Oh, not very bad, sir – he wants a glass of grog.'

'And Mr Martin?'

Jack shook his head.

'Why, the surgeon thinks he will do well.'

'Yes, sir, and so I told Martin; but he said that it was very well to give him hope – but that he thought otherwise.'

'You must manage him, Mr Easy; tell him that he is sure of his promotion.'

'I have, sir, but he won't believe it. He never will believe it till he has his commission signed. I really think that an acting order would do more than the doctor can.'

'Well, Mr Easy, he shall have one tomorrow morning. Have you seen Mr Pottyfar? he, I am afraid, is very bad.'

'Very bad, sir; and they say is worse every day, and yet his wound is healthy, and ought to be doing well.'

Such was the conversation between Jack and his captain, as they sat at breakfast on the third morning after the action.

The next day Easy took down an acting order for Martin, and

put it into his hands. The mate read it over as he lay bandaged in his hammock.

'It's only an acting order, Jack,' said he; 'it may not be confirmed.'

Jack swore, by all the articles of war, that it would be; but Martin replied that he was sure it never would.

'No, no,' said the mate, 'I knew very well that I never should be made. If it is not confirmed, I may live; but if it is, I am sure to die.'

Every one that went to Martin's hammock wished him joy of his promotion; but six days after the action, poor Martin's remains were consigned to the deep.

The next person who followed him was Mr Pottyfar, the first lieutenant, who had contrived, wounded as he was, to reach a packet of the universal medicine, and had taken so many bottles before he was found out, that he was one morning found dead in his bed, with more than two dozen empty phials under his pillow, and by the side of his mattress. He was not buried with his hands in his pockets, but when sewed up in his hammock, they were, at all events, laid in the right position.

In three weeks the *Aurora*, with her prize in tow, arrived at Malta. The wounded were sent to the hospital, and the gallant Russian captain recovered from his wounds about the same time as Mr Hawkins, the chaplain.

Jack, who constantly called to see the chaplain, had a great deal to do to console him. He would shake his hands as he lay in his bed, exclaiming against himself. 'Oh,' would he say, 'the spirit is willing, but the flesh is weak. That I, a man of God, as they term me, who ought to have been down with the surgeons, whispering comfort to the desponding, should have gone on deck (but I could not help it), and have mixed in such a scene of slaughter. What will become of me?'

Jack attempted to console him by pointing out, that not only chaplains, but bishops, have been known to fight in armour from time immemorial. But Mr Hawkins's recovery was long doubtful, from the agitation of his mind. When he was able to walk, Jack introduced to him the Russian captain, who was also just out of his bed.

'I am most happy to embrace so gallant an officer,' said the Russian who recognized his antagonist, throwing his arms round the chaplain, and giving him a kiss on both cheeks. 'What is his rank?' continued he

320

addressing himself to Jack, who replied, very quietly, 'that he was the ship's padre.'

'The padre!' replied the captain, with surprise, as Hawkins turned away with confusion. 'The padre – *par exemple*! Well, I always had a great respect for the church. Pray, sir,' said he, turning to Easy, 'do your padres always head your boarders?'

'Always, sir,' replied Jack; 'it's a rule of the service.'

Secret Mission

Alistair Mars D.S.O. D.S.C.

During 1942, the submarine Unbroken *took part in four secret operations in the Mediterranean.*

Her Commander, Alistair Mars, here tells of one such enterprise – 'Operation Pedestal', which begins with an attempt at train-wrecking . . .

The *Unbroken* was the first of the 'U'-class submarines to be fitted with a three-inch gun. Former boats had been equipped with twelve-pounders, toys of little use against anything bigger than a rowing boat. Because of this, train-wrecking had been a hazardous, cloak-and-dagger affair carried out by intrepid gentlemen operating from folboats. Outstanding among them was the army's Captain 'Tug' Wilson who did magnificently courageous work paddling ashore from submarines and laying explosive charges along the lines.

Ours, however, was to be a more elaborate and snappier job.

During the afternoon of 8 August we examined the shore between Paola and Longobardi through the high-power periscope; a short stretch of coast high on Italy's instep along which the electric track was in full view. After a conference in the ward-room I decided to do my strafing at a point a mile north of Longobardi. It held many advantages, including the useful landmark of Mount Cocuzzo, an absence of civilian houses, and deep water inshore.

After sunset, as the dusk melted into night, we steered to within three-and-a-half miles of the coast. At 9 p.m. we surfaced and crept towards land at four knots, propelled by our near-silent motors.

Fifteen hundred yards from shore we stopped – and waited.

The next hour passed in dark gentle silence. The night was black and starless, relieved only by the red and green railway signals and tiny pin-points of light sneaking through the curtains of the Longobardi cottages. With luck we would soon be giving the inhabitants a new item of conversation with which to enliven their small-town gossip . . . I stretched my arms and turned my face into the soft, off-shore breeze. There was only the slightest of swells to give any feeling of movement, and the look-outs saw nothing around them but dark, empty sea. Below, the crew were at diving stations. It would be a hot, sticky night for them, for there was little ventilation without the engines running, and the boat was already an oven after a day submerged. In the control-room Thirsk studied his charts and checked them against the echo-sounding. The area was well mapped and we were able to determine our gun range to within fifty yards. The gun's crew were huddled on the casing, their feet but a few inches from the water, the first round of flashless night ammunition ready in the breech.

One grave fear was uppermost in our minds – that our target might be blacked-out and we would have to fire blind at the distant sound of its electric motors. If that were the case, our charts giving us the range only to within the nearest fifty yards, we could fire a hundred rounds without doing an iota of damage. I could, of course, fire a star shell, but that would reveal our presence to every sentry, aircraft and ship within a radius of thirty miles. The problem caused me a great deal of concern until, at ten-ten, a train came into view heralded – to our joy – by a large headlamp. Its seemingly disembodied beam moved mysteriously through the night, and we were able to obtain an accurate last-inch, range from it. A few minutes later an up-train passed – assuming they did travel 'up' to Rome – and at ten-forty our own bundle of fun came into sight. She, too, was adorned with a great lamp.

We had moved to within 900 yards of the shore, and at a whispered order the gun's crew closed up. Archdale leaned across the bridge. 'Range a thousand yards, deflection twenty right. Independent firing. Open fire when she reaches the datum point.'

'Aye, aye, sir.'

There was a long pause as the gun held the train in its sights until it reached the datum point.

Ten-forty-six.

With a roar the gun opened fire, its tiny spurt of crimson swallowed quickly in the darkness. The shell screamed through the air and exploded with a tremendous crash.

A hit, by God!

Indeed it was. There was a vivid blue flash as the overhead wires were brought down and in its brilliance I saw the engine detach itself from the coaches and idle on down the track. Again the gun roared, and again. After five rounds, all of them hits, the carriages and trucks crackling merrily with dancing yellow fires. The signal lights were out – the power was off. Archdale transferred his attention to the engine and methodically blew it to pieces.

By 10.48 it was all over. With cold-blooded ease we had deprived Rommel of at least twenty-four hours of supplies – 14,000 tons' worth. It had been achieved in precisely two minutes at a cost to ourselves of ten rounds of three-inch ammunition. I was elated with the brilliant shooting of Fenton and Co., for it was an extraordinary feat, performed with the smooth, effortless ease of a not too difficult gunnery exercise. But congratulations would have to come later, for it was essential to get out of the area and start south towards our rendezvous near Stromboli.

Half an hour later I saw the train still ablaze in the distance. It was a reassurance that I had not dreamed it all.

Our daylight patrol position for PEDESTAL was two miles north of Cape Milazzo lighthouse which lay eighteen miles west of the Messina naval base. It was not a comfortable spot, for the enemy were certain to have the area bristling with every anti-submarine device they could muster. I had said as much at Malta, but it was pointed out that the Admiralty at Whitehall were organizing the convoy operation, and it was they who had chosen my position. I felt the Admiralty should have confined themselves to giving the route of the convoy, and should have left the business of choosing covering positions for the submarines to on-the-spot authorities at Malta, but I thought it as well to say no more than: 'It's a bit close.'

At 12.15 on the morning of 10 August, at about the same time as the convoy was passing through the Straits of Gibraltar a thousand miles to westward, we reached a point four miles from our position, and took a look round. Visibility was good, the sea was calm, only a slight breeze blew from the north-east. Owing to a combination of minor faults and bad sea conditions, the Asdic was out of action. But the hydrophones, which picked up audible sounds as distinct from the supersonic noises picked up on the Asdic, were working, and we had not long been there when the report came up the voice-pipe: 'Mushy HE[1] bearing one-eight-five.'

Puzzled, I went below and listened. Through the ear-phones I could hear a soft tapping; a sound quite unlike any I knew. It seemed to come straight from Cape Milazzo. It was constant, its bearing did not change, and the disturbing thought struck me that we had been picked up by some new-fangled detection device. I said nothing, however, but waited until dawn, when we dived and closed towards our patrol position.

Still the soft, monotonous tapping.

At 9 a.m., four miles north-west of Milazzo lighthouse Thirsk summoned me to the control-room. 'Ship coming towards us from the direction of the Cape, sir.'

I grasped the handles of the periscope and looked. An enemy patrol tug coming straight towards us. As there was no harbour or anchorage under the lighthouse it suggested she was being 'beamed' on to us. I thought at once of the mysterious tappings and did not like the situation one bit.

'Eighty feet. Starboard twenty-five.'

Down we plunged, and the next fifteen minutes passed in uneasy silence. And then, just as I was deciding it had been a false alarm, there was a *krrump*, and the boat shuddered to the explosion of a depth charge. From experience I assessed it at being some four hundred yards off – as were the four others that followed. We promptly went into 'silent routine' which meant that in order not to transmit noises for the enemy to pick up, all machinery, such as ventilation, refrigeration and water circulation systems were shut off, leaving only the motors and gyro-compass running.

I glanced around the control-room. Apart from the licking of lips and the wrinkling of foreheads, the others gave no indication of the tense anxiety they must certainly have been feeling.

[1] HE, Hydrophone Effect from propellers.

But no more depth charges followed the first pattern of five and after a while we crept back to periscope depth. The patrol tug was about a mile away – steering back towards the Cape. All very peculiar.

We returned to our patrol position, and for an hour nothing happened. At 11.15, however, smoke was sighted – a *Cretone*-class minelayer steaming towards us from the Straits of Messina, escorted by a Cant flying-boat. The hydrophones were still picking up that extraordinary tapping, which seemed to confirm that the enemy was beamed on to us.

We went to a hundred and twenty feet, and half an hour later depth-charging commenced.

For an hour it went on: patterns of four or five, with an interval of perhaps ten minutes between each pattern. Oddly – and fortunately – they were seldom closer than within three hundred yards of the *Unbroken* – far outside their lethal range. As a result, we were disturbed by nothing more than heart-jumping *krrumps* and occasional shudders – but all the time there was the nerve-fraying fear that the next one might hit the bull's-eye, and the *Unbroken* would be the subject of another solemn 'Admiralty regrets' announcement. At 1.15 our tormentor was joined by a pal, and the two of them continued the bombardment. We kept to our irregular zigzag, and while I cursed the infernal device that had beamed the tugs on to us, I blessed its lack of absolute accuracy.

My clothes were soaked in sweat, the air in the boat was thick and oily, and my nerves were in a wretched state. If only we had been able to hit back! If only there had been some movement or action to take our minds from the agony of the situation! But no. We could only wait and hope and pray, brooding and exaggerating, picturing a torn, smashed hull and a bubbling, choking, lung-bursting death . . .

Then, at three o'clock, they moved away. The tension eased. I 'fell out' diving stations and told Leading Stoker Fall that he could pass round tea and sandwiches. I was tempted to sneak back to periscope depth for a look round, but reason prevailed and we lumbered along as before – course, oh-three-oh, speed one-seven-five revs., depth a hundred and twenty feet.

It was getting on for 6.30 before the enemy made the next move. That was when Cryer reported 'HE to starboard!' and before the words were fully out of his mouth a pattern of charges dropped close enough to shake the rivets from our plates.

I felt sick in the stomach. It was approaching dusk, and we simply had to surface before midnight in order to recharge our batteries and replenish our air. If we failed to do this we would be able to survive for no more than a further twelve hours . . .

We've got to get out of here!

After the first teeth-rattling pattern the enemy reverted to his curious behaviour of bombarding the sea a quarter of a mile away from us, and I took advantage of the fact to slip into the ward-room to study the charts and plot my next move. We were half-way between Cape Milazzo and Stromboli, having steered roughly north in our attempt to dodge the depth charges. Apart from the fact that the position ordered by the Admiralty was a 'natural' for underwater suicide, it was obvious that the enemy, knowing of our presence, would not send his cruisers into the Cape Milazzo area. I decided to choose another position, although it would be impossible to inform 'Shrimp' Simpson at Malta of the change. One pip on the W/T and the ever-watchful enemy would be able to fix our position to within the nearest hundred yards. For an hour, to the disturbing background music of distant *krrumps*, I made a careful appreciation of the inland sea between Malta and Gibraltar. In the end I decided on a position half-way between the islands of Stromboli and Salina, reasoning that it was the best point of interception if the cruisers were using the port of Messina. It puts us thirty miles from our ordered position and if it turned out to be a miscalculation, I was well aware of the fact that I'd be hung from the highest yard-arm in Whitehall 'as a mystery and a sign' – probably with a cowardice charge thrown in for good measure.

At 7.15 the enemy pushed off, and I assumed that as good Italians they were more concerned with going home than with sinking a British submarine. On the strength of this assumption I told Joe Sizer, the cox'n, to issue tins of tongue for a cold supper.

Paul Thirsk did a little simple arithmetic and informed me that exactly seventy depth charges had been hurled in the general direction of the *Unbroken* that day.

At 10.30, fifteen miles from Milazzo, I decided to surface. It was a tricky, yet necessary, decision, for the enemy might well have returned to the area and could be waiting with stopped engines for the *Unbroken* to refill her lungs.

Quietly we went to diving stations and crept up to eighty feet.

We listened. All was silent.

Sixty feet. Still silence.

Periscope depth. I stared intently into the big periscope. The night was so dark that only a solitary star confirmed that the periscope was actually out of the water. The horizon was indistinct, and a careful sweep did not reveal even the suggestion of a shadow to mar the evenness of the night.

I handed the periscope to Thirsk and told Haddow to plane the boat to the surface and blow number Four main ballast tank with low-pressure air when we reached twelve feet. In this way we would surface slowly and in silence. As the conning-tower broke from the water I leapt to the bridge followed by Archdale and Osborne. Quickly we swept sky and sea through binoculars. Nothing in sight. I reckoned that if we were unable to see the enemy – if he was there – then he couldn't see us, either.

With the faint glow of Stromboli's volcano to port, I ordered: 'Half buoyancy. Group up. Half ahead together. Start the engines.'

Let's get out of here!

★   ★   ★   ★

Shortly before dawn we dived fifteen miles north-west of Stromboli, and looked forward to a quiet, lazy day catching up on lost sleep. Having made certain a thorough periscope watch was being kept, I turned in and managed to grab four hour's rest. This was double the stretch I usually enjoyed, and gives some indication of my exhaustion after the strain of the depth-chargings. I had trained myself to sleep with my ears open, as it were, and any sounds, such as alterations to course, immediately wakened me. Apart from these interruptions, it was a standing order that I should be given a shake by the officer coming off watch every two hours in order to know exactly what had been happening – if anything. But on this occasion I slept for an undisturbed four hours – until 12.30 p.m. when we reached the 'Mars Patrol Position' twelve-and-a-half miles west-south-west of Stromboli peak. The rest of that and the following day were quiet.

We watched and waited off Stromboli, and spent Wednesday night baking in a midnight temperature of eighty-eight degrees. I was asleep in my deck-chair when Tiger Fenton tapped my shoulder. 'Captain, sir! The P.O.Tel. has a signal in the control-room. It's emergency.'

Automatically, as I crossed the bridge, I noted the absence of moon, the dull glow of Stromboli, the flat calm of the sea and the part-clouded sky.

Below, Petty Officer John Willey handed me the pink slip. From Vice-Admiral Commanding at Malta, it read: 'Enemy cruisers coming your way.'

My heart sank and I could have groaned aloud, for 'your way' referred to Cape Milazzo, thirty miles to the south. As I wondered what on earth I should do, an explanatory signal came from 'Shrimp'. At 3 a.m. an aircraft had reported enemy cruisers off Sicily's Cape de Gallo steering east at twenty knots. This meant that they would pass my original position off Cape Milazzo at 7.30 a.m. – in two-and-a-half hours' time.

My immediate reaction was to order a full-speed return towards Cape Milazzo. I could get half-way there by dawn. And the enemy, making a detour around the area of the depth-charging in case we were still there, might well fall into our hands.

I lighted a cigarette and had another look at the charts. As I did so I was struck by a second possibility. The enemy Admiral would know he had been reported because the aircraft which spotted him would have been bound to have dropped a flare. That being so I reckoned he would have the good sense to alter course at least twenty degrees. Since he could not alter to starboard because of land, he would have to alter to port – and into our welcoming arms!

I could see no other alternatives and made a decision which, as far as Lieutenant Mars was concerned, was momentous. We would stay where we were!

We dived early and I altered the breakfast-hour to seven o'clock on the time-honoured principle of food before battle. In the middle of my bacon and eggs, assailed by doubts as to the wisdom of my decision, I heard Cryer report to the officer of the watch: 'HE ahead, sir.'

That was all I needed. With a bound that sent my breakfast crashing to the deck I was in the control-room and holding the big periscope in my hands.

'Diving stations!'

The crew knew what was afoot and hurried eagerly to their positions.

'H.E. bearing two-three-oh . . . Heavy units . . . Fast.'

I swung the periscope. The morning was fine but for a distant haze hanging over the surface of the sea. I could see nothing from the direction from which the HE was coming. I took the earphones and could hear a confused jumble of noise. It certainly came from heavy ships, but they were a long way off. I went back to the periscope.

My heart thumped like a trip-hammer, but I noticed with satisfaction that my hands were steady and my eyes were clear.

Then I saw them as their masts broke through the haze on the horizon. In my joy I could have danced a jig.

'Bearing now?'

'Green one.'

They were now well over the horizon. 'Two . . . Three . . . *Four!* Yes, four cruisers in line ahead, coming straight towards . . . Range?'

Chief ERA[1] Manual read off from the range scale above my head. 'Range, twelve thousand, sir.'

'Down periscope. Port twenty-five. Group up . . . Up after periscope.'

As the smaller periscope cut the surface I had a quick look round for aircraft close to. There were none; but two anti-submarine Cants hovered over the cruisers.

'Down after periscope. Fifty feet.'

Fifty feet would have to do. I wanted to keep my eye on this magnificent array of ships, and it would take too long to get down to eighty feet and back.

As the needles passed thirty-five feet I ordered: 'Full ahead together.' I turned to Haddow. 'Two eight-inch cruisers and, I think, two six-inch. Anyhow, four cruisers for certain.'

Haddow raised an eyebrow. I nodded. He passed the glad tidings over the broadcaster in a commendably calm quiet voice.

Archdale was manipulating the fruit machine, knowing it was my intention to get into a position whereby, as the cruisers passed, I would have the entire lengths of their sides at which to aim. 'Course for a ninety-degree track, sir, one-four-oh.'

'Steer one-four-oh.'

[1] ERA Engine-room Artificer.

The helmsman eased his wheel. The planesman levelled up.

'Course, sir, one-four-oh.'

From Sizer: 'Depth, sir, fifty feet.'

We shuddered as the propellers lashed the water and the submarine leapt across the enemy's bows at her top speed. Assuming the cruisers kept to their course we would have to get some eight hundred yards off their path, turn around and fire. I had fifteen minutes in which to do this – just time enough.

I then announced an item of information I had kept to myself. 'There are eight modern destroyers and two sea-planes escorting. Shut off for depth-charging.'

As Haddow relayed the information to the rest of the boat, I felt a moment of queasiness. It was a feeling I knew of old – a boyhood memory of a twelve-stone brute flashing down the touchline of a rugger field, the full back at the other side of the field, and only myself to bring him down . . .

This time, however, I was not alone. I looked at the faces around me.

Haddow, an enigmatic smile on his lips, watched the depth gauges like a lynx. On him depended whether I would be able to see or not when the moment of firing came. Thirsk was crouched low over his chart, oblivious to everything save the job in hand. Archdale gazed oddly at the fruit machine as though it was about to give birth. On him depended the director angle. Cryer, humped over the now repaired Asdic, had a grin on his face I can only describe as fiendish. ERA Lewis hovered by the telemotor and blowing panels, watching the pressure indicators with deep concentration. Manuel stood behind me ready to read off the periscope and keep me clamped to the director angle at the time of firing. The planesmen, communicating numbers and helmsmen sat with their backs to me, working their controls with practised ease.

Throughout the boat it was the same. Men going about their duties calmly, intelligently and efficiently, well aware that this was a 'now or never' opportunity – a torpedo attack against heavily escorted units travelling at high speed. There would be no second chance. We had to deliver a single, swift knock-out punch.

'Bring all tubes to the ready', I ordered. 'Torpedo depth settings fourteen and sixteen feet.'

After a run of three minutes we crept it back to periscope depth. I lifted my finger and the attack periscope was raised until the eyepiece was just clear of the deck. I curled into a squatting position and looked. Still under water. Lewis raised the periscope, slowly dragging my body up with it. As soon as the top glass cut the surface I whisked around to see if anything was too close to us. Then on to the target.

'Down after, up for'ard periscope.'

The line of cruisers had altered course to starboard – away from the direction in which we were heading – and had taken up a form of quarter-line. This meant the nearest would be one of the eight-inch cruisers. She would be my target. Although the range was rather more than one could wish, the disadvantage was cancelled by the fact that the new formation presented an excellent multiple target – one of the more distant six-inch cruisers might be hit by a torpedo that missed the eight-inch job. I congratulated myself on this stroke of luck, and turned to study the eight evil-looking destroyers and their accompanying aircraft – the boys who could well wreck my chances.

Fortunately five of the destroyers were well out of it on the far side of the cruisers. Obligingly, the aircraft had gone that way, too. The aircraft might come back, but I reckoned I was safe at periscope depth for the time being. The other three destroyers were still in line ahead, and if they did not alter course I would be able to sneak across their bows and fire from inside the 'screen' – from between them and the cruisers.

'Down periscope.'

Archdale looked round. 'New enemy course, oh-seven-oh. What speed shall I allow, sir?'

Thirsk said: 'Speed from plot twenty-two knots.'

Cryer reported: 'Two hundred revs., sir. That gives twenty-five knots according to the table for Italian eight-inch cruisers.'

'Give them twenty-five knots', I said. Archdale manipulated the fruit machine.

'Director angle, green three-six-and-a-half.'

Thirty-six-and-a-half degrees. That was the amount I would have to 'lay off' from the direction in which our bows were pointing. A big angle. It would need care.

'All tubes ready, sir. Torpedoes set at fourteen and sixteen feet.'

'Very good.' Torpedoes set at that depth, hitting a ship doing twenty-five knots, would make as big a mess as anyone could wish for. I glanced at my watch. Exactly eight o'clock. *They'll be having break-fast now, or getting ready for a run ashore at Messina. They'll be lucky!*

I felt good. In my pint-sized submarine I was going to tackle twelve enemy warships all at one time. A story for my grandchildren – if the destroyers and aircraft let me live to tell it!

'Slow together . . . Stop starboard. Up periscope.'

The tip of the attack periscope nosed out of the water. I grasped hard the handles as though to stop it protruding too far, and raised my little finger when six inches were exposed. Lewis stopped it dead. I swept round quickly to fix the covering aircraft. They were still over the other side of the 'screen'.

From Archdale: 'Target bearing green five-oh.'

'How much longer to go?'

'Three-and-a-half minutes, sir.'

The three destroyers in line ahead were still tearing towards me, al-though I was just a fraction inside them. With luck I would have a clear view of my target. They could not have picked us up on their Asdics or they would be circling ready to drop depth charges, but they were going to pass us too damn near for comfort. I could go deep and fire by Asdic, but I was reluctant to do this as firing at a noise is obviously less accurate than firing at a seen object. None the less, we set the Asdic angle, just in case.

All this flashed through my mind in less than a second, and a moment later I uttered a loud curse as I saw the nearest destroyer alter course straight towards us. She was no more than fifteen hundred yards off. I did some quick thinking.

'How much do *Navigatori*-class destroyers draw?'

'Fifteen to eighteen feet, sir.'

It meant she would pass over our hull but not over the conning-tower. Unless she missed us by the narrowest of margins, her keel would snap off the periscope and slice our conning-tower with the ease of a tin-opener. It was a risk we would have to take. I had no intention of losing my target.

Our target . . . I swung the periscope. There she was, still on the same course. To my joy I saw that overlapping her was one of the six-inch cruisers. I had a double length at which to aim.

I winced as I swung back to the destroyers. The crashing bow-wave of the nearest was less than a thousand yards off. A little voice nagged at the back of my brain: *Remember your command course training. A fast destroyer, head on at about a thousand yards. Go deep! Go deep, you bloody fool! You haven't a hope* . . . 'Down periscope.'

Archdale said: 'Just under a minute now, sir.'

'Stand by all tubes . . . Lewis, if my periscope is knocked off as the destroyer passes over, put up the for'ard periscope without further orders. Understand?'

'Very good, sir.'

'Director angle green three-six-and-a-half,' Archdale reported.

'Asdic bearing of target green four-two.'

'Up periscope. Bearing now? Range now?'

'Green three-nine. Range three thousand.'

I swung the periscope. Two destroyers had passed fairly close. The third towered above me. I felt very calm. I could see the stem cutting the water like a monster scythe . . . The for'ard gun . . . A part of the bridge. She was too close for me to see more, but I was a hair's breadth off her port bow and unless she altered course she would not ram us. With a deafening roar she rushed past, and I caught a momentary glimpse of a scruffy-looking sailor smoking a 'bine as he leaned against a depth-charge thrower.

Manuel's breath was hot on my neck as he strained to keep me clamped to the director angle. As the destroyer's stern flicked past my nose, the target came on my sights.

'Fire One!'

The boat jumped with the percussion.

'Half ahead together. Down periscope.'

'Fire two!' Archdale gave the order from his stopwatch. The fast target allowed for an interval of only eight seconds between torpedoes.

'Fire Three!'

From Cryer: 'One . . . Two . . . Three torpedoes running.'

'Eighty feet! Group up!'

'Fire Four!'

'Hard a-starboard. Full ahead together.'

'Fourth torpedo running, sir.'

We spiralled downwards . . .

I swung the periscope and the target came into my sights. 'Fire One!'

★   ★   ★   ★

On a south-westerly course eighty feet deep we hurried from the firing position at a rattling nine knots.

I was very aware that the passing destroyer had caused me to fire late and I hoped the speed of my target had been over-estimated.

The seconds crawled past.

The scene in the control-room might have been transplanted from a militant Madame Tussaud's – the tense, still figures, some standing, some sitting, others crouching, all rigidly silent, unblinking and tight-lipped, straining to catch the sound of a torpedo striking home. For two minutes and fifteen seconds we were like that, until a great clattering explosion brought a back-slapping roar of triumph to shatter the illusion.

'We've done it! We've hit the cruiser!'

Then, fifteen seconds later, a second explosion.

'Tell the boys it's two hits for certain!'

What a moment that was! Fused into one mighty brain and body, the 600-ton *Unbroken* had tackled four cruisers, a couple of aircraft, and eight submarine-killing destroyers. Had tackled them and beaten them. Were we capable of lyric poetry we'd have composed a Psalm of Thanks, for we felt as boastful and as proud as David must have felt that afternoon in the valley of Elah.

The Sinking of the Bismarck

William Shirer

The huge German battleship Bismarck *had sunk the pride of the British Navy* HMS Hood *in a fierce naval battle in the North Sea.*

Instantly, the cry went out: 'Avenge the Hood*!' 'Destroy the* Bismarck*!', and within 24 hours allied battleships, cruisers and an aircraft carrier were chasing the German fox like a pack of hounds, hell-bent on revenge.*

After many incidents, mistakes and near escapes, related in William L. Shirer's book, 'All About The Sinking of the Bismarck*', the final dawn battle approached.*

Already the Bismarck *was crippled; and the allied ships,* Norfolk, Ark Royal, King George V, Rodney *and* Dorsetshire *amongst them, waited impatiently for the kill. . . .*

To the men on the battleships *King George V* and *Rodney*, waiting impatiently for the kill, it seemed, as one officer later wrote, that the dawn would never come.

The crews were at their battle stations all through the long night, though half of them at a time were given permission to snatch some sleep at their posts. The captains of the two ships remained at their compass platforms. They kept track of the plotting of their own positions and that of the enemy, as reported during the night by the destroyers which were snapping at the heels of the *Bismarck*.

They also kept scanning the eastern sky for the first faint hint of dawn. When Commander W. J. C. Robertson, chief of staff for operations, thought he saw it, he went down to his cabin on the *King*

George V to fetch his steel helmet. He was amused to see four large rats scurrying about in terror. Apparently even the rats aboard knew the ship was going into battle.

The Commander in Chief also had been up most of the night, taking in the signals from the destroyers and waiting as impatiently as everyone else for the daylight to break. Admiral Tovey still didn't know exactly where his prey was. For nearly a week the thick clouds had hidden the sun by day and the stars by night. The ships could not get a bearing. They had to plot their position as well as that of the *Bismarck* by dead reckoning. This was never completely accurate.

For this reason the Commander in Chief during the night had asked Captain Vian's destroyers to fire star shells to indicate the *Bismarck's* location. But in the rain and low clouds he had not been able to see them over the horizon.

It soon became obvious that daylight was not going to bring any improvement in the weather. As the skies began gradually to lighten on 27 May, the clouds still hung close to the sea. The rain did not let up. The seas remained high. The wind blew out of the northwest as strong as ever. In the wretched visibility Sir John began to search for the *Bismarck*. Because of the fuel shortage of both his battleships, he knew he had to find the German leviathan and sink her within two or three hours at the most. By 10.00 AM they would have just enough oil to limp home.

At this critical juncture the cruiser *Norfolk* came to his aid, as she had at the beginning of the chase off Iceland. Though herself dangerously low on oil, she had been racing south all night to get in on the fight. At 8.15 AM her lookouts sighted the *Bismarck* eight miles dead ahead. Captain Phillips turned his cruiser hard over to get quickly out of range of the big ship's guns. As he swerved he sighted the *Rodney* and the *King George V* in the distance. He could thus serve as a visual link between them and the enemy.

Admiral Tovey's two ships were actually off course. Had it not been for the *Norfolk* the Commander in Chief might have missed the *Bismarck* once again. Quickly he altered course. Twenty-eight minutes later he finally sighted his target twelve miles directly ahead. It was the first time he had actually seen the *Bismarck*. After nearly a week of frustrating, nerve-wracking pursuit, he had cornered her at last.

Captain Phillips turned his cruiser hard over to get quickly out of range.

He moved in at once for the kill. He could see that the *Bismarck* was moving very slowly, headed into the wind. But he had no reason to doubt that Admiral Luetjens could still use his excellent guns with customary accuracy. The German battleship had managed to dispose of the *Hood* in a few minutes.

Admiral Tovey signalled to the *Rodney*, which was about a mile off to his port side. He told her she was free to move and to fire as she thought best but should conform generally to the flagship's manoeuvres. He was not going to fight the rigid battle that had already cost the fleet the *Hood*.

At precisely 8.47 AM on 27 May the *Rodney* opened fire with her 16-inch guns. Within the minute the *King George V* got off her first salvo of 14-inch shells. The *Bismarck* did not reply for about two minutes. But when she did, her fire was accurate. Her third salvo straddled the *Rodney*, on which she concentrated her big guns, and almost scored a direct hit.

Captain Dalrymple-Hamilton on the *Rodney* turned a little to port so he could bring all his guns into action. Soon he was pounding the *Bismarck* with full broadsides. The *King George V* ploughed straight ahead. In this position she was unable to use her aft guns. But she was rapidly closing the range. The cruiser *Norfolk*, which had refrained from firing at the *Bismarck* during the earlier action with the *Hood* and the *Prince of Wales*, now joined in the battle. She began firing with her 8-inch guns at 20,000 yards.

A second British cruiser soon entered the fray. This was the *Dorsetshire*. She had been escorting a convoy 600 miles west of Cape Finisterre on the morning of 26 May when she picked up the signal that the *Bismarck* had been found again. Captain B. C. S. Martin saw that the enemy was a mere 300 miles almost due north of him. On his own he left the convoy and steamed off at twenty-eight knots to try to get in on some action. He had arrived on the scene just in time. At 9.04 AM the *Dorsetshire* turned her 8-inch guns on the enemy and opened fire.

Thus by shortly after nine o'clock the *Bismarck*, helpless to take avoiding action because of the damage to her rudders, was being shelled by two British battleships and two heavy cruisers. Such superiority soon began to tell. The British warships were now scoring direct hits with their big shells. One of the first salvos was seen to knock away part of the *Bismarck*'s bridge. The German guns, though still blazing away, were losing accuracy.

At one minute before nine o'clock, Sir John turned his flagship south so he could bring a full broadside against the enemy. The *Rodney* followed her. They were both now only 15,000 yards from the German ship, which was yawing roughly north. After fifteen minutes of continuous exchange of salvos Admiral Tovey found that he had passed the *Bismarck*. He turned his ships around for another run parallel to the enemy, this time northward.

The range had lowered to a bare 8,000 yards. Both the *Rodney* and the *King George V* were delivering full broadsides as fast as their big guns could be reloaded. The *Bismarck* was obviously hurt from such a murderous fire at such close range. A large fire was seen belching smoke and flame amidships. Some of her 15-inch guns were no longer firing. A lookout on the *Norfolk* saw two of them drop almost to the waterline. Others pointed crazily at the sky. Their hydraulic controls, it was evident, were no longer functioning. One gun turret was blown clear away, its twisted metal toppling against the bridge.

About ten o'clock, a little more than an hour after the action had started, the last of the *Bismarck*'s guns were silenced. She had been reduced to a flaming, smoking, battered hulk. Through the jagged shell holes in her side could be seen the bright flames of fires consuming her insides.

And yet above the blazing inferno the *Bismarck*'s flag still flew. She was beaten. She was finished. But she would not surrender.

It is impossible to reconstruct the holocaust as it was experienced at this hour by the 2,400 Germans aboard the battered battleship. Each of the 118 survivors later had a tale of horror to tell. But only three of them were officers, all of junior rank. The overall picture as seen from the bridge can never be told. Admiral Luetjens did not send out a single message about this last battle. He did not even signal, as was customary, that it had begun.

He could not, in any case, have sent many messages. One of the first salvos from the British battleships blew away the admiral's bridge and with it Admiral Guenther Luetjens. Captain Lindemann might have survived. Miraculously he escaped injury even when *his* bridge was

demolished by a British shell. Junior officers urged him to jump overboard with them when it became clear that the ship was doomed. But
he stuck to his post to the end.

Battered and silent and afire though she was, the *Bismarck* would
neither surrender nor sink!

Admiral Tovey thought his guns had poured enough heavy shells
into her to sink a dozen battleships. During the run to the south the
Rodney had fired six torpedoes at the *Bismarck* and the *Norfolk* had fired
four in an effort to dispatch her by this means. All had missed. But the
bombardment by both heavy and light guns had not let up for a
moment. And still the flaming enemy hulk kept afloat.

The Commander in Chief was both puzzled and impatient. He had
never imagined that a ship could take so much punishment and not go
down. Time was getting short. German long-range bombers from
France had been reported approaching. German U-boats were known
to be converging on the scene. The *Rodney* and the *King George V* were
already zigzagging as they fired. This was a necessary precaution against
hostile submarines. Worst of all, the oil tanks on the two British battleships were so low by ten o'clock that Tovey was not sure he would
have enough fuel to get them home.

Impatiently the Admiral sent orders to Captain Patterson on the
bridge of the *King George V*.

'Get closer! Get in there closer! I can't see enough hits!'

The two battleships ploughed in closer, the *Rodney* turning so she
could fire with all her nine 16-inch guns. She also dispatched her last
two torpedoes at a range of only 3,000 yards. One of them hit – the
first occasion in naval history that a battleship had ever torpedoed
another. The *Norfolk* also launched her last four torpedoes at 4,000
yards. One of them hit, but still the *Bismarck* did not go down.

Vice-Admiral Somerville asked for another try at it with his Swordfish from the *Ark Royal*. They had disabled the *Bismarck* in the first
place. Perhaps they could finish the job!

The planes took off from the carrier at 9.25 AM, but as soon as they
arrived over the German battleship they saw that it would be impossible
to get down to launch their torpedoes. The shell fire from their own
ships was too intense. The squadron leader signalled Admiral Tovey
asking that he cease fire while the planes made their run to the target.

There was no reply – except from the *King George V*'s anti-aircraft guns, which started to fire at the Swordfish in the belief that they were German planes. Captain Patterson noticed the mistake at once and told the officer commanding the flak guns to desist.

'Can't you see our airmen waving at you?' he asked.

'I thought they were Huns shaking their fists at us,' the officer replied.

It was now 10.15 AM, and Admiral Tovey had to make a hard decision. It was absolutely imperative for him to turn his big ships home. On their dwindling oil reserves, they could make only a slow speed as it was. This would add to their peril if the German bombers and submarines attacked.

He looked over a last time at the burning wreck of the ship he had been firing at with all the guns and torpoedo tubes of the fleet. She still floated. But he knew she was finished. She would never make port. Satisfied that he had destroyed her but disappointed at not having sunk her, he ordered the *Rodney* to form behind him as he set course northeast for Britain.

As he steered for home he sent back one last signal. If any of the cruisers or destroyers had any more torpedoes they might launch them point-blank in a final effort to send the battered *Bismarck* to the bottom.

The cruiser *Dorsetshire*, which had arrived just in time to see some action, had three torpedoes left. Her skipper, Captain Martin, had not waited for the Admiral's last order. When he saw the two big battleships turn for home he acted on his own. He closed in to within 3,500 yards. Two of his torpedoes were sent skimming towards the *Bismarck's* starboard side. One of them hit just under the remains of her bridge, toppling over what was left of it. The time was 10.20 AM.

Then he circled to the port side and at 10.36 fired his last torpedo at 2,500 yards. It tore a big hole at the water-line. Slowly the *Bismarck*, her flag still flying, heeled over to the port side and turned upside-down. Then she sank beneath the waves. The clock on the *Dorsetshire* bridge read 10.40 AM.

At that moment Captain Martin took in the Admiral's signal to try to sink the *Bismarck* with his remaining torpedoes. He replied that he had just done so and that the *Bismarck* had gone down.

Clive goes to War

Lord Macaulay

During the 18th century a great struggle took place between the British, French and Mahrattas for control of the coastal strip of Eastern India from Nellore, north of Madras, and south towards the Tamil country. These wars were known as the Carnatic Wars.

At first, the French, under Joseph Dupleix were so successful that Dupleix was known as 'Governor of India'.

Dupleix sent his ally Chunda Sahib to put Trichinopoly under siege and to attack the pro-British army of Mahommed Ali and so lay claim to the rich and powerful House of Anavedy Khan

With Madras and the British East India Company stationed at Fort St George also under siege by the French, prospects looked very bleak for the British . . . .

Robert Clive was now twenty-five years old. After hestitating for some time between a military and a commercial life, he had at length been placed in a post which partook of both characters, that of commissary to the troops, with the rank of captain. The present emergency called forth all his powers. He represented to his superiors that, unless some vigorous efforts were made, Trichinopoly would fall, the House of Anaverdy Khan would perish, and the French would become the real masters of the whole peninsula of India. It was absolutely necessary to strike some daring blow. If an attack were made on Arcot, the capital of the Carnatic, and the favourite residence of the Nabobs, it was not impossible that the siege of Trichinopoly would be raised. The heads of the English settlement, now thoroughly alarmed by the success of Dupleix, and apprehensive that, in the event of a new war between France and Great Britain, Madras would be instantly taken and destroyed, approved of Clive's plan, and intrusted the execution of it to himself. The young captain was put at the head of two hundred English soldiers, and three hundred sepoys armed and disciplined after the European fashion. Of the eight officers who commanded this little force under him, only two had ever been in action, and four of the eight were factors of the company, whom Clive's example had induced to offer their services. The weather was stormy; but Clive pushed on, through thunder, lightning, and rain, to the gates of Arcot. The garrison, in a panic, evacuated the fort, and the English entered it without a blow.

But Clive well knew that he should not be suffered to retain undisturbed possession of his conquest. He instantly began to collect provisions, to throw up works, and to make preparations for sustaining a siege. The garrison, which had fled at his approach, had now recovered from its dismay, and, having been swollen by large reinforcements from the neighbourhood to a force of three thousand men, encamped close to the town. At dead of night Clive marched out of the fort, attacked the camp by surprise, slew great numbers, dispersed the rest, and returned to his quarters without having lost a single man.

The intelligence of these events was soon carried to Chunda Sahib, who, with his French allies, was besieging Trichinopoly. He immediately detached four thousand men from his camp, and sent them to Arcot. They were speedily joined by the remains of the force which Clive had late scattered. They were further strengthened by two thousand men from Vellore, and by a still more important reinforcement of a hundred and fifty French soldiers whom Dupleix despatched from Pondicherry. The whole of this army, amounting to about ten thousand men, was under the command of Rajah Sahib, son of Chunda Sahib.

Rajah Sahib proceeded to attack the fort of Arcot, which seemed quite incapable of sustaining a siege. The walls were ruinous, the ditches dry, the ramparts too narrow to admit the guns, the battlements too low to protect the soldiers. The little garrison had been greatly reduced by casualties. It now consisted of a hundred and twenty Europeans and two hundred sepoys. Only four officers were left; the stock of provisions was scanty; and the commander, Clive, who had to conduct the defence under circumstances so discouraging, was a young man of five-and-twenty, who had been bred a book-keeper.

During fifty days the siege went on. During fifty days the young captain maintained the defence, with a firmness, vigilance, and ability, which would have done honour to the oldest marshal in Europe. The breach, however, increased day by day. The garrison began to feel the pressure of hunger. Under such circumstances, any troops so scantily provided with officers might have been expected to show signs of insubordination; and the danger was peculiarly great in a force composed of men differing widely from each other in extraction, colour, language, manners, and religion. But the devotion of the little band to its chief surpassed anything that is related of the Tenth Legion of Caesar, or of the Old Guard of Napoleon. The sepoys came to Clive, not to complain of their scanty fare, but to propose that all the grain should be given to the Europeans, who required more nourishment than the natives of Asia. The thin gruel, they said, which was strained away from the rice, would suffice for themselves. History contains no more touching instance of military fidelity, or of the influence of a commanding mind.

An attempt made by the government of Madras to relieve the place had failed. But there was hope from another quarter. A body of six thousand Mahrattas, half soldiers, half robbers, under the command of a chief named Morari Row, had been hired to assist Mahommed Ali; but thinking the French power irresistible, and the triumph of Chunda Sahib certain, they had hitherto remained inactive on the frontiers of the Carnatic. The fame of the defence of Arcot roused them from their torpor. Morari Row declared that he had never before believed that Englishmen could fight, but that he would willingly help them since he saw that they had spirit to help themselves. Rajah Sahib learned that the Mahrattas were in motion. It was necessary for him to be expeditious. He first tried negotiation. He offered large bribes to Clive, which were rejected with scorn. He vowed that, if his proposals were not accepted, he would instantly storm the fort, and put every man in it to the sword. Clive told him in reply, with characteristic haughtiness, that his father was an usurper, that his army was a rabble, and that he would do well to think twice before he sent such poltroons into a breach defended by English soldiers.

Rajah Sahib determined to storm the fort. The day was well suited to a bold military enterprise. It was the great Mahommedan festival which is sacred to the memory of Hosein the son of Ali. The history of Islam contains nothing more touching than the event which gave rise to that solemnity. The mournful legend relates how the chief of the Fatimites, when all his brave followers had perished round him, drank his last draught of water, and uttered his latest prayer, how the assassins carried his head in triumph, how the tyrant smote the lifeless lips with his staff, and how a few old men recollected with tears that they had seen those lips pressed to the lips of the Prophet of God. After the lapse of twelve centuries, the recurrence of this solemn season excites the fiercest and saddest emotions in the bosoms of the devout Moslem of India. They work themselves up to such agonies of rage and lamentation that some, it is said, have given up the ghost from the mere effect of mental excitement. They believe that whoever, during this festival, falls in arms against the infidels, atones by his death for all the sins of his life, and passes at once to the garden of the Houris. It was at this time that Rajah Sahib determined to assault Arcot. Stimulating drugs were employed to aid the effect of religious zeal, and the besiegers, drunk with enthusiasm, drunk with bang, rushed furiously to the attack.

Clive had received secret intelligence of the design, had made his arrangements, and, exhausted by fatigue, had thrown himself on his bed. He was awakened by the alarm, and was instantly at his post. The enemy advanced driving before them elephants whose foreheads were armed with iron plates. It was expected that the gates would yield to the shock of these living battering-rams. But the huge beasts no sooner felt the English musket-balls than they turned round, and rushed furiously away, trampling on the multitude which had urged them forward. A raft was launched on the water which filled one part of the ditch. Clive, perceiving that his gunners at that post did not understand their business, took the management of a piece of artillery himself, and cleared the raft in a few minutes. Where the moat was dry, the assailants mounted with great boldness; but they were received with a fire so heavy and so well-directed that it soon quelled the courage even of fanaticism and of intoxication. The rear ranks of the English kept the

347

Clive took management himself and cleared the raft in a few minutes.

front ranks supplied with a constant succession of loaded muskets, and every shot told on the living mass below. After three desperate onsets, the besiegers retired behind the ditch.

The struggle lasted about an hour. Four hundred of the assailants fell. The garrison lost only five or six men. The besieged passed an anxious night, looking for a renewal of the attack. But when day broke, the enemy were no more to be seen. They had retired, leaving to the English several guns and a large quantity of ammunition.

The news was received at Fort St George with transports of joy and pride. Clive was justly regarded as a man equal to any command. Two hundred English soldiers, and seven hundred sepoys were sent to him, and with this force he instantly commenced offensive operations. He took the fort of Timery, effected a junction with a division of Morari Row's army, and hastened, by forced marches, to attack Rajah Sahib, who was at the head of about five thousand men, of whom three hundred were French. The action was sharp, but Clive gained a complete victory. The military chest of Rajah Sahib fell into the hands of the conquerors. Six hundred sepoys, who had served in the enemy's army, came over to Clive's quarters, and were taken into the British service. Conjeveram surrendered without a blow. The governor of Arnee deserted Chunda Sahib, and recognized the title of Mahommed Ali.

Had the entire direction of the war been intrusted to Clive, it would probably have been brought to a speedy close. But the timidity and incapacity which appeared in all the movements of the English, except where he was personally present, protracted the struggle. The Mahrattas muttered that his soldiers were of a different race from the British whom they found elsewhere. The effect of this languor was, that in no long time Rajah Sahib, at the head of a considerable army, in which were four hundred French troops, appeared almost under the guns of Fort St George and laid waste the villas and gardens of the gentlemen of the English settlement. But he was again encountered and defeated by Clive. More than a hundred of the French were killed or taken, a loss more serious than that of thousands of natives. The victorious army marched from the field of battle to Fort St David. On the road lay the City of the Victory of Dupleix, and the stately monument which was designed to commemorate the triumphs of France in the East. Clive ordered both the city and the monument to be razed to the ground.

He was induced, we believe, to take this step, not by personal or national malevolence, but by a just and profound policy. The town and its pompous name, the pillar and its vaunting inscriptions, were among the devices by which Dupleix had laid the public mind of India under a spell. This spell it was Clive's business to break. The natives had been taught that France was confessedly the first power in Europe, and that the English did not presume to dispute her supremacy. No measure could be more effectual for the removing of this delusion than the public and solemn demolition of the French trophies.

The government of Madras, encouraged by these events, determined to send a strong detachment, under Clive, to reinforce the garrison of Trichinopoly. But just at this conjuncture, Major Lawrence arrived from England, and assumed the chief command. From the waywardness and impatience of control which had characterized Clive, both at school and in the counting-house, it might have been expected that he would not, after such achievements, act with zeal and good humour in a subordinate capacity. But Lawrence had early treated him with kindness; and it is bare justice to Clive to say that, proud and overbearing as he was, kindness was never thrown away upon him. He cheerfully placed himself under the orders of his old friend, and exerted himself as strenuously in the second post as he could have done in the first. Lawrence well knew the value of such assistance. Though himself gifted with no intellectual faculty higher than plain good sense, he fully appreciated the powers of his brilliant coadjutor. Though he had made a methodical study of military tactics, and, like all men regularly bred to a profession, was disposed to look with disdain on interlopers, he had yet liberality enough to acknowledge that Clive was an exception to common rules. 'Some people,' he wrote, 'are pleased to term Captain Clive fortunate and lucky; but, in my opinion, from the knowledge I have of the gentleman, he deserved and might expect from his conduct everything as it fell out; – a man of an undaunted resolution, of a cool temper, and of a presence of mind which never left him in the greatest danger – born a soldier; for, without a military education of any sort, or much conversing with any of the profession, from his judgment and good sense, he led on an army like an experienced officer and a brave soldier, with a prudence that certainly warranted success.'

Acknowledgements

The editors would like to thank the following authors, publishers and literary agents for their kind permission to include the following copyright material in this book:

Alistair MacLean for THE MARCH ON AQABA from *All About Lawrence of Arabia* published by W. H. Allen & Co. Ltd and Random House Inc.

Howard Jones and Rupert Crew Ltd for AGAINST THE KING from *The Spur and the Lilly* published by MacDonald & Co. Ltd.

Anthony Buckly for THE BEGINNING OF THE END.

Mrs N. P. Yeates for THE TROUBLE WITH CAMELS from *Winged Victory* published by Jonathan Cape Ltd.

Charles McCormac for ESCAPE OR DIE from *You'll Die in Singapore* published by Robert Hale Ltd.

The estate of the late Baroness Orczy for THE SCARLET PIMPERNEL from *The Scarlet Pimpernel* published by Hodder and Soughton Ltd.

Richard Hillary for BLAZING COCKPIT from *The Last Enemy* published by Macmillan, London and Basingstoke.

Sir Irving Benson for THE MAN WITH THE DONKEY from *The Man With the Donkey* published by Hodder and Stoughton Ltd.

Pierre Closterman for FIGHT IN THE FOG (translated by O. Berthoud) from *The Big Show* published by Chatto and Windus.

George Martelli for THE EXPERT COMES TOMORROW from *The Man Who Saved London* published by William Collins, Sons & Co. Ltd.

John Simpson for NELSON'S LAST DAY.

The estate of the late Henry Williamson for A BICYCLE RIDE from *A Fox Under My Cloak* published by Macdonald and Jane Ltd.

Sidney Hart and Rupert Crew Ltd. for SUBMARINE TRIAD PENETRATES OSLO FJORD from *Discharged Dead* published by Odhams Press.

Kendal Burt, James Leasor and David Higham Associates for A MILE FROM FREEDOM from *The One That Got Away* published by William Collins, Sons & Co. Ltd and Michael Joseph.

The estate of the late Dennis Wheatley for THE BOGUS GENERAL from *The Scarlet Imposter* published by Hutchinson & Co. Ltd.

Alexander McKee for THE RED KNIGHT DIES from *The Friendless Sky* published by Souvenir Press.

The estate of the late Sir Lewis Ritchie for THE SURVIVOR from *Navy Eternal*.

Hayden McAllister for THE MAN WHO KILLED HITLER.

Captain W. E. Johns and R. A. Kelly for THE BATTLE OF THE RIVER PLATE from *No Surrender* published by George G. Harrap and Co. Ltd.

John Frayn Turner for TWO V.C.s OF THE AIR from *V.C.s of the Air* published by George G. Harrap and Co. Ltd.

Eric Williams for WELCOME TO OFLAG XXIb from *The Tunnel* published by William Collins, Sons & Co. Ltd and Abelard Schuman.

Alex Bowlby for A DAY IN THE LIFE OF 'D' COMPANY from *The Recollections of Rifleman Bowlby* published by Leo Cooper.

Andrew Wilson for FLAME TANK COMMANDER from *Flame Thrower* published by William Kimber & Co. Ltd.

Brigadier James Hargest for ESCAPE FROM CAMPO 12 from *Escape from Campo 12* published by Michael Joseph.

Arthur Gold Lee for DAWN PATROL from *Open Cockpit* published by The Hutchinson Publishing Group Ltd.

Alistair Mars, D.S.O:, D.S.C. and bar for SECRET MISSION from *Unbroken* published by Frederick Muller Ltd.

Every effort has been made to clear copyrights and the publishers trust that their apologies will be accepted for any errors or omissions.